He looked like a guy who could break your heart just by smiling at you.

"Why are you going to Edinburgh?" she asked.

"I'm on holiday."

Everything she'd read about in mom's journal had painted Scotland as such an open and friendly place. Beautiful, rugged country; generous, warm people.

Her mother's people. She sighed.

Bobby Finn reached over and touched her knee. She glanced at his hand, so strong and firm.

The truth was, his touch grounded her a bit.

"You said you're with Scotland Yard—"

"Was. I've taken a leave to do some private work."

"What kind of private work?"

"I work for a team of private investigators, an international group that takes on unsolvable crimes. Quite fun, actually, when things work out."

"And when things don't work out?"

The intensity of his dark eyes touched her heart. She couldn't look away.

"When things don't work out, I get sent on holiday."

PAT WHITE

MISS FAIRMONT *and the* GENTLEMAN INVESTIGATOR

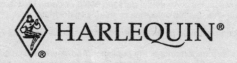

HARLEQUIN®

TORONTO • NEW YORK • LONDON
AMSTERDAM • PARIS • SYDNEY • HAMBURG
STOCKHOLM • ATHENS • TOKYO • MILAN • MADRID
PRAGUE • WARSAW • BUDAPEST • AUCKLAND

This book is dedicated to Heather Davis Koenig, talented writer and good friend.

ISBN-13: 978-0-373-88754-5
ISBN-10:   0-373-88754-X

MISS FAIRMONT AND THE GENTLEMAN INVESTIGATOR

ABOUT THE AUTHOR

Growing up in the Midwest, Pat White has been spinning stories in her head ever since she was a little girl, stories filled with mystery, romance and adventure. Years later, while trying to solve the mysteries of raising a family in a house full of men, she started writing romantic fiction. After six Golden Heart nominations and a *Romantic Times BOOKreviews* award for Best Contemporary Romance (2004), her passion for storytelling and love of a good romance continues to find a voice in her tales of romantic suspense. Pat now lives in the Pacific Northwest, and she's still trying to solve the mysteries of living in a house full of men—with the added complication of two silly dogs and three spoiled cats. She loves to hear from readers, so please visit her at www.patwhitebooks.com.

Books by Pat White

HARLEQUIN INTRIGUE
944—SILENT MEMORIES
968—THE AMERICAN TEMP AND THE BRITISH INSPECTOR*
974—THE ENGLISH DETECTIVE AND THE ROOKIE AGENT*
980—MISS FAIRMONT AND THE GENTLEMAN INVESTIGATOR*

*The Blackwell Group

CAST OF CHARACTERS

Bobby Finn—Investigator for the Blackwell Group, Bobby resents his assignment playing babysitter to a spoiled American girl in the UK, especially when she denies she's in danger.

Grace Fairmont—Her mother died when she was a baby, and Grace is on a soul-searching mission to find herself by touring Mom's homeland of Scotland. She never expects to encounter danger on her trip.

Max Templeton—Director of the Blackwell Group—a private investigative team hired to protect Grace Fairmont while she tours the UK.

Harry Franklin—Seems like a gentleman when he helps Grace after she's knocked down at King's Cross railway station. Yet appearances can be deceiving.

Uncle Gerry, Aunt Rose, Cousin Anne and Cousin Jimmy—The family Grace aches to meet. She hopes they will give her answers about her mother's mysterious life in Scotland.

Chapter One

"So, who is she?" Art McDonald said. "A murder suspect? Thief, what?"

Bobby Finn glanced at his former Scotland Yard partner then to his assignment: American Grace Fairmont, helpless rich girl whose father didn't want her traveling the U.K. alone.

She sat across the pub from Bobby and Art, leafing through travel brochures and analyzing maps. This was a fancy holiday for her, a diversion from her dull life.

For Bobby, this was a jail sentence. He'd jeopardized the Blackwell Group's last case, and he'd been sent back to London as punishment. A private dick working as a babysitter.

"She's a bloody schoolteacher," Bobby explained. "And a thorn in my side."

"A school teacher?" Art said. "What's she done?"

"Besides bore me to tears?" Bobby swallowed back his ale. "She's nothing, Art. She's not a suspect or an informant."

"I think you're overreacting, mate."

"I should be back in the States, working on a murder case for Blackwell. Instead, I'm stuck following that female around for two weeks."

Miss Grace Fairmont had been sitting at a table in the corner for nearly an hour. Her shoulder-length blond hair floated about round cheeks that made her look more like a teenager than a twenty-six-year-old woman. She wore a denim jacket, a purple scarf and soft pink lipstick, accentuating full lips, lips that looked too sexy to be on such a youthful face. A shopping bag sat by her side carrying her spoils from a prestigious lingerie shop.

Bobby had spent the day following a woman on her shopping spree. Could there be a harsher sentence?

"It's great to see you," Art said, leaning across the table. "Tell me about Blackwell, give me all the details."

Details of a missing boy, almost lost forever thanks to Bobby?

"I cocked-up, mate. That's why they sent me back."

"You know Max wouldn't punish you for being human. We all make mistakes, Bobby."

Yeah, but Bobby more than most, right? What made him think he could shake his past? Bobby was a failure at protection. Why had Max picked him for this assignment?

"Bobby?"

He glanced at Art, his mate from the Special Crimes Initiative at Scotland Yard. Art was a good friend, a mentor, and Bobby had missed him. He wished Art had stayed with the private investigative team back in the States, but the man had a wife and kids. He had a life.

Bobby envied him.

"What happened?" Art pushed.

"We were investigating a case of a missing boy." Bobby leaned forward in the booth. "I looked right into the bastard's eyes, Paul Reynolds was his name, and I didn't realize he was the man who was demanding the ransom." He hesitated and shook his head. "What the hell's the matter with me?"

"Nothing, it happens to all of us. We misjudge people."

"Not Max, he doesn't make mistakes."

"He's human, Bobby, just like the rest of us. And consider what he had to struggle with to get back on his feet. I can see why you admire him, but don't put him on a pedestal. He wouldn't like it."

He couldn't help it. Max was the man who'd challenged Bobby out of a life of crime and pushed him into a career in law enforcement. Max was Bobby's only father figure, although only ten years his senior. Max had encouraged Bobby, given him a chance.

And Bobby had let him down.

"I was doing it by the book, asking the right questions, digging for secrets. I've watched Barnes. He's so analytical and I thought I could learn from him. It all fell into place when Reynolds helped me draw my conclusions."

Bobby had been trusting and gullible. Just like when he'd trusted his mum to come back for him. Bobby should have known she couldn't stand the sight of him, not after what he'd done.

"The man had no criminal background?" Art asked.

"None. He was an upstanding citizen."

"Then you had no reason to suspect him. People lie, Bobby. You can't control that."

"But I don't have to believe them."

Art took a sip of ale.

"The odd thing was," Bobby continued, "even as I drove off with the information Reynolds gave me, feeling all proud of myself…" Bobby hesitated.

"Even as you drove off, what?"

Bobby looked into Art's gray-blue eyes. "I got this feeling, like something wasn't right, like there was something off about Reynolds."

"But you didn't act on that feeling?"

"It's a feeling, mate. Not proof of anything. Barnes always says—"

"Screw Barnes."

"I'd rather not, thanks."

Art smiled. "Barnes has his way of working cases and you have yours. Max always thought you'd make an excellent investigator because you were able to get into the devilish mind of a criminal."

Sure he could. It was his mind, as well.

"Stop thinking so much and follow your gut," Art said.

The waitress served their fish and chips.

"Ah, my gut's been missing this," Bobby joked. He forked a piece of fish and took a bite. Closing his eyes, he moaned with appreciation. There were some things about London he missed desperately.

And others he was glad to leave behind, like the shame of his past.

"Uh, Bobby?" Art said.

Bobby opened his eyes as he savored the taste.

"You'd better eat fast. It looks like your girl is leaving."

Bobby glanced at Grace Fairmont's table. Blast, she was handing her waitress her credit card.

"Bloody hell," he muttered, glancing at his full plate of food.

"We'll get the waitress to box it," Art offered.

Bobby pulled out his wallet.

"Don't even try it," Art said, not looking at him.

Art hailed a waitress and asked for a box. Bobby kept his eyes trained on Grace Fairmont. This was going to be torture, for sure, more waiting while she shopped for sexy nightgowns and bras.

Unbeknownst to Miss Fairmont, her father had hired Blackwell to protect her while on her trip. She was a schoolteacher with a steady boyfriend; she lived an unremarkable life in a suburb of Chicago.

Still, Max had given Bobby the directive: *Follow her. Protect her.*

From what? Abusing her bloody credit cards?

She signed her receipt and grabbed her things: a small red suitcase, light-gray backpack and shopping bag. She headed for the door.

"It was great catching up." Bobby shook Art's hand. He watched Grace leave the pub and head west in the direction of more shopping.

Art smiled. "Remember what I said."

"Yeah, I'll be sure to tell Barnes you think we're made for each other," Bobby joked, heading for the door. The waitress handed him his box of fish and chips.

"Behave," Art called after him.

"What, are you kidding?"

GRACE FAIRMONT waited at King's Cross Station for the 6:00 p.m. train to Edinburgh.

This was it.

The beginning of her journey to find answers.

She leaned against a wall to do some people-watching. Everyone looked so absorbed in their worlds. A mother knelt down and pointed to the schedule board. Her daughter, maybe six, looked up, eyes wide, so trusting and innocent.

Grace snapped her gaze from the mother and child and caught sight of a man, racing across the station, looking for someone. Maybe his lover?

She thought about Steven back in Chicago, about what he'd be like as a husband and a father—wonderful, attentive, loyal. For some reason, that gave her little peace.

What on earth was the matter with her? Steven was a great guy, a little over-protective, like Dad, but he meant well.

Yet Grace could not give herself completely until she understood herself better; understood herself by walking in her mother's footsteps.

Her mother, whom she'd never known.

Grace Fairmont needed to exorcise her ghosts and heal that empty spot in her heart. She needed answers and was convinced this trip to the United Kingdom would bring her closure somehow.

Dad had argued with her, told Grace it was a waste of time, that she was only torturing herself. But once he knew she was determined to do her soul-searching, he relented and gave her a treasured gift: a journal her mom had left behind.

Grace had wondered why Dad had never shared it with her all these years. When she asked him, he said he was trying to protect her, once again, from hurt and pain. That seemed to be his primary focus in life: to protect his little girl.

But Grace wasn't little anymore, and she ached to stand on her own.

Grace had coveted Mom's journal, filled with private thoughts about her life and her family.

About her baby girl.

She wrote with such love on those pages. Yet she'd only known Grace for a year before being killed by a drunk driver.

Grace shook off the melancholy and headed for the train, anxious to get away and clear her head. If nothing else, this could be a good diversion from her routine life.

She'd always been routine, accountable, the perfect daughter, probably because she didn't want to risk losing the love of her only parent. Then, after Dad had married Andrea, she'd worked hard to please her stepmother, as well.

But inside something had always felt off, crooked.

Which is what started this self-identity quest.

Passengers began to board the train for Edinburgh. She lined up, feeling a little claustrophobic. At only five foot three inches, she tended to feel that way when surrounded by a large group of people. It was even more hilarious when her eighth-grade science students towered over her.

She let her gaze wander to the passengers boarding the next car: couples holding hands and families beginning a holiday in Scotland.

Some day, she thought. Some day she'd have a family and take trips with her children. Grace would always be there for her—

SMACK!

Something slammed into her, knocking her off balance. She braced her fall with her hand and pain shot up her arm. Adrenaline rushed to her head as she struggled to catch her breath. She looked up to see three teenage boys whizzing away on skateboards, security officers chasing after them.

Someone touched her shoulder.

"You okay, miss?"

She glanced up at a businessman in a gray suit with an angular face and blue eyes.

"Fine, I think," she said.

He pulled her to her feet, his hand pinching

her arm. He was trying to be helpful and didn't realize the grip he had on her.

"Thanks," she said.

"Those boys should be strung up for knocking you down."

"They're kids," she excused, knowing how energetic teenagers were.

"Yes, well, they should have better sense."

Now he sounded like her father.

"Please." He motioned for her to board ahead of him.

She climbed onto the train, shooting him one last smile of thanks, and made for the first-class section. She wanted to be pampered, to have someone take care of *her* for a change.

It had been so long since she'd put herself first. She'd spent her life worrying about Dad, her stepmom, her half sisters, Annie and Claire, and even her students at Inglewood Junior High.

Grace found a seat and settled by the window so she could get a view of the ocean as they got closer to Newcastle.

The helpful businessman took a seat across from her.

"Are you on holiday, then?" he asked.

So much for peace and quiet.

WHAT'S THIS? The boring American girl had already snagged a new boyfriend?

Bobby had chosen a seat a few rows down, watching the bloke in the suit make conversation with Grace.

Bobby sensed it was an effort for her to respond. Why? Was she the unsociable type? Or did she sense something creepy about the man? Bobby had. Nonsense, she wouldn't have given him so much of her time if that were the case. They'd chatted on and off for nearly half the trip to Edinburgh.

Bugger, they were headed to Scotland and Bobby hadn't had time to grab his things from the hotel. He'd have to buy some new clothes, courtesy of Blackwell.

Bobby eyed Miss Fairmont's train companion. The man wore an expensive suit and a gold earring, but worn, cheap trainers. There was something off about him. The bloke was working too hard to charm Miss Fairmont.

Why? Sure, she was mildly attractive, but

not a model type who would draw the attention of a hoity-toity like suit man over there.

It made him ill to watch the businessman lean toward her, whisper a joke and laugh at it himself. She shot him a strained smile and pressed her forehead to the window. She looked as if she wanted to jump to get away from him.

How could he be so blind?

A few minutes passed. The suit glanced at Bobby, who refocused on newspaper headlines: the Prime Minister had struck a deal with the French regarding nuclear power; G8 aid pledges were not meeting expectations; a new program was in the works to improve students' handwriting.

When Bobby glanced up, Grace was heading into the next car. What's this? Was she finally getting away from the wanker, or just making a trip to the toilet?

Five minutes passed. Ten. The suit checked his watch, looked impatient. It was almost as if he was afraid she'd left for good. The bloke stood and went into the next train car.

Bobby folded his newspaper. Suit man's interest in Grace was beyond obsessive.

Follow her. Protect her.

Bobby went into the next train car in search of Grace and her suitor. It was half-full, but there was no sign of the girl or the businessman.

What could this be about? A random stalker? More like a prick who couldn't take no for an answer.

Bobby pushed through to the next car. The conductor announced they were approaching Newcastle. The train slowed and Bobby held on to the back of a seat as his weight shifted with the motion of the brake.

A few passengers stood and gathered their things, blocking his view of the next car.

The train stopped, passengers got off and the doors closed. Bobby glanced out the window and spotted the businessman racing across the platform. Had Grace gotten off the train and he was following her?

Bloody hell.

The train pulled away and Bobby raced through the car peering through windows, trying to catch sight of her. This was all wrong. Her father had said she planned a trip to Edinburgh, where she'd start her tour of Scotland.

This was supposed to be an easy assignment: follow and protect a girl. How hard could that be?

For you, bloody impossible.

He pushed through another car, peered out the window and spotted the businessman march down the steps, out of sight.

Bobby pounded his fist against the back of a seat. He'd cocked-up in less than twenty-four hours. Max wouldn't be able to ignore this one.

And Bobby couldn't ignore the voices in his head: *How could you let this happen? Of course your mother didn't want you.*

The sound of muffled tapping drew his attention to the back of the car. It was coming from the toilet.

He went to the door and knocked. "Anyone in there?"

A woman's whimpers echoed through the door.

Blast. The door couldn't be locked unless she'd locked it. And if that were the case, why hadn't she let herself out of there. Was she bound or worse?

"Miss? I'm going to push open the door," he said.

He cracked open the door and she blinked back at him through teary eyes, a white handkerchief stuck in her mouth, her wrists bound with flex cuffs.

"Good God," he hushed. "Here." He helped her to a seat. She shook with fear.

"Let's get this off you." He pulled the gag from her mouth, guilt ripping him up inside.

He let this happen. Wasn't there to protect her. Again.

"He t-t-took." She could barely speak without stuttering.

"Shh. Have a rest."

"He took…my mom," she said.

"It's okay, you're okay now."

He pulled out his pocketknife to cut her bindings.

"Hold it right there," a male voice said behind him.

Chapter Two

Bobby's hands went up and he glanced over his shoulder. A bloke holding Met Police identification in one hand and a gun in the other towered over him. Relief that it wasn't the businessman was quickly replaced by shame. Old, bitter memories tore at his chest.

You're a bad seed, a delinquent who will spend his life in prison.

No, things were different now; Bobby was one of the good guys.

"I'm trying to help," Bobby said.

The officer glanced at Bobby's hand. "By threatening her with a knife?"

"I was going to cut her loose."

He held the man's gaze, struggling to keep the guilt from his eyes. Guilt for the many sins he had yet to be absolved of; guilt for letting the stranger hurt the American Grace.

"Hand over the knife."

Bobby did as ordered, very slowly. "I'm a former inspector with Scotland Yard."

"And I'm Prince William." The cop pocketed the knife. "Stand up, arms behind your head."

"No," Grace said.

Bobby studied her as she addressed the officer.

"He helped me," she said. "He's not the bad guy."

The officer eyed Bobby, who fought off buried shame and held his gaze.

"How about some identification?" the officer asked.

"Cut her free first."

The policeman holstered his gun and pulled out his own pocketknife. Grace raised her bound wrists and he cut them loose. She rubbed the skin, raw from the unforgiving plastic.

"ID," Bobby said, handing him his driver's license and Blackwell business card.

"Robert Finn."

"Bobby," he corrected.

The detective eyed it and nodded. "You used to be with Scotland Yard? Doing what?"

"I was an inspector with the Special Crimes Initiative."

"And you left because?"

"Shouldn't you be more worried about this woman than my employment history?"

Bobby didn't want him wasting time trying to analyze his motives; he was furious about the girl's attack and he wanted answers.

Considering her teary eyes and trembling fingers, he wasn't sure if *she* had any.

"Miss?" the detective said.

"Grace, Grace Fairmont."

"Miss Fairmont, I'm Detective Adam Parker with the Metro Police. Can you tell me what happened?"

"A man," she started, then paused. "He was sitting by me, making conversation. A stranger…" Her voice trailed off.

"I saw him get off the train at Newcastle," Bobby offered.

The detective narrowed his eyes at him.

"I noticed how he pushed himself on the girl. Something about the bloke didn't sit right."

The detective redirected his attention to Grace. "What did you talk about?"

"The weather, London, my trip. He said his name was Harry Franklin, Esquire."

She glanced at her fingers, fiddling with a ring she wore on her right hand. She was keeping something private, to herself. Bobby could sense it.

"He asked me a lot of questions," she continued. "I tried pretending to be asleep, but he didn't get the message. I…I excused myself and went to another car, hoping he'd leave me alone."

She coughed and Bobby wanted to reach out and comfort her. But he, too, was a stranger and after what had just happened he knew she'd most likely recoil from the gesture.

"He followed me," she said. "And I got this feeling." She looked up at the detective. "Like he was going to hurt me. So I went into the bathroom, but he shoved the door open and pressed himself up against me and…" She waved her hand, then placed her fingers to her mouth, as if to fight off sobs.

Bobby fisted his right hand, wanting to find

the bastard and break his nose. If he had touched her inappropriately—"What did he do to you?" Bobby said. He couldn't stop himself.

"No," she said. "Nothing like that."

She held his gaze, her clear blue eyes penetrating and intense as if she could see into his soul. Bobby snapped his attention to the detective.

"It's okay, now, miss," Detective Parker consoled. "He's gone, he's off the train according to Mr. Finn." The detective knelt beside her. "Your attacker can't hurt you anymore. But I'd like to call in a description to the Transport Police."

She nodded and cleared her throat. "He was tall—"

"About six two," Bobby offered.

"Short, trim hair, blue eyes, this one," she pointed to her right eye, "had a brown spot by the pupil. He had an accent, but it wasn't like yours, Detective." She glanced at Bobby. "It was more like yours."

He'd called Dublin his home until his mother had sent him to live with Uncle Thomas in London. Had she recognized an Irish accent?

"What else?" Detective Parker prompted.

"He had a gold earring in his left ear," Bobby said. "And he wore an expensive suit, maybe Armani, but not his shoes," Bobby said, puzzling for a second. "The bloke wore trainers, beat-up trainers."

"Did he say anything to you when he assaulted you in the bathroom?" Parker asked her.

"He said 'You can't run like your mother.'" She glanced up at the detective. "But I never even knew my mother. She died when I was a year old."

"Mistaken identity?" Bobby said to the detective.

"Sounds like. How about your luggage?"

"He took my backpack."

"But he wasn't carrying it when I saw him on the platform," Bobby added.

"It might still be on the train," Parker said. "I'll start a search after I radio in."

"I didn't know they put Metro detectives on the rail system," Bobby said.

"They don't. Lucky for you I'm on my way to meet family in Edinburgh."

"Very lucky," Bobby added, nodding at Grace.

"I'm going to call it in, then search for your pack." He glanced at Bobby. "Could use a hand if you're interested."

"No," she said again, reaching out to Bobby.

Her hand landed on the sleeve of his leather jacket. "I'd rather he stay here, with me."

She looked at him with such trust, such gratitude…and for a second, he welcomed her confidence. Then he remembered why he was here: as an employee, hired by her father.

Mr. Fairmont had specifically said he didn't want his daughter finding out he'd hired Blackwell. He feared she'd be furious and would try to shake off the secret bodyguard.

"It's okay," she said to Bobby after watching him for a moment. "You don't have to stay with me."

She must have read the internal struggle in his eyes.

Bugger, he'd always been so good at hiding his demons behind a layer of smiles and charm.

"I'll sit with you." He smiled.

Relief eased the tension lines on her face.

"I'll check back." The detective left.

"Your cheek is red," Bobby said. "Let me get you some ice."

He started to get up but she grabbed his jacket sleeve. "No, please, would you mind staying here and talking to me?"

"Of course."

She glanced out the window, hugging her midsection.

"Are you chilled?" he said.

She shook her head that she wasn't. She looked absorbed in the landscape, yet there was nothing to see outside but the black horizon of the North Sea.

He studied her young features: round cheeks and freckles dotting her slightly upturned nose. She wore little makeup to speak of, but her cheeks were a natural rose color, so she really didn't need it. She'd look fourteen if it weren't for something wary in her eyes and a full lower lip that gave her a natural pout.

She had plenty to pout about. She'd been accosted on a train in a strange country. How could she let the bastard get the advantage? Didn't the girl have any protective instincts?

"What did you mean, he took your mum?" Bobby asked.

She sighed and seemed to melt into the seat.

"He ripped my locket off my neck. It had a picture of my mom and my dad."

It was the only photograph she had of her, Grace realized. She closed her eyes and fought back more tears. No, she wasn't a fragile girl who'd fall apart because she'd been mugged. People were mugged all the time. They survived. She would.

But it wasn't the mugging that tore at her heart. That photograph of her mother had been Grace's only link to her, her only connection.

"Aw, come on, love, it's not that bad. I'm sure your father can find you another."

The man in the black leather jacket had such a calming nature. She couldn't help but be drawn to him.

To think when she'd noticed him earlier on the train, she'd thought him rough and dangerous. It was the intensity of his dark eyes whenever he glanced her way that made her nervous. That and his two days' growth of beard.

He looked like a tough guy, a guy who could break your heart by smiling at you.

How could she have known that Bobby Finn was the kind man, and Harry was the danger?

"He seemed nice," she blurted out.

"Who, the hoity-toity bloke sitting next to you?"

"Yeah."

And he did. He'd helped her up after she'd been knocked down by the teenagers and he'd sat by her on the train as if protecting her.

Could she have worse instincts?

"Gawd, I'm so stupid," she muttered.

"Don't go beating yourself up, miss. When someone's nice to you there's no reason to think he's going to hurt you. Still…" He hesitated and rubbed at his beard. "He *was* prepared, wasn't he? He carried ties and a gag on him like women carry handbags?"

"He's a lawyer." She wasn't sure what that had to do with anything.

"Well, that explains it then." He smiled, his cheek dimpling.

She almost felt herself smile.

"You sure you didn't know him?" he asked.

"No, I've never seen him before today."

"And he didn't say anything besides the comment about your mum?"

"No." Her gaze drifted to the center aisle of the train.

She wasn't sure why she lied, other than she didn't want to impose on this man's kindness. What purpose would it serve to tell him about the other comment, the one about the dangers of a single girl traveling north of Edinburgh?

That threat was meant for someone else. He'd obviously mistaken her for another woman traveling alone to Scotland. It had to be. Grace didn't have enemies, no one who'd threaten her life.

Everything she'd read in Mom's journal had painted Scotland as such an open and friendly place. Beautiful, rugged country; generous, warm people.

Her mother's people. She sighed.

"Whoa there, love." Bobby Finn reached over and touched her knee.

She glanced at his hand, so strong and firm.

He snapped it back. "Sorry. You looked so sad like you'd lost your dog or something."

Or something.

"It's okay," she whispered. "I'm really tired, I guess."

The truth was, his touch grounded her a bit. She should be ashamed of herself for so willingly accepting comfort from yet another stranger.

A stranger she knew nothing about.

"Why are you going to Edinburgh?" she asked.

"I'm on holiday."

"You said you're with Scotland Yard—"

"Was. I've taken a leave to do some private work."

"What kind of private work?"

"Twenty questions, is it?" he said with a smile.

She shook her head. "I'm sorry."

"Don't be. You're wary, you should be. Okay then, I work for a team of private investigators, an international group that takes on unsolvable crimes. Quite fun, actually, when things work out." He glanced at his fingers, loosely interlaced in his lap.

"And when things don't work out?"

He looked her straight in the eye. The intensity of those dark eyes touched her heart. She couldn't look away.

"When things don't work out, I get sent on holiday." He smiled, but it looked forced, as if there was great pain behind his words.

"I'm sorry," she said.

"Don't be. I haven't taken a break in over ten years. I could use a little sightseeing, tour the castles and walk the battlegrounds."

"Culloden?"

"That tops the list."

She nodded. A few minutes passed.

"What else are you going to do?" she said, to distract herself. She'd been attacked, in a strange country, in a public place. She'd suddenly wondered if Dad was right to be so protective, right when he'd said she was incapable of taking care of herself.

No, she'd lived with his overprotectiveness for years, and she finally needed to get away on her own, find some answers about her mother.

"I'll probably head up to Inverness," Bobby Finn said. "Make some stops in between, play golf. Haven't finalized everything."

"What's Edinburgh like?"

"What, you've never been?"

"No."

"Make sure you tour Edinburgh Castle and Holyrood."

"I'm only going to be there a day. I'm not much for big cities."

"You might be able to do both in a day." His enthusiastic smile faded. "Hold on, I'm such a bloody sod. That bastard lawyer got your money and your credit cards, didn't he?"

"Yeah, but at least he didn't get my suitcase. I checked it with the guard's van before getting on board." She sighed with relief. He hadn't taken her prized possession: Mom's journal, the roadmap Grace would use to make this journey.

Bobby Finn leaned forward in his seat and pulled out his wallet. "Do you need money? I think I've got a few hundred pounds in here."

"No, don't." She placed her hand to his. The intimate connection warmed her fingertips. "I'll be fine. I'll wire my…" Who? If she wired Dad she'd have to tell him the whole story. He'd demand Grace come home, they'd get in another big fight. And Steven? He'd practically followed her onto the plane he wanted to come with her so badly.

This was something she needed to do alone.

"I'll be fine," she said. She realized her fingers still touched the back of his hand. He slipped his hand from hers and shoved his wallet back into his pocket. She studied this tough-looking man whose eyes warmed with tenderness.

"I'm hot-blooded," he said.

"Excuse me?"

"When you touched me you noticed how hot my skin was?"

Actually, she thought it was a combination of coming off an adrenaline rush and needing a friendly connection.

"My temperature runs about two degrees above normal. You know, hot-blooded, hot-headed. At least that was the excuse they came up with in school."

Chatting with him was a nice diversion. It

distracted Grace from the violent flashes of being assaulted. She could pretend to be normal again and deny feeling victimized.

"Did you get in trouble a lot?" she said.

"Every bloody day. I was ba-a-ad."

"I doubt that."

His gaze snapped up to meet hers. He looked frightened for a second. Then his lips curved into a mischievous grin.

"I was so bad I was expelled from three primary schools," he said.

"And yet you became a policeman."

His smile faded. He looked almost embarrassed.

The door opened and Detective Parker stepped up to her. "No sign of your backpack, yet, miss."

"Thanks. At least I've got my cell phone. Kept it in my jacket."

"Is there someone you can phone when you get to Edinburgh?"

No way around it. She'd have to call Steven to wire her money. She'd make him promise not to tell Dad what had happened. "I have a friend I can call."

"You're sure? Because I could always front you a few pounds."

"I already tried that," Bobby said. "She won't take money from strangers." He winked.

"Hey, taking help from a stranger got me into this mess in the first place," she said.

"How's that, miss?" Detective Parker asked.

"That man, Harry, helped me after I was knocked down by teenagers at the train station."

"This feels like a set-up," the detective said. "He probably paid those boys to knock you over so he could get into your good graces and stay close to you."

"Why?" Her voice squeaked a pitch higher than usual. "What have I done to deserve this?"

"Nothing, you've done nothing wrong," Bobby said. "It's not your fault. They'll get the bastard."

"Transport Police will do their best," Parker offered. "They've notified Newcastle Police to be on the lookout. In the meantime, we don't have to worry about a repeat attack. He's miles away from Edinburgh. You're safe now."

Her attacker's warning echoed in her mind:

Traveling north of Edinburgh can be dangerous for a single girl.

It was a hollow threat from a bully who picked on naive tourists. She'd be strong, gather her courage and finish what she came to do.

SHE LOOKED adorable when she slept, Bobby thought, studying Grace Fairmont's young features. She'd fallen asleep after an hour's worth of conversation with Bobby and Detective Parker, but most of it had been with Bobby. With every passing minute he sensed she grew more comfortable with him, more relaxed.

There was something open about her, yet fragile. A part of him wanted to shout in her face: *Don't trust me, I'm no good. I'm pretending to be something I'm not.*

And I obviously can't protect you.

But he couldn't for so many reasons, his position with Blackwell topping the list.

He'd been hired to do this simple job. If he wanted to make his way back to the Blackwell team in the States, he needed to follow orders and make sure she got safely home from her holiday.

If he succeeded he could earn a bonus or maybe a higher spot on the team. There was a rumor that the Patron was going to start a second team and maybe Bobby could get in line for that promotion.

He glanced at the sweet-faced Miss Fairmont. Her safety was worth nothing but a promotion to him.

You really are a bastard, Finn.

Detective Parker returned from making a call. "Someone spotted the man she described leaving the train station. Transport Police did a background on Harry Franklin, but nothing turned up on their wanted lists."

"It's probably an alias," Bobby said, watching Grace sleep. Fitfully, of course. He guessed she was both exhausted by her experience and terrified, as well.

"What do you make of it?" Parker said, eyeing Bobby. "Simple mugging or something more?"

"Sounds like a case of mistaken identity, but feels like more, doesn't it?"

Parker nodded. "What do you know about her?"

"As much as you do," he lied. He didn't want to reveal his true assignment and complicate matters further. "She's a fragile one."

And a bit secretive. Bobby sensed the American wasn't being completely truthful about the attack. Why? What was she hiding?

He'd read her file and had become familiar with the life of Grace Fairmont. An only child, her father raised her by himself until she turned eight, when he married. Grace was a straight-A student, a high achiever, yet instead of pursuing business she opted to teach science to teenagers.

Bobby couldn't understand it. He remembered what teenagers were like: emotionally fractured, insecure and angry. Why would anyone choose to be around that day in and day out?

He didn't understand her choice of careers any more than he understood today's attack. There was definitely more to it than a random mugging. After all, the bloke had used flex cuffs and knew exactly how to subdue her without drawing unwanted attention. He'd timed it perfectly.

Bobby's ground his teeth at the thought of Grace being seriously injured while under his watchful eye.

He wouldn't let that happen.

Yet he couldn't protect her if he didn't have her whole story. He stood and pulled out his mobile.

"I'll be right back," he said to Parker.

He went in between cars and called Eddie, Blackwell's computer expert.

"Eddie Malone."

"Hey, mate, it's Bobby."

"Bobby! Hey, it's Bobby from London," he called out to the rest of the team. "What's up, man?"

"I need background. Grace Fairmont."

"Our client's daughter? The one you're playing bodyguard for?"

At least he didn't call Bobby a babysitter.

"That's the one," Bobby said. "I want what the father might be keeping from us. Dig into the family's background, her job contacts, mates from college, that sort of thing."

"So, let me get this straight: you want me to investigate our client?"

"There's been a development and I need to know intimate details about Grace and the Fairmont family."

"Okee-dokee."

"Also, do a search for Harry Franklin, Esquire. It's probably an alias, but see what you can find. And…" He hesitated, not sure what compelled him to make the next request. "Get me everything you can on the girl's boyfriend, the name's in the file."

"This doesn't sound like a simple body-guard job."

"Just trying to get the key players straight in my head, mate. Nothing covert."

"Wait, Max wants to talk to you."

Great. Max would hear the tension in Bobby's voice and inquire about his day.

"Bobby? How's the weather in London?"

"Actually, guv, I'm in Scotland. Taking the rail up to Edinburgh."

"Everything okay?"

Blast, did Max have such little faith in Bobby?

"Fine, guv, why?"

"I know this wasn't the assignment you'd

hoped for. But I gave it to you because I trust you, Bobby. I know you'll take care of the girl."

"Well, actually, it got off to a rocky start. She was assaulted on the train."

"What? A random attack?"

"Looks that way." Bobby paused. "But it doesn't feel that way."

"Follow your instincts, Bobby. Trust them."

"Like I did with Paul Reynolds?"

"Let go of it, mate. He had everyone fooled, even his best friends. You said you thought he was too charming, too happy with the world. You knew something was wrong. You didn't trust yourself. Sometimes you have to look beyond the facts."

Like into Grace Fairmont's unsettled eyes?

"I'll press the father for more personal information," Max said. "Maybe he's keeping something from us."

"Thanks, guv." Bobby heard the door slide open behind him. He turned and spotted Grace holding her mobile in her hand.

"It's a good thing she's got you as her shadow, isn't it?" Max said.

"Sure. I've got to run."

"It's two weeks, Bobby. Then you'll be back with the team."

"Yes, sir." He ended the call and smiled at Grace. "Everything okay?"

"Yeah, Detective Parker said the reception's better out here." She motioned to her phone.

"I'll give you privacy, then." He brushed past her, and she touched his jacket sleeve.

"Thanks, again."

Glancing down into those green eyes of hers, Bobby read vulnerability, yet determination. But determination for what?

Bobby Finn went into the passenger car and sat down across from the policeman. Grace sighed. She'd been so lucky that both of them were on her train. They were the strength she needed to ground herself after the attack.

She gripped the metal pole as the memories flashed to the surface. She'd thought Harry a nice, albeit pushy, guy who needed attention. There was no indication that he was dangerous.

What did you expect, girl? It's not like you've got street smarts, what with your father hovering over you most of your life, protecting you, sheltering you.

If only Mom had been alive to balance things out, Dad wouldn't have been so smothering. Yet he was trying to make up for that empty spot in Grace's life where there should have been another parent.

A loving, nurturing mother.

"Enough," she said, trying to shove back her frustration. That's what this trip was about: Grace's personal elixir, a way to finally let go of the questions and confusion, a way to look ahead instead of dwelling in the past, dwelling in the sadness of not knowing her mom.

After she visited her mother's hometown, and toured some of the spots written about in her journal, Grace would start a new, fresh life.

At some point you have to let go.

Grace called Steven. She'd calmly tell him what happened and ask him to wire her a few hundred pounds until she could replace her credit cards. She had to do it in such a way that he wouldn't worry, or board the next British Airways flight to London.

Sometimes, between her father and Steven, she felt as though she was being suffocated.

Her call went into voice mail.

"Hey, Steven, it's Grace. I lost my wallet on the train to Scotland, can you believe it? Anyway, I was wondering if you could wire me some cash until I can get access to my bank account, just enough for a day or two. Sorry I have to ask. And don't worry about me. There's a former Scotland Yard inspector and Metro policeman on the train. They're taking care of me. Anyway, we'll be pulling into the station in a few minutes. You can reach me on my cell. Thanks."

She pressed End. Something at the bottom of the steps reflected back at her.

Her breath caught in her throat. Her locket. She picked it up and rubbed the worn gold, its shine faded with age.

She opened it.

The picture of her mother was missing.

Chapter Three

Mom's photograph. Gone.

This trip was off to a horrible start for sure. First the mugging, now the missing picture. She wanted to call Dad and ask if he could send another, but then she'd have to tell him the whole ugly story. She wasn't in the mood for lectures.

She wanted a nice, quiet room where she could unwind, have a hot cup of tea and read through Mom's journal. Again.

At least she still had that. Thank God she'd packed it in her suitcase.

She slipped the phone into her pocket and went back to her seat.

"Everything okay?" Bobby asked.

Bobby, the private detective on holiday. She could use his help right about now.

No, she had to do this on her own, couldn't trust anyone, especially not a stranger.

"Good news, actually." She held out the locket. "Found my locket."

"Brilliant," Bobby said.

"Mom's picture is missing, though."

"Probably fell out when he dropped it," Detective Parker offered.

She squeezed it in her hand, the warmth of the metal easing the chill around her heart.

A heart that had never felt completely whole as a child without a mother.

She glanced at Bobby Finn whose eyes were intent on her. She was sure he could read her thoughts. Her gaze drifted out the window. She was anxious to reach the small town of Pitlochry where her mother had grown up.

But now it would take her a few days to get there. She had to cancel her credit cards and wait for their replacements so she could continue her trip.

She should call Dad, especially now that Steven knew something was up. Dad would probably lecture her about always keeping a stash of traveler's checks handy. But she'd been rushed at work, organizing material for her substitute. She'd barely made it to the airport on time. It was only thanks to practical Steven that she'd made her flight.

Steven, a nice, practical man, like her father. Not wild, passionate or unpredictable.

Steven was exactly the type of man she knew she'd marry.

Then why are you here, girl? Why didn't you stay home and marry the guy?

Good question. And one of many.

They pulled into the station and climbed off the train. Bobby Finn grabbed her suitcase from the platform by the guard's van. A British Transport Police officer was waiting for her.

"Here's my card," Detective Parker said, writing something on the back. "I'm giving you my mobile number, as well." He handed it to her. "Don't hesitate to phone me if you need anything."

"Thanks for everything," she said.

"Nonsense, I didn't do anything, but they'll be able to help." He nodded at the

Transport Police officer. "Take care of her."
He offered his hand to Bobby. "Nice meeting
you, Mr. Finn."

"Likewise." They shook.

Parker hailed a cab and disappeared into
the night.

"Miss?" The officer motioned for her to
join him in the police car.

She hesitated.

"Want me to come with you?" Bobby said,
slipping her suitcase onto the seat.

"No, no, you've done enough."

"Here's my mobile number, as well." He
handed her a card that read: Agent Bobby
Finn, The Blackwell Group, with a Seattle
address and phone number. "I'm just
bumming in Scotland; I've got nothing
pressing on my schedule."

"Okay, thanks." She got into the car, panic
filling her stomach, but she wasn't sure why.

"Don't keep her too long," Bobby said to
the officer. "She's had a rough go of it."

"We'll make it brief," he said.

She shot Bobby one last smile, hoping he
didn't read the panic in her eyes.

She felt a kinship with him. She knew intense experiences made a person crave a warped kind of security. And she sensed Bobby Finn wasn't out to hurt her.

"Ah, move over, I'm coming with." He climbed in beside her.

"Excuse me, sir?" the officer said.

"I saw the man, as well. Maybe I can help."

He winked at Grace, and she knew he wasn't coming along to help with the investigation. He was coming to support her. There were good people out there, too, people you could trust.

"So, miss, your attacker stole your backpack and tied you up? Why do you think he'd do that?" the Transport Officer asked, pulling away from the station.

"I have no idea."

"Do you have any personal enemies?"

"None." She'd lived her life as a pleaser, pleasing her father, her stepmom, even Steven.

"And your mother?" the officer said.

"I'm sorry?" A shudder raced across her shoulders.

"Did she have any enemies?"

"My mother's been dead for years."

"I must have misunderstood. Didn't the man who attacked you make reference to your mother?"

"Yes, but Detective Parker and Mr. Finn thought it was a case of mistaken identity." She glanced at Bobby, who narrowed his eyes at the officer.

"Did he say anything else?" the officer pushed.

Something felt odd about the interrogation in the police car. "He said," she glanced at Bobby, "he said it can be dangerous for single girls traveling in Scotland."

"He said that?" Bobby said. "You didn't mention it before."

"You're on holiday. I didn't want to involve you in all this."

Bobby glared at the back of the officer's head. "Are we nearly there?"

What, was he in that big of a hurry to get away from her, just because she didn't tell him everything the mugger had said?

Sure, of course. She'd attracted another controller into her life, a stranger who thought she owed him every last detail of her attack, probably so he could save her.

Grace didn't want to be saved or protected or smothered. She wanted a life where she could make her own decisions and plan her own future.

But first she had to resolve the past.

"What did you have in your backpack?" the officer asked. "Anything valuable?"

"My wallet, a camera, makeup, a book, things like that."

"A mobile phone?"

"No, I've got my phone with me."

"If you're going to do the complete interview in the car, we'll skip the trip to the station and you can drop us at a hotel," Bobby said.

"I'm just trying to get the details while it's fresh in the girl's mind."

The officer didn't ask any more questions, and she wondered what had happened between the two men. Grace studied Bobby, who stared at the back of the guy's head.

He was angry. Why? It's not like he was the one who was assaulted and had his belongings stolen. He was angry because she hadn't taken him into her confidence, because she hadn't given him control of her situation?

The officer's cell phone rang and he answered it. "I'm with the girl and her friend. Yes… I understand. We'll be there momentarily." He turned the car around and glanced into the rearview mirror. "Apparently there's been a miscommunication," he explained to Grace and Bobby. "They're waiting back at Waverly Station. I apologize."

Grace just wanted some food and a hot bath.

"Where are you from, mate?" Bobby asked him. "Your accent sounds familiar."

The officer didn't answer. Bobby shook his head and glanced out the car window. Grace wondered what was going on between them.

A few minutes later they pulled up to the station and Bobby got out, grabbing her suitcase.

"They're waiting for you inside," the officer said.

She and Bobby went into the station. She glanced around, expecting someone to greet them. There were few people left at the station at this time of night.

Bobby motioned for her to sit on a bench and he sat beside her. "I'm sure they'll find us."

A few minutes passed, and Grace fantasized about finally climbing into a soft bed after this mess of a day.

"It will be over soon," Bobby said, as if he'd read her thoughts.

A man dressed in a British Transport Police uniform walked in their direction.

"Excuse me," Bobby said. "We're here to make a report about a mugging." The man seemed puzzled. "The mugging on the rail from London?"

"Oh, yes, I thought… Never mind. I can help you. I'm Officer Markham." He shook hands with each of them. "Right this way."

He led them down a long hallway into an interview room. "We'll get the details as quickly as possible so you can be on your way."

"The officer who picked us up got plenty of details," Bobby said.

"The officer who picked you up?"

"I didn't catch his name."

"Odd," he said, and motioned for them to sit at a table across from him.

"So, you are Mr. Fairmont?" the officer asked Bobby.

Grace nearly choked at that one. She'd never fall for a man like Bobby Finn, a self-proclaimed troublemaker turned private detective. Although he was charming, she recognized his need to dominate and control.

Grace needed a man who would trust her to take care of herself, a man she could trust, as well. She'd been fooled by her share of boyfriends, lured into romance with false promises.

Trust was key with Grace. And respect.

Although he'd been kind to her, she suspected Bobby Finn was an expert at tempting women into his bed. Not much respect in that.

"I'm just a friend," he clarified. "Bobby Finn."

"And Mr. Finn, you're traveling with Miss Fairmont?"

"We met on the train."

"And you've accompanied her here? What a gentleman."

"Thank you, sir."

Markham narrowed his eyes at Bobby as

if trying to make out his character. "I'd like some basics from you, Mr. Finn, then I'll interview Miss Fairmont." He pulled out a pen and wrote something across a pad of white paper.

Grace sensed that Bobby was uncomfortable, but she couldn't figure out why.

Markham asked questions about home addresses, employment and the reason for Bobby's trip to Scotland. She noticed Bobby fisted his right hand in his lap. Maybe, as doctors make terrible patients, former Scotland Yard detectives make uncomfortable interviewees.

Or maybe he was hiding something.

She was being completely paranoid. Sure she was, she was tired, hungry and still rattled.

The officer moved on to Grace. She answered the questions about her life and recalled what she could about the attack.

A knock interrupted them. The door opened and a second officer walked in holding her backpack.

"You found it!" She shot to her feet and he handed it to her.

"Someone from the train turned it in," the officer explained.

"Excellent," Officer Markham said.

"Not excellent," Bobby argued. "Why did he attack her if he didn't want her pack?"

"Money? Check inside, miss," Markham said.

She dug though her things, makeup case, books and emergency underwear in case her luggage had been lost. "He took my wallet, but nothing else. The rest of it's here, even the pepper spray. A lot of good that did me," she muttered.

Relief settled low. She could put this incident behind her and move on with her trip. That is, after she notified the credit card companies.

Bobby's cell phone rang. "Will you excuse me?"

"Of course, we're nearly done," Officer Markham said.

Bobby touched her shoulder for support and left the room.

"So, miss? You didn't know Mr. Finn before today?" Markham jotted something down.

"No, why?"

He leveled her with a serious expression. "How much do you know about Bobby Finn?"

BOBBY WENT OUTSIDE to get better reception on his mobile.

"Finn," he answered.

"It's Eddie."

"That was fast."

"Fast is my middle name. Listen, this is one complicated family.

"The mother left. Poof, disappeared one day. Then, about five years later, there's a death notice for Mary Logan, that was her last name. Died in a terrorist bombing in London. Body was messed up. Closed-casket service."

Abandoned by her mother. He glanced toward the station. Bobby knew what that felt like.

"Oh, and this is weirdo stuff," Eddie continued. "The boyfriend, Steven Hunter? I can't find much on him. What's that about, anyway?"

"I'm not sure. But I'm beginning to think the assault on the train was not a coincidence. The bastard said Grace couldn't run away like her mother. That's too close to the truth. Is Max around?"

"Just left with Cassie. Date night."

Good for him, Bobby thought. Max deserved a night out with the woman he loved.

"I'll check back tomorrow," Bobby said. "Fill Max in. He should know what's going on."

"Aye-aye, captain."

Bobby shook his head. "Good night."

Eddie was a character to be sure, and a gifted computer expert. Bobby shoved his mobile into his jacket pocket, puzzling over this new information.

Grace had made it sound as if the mother had died when she was a child. Did she even know the truth—that her mother had disappeared five years before her death? And did the father have anything to do with it?

It amazed Bobby how families could lie so easily.

Da's gone off on a sea journey and wun be back till next year.

You're just stayin' with Uncle Thomas until school lets out. Schools are better in London.

Lies, lies and more lies.

Feeling his life was completely out of control, Bobby had reached out to his aunt and uncle who had nothing to give their precocious nephew.

Feeling unloved, Bobby had reacted the only way an eleven-year-old boy could: he found another family—a local gang.

Those were dark days. Then came Max Templeton, who'd challenged Bobby out of his anger and away from his criminal career.

Max had saved his life, and Bobby would do anything to return the favor.

Which right now meant protecting Miss Grace Fairmont, a woman who was turning out to be her very own mystery. She'd been attacked at random and happened to be dating a man with no past?

He went back into the station to the interview room. He pushed open the door. Grace was gone.

"Where is she?" Bobby asked.

"One of my officers gave her a lift."

"What? To where?"

"She'd made a reservation at a bed and

breakfast for the night, paid in full so the missing credit cards are not an issue."

"But…" Bobby glanced out the door, confused and frustrated.

"But what, Mr. Finn?"

"I need to find her."

"She doesn't want to be found. She wants to be left alone."

Bobby stared at him.

"Yes, even from you."

"Bloody hell." He turned and raced out of the station.

Searching the street left, then right, he panicked.

He rang Eddie.

"Hey, long time no talk," the computer genius quipped.

"Grace Fairmont's credit cards: find the numbers, trace them. I need to find out where she's staying tonight."

"What, you lost her already? I thought—"

"Just do it, please."

Bobby paced the sidewalk. Blast, if she was hurt again while out of his company—

No, he wouldn't let it happen. He'd only

been gone minutes when she'd sneaked out of the station.

Sneaked away. Was she scared of him? Why? What had the Transport Police officer said to make her leave without even saying goodbye?

Now he sounded like a twit. He was a stranger who had offered comfort on a train, nothing more. He didn't deserve another thank-you or goodbye.

"Got it," Eddie said. "The Guest House of Edinburgh at 8 Newington Road."

"Thanks." Bobby clicked off his mobile and hailed a cab.

Instinct told him this wasn't a routine mugging, and this was anything but a routine American woman.

Now, if he could only get to her in time.

HE LIT a fag and glanced across the street at the dark-haired stranger in the leather jacket. This could be a problem.

The man named Bobby Finn climbed into a cab and took off, probably in search of the girl. Why? Who was *he* working for?

He stepped into the phone box and called in. "Eleven o'clock check-in. She's safe in Edinburgh for the time being."

"What does she know?"

"Can't be sure. She had company so I couldn't ask too many questions."

"Intel indicated she'd be traveling alone."

"She made a friend on the train. A man named Bobby Finn. Must be a cop, or former cop. He made me."

Silence.

"No," he clarified. "He doesn't know who I am but he suspected something."

"And the girl? Where is she now?"

"On her way to the inn."

"Did you identify her attacker?"

"Not yet. I'm worried about her new friend. He could complicate things."

"We'll have to take care of him."

"Yes."

"Set him up. Be creative."

"And if he's a cop?"

"All that matters is the girl and finding out what she knows."

"And if she knows nothing?"

"Unfortunate for her. If she doesn't know anything, she's as good as dead."

Chapter Four

Grace sat on her bed, paging through the worn leather diary. As she traced her fingers across the faded pages, she struggled to absorb her mother's thoughts and feelings.

An inquisitive little girl, Grace reaches for everything, especially my gold locket. I will give it to her one day, when she's all grown up.

Grace squeezed the locket in her hand. She could no longer wear it around her neck, thanks to the jerk who'd broken the clasp when he'd ripped it off.

The image of Bobby Finn's soft brown eyes taunted her. She should have said something before leaving, but the officer had a point: she knew nothing about Bobby. He could be a part of the attack on the train.

No, she didn't believe that. She'd left him behind because she felt herself relying on him, appreciating his steady hand and virile strength. She found herself falling into an old pattern of being taken care of by a man and she didn't like it, especially not with a stranger, for Pete's sake.

Still, he'd been helpful and gracious. She'd do the right thing and call his cell phone in the next day or two, apologize for running off and thank him again for his help. After all, she wasn't rude by nature.

And apparently not cautious, either.

She flipped a page in her mother's diary.

She has her father's blond hair and blue eyes. I hope she'll grow up looking more like him than me.

"Why did you want me to look like Dad?"

Someone knocked on her door. She sat straight and closed the diary, marking her place, with her locket chain.

"Yes?"

"Miss Fairmont? You'd mentioned wanting to take a bath? It's available," the innkeeper, Mrs. McCarthy, said through the door.

"That would be great."

"I'll put a note on the door and you can have it for thirty minutes then."

"Thanks."

She slipped on her footies and tied her robe around her waist. Her cell phone rang. The caller ID read Dad and she sighed. Well, she couldn't avoid this forever.

"Hi, Dad," she answered, trying to sound perky.

"Gracie," he said in that dad tone. "You were supposed to call when you'd checked in."

"I just got here."

"Just?"

"Have you spoken to Steven?"

"No, why?"

Odd. She figured Steven would have called her father for reinforcements, to convince her to come home.

"There was an incident on the train. I'm fine but it delayed my getting here."

"What kind of incident?"

"Someone stole my backpack. It's okay, though. They found it. Everything is fine."

"You're trying too hard."

"Dad, really, I'm fine. I'm about to take a bath and the clock's ticking on my thirty minutes so if you wouldn't mind, I'll call you tomorrow."

"You promise you're okay?"

"Promise."

"Gracie—"

"Love you, Dad."

"Love you, too, sweetie."

She hung up. Tension started around the base of her throat, that feeling she used to get when she'd try hanging out with a new friend, only to have Dad call the parents. Then he'd call his friend at the police department to do a background check and make her wait until the family had been approved before she could go over to play.

By the time she got there, playtime had been cut in half and the new friend thought Grace a freak with a bossy dad.

Grace knew he meant well. But after all

these years would she ever break free of his micromanaging? Ever become her own woman?

She dug in her backpack and pulled out the pepper spray. Maybe she was being paranoid, but she wasn't going anywhere without it from now on. She hoped she'd never have to use it, but holding it in her hand made her feel safe.

She headed down the hall to the bathroom, closed the door and locked it. Filling the tub, she sat on the toilet seat and dropped lavender bath salts into the water.

When she'd started dating Steven she'd thought it progress that Dad hadn't demanded Steven be fingerprinted and checked against the FBI database before her second date. Working for the government, Dad had connections and friends in all kinds of places.

But he'd seemed to trust her decision to date Steven. Dad's confidence made her feel a bit independent, like a mature, grown woman who could make her own choices and take care of herself.

For the most part Steven supported that concept, but every once in a while he'd slip, and it seemed that he was falling into the overprotective role, as well.

Was that because women are attracted to men like their fathers? Had she unwittingly attracted another controlling man into her life?

God, she hoped not. But here, thousands of miles and an ocean away, things looked a bit clearer than they did back home in Illinois. Things seemed a bit clearer since she'd had time to breathe and think without the pressures of school, lesson plans and paper-grading.

Now, if she could recover from the trauma of being attacked on the train she'd actually relax and enjoy this trip.

A trip designed to help her find peace.

She took off her clothes and slipped into the water, letting it warm her skin. She turned off the faucet and leaned back, her arms resting on the rim of the tub.

It felt heavenly, the quiet, the solitude.

After Dad had married Andrea and had two more children, life had been anything but quiet. Grace had wanted to please her new mother, maybe even find love there. Andrea did love Grace, but not the same way a biological mother would love her child. Grace was convinced of this.

She slid down, letting her shoulders rest deeper in the water. It had been Dad who had bathed her as a little girl, fed her and read to her at night.

Dad. He'd always seemed sad growing up, which is why Grace tried so hard to please him, not disobey his wishes. But at what cost? She was now in her twenties and still felt that tug to please him instead of pursuing her own dreams. Sure, she loved teaching science, but a part of her yearned for something more, something exciting.

"Girl, getting away has really mixed you up," she muttered.

Exciting? Grace was the definition of predictability. She didn't need or want anything outside that safe circle.

Or did she?

The lights went out and she was plunged into complete darkness. She sat up and reached for the pepper spray. Gripping it in her hand she heard the doorknob rattle.

Her heart slammed against her chest. Naked, wet and alone.

Vulnerable.

A flash of memory sparked panic.

Lights out. A stranger's presence. Grace was only five.

But she wasn't five now.

"Who's there?" she called.

Pepper spray in hand, she got out of the tub and fumbled in the dark, drying off the best she could. It wasn't pitch-black, thanks to the streetlight outside.

"Miss Fairmont?" the innkeeper called through the door. "We've had a power outage. I'm terribly sorry. Are you okay?"

"Fine, thanks."

She managed to get her robe on and tie the sash, her fingers trembling from the cold. Or was it fear?

"I've put a lantern in the hallway so you can find your way back to your room."

"Thank you."

Grace heard the floorboards squeak as the woman went back downstairs.

"It's okay. Breathe," she ordered herself.

With arms straight out and a finger on the pepper spray, she opened the door. She grabbed the lantern and went to her room, shaking off the sensation that someone was behind her, too close, within reach.

She'd always been scared of the dark. Ever since the lights had gone out when she was five and had waited for Dad to return with the flashlight. She could have sworn someone was there, with her in the bathroom.

Just like she felt someone was behind her now.

She spun around pointing the pepper spray at her imaginary stalker. The short hallway was empty.

"Get a grip," she muttered.

She turned and opened the door to her room.

"Grace," a deep voice said from the corner.

She screamed and fired off the pepper spray.

"Bloody Christ," a man said, coughed and collapsed to the floor. "Grace, don't. It's Bobby."

Bobby struggled to breathe, his eyes burning, his chest tightening as if someone was squeezing the air out of his lungs.

"How did you find me?" she cried.

"I'll explain." Cough. Cough. "I have to…talk to you."

He wheezed, struggling to breathe. Blast, if she called the police on him he'd be taken away for questioning and she'd be vulnerable again.

"What's all this?" Mrs. McCarthy said, rushing to Grace's room.

"Grace, please," he said.

"Call the police," she said to the innkeeper. The woman dashed off.

"You have to—" Cough. "Listen."

"The detective was right. You were part of the attack on the train, weren't you?"

She got down in his face, as he struggled to breathe.

"Tell me what you want," she demanded, then she shoved that bloody pepper spray at him again.

He lost it and grabbed her wrist away from his face. Although he couldn't focus his watering eyes, he could feel the warmth of her breath on his skin.

"I'm not the enemy," he rasped.

He snatched the spray canister from her

hand, tossed it aside and stood, knocking something off a dressing table. He leaned against the wall wishing the effects of the spray would pass, so he could explain why he was here.

And how would that conversation go, mate? I'm the babysitter hired by your daddy?

"What do you want?" she said.

His eyes burned as if they were on fire. "I need cold water." He stumbled out of her room and down the hall to the toilet.

He bent over the sink and turned on the cold water, cupping his hands. He splashed his eyes three, four times. Bugger, too many coincidences: the assault, the imposter officer who drove them around tonight and now the lights going out.

The bathroom door closed with a click. Grace stood there holding the damn pepper spray.

"Don't do that again," he said. "Please."

"Then tell me what this is really about."

"It's about your safety."

"And you care why?"

"It's my job."

"As a private detective?"

"Yes."

He splashed more water on his face.

"Who hired you?"

Now what? If he told her she'd be furious and if he didn't tell her she'd demand the police take him away.

Bugger, she'd probably insist they lock him up anyway.

"Your father hired me," he admitted.

"How could he?"

"Simple. He rang my boss, asked for help protecting his little girl, and I'm practically blinded for my trouble." He pressed a cool washcloth to his eyes.

"How much is he paying you?" she said.

"I'm sorry?"

"I'll double it if you leave me alone."

He slowly lowered the washcloth and looked at her through the mirror. Was she that offended by his presence?

Sure she was. Grace was about dignity and class; Bobby came from street rubbish.

No matter. He had a job to do.

"I'm not leaving you alone," he said. "This job is important to me and I'd rather you not muck it up because you're on an independent streak."

"You make it sound so frivolous."

"Isn't it?"

"You wouldn't understand."

"I understand this." He turned and squared off at her. "You've got a father who wants you safe. He knows you have a sweet look about you that makes you a target and he cares enough to hire someone to watch after you. You're lucky you've got someone who cares so much."

"I'm twenty-six, dammit, I don't want a bodyguard."

"Maybe it's not about what you want. Do this for your father. Give him peace of mind."

And help me keep my job. He didn't say it. He knew she thought him the enemy. She couldn't care less about Bobby's job, his future.

She wrapped her arms around her midsection. "It always has been about him. I was doing this for me."

"No one's stopping you." He sighed and placed his hands to his hips. "Look, everyone can get what they want. You can have your holiday; your father can have peace of mind and I can keep my job."

Grace had imagined the compassion in his eyes, earlier, the tenderness. It wasn't real.

"This was all about your job," she said in a flat tone.

"It's my life. I don't have family like you."

"Aren't you lucky."

"Miss Fairmont?" a man called through the door. "This is the police."

She pressed the back of her head against the door and studied Bobby Finn. He was a charmer to be sure, convincing her that he cared about her safety.

"Please, Grace," Bobby said, his eyes still red and watering. "If they take me in I can't protect you."

"From what? There's nothing to protect me from. I got mugged. It's over."

"I couldn't stand it if anything else happened to you."

"Why, because they'd dock your salary?"

He stared at her, but didn't answer.

"Miss Fairmont?" the officer called again.

She opened the door. "I'm sorry, but there's been a misunderstanding. It was dark and I couldn't see who it was."

"Are you saying you know this man?"

She glanced over her shoulder. "Yes, he's a friend. He wanted to surprise me."

"Scared the wits out of me," Mrs. McCarthy said.

"Please, come into the hall, miss," the officer said.

She followed him and shut the bathroom door.

"You're sure you're all right?" he asked.

"I'm fine." *Just angry as hell.*

"But he broke into your room," Mrs. McCarthy said.

"My fault, actually," she lied. "I left the door unlocked. It's okay. He was trying to surprise me."

"Looks like he got the surprise with pepper spray in the face." He glanced at the cylinder in her hand.

"Yeah, well." She slipped it into her robe pocket.

"Since all's well then." The officer nodded

and started down the stairs. Grace heard Mrs. McCarthy offer him tea for his trouble.

Grace glanced at the bathroom door. Great, just what she didn't want on this trip: a shadow. Wasn't that part of the purpose? To prove she could live her own life independently of men like her father?

She opened the door to find Bobby coughing and splashing water on his face. Regret settled across her shoulders. She did feel bad that she'd sprayed the very man who'd given her comfort on the train.

Because it was his job.

"Here's the deal," she said.

He turned and blinked repeatedly.

"I need my space. Lots of it. I have things to do on this trip. Personal things."

"I understand."

She sighed. "If I'd wanted company I would have invited Steven."

"Of course," he said, his face set like stone.

"Fine, I'll see you in the morning." She opened the door and started down the hall. "I'll be stopping by the American Express office to pick up a new credit card. The rest will take a few days to get here, so I'll probably do the sights." She opened the door to her room. "Good night."

Bobby glanced down the hall. She had a corner room, which was good. He'd curl up against the wall and sit outside her door. Might be overkill, then again, might not be.

He still wasn't sure what to make of this assignment.

Although, he was getting a clearer picture of Miss Grace Fairmont. She was tougher than he'd originally thought, determined as hell, and a bit self-centered. All she could think about were her own needs, taking this trip regardless of her father's worry.

And he should be worried. Bobby wasn't fibbing when he'd said she had a look about her that drew unsavory characters. Sweet, innocent and trusting. That's what Miss Fairmont looked like on the outside.

But then people weren't always what they seemed if Bobby's last case was any indication.

If his own family was any indication.

Mum had always seemed so loving.

Loving parents don't abandon their children.

"Ah, that's what happens when you come home, Bobby," he muttered.

Home? He sat on the hardwood floor and studied the knickknacks on the table in the hallway. This is what a real home looked like: warm and cozy.

He'd never lived in any home like this. No, his first home was filled with sadness, and his second home with judgment and disappointment.

In Bobby.

He wouldn't disappoint Max Templeton. He didn't care what hoops she made him jump through; he'd do whatever it took to stay close to Grace Fairmont and complete his assignment.

Crossing his legs at the ankles, he leaned against the wall. He took a deep breath, inhaling the scent of lavender, realizing it was Grace's scent that hovered in the hallway outside her door.

It was a good thing he was methodical when it came to women. He always called the shots, deciding when a relationship would start and how long it would last. Never more than a few months, of course. He wasn't a fool. He wouldn't completely give his heart, knowing that in the end the woman would abandon him for a smarter chap, a better provider.

No, you couldn't count on a woman for anything but great sex. Most of the time, anyway.

He glanced at Grace's door. He'd bet she was a wild one between the sheets, the outwardly reserved ones usually were. Not that he'd ever know firsthand. Becoming intimate with this woman was dangerous on so many levels.

Grace Fairmont was the type you wanted to take care of and protect. The most dangerous kind. They drew you in and stole your heart while you were busy buying them flowers or tickets to Elton John concerts.

SMACK! Just like *that* you'd be knocked on your bum and wouldn't even know what hit you.

Because she was smarter than you.

Because she stole your heart and now you were half a man.

Not that he'd ever lost his heart completely.

He'd come close twice, and both times he'd managed to rip himself out of the fire before he got burned too badly.

It was good experience to recognize the dangerous ones.

And Grace Fairmont was dangerous as hell.

SHE PACED her small room, did the deep-breathing technique Steven had taught her and opened her cell phone to call Dad.

Bobby's words taunted her. *You're lucky you've got someone who cares so much.*

Is that what you called it? Luck?

Grace called it a curse, especially as she'd gotten older and Dad had never loosened up. She was an adult woman. When was he going to get that through his head?

She hit the speed-dial number and it rang.

"Hello?" he answered.

"Dad?"

"What's wrong?"

"Your bodyguard."

Silence.

"Dad, I'm twenty-six. You can't do stuff like this."

"How did you find out?"

"He told me."

"Out of the blue a complete stranger walks up to you and announces he's your bodyguard?"

"No, it's complicated."

"It started on the train, didn't it? When you had your little incident?"

"Yes, that's how we met. Then he showed up in my room and now I want him out of my life."

"Why was he in your room?"

"I didn't ask. I got him with pepper spray."

"You were prepared. Good girl."

"I don't feel very good. You know what a guy looks like after he's been sprayed?"

"I can imagine."

Grace didn't have to. The image of Bobby's bloodshot eyes and vulnerable position on the floor haunted her. She hated inflicting that kind of pain, especially to someone who'd helped her only hours earlier.

Helped her because he was paid to help her.

"I want to do this alone, Dad. I want to tour Scotland and learn about my mother. On my own."

"Let him follow you, Grace. You won't even know he's there."

She heard Bobby cough outside her door.

"Dad, I'm not a little girl anymore. It's time you let go."

Silence.

"Dad?"

"I will, honey. I promise. As soon as you return from your trip I'll give you your space."

"I need it now."

"No."

"No? Okay, now I have to play Mission Impossible and escape from my bodyguard?"

"Grace, please don't do that. For my peace of mind please let him do his job. I…" He hesitated. "I have my reasons."

"Dad, I love you but you've got to stop—"

"I can't, Gracie. Not while you're out of the country. There are things you don't know." He hesitated. "Things about your mother."

Chapter Five

Her heart beat a little faster. "What kind of things?" she asked.

"This isn't something you talk to your daughter about over the phone, Grace."

Oh, God, what was it?

"Dad, you're freaking me out here."

"Your mother was and will continue to be a mystery to me in many ways. We loved each other, but she had her secrets."

Grace sat on the bed and thought about Steven, and how she kept a part of herself hidden from him, not entirely sure why.

"What do Mom's secrets have to do with me?"

"She ran with a wild group back in the U.K.," he said. "I'm not sure what they were into, but when I'd ask her about her life there she'd withdraw and look so terribly sad. After a few months I stopped asking. I'm afraid it might have been illegal and I wouldn't want anything to happen to you because of things your mother did."

"Wait a second, you always made her out to be this loving, compassionate mother who'd do anything for her child."

"She loved you so very much."

Grace couldn't remember that love thanks to a drunk driver hitting mom's car head-on. Hell, if it wasn't for the photo in Grace's locket she wouldn't know what her mother looked like—and now that was gone.

"What do you think she was into, exactly?" she said.

"I have no idea. But it was ugly. She may have even spent some time in jail."

"Jail… Is that why you didn't want me to take this trip? Because you were afraid I'd find out the truth?"

"There's only one truth, Gracie. Your mother loved you. Whoever she was ten years before she gave birth to you, she was no longer that person."

That *really* didn't sound good.

"Do you know why she was in prison?"

"I don't even know for sure she was in prison. She wouldn't talk about her past or her family. But the way she acted in public, suspicious, like she was on the alert all the time, made me wonder."

"I wish you had told me this before."

"I know, honey. I'm sorry. I didn't want you to think ill of your mom."

Grace wasn't sure what this trip would reveal, but whether good or bad, she was determined to find some kind of resolution. Even if it meant she'd discover the dark side of her supposedly loving mother.

No, not supposedly. It didn't matter what her mom had been into, because she *was* a loving mother. Her diary proved it with every word about her baby girl, Gracie.

"Can we compromise?" he said.

"How?"

"You finish out this trip with the body-guard close by and I'll work on easing up when you get home. Please, Gracie, just this one last time."

She sighed. It started to make sense: Dad's overprotectiveness and micromanaging. He'd been left alone to raise a baby girl. A big responsibility when you shared it with someone and even bigger when you were doing it on your own. Isn't that what she'd learned from the parents of middle-schoolers? The single parents struggled so hard to give their children everything they needed, fighting time constraints and just plain exhaustion from burning the candle at both ends.

She thought about the time Dad had rushed her to the hospital after she'd broken her wrist, the times he sat up with her because of night terrors. She used to dream of monsters hiding in the shadows of her room; she used to hear someone breathing.

Dad had done so much for her, on his own. And he was asking this one simple thing.

"Okay," she said. "I'll keep the bodyguard."

"Thank you, Gracie." He sounded tired, weary.

"I'll even try not to blast him with pepper spray again," she joked.

"That's a good girl."

She smiled. She'd be fifty and he'd still be calling her a good girl.

"What's on the agenda for tomorrow?" he asked.

"The Royal Mile. Edinburgh Castle and Holyrood, I think." She thought about her chat with Bobby on the train. "I heard it's fantastic."

"I thought you were heading up north right away."

"I have to wait for replacement credit cards. I can pick up a new Am Ex card, but I have to hang around for the others."

"You should have brought traveler's checks."

"Thanks, yeah, I've figured that out."

"I'm sorry, of course you have. I'm doing it again. Okay, sweetheart. You have a wonderful time. Check in once in a while, okay?"

"I will, Dad, promise."

"Love you."

"Love you back. 'Bye."

She pressed the End button and placed the phone on her nightstand. Mom's diary caught her eye. Would Grace find hidden meanings there? Something to reveal her mother's secrets, her dark past?

"Oh, stop. Dad's overreacting," she muttered.

True, but he overreacted because he cared. She could hardly fault him for loving her so much.

For eight years Dad had done so many things for her without help from a wife. He'd done pretty darn well for a single father.

She had to respect him for that. And now that she knew the truth about Mom, Grace understood why this trip in particular made Dad nervous. She wished he'd spoken with her in person instead of hiding the truth.

Was he worried that she couldn't handle it? That she'd idolized her mother so much the truth would destroy Grace?

No, regardless of what her father thought, Grace knew she was stronger than that, tougher. She didn't need to be protected and she surely didn't need a bodyguard.

Yet she was stuck with the handsome Bobby Finn.

She opened the door and there in the corner of the hallway sat her bodyguard.

"You can't sleep out here," she whispered.

"Sure I can. Unless they call the police back."

He sniffed and rubbed his eyes.

Guilt snagged her conscience.

She went back into her room and grabbed a spare pillow and blanket.

"I spoke with Dad." She tossed the pillow and blanket at him. "You've still got a job."

"Lovely," he said with a forced smile.

"Look, I'm sorry about the pepper spray."

"I'm not. It means you're on the ball this time."

This time, right, not like when she'd been attacked on the train. The stairs creaked, and Grace took a step toward her room. Bobby stood as if ready for a confrontation.

Mrs. McCarthy stepped into the hallway and glanced at Bobby and then Grace. "What's this?"

"He's…we're…" What should she say? If she admitted Bobby was her bodyguard it would surely alarm the woman. "We're having an argument," Grace blurted out.

"Well, I'm sorry, but your friend is going to have to leave. He can't sleep on the floor and we don't have any rooms available tonight."

Bobby looked so completely disheartened.

"Come on now," the innkeeper said. "You'd best be off. I think the Greystone Inn down the block has a few single rooms open." She motioned with her hand.

Bobby didn't move. He was going to get them both kicked out of the inn.

"No, it's okay," Grace said. "He can stay in my room." She glanced at Mrs. McCarthy. "Can't he?"

"I'll have to charge you an extra ten pounds."

"Of course." Grace glanced at Bobby, who clutched the pillow and blanket, but hadn't moved.

"Well?" Mrs. McCarthy prompted.

Bobby grudgingly walked toward Grace and hesitated as he passed her. His eyes were dark and intense as if he was furious, and for a split second she thought better of inviting him in to spend the night.

He disappeared into her room.

"Thank you so much," she said to Mrs. McCarthy.

"I'm not used to so much excitement."

"I'm sorry."

"You'll keep it quiet up here?"

"Yes, ma'am."

What, did she think they were lovers?

With pursed lips the woman nodded and turned to go downstairs. She wasn't happy. Well, neither was Grace. She'd wanted solitude and peace on this trip. Instead, she was stuck with a sexy stranger as her shadow.

She went into her room and shut the door. Bobby stood by the window, peeking through the sheers. "I'll wait a few hours and go back in the hallway."

"Oh, okay." She climbed into bed and turned off the bedside light. "Good night."

He didn't respond.

She lay there, eyes partially closed, watching his silhouette as he stood guard at the window. Strangely enough, she felt safer with him here.

Resentment took hold. She wanted to stand on her own, without her father or a body-guard or Steven holding her hand.

"What happened?" Bobby said.

She opened her eyes. "What do you mean?"

"What made you ask me into your room?"

"My dad explained why he's worried about me. I agreed to keep you around."

"Keep me around? Like a stray puppy?" He laughed.

"I didn't mean it like that."

"It's okay. I'm used to it."

A few more minutes passed. She suddenly wished she knew more about this man's personal life. No, it was better not to know. There was something about Bobby that excited and intrigued her.

"I have to admit this is a first," he said.

"What?"

"Spending the night with a woman, but not in her bed."

Grace clutched the down comforter tighter to her chest. She'd sensed he was one of those guys, the kind that enjoyed sexual affairs but never engaged in love. She'd dated a few men like that. Thank goodness she'd found Steven.

She sighed. Solid, predictable Steven. Dad

had been so relieved when she'd found him, especially after her wild teenage years.

She was lucky that Steven had come into her life, moved into her apartment complex and soon afterward, introduced himself. That had been two years ago. She wondered why she'd put him off for so long, discouraged him from making his official proposal.

"Are you married?" she asked Bobby.

"You've had a rough day," he said. "Get some sleep."

Obviously she'd hit a sore spot. Well, if she was going to spend the next two weeks in his company, she didn't want it to be awkward.

"Sorry," she said.

"For what?"

She propped herself up and studied his silhouette as he continued to stare out the window. "I didn't mean to pry."

"Don't let it happen again."

She heard humor in his voice and struggled to read his expression in the dark.

"It's fine. Go to sleep," he said.

She lay back down and pulled the comforter up to her shoulders. "Good night."

"Sweet dreams."

Her last conscious thought was how odd those words sounded coming from Bobby Finn's mouth.

THE NEXT DAY, Bobby followed Grace to the American Express office where she got a replacement card. Apparently she'd need it.

She spent the morning buying gifts for family and friends back home. Bobby had never intentionally gone shopping with a woman. He considered it torture.

Yet with Grace it wasn't so bad. She was genuinely enthusiastic about every purchase as if she'd struck gold. It was hard to stay cross with that kind of enthusiasm smiling back at you.

"Look at this wool scarf," she said. "It'll be perfect for Dad, and the girls, they'll love the Scotland flag patches. They'll put them on their denim jackets and they'll feel so cool."

She shoved them back into her bag and shrugged, grinning from ear to ear.

She wore her hair straight today, framing

her round face and full lips. She looked enticing, like a female he'd proposition.

"What? You think I should have gotten Dad a different plaid?"

"It's fine." He recovered, snapping his gaze from hers. Bugger, she'd noticed he'd drifted into lust. *Not good, mate.* "You know whose pattern that is?" he said.

"Who?" She started walking and he kept pace beside her.

"The Black Watch."

"Sounds sinister."

"On the contrary, it's an infantry battalion of the Royal Regiment of Scotland. This country has had quite the history, always fighting for independence, always fighting to establish its own identity."

"I can relate."

"Can you?" he teased. "Well, at least no blood's been shed over your independence."

"Not yet, anyway." She smiled at him and he wondered if the threat was aimed at Bobby or at her father.

"Hey, what about you? You haven't bought anything today," she said.

"Shopping isn't my favorite pastime, although now that you mention it, I could use a few pairs of trousers and shirts. I didn't have time to pack before I got on the train."

"Okay, great. I used to love helping Dad shop for clothes, especially when he started dating."

"You didn't feel threatened by that? The other women?"

"He didn't date all that many and besides, I wanted a mother so badly. For a long time I thought it was my fault I didn't have one."

He hesitated and touched her jacket. "Your fault?"

"Yeah, y'know, if he didn't have me around he would have found a wife faster, stuff like that. You think weird stuff when you're a kid."

Or not so weird. Bobby had cried so hard when his mum left him with Uncle Thomas. She'd said he needed a male role model, but Bobby knew it was something else. He'd failed. Miserably, and she couldn't stand having him around.

"Hey, I'm over it," she said. She studied him with worry in her eyes. "You know, before this trip is over you're going to have to tell me what puts that look on your face."

"What look?"

"You go like this." She clenched her jaw and narrowed her eyes.

"I do not look like that."

"Uh, yeah, you really do."

Blast, he was that transparent?

"Help me pick out some clothes," he said, picking up the pace.

"My pleasure."

Bloody marvelous, now he was her pet project. She'd probably dress him in fancy trousers, a tailored shirt and stuffy tie.

"Why is it so important to you?" she said.

"What, clothes?"

"Your job?"

"It's my life's work."

"Following American girls around?"

"Catching bad guys, putting them away where they can't hurt anyone. This—" he motioned to the space between them "—is a temporary diversion."

A pleasant diversion.

She glanced away and he thought he might

have hurt her feelings. How could that be? He didn't say anything out of order.

Yet Bobby, the master of flirtation, put his foot in it on more than one occasion with this girl.

"I'll bet you can get something in here." She steered him into a shop selling wool sweaters, tartan trousers and colorful souvenirs. "Look at all this stuff," she said, her eyes wide as they scanned the wares.

"What's your plaid?" she said.

"I don't have one."

He didn't have a plaid; didn't have a homeland, although he was born in Ireland, he'd been shipped off to England for the better part of his life.

"Everyone's got a plaid, right?" she said.

He shook his head. "Americans."

"I'll pick one out for you. Something that complements your eyes."

"I wear black," he said, sounding like a child. "Black trousers, black jacket."

"Okay, then we'll find you a shirt. Black plaid, perhaps?" She winked.

He stood behind her as she sifted through

the rack of clothes. Instincts always on alert, he scanned the tourists filling the shop, paying attention to any oddities or anyone unusually interested in Grace.

Could the attack on the train and the power outage at the inn be simple coincidences? Possibly. He hoped so. He didn't like the thought that this girl on holiday was at risk.

"This one," she said, pulling a plaid shirt from the rack. "Large, right?"

"It's bloody purple," he said.

"It's maroon and it will look great. Hold it for me." She handed it to him and glanced behind him. Her brows furrowed.

He turned to see what she was looking at.

People milled about picking through the scarves and hats on sale. He looked back at her.

"I'm seeing things," she said.

"What things?"

"My boyfriend. I swear I just saw him walk out the front door. They say everyone's got a double. That must have been him." She turned back to the rack of shirts.

Bobby glanced out the front window of the

store. He wished he knew what the bloke looked like. He made a mental note to have Eddie send him a photograph of the boyfriend.

She turned and handed him another shirt.

"No, absolutely not," Bobby said. "I may be color blind, but I know pink when I see it."

"Just kidding." She shot him that silly smile of hers and put it back.

When she smiled he wanted to touch her cheek, trace his thumb across her soft skin.

He took a slight step back. He really didn't need to fall into lust with this girl. She was classy, had a boyfriend, led an uncomplicated life.

Unlike Bobby.

Bobby was broken in more ways than he could count, and he'd never be capable of giving true love to a woman. That was just fine with him.

"Okay, try these on and I'll be waiting outside the dressing room," she said.

"Right outside?"

"Of course, I wouldn't want to miss the fashion show."

With her hand to his back she pushed him

to a dressing room. He peeked through the slit between the drape and the wall to make sure she hadn't strayed too far. She was right outside the dressing room.

In record time he changed into the wild plaid trousers and a clashing shirt. Colors to complement his eyes? Rubbish. He looked in the mirror and nearly burst out laughing. He only hoped it had the same effect on Grace.

He flung open the drape. "I may be color blind but—"

She was gone.

"Grace?"

Maybe she was looking for more clashing patterns.

"If you're looking for the blond woman, she ran out the front door," a teenage girl said.

Bobby glanced through the storefront window and spotted Grace outside.

"Grace!" he called after her. He raced through the store, the clerk calling after him.

What on earth was she doing running away? Was it all a ruse? A game to get free of him?

Bobby pushed through tourists and raced

into the street, only now aware that he wasn't wearing shoes and had left his wallet in the dressing room in his pants.

Bollocks, where had she gone?

"Grace!" he called down the street.

He thought he saw her blond head through the crowd of tourists and pushed through to get to her.

"Stop! Thief!" someone cried behind him.

"Grace!" he shouted again.

Sirens echoed down the street. God, no, she wasn't hit by a car or injured or—

"I don't think so," a man said, grabbing Bobby's arm. He wrenched free, racing after her, desperate to keep her safe.

Maybe if he had kept Wendy safe Mum wouldn't have sent him away.

For crying out loud, where had that come from?

Something tripped him and suddenly there were three men pinning him to the sidewalk. He heard a woman's cries. His heart clenched with panic.

The sirens wailed. She couldn't be hurt. He'd never forgive himself.

"Get off me." He struggled against his aggressors. He couldn't budge.

The dozen faces standing over him parted and two police officers looked down at him.

One of the officers shook his head in disgust. "All this for a pair of purple trousers?"

Chapter Six

"Hold on a bloody minute, it's a misunderstanding," Bobby protested as the police pulled him to his feet and walked him to the squad car.

He still couldn't believe they'd cuffed him for running off with a pair of ridiculous purple trousers. He hadn't given much thought to dashing into the crowded street wearing the store's gear. He'd been too worried about Grace.

As they shoved him into the back of the police car he fought back his shame. He'd failed at so many things in his life. Why should this be any different?

Bugger, where had she disappeared to and why? Was this shopping lark her clever way of giving him the slip?

"Hey, wait!" a woman cried.

Grace. He turned and looked into her concerned blue eyes.

"Why are you arresting him?" she demanded.

"He stole these trousers right off the rack."

"No, it's a mistake. It's my fault."

"Sorry, miss, we're taking him in."

"My clothes are still in the fitting room," Bobby shouted as the officer shut the door.

Grace said something to the copper, probably asking where they were taking Bobby, then she ran off.

Alone.

And Bobby was stuck in the back of a squad car, helpless and unable to protect her. When he was released he should call Max to have someone else assigned to this case. Eddie maybe. He'd be a lot of fun for Grace and good American company.

"So, you do this often, Finn? Run off in other peoples' trousers?"

Bobby's blood ran cold. "You know my name?"

The cop didn't answer. Bobby glanced out

the car window. They headed away from the Royal Mile, away from town.

"Where are we going?" Bobby asked.

"Some place where we can talk."

Not good. Were these blokes truly the police?

"Talk about what?"

"About how we don't appreciate known criminals showing up and mingling with our tourists."

"I wasn't mingling with anyone."

"No, you were just caught stealing. We know all about you, Bobby. Officer Markham at Transport Police pulled your criminal history. We know about the breaking and entering and drug-peddling."

"That's not true." His temper flared.

"Records never lie, mate. We're going to give you a re-education before you decide to hook up with your old friends."

"A thorough background check would also reveal I'd been with Scotland Yard."

"He's got a sense of humour, that one," the driver said to his partner.

"Either that or he's off his trolley."

"I was with the Special Crimes Initiative," Bobby said.

"Definitely off his trolley."

It didn't matter what they did to him, but someone had to watch out for Grace.

"I've been hired to look after the girl," he said. "At least call in and have someone check on her."

"Why, she looked pretty independent to me," the driver said.

"You should have heard her read me the riot act because I was taking her boyfriend into custody. She's got a mouth on her."

"Her father hired me to accompany her on this trip," Bobby explained.

"Now why would he do that?" the driving cop said.

"He didn't tell me why. He just said he was worried about her."

"Ah, she'll be fine. She's meeting us at the station," the other one said.

"She'll be waiting a long time," his partner said.

They chuckled.

"Listen to me!" Bobby pounded on the seat between them. "I need to get back to her."

The lead cop turned around and eyed Bobby. "You'll get back when we're done."

THEY PULLED into an old warehouse parking lot.

"In there," the driver cop said. "No one will hear anything."

Adrenaline pounded through Bobby's veins. He was going to be beaten and tortured. Why? Because of his criminal background? No, there was something else going on here.

They parked and the lead cop opened his door. "Out with ya."

Bobby took a deep breath, scooted out and shouldered the guy in the gut. They both went down.

"Christ almighty!" the guy said.

Bobby was pulled off by the second cop, who spun him around and slugged him in the gut. Bobby went down gasping for breath.

"He messed up my uniform," the first cop said, kicking him in the chest.

Bobby rolled away, his ribs aching from the kick.

"Let's get this over with. Hold him."

Bobby was pulled to his feet and held up by one cop while the other slugged him again. Sure, they didn't want to damage his face or anything so obvious.

As he struggled to recover, something pricked his arm. He was tossed to the gravel drive, his head slamming against the rugged stones.

He lay there, dazed, trying to make sense of what was happening. All this for stealing a pair of trousers and a shirt? Bollocks. Even with his record, his criminal background was nothing compared to his years at Scotland Yard, where he'd tried desperately to make up for his sins.

Where he'd met Max Templeton and got a second chance, and a third with the Blackwell Group: finding a serial killer, saving a lost boy, protecting Grace.

Max. Cassie. Grace.

She was vulnerable, too innocent. Too sweet to be involved in anything like this.

Like what? Like violence and torture?

Torture. Failure. Grace. He was failing again.

Couldn't think. Thoughts spinning as if he'd drunk too much ale. A pint. Three pints. How much had he had with Art last night? He couldn't remember. Couldn't remember why he was here on the ground, gravel digging into his cheek.

Suddenly sitting up.

Who hired him? Why was he watching Grace? What about her mother?

That's why Grace was here, in Scotland, yes, that's why she'd come. She wanted to find out about her mum, where she'd lived as a girl.

The past. Leave the past alone. Bobby knew that. Hadn't spoken to Uncle Thomas since his aunt's funeral. Bastard.

The man on the train. His name? Harry Franklin. Earring, worn trainers, expensive suit. Inspector Parker. Helpful chap. Gave her his card.

His brain fast-forwarded through the last forty-eight hours. He could hardly focus. The fall must have knocked him senseless.

Brains rattled. Would be fine in the

morning. They were trying to help him, keep him on the straight and narrow.

Like Max. Max always helped. Had faith in Bobby.

Where was he going next? Up north, where? Maybe Pitlochry. Mentioned in her diary.

Diary?

Dark leather, with ties. Saw it on her nightstand. Mother's notes to her daughter. Dead mother.

What happened to mother?

Died in a car accident. Died when Grace was a baby. Didn't know her mum.

Where did Mum grow up?

Don't know. Mum was gone, dead. Grace was a baby. Grace…she didn't like having someone follow her, act as her bodyguard.

Not much of a bodyguard, is he? They're calling. Have to report back.

Pulled to his feet. Bobby struggled to get balance.

Must have hit his head when he fell outside the shop. Probably a concussion. Will take him to a clinic, call the girl. He'll be fine.

In the backseat, spinning, everything spinning.

Thought they were going to torture him. Paranoid chap.

Blur of images, buildings, steel fence. Feeling sick. Close eyes.

Relax, mate. Would be over soon. Would wake up right as rain.

"Grace." He breathed her name.

Save her. Had to help her. Had to…sleep.

GRACE PACED around Bobby's hospital bed. The police believed he'd knocked himself stupid when his head hit the sidewalk. Bull. He was conscious when they drove off. Something else had happened to him. He'd been out for three hours.

If this wasn't a case of brutality, she didn't know what was. He'd obviously been knocked unconscious by the two cops who'd arrested him outside the shop.

Why? It was a misunderstanding. Guilt tore at her stomach. If she hadn't run off, chasing after a ghost who looked like her boyfriend, Bobby wouldn't have run out of the store after her. He wouldn't have been taken away by the cops and wouldn't be lying in a hospital bed.

"Miss Fairmont?" A man wearing a navy suit, crisp white shirt and maroon tie stood in the doorway.

"Yes?" She stepped closer to Bobby and touched his hand in a protective gesture.

"I'm Detective Inspector Owen. I want to apologize for any misunderstanding." He took a few steps into the room.

"No misunderstanding," she said. "Your men abused my friend."

"I'm sorry you think so, miss. I'll look into it."

"You do that."

She stroked the back of Bobby's hand. She and Bobby had the absolute worst luck.

"It's an easy fix," the inspector said.

She glared at him. "Really?"

"We'll drop the theft charges and you don't pursue this line of thinking."

"You mean the one that dictates I notify your superiors about police brutality?"

He glanced at the floor and crossed his

arms over his chest. "There's no point in that, miss. If your boyfriend hadn't stolen the clothes none of this would have happened."

"He didn't steal anything. He ran out of the shop because he was worried about me."

"Why's that, miss?"

She shook her head. Bobby seemed to be sleeping so peacefully.

"You're here on holiday then?" the inspector asked.

"Yes."

"I'd hate to hold you up with unnecessary paperwork. I'll give your bloke the benefit of the doubt and you can be on your way."

"Gee, thanks."

"Unless you feel that's unfair."

"It's fine," she said, frustrated, wanting to head north sooner than later.

"Good day, then."

She didn't look up, but sensed the inspector leave the room.

She squeezed Bobby's hand, remembering what the doctor had said. It seemed like a minor concussion, nothing to be alarmed about. Then why was he still asleep?

She sat in the chair and rubbed the back of his hand. He looked so still and broken, nothing like the man who'd protected her on the train or stood watch outside her room at the inn.

He seemed completely drained of energy. Because of her.

No, she wouldn't take full responsibility. She didn't want him tagging along on this trip. That had been Dad's idea.

"Wendy," Bobby muttered.

Great, now he was dreaming about old girlfriends.

"Bobby? It's me, Grace. Can you hear me?"

He moaned and squeezed the sheets between his fingers.

"Shh. It's okay now," she said.

"No!" He sat up, gasping for air. His eyes were open but not totally focused.

"Bobby, look at me. It's Grace. Do you know who I am?"

"Grace?" His brown eyes widened, he swallowed, then fell back against the bed. "Where am I?"

"At the hospital. You lost consciousness."

"How?"

"They said when you fell and hit your head on the sidewalk, remember? Outside the tartan store?"

He pinned her with his gaze. "You were gone."

"I'm sorry, really, I'm an idiot."

"Where did you go?"

"It's stupid, and now it caused this. I feel like a jerk."

"Where?"

"I saw that guy, the one who looks like Steven, and I thought it was him. He glanced at me through the window and gave me this weird look. I ran outside but lost him in the crowd. You ran after me and forgot to change your pants. The cops came for you and you fell and knocked your head on the cement, which makes no sense because you spoke to me before they took you away."

"What did I say?"

"You said that your pants were still in the fitting room. I got them, and your wallet and went to the station. Then the cops called and said you were being brought to the hospital."

"I fell. Hit my head on the rocks."

"Not rocks, the sidewalk. Do you remember?"

"Not really."

"He's awake?" A doctor came into the room with a clipboard in his hand. "Excellent."

"He doesn't remember things," she said.

"To be expected. There's minor swelling around the brain, nothing serious, but even a slight contusion can cause memory issues. You remember this pretty lass, eh, Bobby?" the doctor said.

Bobby looked at her. "I remember Grace."

"Very good. How about where you are?"

"Ireland."

She looked at the doctor.

"You're in Edinburgh," the doctor corrected. "Do you know why you're here?"

"I'm with Grace."

"When is your birthday?"

"October 7, 1974."

"Good, excellent. We need to keep you overnight, young man." He glanced at Grace. "Just as a precaution."

"But you said it wasn't serious." She'd kick herself if he was seriously injured because she'd flaked out and gone chasing after a ghost.

"I don't think it is. But my recommendation is to let him spend the night to be sure. You may stay for another few hours if you wish." The doctor smiled and left.

She studied Bobby, who didn't seem to have any visible head injury, yet looked out of it. "What happened?" She took a step toward him and he glanced away, out the window. He was angry with her.

"Look, I'm sorry," she said. "I saw this guy who looked like Steven and I thought he'd come over to check on me, but that's impossible because he could never get here that quickly."

"Like the police."

"Excuse me?"

"They showed up too bloody fast." His eyes met hers. "It's like they were around the corner waiting to arrest me. I'm not even sure they were legitimate police."

"Then what were they?"

He closed his eyes.

A few minutes passed in silence.

"Just relax, let them take care of you tonight," she said.

"I can't relax." He pinned her with his dark-brown eyes. "I need to keep you safe."

For a second he sounded as if he cared about her. No, he didn't respect her, didn't think her able to take care of herself. Yet he was the one lying in the hospital bed.

"How did you hurt your head?" she said.

"I don't remember, exactly."

"They claim you fell."

"Against the gravel, yes, I remember that."

"There wasn't any gravel on the sidewalk."

He sat a little straighter and fisted his left hand. His usual expression, one of mild humor, faded and he stared into space as if remembering something.

"Bobby?"

"You need to get me out of here." He pulled the IV needle from his hand and climbed out of bed.

"You sure that's a good idea?" she said.

"I'm fine. I can't be here, especially if they're going to send you home in a couple of hours."

"I can take care of myself."

He shot her a look of disbelief. She was tempted to hightail it out of there, but he'd find her eventually, or worse, chase after her in his hospital gown and get arrested for indecent exposure.

Why did she care? She didn't want his company on this trip.

She stepped outside his hospital room and waited for him to dress. Maybe she didn't welcome Bobby's company, but she'd promised Dad. And in return he'd promised that he'd back off after this trip.

Most twenty-six-year-olds wouldn't care about what their fathers thought, they would have moved far away by now—to the West Coast, or another country even. But Grace has always wanted to please her father, desperate to make him happy because for the longest time he'd always seemed so sad.

Because Mom had died.

Grace couldn't bear to make him angry, to see that disappointment on his face. He'd frowned at her quite a bit during high school. Even though she'd kept her grades up, she'd had some fun, experimenting with alcohol and boys. She'd had her heart broken in high school when, behind Dad's back, she'd managed to date bad boy Andy Peters. But instead of rubbing it in her face, when Dad found out he only said he was sorry and that although this was her first heartbreak, it would probably not be the last. He held her and told her it would be okay.

Thinking back, he'd always been there for her, when she'd succeeded and when she'd failed, and he'd never made her feel bad about her mistakes.

He'd been a great dad and still was.

Bobby stepped into the doorway and grabbed the frame to steady himself. "Let's go."

He took a few steps and wavered, so she placed his arm around her shoulder and steadied him.

"I can manage," he said, looking down at her.

"I'm sure." She pushed the elevator button and eyed the hallway. No one seemed to notice their escape.

"Did you find him?" Bobby said.

"Who?"

"Your boyfriend."

"No." The elevator door opened.

"Why do you think you keep seeing him?"

"Because I'm a nut. Who knows?" They rode the elevator to the first floor.

Not only was she nuts but she was a liar. She was lying to herself. She kept saying she wanted her independence, wanted to be her own woman and live her own life. Yet even now, in another country, she imagined Steven close by. Why? Because it made her feel more secure.

She'd never be a strong, independent woman this way. Damn, how had she ended up here?

She hailed a cab and they took off for the inn. The charges against Bobby had been dropped once she'd paid for the outfit and explained to the retailer what had happened. She studied him as he stared out the cab window, a dazed expression on his face.

They pulled up to the inn and she helped Bobby upstairs to her room. He kept shaking his head as if he were trying to clear it. She couldn't very well make him sleep on the floor tonight. Maybe she'd get lucky and Mrs. McCarthy would have an opening.

They got to her room and he sat on the floor, tipping his head back against the flowered wallpaper.

She pulled down the covers and turned to him. "Come on, get in bed."

"I'm fine," he said, his eyes closed.

"Right. You could barely make it up the stairs."

He got to his feet and stood firm for a second, then stumbled to the bed. "Bloody hell."

She pulled the covers up to his shoulders, realizing they hadn't found him a change of clothes, save the wild pants and shirt he'd worn out of the store. She doubted he'd put those on again.

Sprawled across the double mattress, Bobby looked like a giant in a junior bed. He rolled onto his side, away from her, and she decided this was the perfect time to make her escape.

She opened the door.

"Don't go," he said.

She hesitated, her hand on the doorknob. "What?"

"Don't...leave."

"I'm just going to get us something to eat. Okay? I'm hungry, it's nearly supper time."

"Grace," he muttered.

Then nothing. She waited a minute.

"Bobby?"

No response. Good, she could zip out and buy him some clothes, then pick up dinner. She left the room, making sure the door was locked.

She walked a few blocks and found a cab to take her to the shopping district. In record time she picked up three pair of jeans and a few plain black shirts. She also picked up underwear and socks, and thought how odd it felt to shop for Bobby. She'd never shopped for Steven.

She picked up a green shirt on sale. Wouldn't hurt to try something different, she thought.

On the way back to the inn she stopped at a pub hoping for some fast, hot food to take back.

Surely food would make Bobby feel better.

Why are you worried about him, girl? He's an employee, not a friend. Heck, she didn't even know him that well.

But she certainly felt ashamed about the incident at the store today. She felt responsible. That's what this was about—making things right. Things were still not quite right with Grace, and they wouldn't be until she finished her quest and found peace.

Sitting on a pub stool, she thought about her plans for tomorrow: Edinburgh Castle. Mom had written about it in her diary, about its great strength and history, about its integrity.

About how she wanted to take Grace there someday.

"I'm here, Mom," she whispered. "I wish you were."

The waitress brought over two boxes of fish and chips, and Grace headed back to the inn. Since it was a beautiful night and not dark yet, she decided to walk to clear her head.

As she walked down Newington Street, she wondered if she could really accomplish what she'd set out to do with Bobby as her shadow. Sure she could. If he'd loosen up a bit, not panic and chase after her wearing a store's merchandise. What was he so worried about, anyway? What could happen to her on a public street in broad daylight?

"Miss?" a male voice said behind her.

She reached for her can of pepper spray, tucked safely in her pocket. Heck, she didn't even know if the thing shot more than once. In any case, she was ready.

Cripes. Now Bobby was making her paranoid.

She turned and froze at the sight of Harry Franklin smiling back at her.

Chapter Seven

"Didn't expect to see me again, did you now?" Franklin grabbed her wrist.

Grace pointed, sprayed and ran. She heard him coughing, swearing between gut-wrenching gags.

Clutching her bags of clothes and food, she fled from him, determined not to let him take anything from her ever again.

She raced down the street, turned a corner and hailed a cab. She'd get to the inn where she'd call the police immediately. The man who'd assaulted her on the train would not hurt her as he had before.

Adrenaline addled her nerves, and she struggled to remember her destination. "Guest House of Edinburgh," she said.

It was a good mile to the inn, far enough that she felt sure Harry Franklin couldn't follow her. What did he want? He already had her credit cards and money.

The cab dropped her at the inn and she raced up the stairs. She put down her packages and fumbled in her pocket for her key. Not there. Oh, God, had Harry Franklin picked her pocket when she wasn't paying attention, when she was too busy buying clothes for her bodyguard, buying him fish and chips?

"My key, my key," she whispered, her fingers shaking at the memory of his eyes, dark, like death, with a twisted, sick twinkle in the black pupil.

If he got her key, what else did he get? Could he know where she was staying? They had to get out of here. She knocked on the door and it swung open.

Bobby towered over her, anger filling his eyes. "Where the hell did you go?"

"For clothes, then food, then Harry Franklin found me," she said, her voice catching.

His expression softened and he pulled her into the room with a gentle grip of her elbow.

"Slow down, Grace. You saw Harry Franklin? The guy on the train?"

"He was...he was outside the pub—"

"A pub?"

"I went for food, after I got clothes," she said, shoving the shopping bag at him. "I got jeans and shirts and...and..." Her voice hitched.

"Grace, it's okay now. You're safe." Bobby led her to the bed and she sat.

"My key, I can't find my key. What if he got it?"

He unpried her fingers from the food bag and placed it on the nightstand, then knelt beside the bed and held her hands in his. "Where did you put the key when you left me earlier?"

"Um...jacket, jacket pocket."

"Check it."

She couldn't move, still dazed by the thought that on her one trip out of the country she'd snagged herself a stalker.

But why? She was a middle-school science teacher, for heaven's sake.

"I'm going to search for your key." Bobby reached up and stuck his hand in her left coat pocket. Grace watched his eyes as they filled with concern. If Harry Franklin had taken her room key…

"Not in this one," Bobby said. "Grace, it will be okay. He can't hurt you with me here."

"You were unconscious when I left."

"I'm okay now. Let's check your other pocket."

Something snapped. This is exactly what she'd been fighting: depending on a man to make everything okay.

"No," she said, pushing his hand away. "I'll do it." She reached into her pocket and fished around. If she wanted to be an independent woman she had to start acting like one.

If Harry Franklin had stolen her key she'd just have to deal with it.

Her fingers grazed cool metal. She sighed and pulled the key from her coat pocket.

"It's here. It's fine."

"See? I told you it would be," Bobby said, with compassion in his eyes.

And for some reason she resented it.

She stood and took off her jacket. "I'd better call the police and tell them I saw Harry."

Someone knocked on her door. She jumped back, then took a deep breath and called, "Who is it?"

"Detective Inspector Owen. May I have a word?"

Bobby stood behind the door and motioned for her to open it. She did, and recognized the inspector from the hospital.

"I thought we agreed there'd be no charges brought against Mr. Finn," she said.

"It's not about that. Could you please step into the hall, alone?"

She nodded at Bobby and went into the hall.

"I was about to call the police," she said.

"You were?"

"I just saw the man who attacked me on the train last night. He was following me."

Inspector Owen motioned for her to join him down the hall. "I didn't know you were assaulted. Yes, well, it's beginning to make sense."

"Excuse me?"

"I'm sorry to say that we suspect Mr. Finn may not be the most honorable of chaps."

"Meaning?"

"He has a criminal record, did you know that?"

"I heard something about it." He'd been honest with her and told her about his delinquent teenage years.

"Did you also hear that one of his known partners was a man named Harry Franklin?" Inspector Owen said.

"No." A chill raced down her arms. It couldn't be. Bobby had been hired to protect her. He couldn't have known the man who attacked her.

"Mr. Finn and his partner were suspects in half a dozen burglaries and assaults some years back. Harry got caught and served prison time for one of the crimes, but Bobby Finn's girlfriend provided him with an alibi."

His girlfriend. Of course, always charming the ladies. Charming them into giving alibis, keeping him out of jail. Charming them into buying him clothes, dinner and a place to sleep for the night.

"I...I can't believe it," she whispered.

She glanced down the hall. He was living in her room, touching her things.

She had to get out of here and away from him. Tonight.

Yet something didn't feel right. Dad wouldn't hire a criminal to protect her. Had he been charmed, as well, tricked into hiring Bobby?

"We don't have solid proof of any wrongdoing, but I thought you should be warned," the inspector said.

"Thanks." She wrapped her arms around her stomach.

"He hasn't left your side, has he?" Inspector Owen prodded.

"No. He was supposedly hired by my father as a bodyguard."

"Why would you need a bodyguard?"

"My father is overly protective since I'm his only child." She glanced down the hall. "Why me?"

"Anyone's guess. Is your father wealthy?"

"No, he works as a scientist for the U.S. government."

"Maybe it's about his work. More likely, knowing Mr. Finn's criminal history, it's about money. It's a new angle these days:

chum up to a girl on holiday and keep her happy while you blackmail the family."

"But he told me he was with Scotland Yard before becoming a private detective."

"I checked. Couldn't find any record of a Bobby Finn working at Scotland Yard."

Bobby a bad guy, working with Harry Franklin? She should call Dad to see if he'd received a ransom demand.

Damn, her cell phone was in the room.

She'd have to go back in there. Figure out how to get away from him. She should be afraid of him, afraid he might hurt her, but she wasn't. There was something about Bobby Finn, something…gentle.

Get real, girl! Maybe Dad was right to worry about her. She was too darned trusting.

"I appreciate you stopping by."

"I tried phoning but it went into voice mail. You should check your mobile."

"Okay, thanks."

"I'll put out a bulletin on Harry Franklin, see what we can turn up. In the meantime, be wary of Mr. Finn. Oh, he forgot this at the hospital." He pulled a metal cross on a piece of black cord from his pocket.

She took it from him and thought how ironic it was that a man like Bobby Finn would wear a cross around his neck. Yeah, he needed forgiveness for his sins all right.

"Thanks," she said.

"If you need anything—"

"I won't."

He nodded and left. She went back to her room and took a deep, steadying breath before opening the door. Then she had a thought. She started downstairs. Her door cracked open.

"Grace?" Bobby said.

"I'll be right back," she said softly. "I need to find Mrs. McCarthy."

"You won't leave the inn?" He sounded genuinely concerned.

"No," she said, turning and making her way to the first floor. She had half a mind to keep on walking, but her things were in her room, most importantly, Mom's diary.

She needed to get away from all these games and find her mother's hometown.

Discover that piece of herself that would make her feel whole.

She found Mrs. McCarthy in the den watching television. "Can I help you?" the woman asked.

"I was wondering if you had any openings tonight?"

"I did have a room open up downstairs."

"I'd like to rent it for my friend," Grace said.

The woman went to the reception desk in the entryway and pulled out a key. She handed it to Grace. "I'll charge your card then?"

"Yes, thank you." Grace went upstairs and opened the door to her room. Bobby was standing by the window, her mother's diary in his hand. She clenched her jaw, suddenly feeling naked.

"That's personal," she said, snatching it from his hands. No one had read Mom's thoughts but Grace. She felt violated and suspicious about his motives.

"I'm sorry," he said.

Like hell, he was. He probably wanted to gain insight into her psyche so he could manipulate her more.

"What did the inspector want?" he asked.

"He needed me to sign a statement about your arrest." *Quick thinking, girl.* She handed him the key. "A room has opened up downstairs."

He took the key and looked surprised, maybe even hurt. "I don't want to leave you."

"I'll be fine. Your room is right by the stairs so you can stay up all night and keep watch if you're that worried."

"You were worried, too, a few minutes ago."

She untied the bag of food, resigned to the fact she'd have to eat this one last meal with him. She didn't want to make him suspicious.

Act cool, unaffected, as if nothing has changed.

"I'm starving," she said. With her foam container in hand she sat on the bed. She took a bite of fish hoping to speed up this process. Inside, her stomach rebelled as she fought her frustration. Was this man her enemy or friend?

No, even if he wasn't her enemy, he wasn't a friend. He was hired to protect her. Maybe. She wasn't sure of anything anymore.

Yet an hour ago *she* was protecting *him* in

his hospital bed. Could she really have been so wrong about Bobby? She didn't want to come right out and confront him with the inspector's accusations. She had to figure out another way. She'd start by calling Dad, later, after Bobby left.

She checked her cell phone. The battery was dead.

"You're sure everything is okay?" He walked over to close the door.

"Leave it open," she said. He took a step back and studied her. "Here." She handed him his food. "So, tell me about your work."

"As a private detective?"

She wondered if he was trying to remember which lie he'd told regarding his career.

"That's what you do, right?" she said.

"Yes." He opened his container and analyzed its contents, then closed it. "Maybe later. What else did the inspector say to you?"

He pinned her with those dark eyes of his as if he could read her next lie before she even spoke it. To think she'd thought his eyes warm and charming last night on the train.

"He said they'd put out a bulletin for Harry Franklin. That eased my mind a bit."

"Which doesn't mean they'll find him," he muttered.

Was that wishful thinking?

"Oh, I don't know. Stranger things have happened."

Like I was seduced by a major charmer named Bobby Finn.

"I almost forgot." She pulled the cross from her pocket. "He also came to return this. You left it at the hospital."

He didn't reach for it at first, his expression suddenly younger, a bit lost.

"Thanks," he said, his voice hoarse. He took it from her and placed it around his neck.

"Who gave that to you?" she said.

"My mother, after…" His voice trailed off. "Before I left."

"Left for Scotland Yard?"

"No, left for England, to live with my uncle." He gently rubbed the metal cross as if to conjure good luck or maybe even solace.

That expression on his face made her want to ask more questions about his childhood, his family and his disappointments. Was he really that good an actor?

"Why did you live with your uncle?" she pushed.

Bobby went to the window and stared down onto the street. Why did he live with his uncle? There were so many reasons, all of them rubbish. He knew the truth from the day mum had dropped him with Uncle Thomas: Bobby had been a grand failure and she couldn't stand the sight of him.

She might have tried to whitewash it by saying the schools were better in Uncle Thomas's area of London, and that Bobby needed special help because of a learning problem, but he knew the truth. Ever since Wendy's accident things were not the same at home. Bobby was no longer welcome. It was his fault Wendy struggled to walk with a cane, his fault she'd become a withdrawn, sad woman.

If only he'd been paying attention. If only he'd moved a little faster, Wendy wouldn't have been hit by the speeding car.

And maybe if he'd spent another twenty

years solving crimes he'd be able to live with himself.

Or not. He'd never forgive himself for his sister's condition, always wondering what kind of woman she would have become if not for the accident.

"Is it for good luck?" she said.

"What?" He'd forgotten what they were talking about. His brain had been a little fuzzy since his arrest, and he suspected it was due to more than a slight knock to his head. Something else had happened when he was with those two officers. If only he could remember.

"The cross." She motioned to his neck.

"Not luck, exactly. More like…" What? What could he say? That it was his constant reminder that even if his mother and sister couldn't forgive him, even if Bobby couldn't forgive himself, there was always hope that God had the compassion to forgive a bastard like Bobby. "A reminder," he said. "To behave."

"Does it work?" She smirked.

"Not always."

"Like with women, right?"

"Excuse me?"

"I sense you're a charmer with women. You use them, right?"

"What if they're using me?" he said.

She shrugged and ate another piece of fish. She was awfully calm and sure of herself compared to when she'd come in earlier.

It must have been Owen's visit that had eased her fear. Even though she had Bobby as her personal bodyguard, a visit from the local police had probably calmed her down.

Sure it had. Bobby was a failure at protection. She probably sensed it.

"Are you well enough to make it downstairs by yourself?" she said.

"You want to be rid of me that badly?" he joked.

An odd look creased her features as if he'd guessed her very thoughts.

"It's been a full day," she said. "I'd like the rest of the night to myself."

Something was off. She seemed colder, more distant than when they'd gone shopping. He could have sworn they'd developed a connection of sorts this afternoon.

But now, watching the woman on the bed

eat her fish and chips, he wondered if he'd imagined it. She suddenly seemed like a complete stranger.

What are you thinking, Bobby? She is a complete stranger.

"Have I done something?" he said without thinking.

"Done something?"

"Offended you in some way?"

"No, why?"

"You seem different, uncomfortable."

"I'm tired." She closed her foam container and sighed. "Exhausted from all the drama."

"Right, well…" He started for the door and her shoulders sagged as if she was relieved. Why? Was she afraid of him?

He thought they'd come to an agreement, an understanding about his role in her holiday. Yet she seemed anxious to be rid of him.

"Good night, then." He opened the door. "Make sure you lock this behind me. And pull the nightstand to the door to block anyone from coming inside."

"The nightstand isn't very heavy."

"The bed then. Something."

"I'll be fine. Will you?"

She said the words, but he sensed she didn't mean them. She wanted him out of her room and quite possibly out of her life.

"Good night," he said.

"Wait." She got up and handed him a shopping bag. "Some clothes I picked up for you."

"Thank you." He closed the door, waited until he heard her lock it and went downstairs to his room. Something felt off, her attitude, her forced smile.

You're suffering from a blow to the head, mate. Maybe it's all in your imagination.

Bobby opened the door to Room Two and flipped on the light. The room was pleasant enough, a wood dresser in the corner and the bed covered with a flowered spread.

He dumped the clothes on the bed. Not bad, he thought. Black trousers, a few black shirts and an emerald-green shirt. Cheeky.

He splashed water on his face at the sink, then dressed in the new clothes.

Well, he couldn't put off the inevitable. Time to call in. He wasn't sure how he was going to break the news to Max that he'd been arrested, although not charged. He'd start by calling Eddie to see if the bloke had any news for him on this case.

"Malone, here."

"Eddie, mate, it's Bobby."

"You okay, man? We got a call from the police asking about your employment with the Blackwell Group."

"Bugger," he swore. "So, Max knows then?"

"Yep. But he thinks something smells fishy, although he didn't say it like that."

"Did you find uncover anything interesting about the Fairmont family?"

"As far as family is concerned, her dad's a scientist, there's an aunt, lives in Madison, and that's about it. Background on the mother, well, Max wants to talk to you about that. But get this: I can't find a record of marriage for her parents. They may not have been married when her mom gave birth to her."

Bobby glanced at the ceiling, picturing Grace sitting in bed, reading her mother's diary. He would bet she didn't know that.

"What else?"

"Couldn't find much on the boyfriend. He must be a boring kind of guy. He's a financial analyst with Baker and Hughes in Chicago. He brings down six figures easy, doesn't really have hobbies. Just works and hangs out with Grace Fairmont. Oh, and something weird about the mother? The death notice appeared five years *after* she supposedly died in a car accident in the States. I tried finding out more but a virus kept attacking my computer. A symbol would pop up, a pinwheel, you know, the kind that kids blow on to make them spin around? Anyway, the virus would try to eat my hard drive." He paused. "But it couldn't get past Tabitha's chastity belt. Max thought he recognized the symbol. Wait, he wants to talk to you."

Bobby was going to get an earful now. A real thrashing for cocking-up in less than twenty-four hours.

"Bobby, how's it going, mate?" Max inquired.

"It's been better."

"Tell me what's happened so far. In detail."

Bloody hell, he had to relive the embarrassment of this morning?

"Before or after I got arrested for stealing purple trousers?"

"You've *got* to be kidding."

"Wish I were. I'm telling you, guv, this is the strangest twenty-four hours of my life. First Miss Fairmont is attacked on the train, then I sensed the man who picked us up at Waverly was a fake, not with British Transport Police. I got shot with pepper spray last night, then I get knocked unconscious this afternoon while being arrested for stealing purple trousers I didn't even want. Don't ask me to explain that one. Some people don't have this much excitement in an entire year."

He didn't dare tell him he'd lost a chunk of time this afternoon, that he couldn't remember the few hours after the cops arrested him outside the shops.

"Bobby, I'm afraid this case is more complex than we'd originally thought. It's probably best if you bring the girl back to the States."

"She'll never go for it, guv. She's got something to prove to herself, something about her mother."

He thought about the few paragraphs he'd read in the mother's diary, about the love that dripped off the pages. He could understand why she was so determined to walk in her mum's footsteps and absorb some of her personal history.

To be loved like that. With such completeness.

But then, why did the mother leave? That's what it sounded like from Eddie's information.

"It looks like Miss Fairmont's mother was on a British Intelligence watch list of suspected PIRA terrorists," Max said.

"Bloody hell." The Provisional Irish Republican Army.

"I doubt Grace Fairmont is aware of this," Max continued. "What also concerns me is the symbol that kept popping up on Eddie's computer when he tried digging into the mother's background. I recognized it as a code symbol used by British Intelligence.

They were key players in the fight against terrorism."

Bobby absently sat on the bed and pressed his fingers to his eyelids. "So, the bloke who picked us up at the train station…"

"Could be MI5 or PIRA. We can't figure out why they'd be interested in the girl. The mother died years ago. Maybe MI5 thinks Grace knows something. It explains why the father has been so overly protective all these years."

"Do you think he knows?"

"I'm not sure. Left him a message, hoping to get answers. Don't mention this to the girl until we know more. The MI5 connection troubles me, but not as much as ties to the PIRA."

Bobby thought about the stolen backpack: stolen, then returned hours later. Was it a ruse by MI5 to plant a bug and track Grace's whereabouts?

"Do you think Grace is in danger, guv?" Bobby squeezed the phone. His protective instincts flared.

"Hard to say," Max admitted. "The mugging on the train could be a part of this, or just bad luck. If he'd been a hired assassin he would have killed her on the spot."

True. Harry Franklin, or whatever his name was, could have ended her life with one slice of a well-placed knife.

A knife…across Grace's throat. That beautiful girl…dead.

"I need to check on her, guv." Bobby hung up and raced to Grace's room.

What was he going to say? Tell her the truth? That her mum had been a PIRA terrorist, possibly under surveillance by British Intelligence? She idolized her mum and trusted her father. She wouldn't believe a word coming out of Bobby's mouth.

He knocked on the door. "Grace? I need to talk to you."

Nothing. He glanced at the bottom of the door. Her room was dark. It was too bloody early for her to have gone to sleep. He knocked again. He had to tell her what they were dealing with, yet he wasn't sure himself.

He persisted, knocking a little louder this time. He didn't want to alarm the innkeeper but couldn't risk Grace's safety.

She still didn't answer. Could someone have broken into her room? Kidnapped her? Killed her?

No, if *they* thought she had information, *they'd* want to keep her alive.

What about the inspector from earlier? Was he legitimate or a fake, planted by MI5? What did British Intelligence want with her? She didn't even know her mother.

Taking the stairs two at a time he started to think up reasons why he was going to ask Mrs. McCarthy to open the door. He found her in the small den watching news reports on the telly.

"Hello, Mrs. McCarthy," he said, as charmingly as possible, fighting back his panic. "I was wondering if you could check on my friend, Grace."

"Oh, she's fine." The older woman waved her hand. "Left a few minutes ago out the front."

Bobby rushed out the front door to the sidewalk and looked both ways. He spotted Grace walking rather quickly toward the heart of town. Where was she off to? Was she lured out of her room by a mysterious phone caller?

It seemed more likely she was running. From him.

A man approached her and she ducked into a pub. The man kept walking. Bobby followed her and tried to spot her blond hair over the top of the crowd in the pub. She went toward the back door and Bobby caught up to her, placing his hand to her shoulder.

She spun around, her eyes wide with... fear? No, more like anger.

"Blast, Grace, where are you off to alone? It's dangerous. Don't you understand how vulnerable you are, how easily someone could hurt you?"

"Yeah, like you?"

Chapter Eight

Bobby let go of Grace's shoulder. "What did you say?" Good God, she thought *he* was out to hurt her?

"Are you and Harry Franklin working together to blackmail my father?"

"Have you gone completely round the bend?"

"Inspector Owen said there's no record of you working at Scotland Yard."

"Owen? That twit doesn't know what he's talking about. He's probably not even a real detective." He reined in his temper.

"What's that supposed to mean?"

"We need to talk." Bobby glanced at the roomful of pub patrons. Any one of them could be associated with PIRA or MI5.

She took a step away from him. "Just leave me alone, okay?"

"Only if you get back on a plane to the States."

"What? Why? What's your angle now?" She narrowed her eyes at him.

"My angle is to keep you safe. I'm not a criminal. I'm not working with Harry Franklin. Inspector Owen's job is to get me out of the picture, probably so they can get to you."

"*They* who?"

"Please." He motioned with his hand toward a booth. "Sit with me and I'll explain."

She glanced around the room, probably feeling safe because she was surrounded by people, and slipped into the booth. Bobby ordered two pints from a waitress.

"First, I would never hurt you, Grace," he started.

She cocked her chin up as if to say she wasn't stupid. She knew he was lying.

"I don't know Harry Franklin," he said. "Yes, I was arrested when I was a teenager— with a boy named Harry Smith. We were young and stupid and thought we could make a quick hundred quid by breaking into people's homes and stealing valuables. I told you I was a bad kid, Grace. I never lied about that. We all have things in our past we're not proud of."

She sat back in the booth, arms crossed in a defensive posture. He wasn't getting through to her, not even scratching the surface.

But he had to.

"I just spoke with my boss, Max Templeton," Bobby said. "He thinks you could be in danger."

She narrowed her eyes. "Why?"

"Your mother may have been involved with the PIRA when she was younger."

"PIRA?"

"The Provisional Irish Republican Army."

"I don't believe it."

"She was young. People do stupid things when they're young."

Like let their sisters get run down by a drunk motorist.

Grace's gaze drifted to her ale.

"When our computer expert tried to get personal information about your mum he got stumped by a virus," Bobby said. "A virus possibly linked to MI5."

"What's that?"

"British Intelligence. My boss thinks that British Intelligence officers might be keeping you under surveillance."

"Sure they are." She shook her head.

"I'm not kidding," Bobby said, frustrated. What now? Tell her to call her father for confirmation? Bobby wasn't sure Max had spoken to the client about this new development, and Bobby doubted she'd believe anything other than her father's word.

"I'm a science teacher, not a spy or a political figure," she argued. "There's no way British Intelligence would be interested in my boring life."

He sensed pain in her words, regret even.

"You have to consider the fact that your mother's activities have put you in danger."

"No. I don't believe it. My mother was a loving, caring woman. She was not a terrorist."

"Think about everything that's happened since you've been in the U.K. The mugging, the lights going out—"

"Stop," she said. "I'll tell you what. I'm going to leave here and you're going to stay away from me for two reasons: one, if I see you again I'll call Inspector Owen and press charges for harassment, assault and whatever else I can think of to keep you locked up long enough so I can finish my trip. Second, because I'll use the spray again if you don't. I didn't tell you that was my dad's concoction, did I? A mild form of a nerve gas he designed for the military. So unless you want to be using a seeing eye dog for the rest of your life…"

"Grace—"

"Enough. Stay away from me." She stood and marched to the door.

He'd done better when he'd lied to her and charmed her. She wasn't a stupid woman, just misled and frightened.

Right now, of him.

And possibly of the information he'd just shared with her. Somewhere deep down, she had to consider the truth of his words. The reality of a loved one being a terrorist would shatter anyone's world. It would especially shatter the world of a woman seeking answers about her mother…and herself.

He got up and headed for the door. He'd follow her, keep to the shadows and do his job.

Whether she liked it or not.

THE PROVISIONAL Irish Republican Army?

British Intelligence?

Bull.

Bobby was not only charming, but he could lie with such sincerity that she'd nearly believed him.

Shaking off the chill, she headed back to the inn. She'd left earlier to find a public phone since her cell battery had died and the inn phone was just outside Bobby's room. She didn't want him listening in as she called Dad, then other inns to find another place to stay.

Yet, before she could find a phone box and make her calls, she'd sensed someone following her, so she she'd ducked into the pub, filled with people for protection.

That someone had been Bobby, with his outrageous tales and forced concern.

She had to get to a phone and call Dad, had

to confirm Inspector Owen's suspicions. Then she'd call other inns. She'd made a mental note of inns she'd seen while shopping today. She'd start with them. She only planned to stay another day to wait for her credit cards.

She found a phone box a block away from her inn and called Dad but got a busy signal. He didn't believe in call waiting. "Focus on one thing at a time," he'd lecture her. She noticed a small black car park across the street and turn off its lights. No one got out.

"Great, now Finn's got you spooked," she whispered to herself.

Pressing the receiver to her ear, she thought about Bobby's wild accusations. Surely Dad would have known if Mom had been involved with a terrorist group, and he would have told Grace.

Then again maybe not. Grace had nothing to hold on to but the faded memory of a loving mother. That's why she felt so empty inside, as if a piece of her was missing. It was all starting to fade, to be lost completely.

Grace was going through an identity crisis, plain and simple.

The things that had once interested her—the opera and playing tennis with Steven—had become boring and routine. To some degree her relationship with Steven had become boring, as well.

Which made no sense at all. He was perfect: solid, steady and he knew what would please her. Steven was the quintessential "perfect" mate.

And she'd been the perfect daughter for Dad.

Suddenly, in her mid-twenties, perfect didn't seem as important as finding answers; finding herself.

She needed her mom.

Since that was impossible, the least she could do was walk in Mom's footsteps, visit the places she'd been and somehow make an emotional connection to give Grace strength to do what she had to: strike out on her own.

Kiss Daddy and Steven goodbye and start a new life somewhere away from them, at least for a while, until she felt like her own person.

"My God, I've really gone…" She hesitated, about to say *crazy* but chose instead "round the bend."

She tried a few inns with no luck. She hung up the phone and decided to go back to her room. Bobby had to know she was serious about reporting him to the police if he attempted to speak with her again.

The flare of a lighter in the car across the street caught her eye.

It had nothing to do with her. The mugging was random, the lights going out were the result of outdated electrical wiring.

What about Mom's picture being stolen? Why steal the photo and not the locket?

She was starting to fall under Bobby's spell, starting to believe his outlandish story about Mom being a terrorist.

You can't run like your mother.

The memory of the mugger's words made her shudder. She'd thought it had been a case of mistaken identity, but if there was any truth to what Bobby had told her…

No, he's liar, a manipulator.

And she had to take care of herself.

She pulled out Inspector Owen's card and called him.

"Owen," he answered.

"Inspector, it's Grace Fairmont."

"Yes, Miss Fairmont, how can I help?"

"I confronted Mr. Finn about his true intentions, and he argued that I was in danger and that my mother had been a terrorist with the PIRA."

"Really?" he said.

"He's lying, of course. But the thing is, I can't find another room for the night and he's staying at the same inn. He's downstairs, but I don't feel entirely safe."

"I'll have him brought in for questioning."

"You can do that? Without me making a formal complaint?"

"We can. I'll send someone over right away."

"He may not be there. I left him at the Royal Oak Pub. I told him if I saw him again I'd press charges."

"I'll post a man outside your inn. Get a good night's rest."

"Thank you, I really appreciate it."

"Would you like me to send a car?"

"That's not necessary."

"Be careful, Miss Fairmont."

"Thanks, I will."

She hung up feeling a bit safer. She'd get to the guest house and lock herself in her room. Then she had to try and get a decent night's sleep. What a joke. How was she going to do that with all this craziness going on around her?

Buttoning her jacket she jogged down Newington Street with one thing in mind: reading Mom's journal. Those pages held the truth, the truth about a loving mother who cherished her baby girl.

Grace sighed. The country. She longed for it, ached to be walking in her mother's hometown of Pitlochry, attend church, visit the sites like Loch Leven Castle and the battleground of Culloden. Mom described these places in her journal as if she'd hoped to take Grace there someday, yet, she almost made it sound as if she was describing the places for the first time, from a tourist's point of view.

There was no sign of anything unusual or

threatening as Grace approached the inn. She went inside and was greeted by Mrs. McCarthy.

"Is everything all right? Your father's called twice," the woman said.

"May I use this phone?" Grace motioned to the phone on the cherrywood table.

"Yes. An extra charge for overseas calls."

"That's fine." Grace picked up the receiver and made her call.

"Hello?"

"Dad, it's Grace."

"Thank God."

"I tried calling you but—"

"I was on the phone with the detective agency. They've uncovered some things, some disturbing things. I need to talk to you, Gracie."

No, she didn't want Dad to tell her Mom was a PIRA terrorist under the watchful eye of British Intelligence. Grace wouldn't believe it, not even from Dad.

"She left us, Gracie," he said. "She didn't die in a car accident."

Grace gripped the receiver and stared at the gold-striped wallpaper. She couldn't make sense of his words. Wasn't sure she'd heard him clearly.

"When you were a year old your mom disappeared," he continued. "She left me a note. She asked that I not look for her and begged me to take care of you, explaining how much she loved us both and that was why she had to leave. Five years later someone sent me her death notice from *The Times of London*. She was the innocent victim in a terrorist bombing that killed five people."

"Terrorist bombing? As in…"

"An attempt to kill the prime minister that failed."

"Dad, do you know if she was involved with the Provisional Irish Republican Army?"

"No, I'm sure she was not. Your mother was about peace and compassion. She would never be involved with an organization that hurt innocent people."

"But what do you know about her, really?"

"I know I loved her."

"And she left you. And me. She left us and you never told me."

"I thought you'd be crushed."

"I had a right to know," she declared.

"I'm sorry, Gracie. I couldn't bring myself to tell you the truth. What good would it have done? It doesn't matter now."

"It does, actually. It matters a lot. It means she didn't want me."

"Don't say that, Grace."

"I've gotta go. I love you." She hung up and went upstairs to her room.

Opening her door, she flipped on the light and grabbed the journal off the nightstand.

Her mother didn't want her.

No, Grace refused to believe that.

She locked her door and frantically leafed through the pages, familiar with them all, having committed most of the entries to memory.

Grace smiled at me today.
Gracie got her first tooth.
Gracie is such a smart girl.
I can't wait to take Gracie home and show her to my family. I can't wait to show her the hills, the lochs, the beautiful coun-tryside. I love my baby girl so much.

"Then why, Mom? Why did you leave?"

She snapped the book shut, unable to read another word without bursting into tears of frustration, tears of loss.

It was as if she'd lost her mother all over again, and she didn't even remember losing her the first time.

What had Dad said? That Mom's letter had asked he not try to find her. That she professed her love for both Dad and her baby girl?

Was it simply that she was a member of the PIRA and loved the fight for Irish independence more than she loved her family?

That wasn't possible. Mom was from Scotland; Dad had said so.

He'd also said her mother had been killed by a drunk driver when Grace was a year old. Now that she thought about it, he'd told her *how* mom had died when Grace was twelve, right before the trying years of teenage rebellion and experimentation with alcohol and drugs. Up to that point he'd just said she'd died in a car accident.

Suddenly she felt incredibly manipulated.

Her father had lied to her all these years.
Who *could* she believe?

Her heart. Her mother's words. They
would lead her to answers. This journey
would still give her peace.

Forget the other credit cards. American
Express was good enough for purchases and
cash advances. She'd head up north first
thing tomorrow.

She needed to prove what she knew in her
heart: her mom was not a terrorist. Her mom
had loved her. What on earth would have
made her run away?

Anger coiled in Grace's chest as she
wondered if someone was responsible for
chasing her mother away, depriving Grace
of her much-needed love.

Grace wanted answers, not only for her
identity's sake, but to honor Mom's memory.
Grace would uncover the truth.

She glanced down and noticed an envelope
had been slipped under her door. She hadn't
seen it when she'd come in. Placing the
journal on the nightstand, she grabbed the
envelope and opened it.

She pulled out a white sheet of paper with three words on it: Please Go Home.

HE LIT a ciggie and glanced at the Guest House of Edinburgh. It would be easy enough to climb in through the window, strangle her and be done with it.

Although it would be rather difficult with agents surrounding the place. Agents and terrorists all out for the same thing: the list. She might have it, or know where to find it. She'd be no use to anyone dead. To think the list could be in the hands of such a naive, fragile creature.

He glanced up the street, wondering if they knew where she was. She'd run into Franklin earlier, but the team had chased him underground for the time being. Franklin's group had to know she was surrounded by invisible agents.

Yet she was so very alone.

Maybe he shouldn't have eliminated her bodyguard from the equation. He was being paid to keep her safe. But the bloke would complicate the mission with his police instinct and attitude.

This had to go smoothly. For England's sake.

Chapter Nine

Grace hadn't seen Bobby Finn since their blow-up at the pub. She wondered if he'd written the note telling her to go home. Why? To keep her frightened and needy? The door to his room had been shut this morning, and Mrs. McCarthy said she hadn't seen him leave. Grace guessed Inspector Owen had detained him to give her the opportunity to get out of town without being followed.

She was standing in line at the rental car agency when her cell phone rang.

"Hello?" she said. She didn't recognize the caller ID.

"Miss Fairmont? My name is Max Templeton. Your father hired my agency to keep watch over you while in the U.K."

"Yes, he told me."

"I'm wondering if my agent, Bobby Finn, is with you. We haven't been able to reach him on his mobile."

"No, he's not with me. I've asked him to leave me alone."

"I'm sorry? Did he offend you?"

"No, the local police came to see me last night and warned me about him."

"Miss Fairmont, Bobby Finn is a loyal agent and was an excellent inspector with Scotland Yard. I wish you hadn't given him the slip."

"But Inspector Owen said—"

"Forget Owen. He doesn't know the whole picture. Bobby is a determined agent. I'm sure he'll find you. When he does ask him to phone in straight away."

"Anything I should know about?"

"Not at this time. Miss Fairmont, please be careful, pay attention to your surroundings and stay in well-populated areas."

"Thanks."

She pocketed her phone and scolded herself for believing Inspector Owen's tale. What was *his* motivation, she wondered?

Anxious to get out of the city, she signed the rental-car paperwork and found her economy car. She opened the trunk and dumped her bags inside, then got behind the wheel and pulled out her map of the area. She'd just figured out how to get out of town when the passenger door opened. Inspector Owen slid into the car and shut the door.

"What the—"

"Sorry, miss, I don't mean to frighten you, but we lost track of Mr. Finn and I wanted to warn you."

"You could have called the inn."

"You were gone."

"You have my cell number."

"I wanted to speak to you in person."

Stay strong, don't let him sense your fear. Was he even a real policeman?

"You need to know a few things, about your mother," he started.

"You knew her?"

"I knew of her. She was…" he hesitated, "involved in the deaths of innocent people."

"I don't believe you."

"What do you know about her?"

"I know she loved me."

"You didn't know about her affiliation with the Provisional Irish Republican Army?"

"That's not true."

"My organization wants your help."

"Your organization?"

"We need information that we think your mother may have left behind when she died."

"She left me nothing," she said. "Except for a locket and that was broken in a mugging." She wasn't sure why she didn't tell him about the diary. Maybe because it was sacred and she didn't want strangers leafing through it, reading a mother's private thoughts meant for her daughter. Or maybe because he hadn't told her who he worked for.

"I'm sorry, but I don't believe you." He grabbed her wrist and pulled her closer to him. "You need to come with me."

"Let go, you sonofabitch." She squirmed to get away from him.

Suddenly the passenger door opened. Bobby grabbed Owen, pulled him from the car and slugged him twice. The guy fell to the ground in a heap. Bobby raced to the driver's side of the car and opened the door.

"Move over," he ordered.

Stunned, she just looked at Bobby.

"I said *move*." With both hands on her shoulders, he gently slid her over and got behind the wheel. He hit the automatic lock button as Owen got to his feet and pounded on her window.

She shrieked, Bobby put the car in gear and they took off.

"That sonofabitch hurt me," she said, rubbing her wrist with her hand.

"He could have done a lot worse. What were you thinking, running off on me this morning? You could have been killed."

"I thought you were the bad guy, remember?"

"Oh, I'm bad, Grace, that's true. But I'm not the one trying to hurt you."

"I know." She hugged herself and glanced out the window. "Max Templeton called my cell looking for you."

"Bugger, that can't be good news. I'm taking you to Heathrow."

"No, you can't."

"This isn't a simple holiday anymore. This is about terrorists and spies and who knows what else."

"They'll find me back in the States, too. We need to get answers, find out what my mom was about. It's the only way I'll be truly safe."

"No, you're going back."

"Dammit, Bobby, I've come this far. I'm too close to give up."

"What's so bloody important that you'd risk your life to go touring the countryside?"

"My life. Finding out who I am and why." She paused. "Why Mom left."

"She died. People die. It happens."

"But she didn't just die. She left us when I was a year old. She died years later. I need to know why she left. I need to know who she was."

"What difference does it make?"

"I guess not a lot to someone like you. You know who you are and what your mission is in life: finding bad guys, protecting good girls." She sighed. "But I'm lost, Bobby. I've been lost for a long time, and the only way I'm going to find myself is by getting some answers."

"You're putting yourself at risk."

"I'll be at risk no matter where I am. I can't stop that now. I've opened some kind of door to danger that only I can close. You've got to help me. Please."

Bobby didn't say anything at first. He still couldn't believe her determination to continue this trip after her encounter with Owen. Was he MI5, or with the PIRA? What did they want with her?

He took a deep breath and headed north out of town. They'd have to ditch the car if they didn't want to be followed. Owen could have put a tracking device on it.

He glanced at Grace, then back out the front window. Bugger, she could have been hurt. But if they'd wanted to hurt her, wouldn't they have done it already? And who were *they*? He wouldn't mind answers himself.

But not about his identity or his mother. He had all those. He knew the sins he'd never shake loose from his soul.

Yet Grace seemed wounded by the news that

she'd been abandoned. It was fresh in her eyes, shadowing the blue with a hint of sadness.

And it resonated someplace deep in his chest.

"I need to speak with Max," he said. "The battery is dead on my mobile. May I use yours?"

"Sure, I can call for you."

"Thanks."

"I'm sorry," she said.

He glanced at her.

"I'm sorry I believed that jerk over you," she said.

"Forget it. I wouldn't have believed me, either."

"Why do you do that?"

"What?"

"Beat yourself up like that?"

"Habit. Phone Max, will you?"

She hit redial for the last incoming call and held the phone to his ear. "It's Bobby," he said, when the phone was picked up.

"We've been worried. Everything okay?"

"Fine. I'm with Grace."

"Brilliant, I knew you'd find her," Max said.

"She was nearly taken by a bloke pretending to be a detective in the Edinburgh police."

"What was he looking for?"

"Not sure."

"After we hang up, talk to her and find out what he asked her. We're still unclear about why this has all surfaced at this time in her life."

"Maybe because she's in the U.K.?"

"Possibly."

"Isn't it the middle of the night there?"

"Early morning, actually," Max said. "I couldn't sleep. I never sleep well when Cassie's away. She's visiting her mum."

"Miss your security blanket, do you?" Bobby joked.

"That, and I'm worried about this case. Eddie was up all night digging for clues. Not that he sleeps much."

"No, only at his desk."

"Here's what we know: Miss Fairmont's mother, Mary Logan, was affiliated with the PIRA when she was a teenager and then into her twenties. But what's odd is that her parents moved to Scotland when Mary was eighteen, during the prime of her activity. She accompanied them, yet spent half the year back in Ireland with relatives. Then she disappeared from the U.K. when she was twenty-three and ended up in the States where she struck up a romance with Don Fairmont. Two years later, she gave birth to Grace. About a year after that she left them to go back with PIRA in Ireland. She was killed in a parade bombing five years later."

"So, she's gone, it should be over." Bobby glanced at Grace, who studied him with such intense blue eyes.

"But it's not," Max said. "It doesn't tally, mate. There's more to this woman's life and I suspect it's dangerous. Are you putting Miss Fairmont on a plane home?"

"She won't go."

"I was afraid of that."

"She says the trouble will follow her back to the States as long as this is unresolved." He glanced at her and nodded. "She's got a point, guv."

"Yes, now that Pandora's box has been

opened we'll have to deal with it. We'll keep digging, see if we can turn up anything to help you arm yourselves."

"Yes, sir."

"Don't let her out of your sight."

"I won't."

"Has she accepted that you're the agent sent to protect her, not some phony?"

"I think so."

"Bobby?"

"Yes?"

"There's no one I'd rather have watching Miss Fairmont."

"Thanks, guv."

"Be careful."

"I will."

Bobby nodded to Grace to hit End, and took a deep breath. What had started as a babysitting assignment had turned into international terrorism and possibly espionage. What was MI5's angle? Did they think her mother might still be alive and they hoped to use Grace to lure her out?

No, by all official accounts Mary Logan had died in the parade bombing. Yet what if she wasn't simply a soldier for PIRA? What if there was more to this intrigue?

"Go on, I can handle it," Grace said.

"I'm sorry?"

"You have this look on your face like you're afraid to tell me something."

"I'm thinking."

"You're stalling. Please, don't keep things from me. I feel like everyone's been keeping the truth from me my whole life. If there's one thing I won't forgive it's people keeping the truth from me ever again."

"We have some facts but not much confirmation."

"What facts?"

"Are you really up for this?"

"Please."

"Fact: your mum was with the terrorist group PIRA as a teenager and up through her twenties. Fact: she came to the States for a few years in the later 1970s, for what reason, we're not sure. That's when she met your father. She went back to PIRA in 1981 and was killed in a bombing in '86. We think both

PIRA and British Intelligence are interested in you, her daughter."

"I feel like I don't even know my own mother," she whispered. "But why is this happening now?"

"Did you make inquiries about your mother before you came to the U.K.?"

"Well, sure, I had to find out where she grew up, if she had family, all that stuff."

"You must have accidentally alerted PIRA to your existence. What I can't figure is what they want from you."

"That makes two of us."

"What did that Owen bloke say to you?" Bobby pushed. "You need to remember every word if possible."

"He asked if my mother had given me anything. I said yes, the locket."

"Did you tell him about the diary?"

"No." She turned to him and held his gaze. "I don't know why. It's silly, I guess, but Mom's diary is private. It's the only thing I have of hers that shows me how much she loved me."

If she'd loved Grace she wouldn't have abandoned her, Bobby thought. The lost look in her eyes made him keep that opinion to himself.

"Was there anything in the diary explaining why her family moved to Scotland?"

"No. She started this diary when she was pregnant with me. She wrote down stories about her childhood and her homeland though."

"Ireland?"

"Scotland. She's from Scotland, that's why the PIRA stuff doesn't make sense."

"She's Irish, Grace. Her family moved to Scotland when she was a teenager."

She leaned back against the seat. "Everything is a lie," she said. "Do you think we'll find any truth in all this?"

"Yes. It may not be the truth you're looking for, but it's there."

"I wanted answers so badly, hoping they would make me whole. Yet all I feel right now," she hesitated, "is ashamed."

"Why?"

"My mother was involved in killing innocent people."

"We are not our parents, Grace." He tried

to believe the words as he spoke them, tried to believe he wasn't a failure to his family like his father: a man who abandoned a wife and five children for the sea.

"What would make someone do that?" she said.

He pulled into a parking lot of another car-rental agency to switch cars. "Make someone…"

"Join a terrorist group."

"They don't consider themselves terrorists. They feel passionate about their cause," he said.

Bobby was starting to feel passionate about protecting Grace. This young woman was faced with a complete upheaval in her life, new information that could forever change her future. Yet he sensed she was determined to deal with it and come out a stronger person.

He'd never known a woman quite like her. Bobby chose to sleep with scatty types who were drawn in by his looks and charm. That was the difference. He wasn't going to sleep with Grace.

Bobby wasn't stupid. He knew the worst pain was caused by love. He'd read that pain in his own mother's eyes with each year that his father stayed away. He'd broken her heart and she'd become a sad, semi-functional woman.

Bobby had no plans to tangle with the romantic type of love.

He could imagine plenty of blokes falling head over heels in love with Grace Fairmont. It was her innocent smile and determination, and maybe even that edgy vulnerability that gave the impression she didn't mind a strong man in her life as long as he respected her independence.

"Why are we here?" she said, glancing across the car-rental lot.

"Need a different car. Don't want to be followed into the country."

Although Bobby knew if MI5 was interested in her, there wasn't much to keep them from finding Bobby and Grace.

Outsmarting British Intelligence? How was Bobby going to do that?

He told her to stay in the car and lock the doors while he rented another car. At least they would reduce their chances of being tracked up north. He got the new car then checked her backpack for a tracking device. Nothing.

Then again, if British Intelligence had known what train Grace would be on two nights ago, they'd surely know where Grace was headed—to her mother's hometown.

Everything Bobby did, he did with Grace in mind. *Of course. Because that's your job, mate. Think of her needs first and put her safety ahead of everything.*

He found A90 and headed north.

"Did you always know you wanted to do this?" she said.

"What, chaperone beautiful women around the countryside?" he joked. She looked so sad and lost. He wanted to brighten her cheeks, maybe even make her smile.

"Beautiful, huh?" she said.

"You're fishing for more compliments, are you?"

She smiled.

His heart filled his chest. Bugger, she was dangerous in a completely innocent sort of way.

"By the way, nice shirt," she said. He heard the humor in her voice.

"Thought I'd try something different," he said. This morning, he'd put on the green shirt she'd bought him.

"Were you always interested in police work?" she asked.

"Actually, no. I figured I'd be in jail by the time I turned twenty. Instead, Max demanded I make something of myself. He's like a father figure, but don't tell him I said that. He's barely ten years older. I think he'd be offended."

"What happened to your father?"

Bobby could feel his smile fade.

"He's gone, isn't he?" she said.

"A long time ago," Bobby answered.

"How did he die?"

"He didn't. He left. Left my mother with five children under the age of eleven. I was the oldest."

"That must have been a big responsibility."

"It was, until I cocked-up and she sent me away." Why couldn't he shut his mouth?

"Cocked-up? What does that mean?"

He glanced at her then back to the road. "It means my little sister was hit by a car and it was my fault."

She looked at her chin pushed in, could he
private nighttime eater. Kiss the boy's ear and it
was too dark.

Chapter Ten

She studied Bobby's expression, his set jaw
and dark penetrating eyes focused on the
road. She sensed he hadn't meant to let the
information slip about his sister, about his
own perceived failure.

"I'm…I'm sorry," Grace said.

Still, how could an eleven-year-old boy be
expected to take care of four younger children?

"It was a long time ago," he said.

Yet he wore it like a favorite jacket,
slipping into it daily. Kind of like his cross.
Did that reminder have something to do with
his sister?

"How were you responsible?" she pushed.

"I'm her older brother. I should have
stopped Wendy from going out into the street."

"Accidents happen, Bobby."

"Not this one. It could have been prevented."

I failed. He might as well have said the words.

Suddenly she realized why protecting her was so important. He was trying to right the wrongs of his past by keeping her safe.

"Thanks, by the way," she said.

"For what?"

"For finding me today; for putting up with my suspicions about you being the bad guy."

"It's important to be suspicious." He paused. "Of everyone."

He was warning her to keep her distance. Why? Did he think she was going to fall for him, on vacation?

"I should call Steven," she said, giving the not-so-subtle hint that her heart belonged to another man, even if she wasn't entirely convinced of it herself.

And maybe it would remind her, as well, because in the past few days she'd found herself attracted to Bobby Finn. Of course she had; he was a real charmer. His natural charisma drew women to him, his smiles, his sense of humor.

Was any of it real? Or was it an act to do his job?

God, she was so desperate for "real." Starting with the truth about her mom.

She called Steven, but again, her call went into voice mail.

"Hey, Steven," she said. "I'm okay now, heading up to Pitlochry for the week. We've got a lot to talk about when I get home." She glanced at Bobby, who pretended not to be listening. "I've learned some things about my mom that are a bit unsettling. Anyway, not to worry. I'm safe. Well," she hesitated, unable to the say the three words shared by lovers. "Talk to you soon."

She slipped the phone into her pocket and glanced out her window. It's not like they had said I love you all the time. No, it was more like a casual love-ya type of endearment, like punctuation on the end of a sentence: necessary and expected.

Of course it was expected. They'd been going out for more than a year, took turns sleeping over on weekends and watered each other's plants when one of them was out of town.

If you disregarded the sexual relations, they sounded more like friends than lovers. Not that she'd know what true lovers acted like. Sure, Dad loved Andrea but Grace always sensed his one true love had been Mom. Mom had drawn out his uninhibited passion and filled his heart completely.

Truth was, Steven didn't do that for Grace. He was nice and courteous and said all the right things, almost as if he'd read a book on how to please a woman. Yet it didn't fill her up.

The thought of living with him for the rest of her life didn't excite her.

Not nearly as much as the thought of Bobby Finn touching her.

Oh, crud, not good.

Being attracted to her bodyguard was disastrous for so many reasons starting with the fact that he was with her because of his job, not because he wanted to be with her. Secondly, wasn't there a name for the warped syndrome of a woman being attracted to her bodyguard? It was a natural progression created by a dangerous situation. This relationship wasn't real any more than the charming ways of the man sitting next to her. His charm was a well-practiced act, she guessed, to get his way with women.

What was really buried beneath his casual charm? *Forget it, girl. You're looking for trouble if you go digging for that answer.*

"I've had some karate training," Bobby said.

She snapped her gaze to meet his. "What?"

"You look worried about me protecting you. I don't need a weapon to defend myself."

Yeah, but how was she going to defend herself against the simmering attraction growing between them?

She'd rely on his honor. He was a gentleman. She could tell by the way he had touched her after she'd seen Harry Franklin. Bobby had knelt in front of her and soothed her nerves by cradling her hands in his. When he'd searched in her pocket for the key, he'd been so gentle, his eyes warm with comfort. And at the pub, when he'd caught her running away, he'd put his hand to her shoulder to stop her.

A gentle hand.

A comforting hand.

Even when he'd been upset with her.

"Look, if you're that worried we'll stop before we get to town and I'll show you a few moves," he said.

"Moves?" Like hugging, kissing, touching in the most intimate of places?

"So you can protect yourself in case we're separated," he explained.

SHE WAS TOO QUIET, Bobby thought an hour into the drive. Something was on her mind. He hoped he hadn't said anything to upset her. She had enough to deal with, especially the potential danger of being watched and hunted.

Was it something the phony inspector had said that had upset her?

He watched her turn a page in the diary, reading intently. "I need to ask you something," he said.

"Sure." She glanced up.

Those blue eyes, so wide and innocent, made his heart race a bit, like when he'd had a crush on Molly Longergan in grade school.

You weren't good enough for her and you're surely not good enough for Grace Fairmont.

"Can you remember anything else the Owen bloke said to you?" he asked.

"Other than Mom being involved with the deaths of innocent people?"

"He said that?"

"Yes."

Then he had to be British Intelligence.

"Did he give you any indication what he wanted from you—" Bobby paused.

"When he practically ripped my hand off?"

He noticed the rise in the pitch of her voice but it was not from fear. She was angry. Good, anger would keep her sharp.

"I'm sorry I didn't get to you sooner," Bobby said.

"You should hardly feel sorry. I ditched you, remember?"

He shot her a pleasant smile, not the one he used when flirting. Grace wasn't a female to warm his bed. She was an intelligent girl on the run, trying to sort out her past.

A girl in danger.

"In case you get the urge to ditch me again,

I've got an idea." He pulled off the side of the road into a gravel drive. "It's time for that self-defense lesson."

He parked and got out of the car. She joined him in a grassy area and stood there, impatient.

"What, you don't think this is important?" he said.

She leaned against the hood of the car. "You're always going to be with me, so what's the point?"

Not always, luv.

"It will be good for you to know, regardless. Pay attention. First, always be aware of your surroundings. If you sense something's off, change direction and be ready to run or find a policeman to help."

She made a face.

"Okay, maybe not a policeman but get into a large crowd. Generally, you're safe when you're surrounded by people."

"And if I'm alone in the middle of nowhere?" She motioned to their surroundings.

"Keep eye contact. Don't show any weakness. Think of everything as a weapon. Your objective is to survive and get safely away. That's the only rule. Scream, bite, scratch, kick, do whatever you have to. Think about things you have on you as weapons."

"I've still got some pepper spray left."

"Excellent. Look around you, everything here can be used as a weapon: dirt, stones, bricks. You have to train your mind to think differently about everything you see. You don't have time to consider if you should or shouldn't. We know we're being followed so take action immediately."

She nodded. Determination flared in her eyes. Good, she was ready.

"How about some physical moves?" he suggested.

"Sure," she said.

He could have sworn she blushed. *Focus, mate. You've got to teach her to protect herself.*

He got behind her and wrapped his arm around her neck. "I'm going to take your money," he whispered into her ear. "Kick me," he ordered.

She did, half-heartedly.

He released her and turned her around to

look at her. "Are you playing with me? Come on now, this isn't fun and games."

"I don't want to hurt you."

"You won't." He turned her around and wrapped his arm around her neck again. "I'm going to take your mum's diary."

She kicked, swung her arms up to hit his head, and he lost his balance. They both went down, Grace on top of him, snickering.

And it angered him.

"This is serious business," he said, unable to keep the irritation from his voice. "This is your safety we're talking about."

She stopped abruptly and cleared her throat. "Sorry, I laugh when I'm embarrassed."

She was leaning on him, like a girlfriend leaning across her boyfriend's body at a picnic. Close, so very close. His breath caught in his throat. How could he be this close and not kiss her? Her tongue licked her bottom lip. Blast, he was going to lose it in a minute. He struggled to hold on to his self-control.

This was not a one-nighter like the rest. She was his assignment, a woman he had to keep safe. He'd have a heck of a time concentrating on her safety if he was kissing her.

"If you don't, I will," she said.

He studied her eyes, filled with need. "Will what?"

She leaned forward and kissed him, the taste so bloody perfect. He'd never paid attention to the taste of a woman's lips before. It never seemed to matter. Just kiss her, get her into your bed, feel the connection for a brief few minutes, then detach. Don't think about how soft her lips felt or how delicious their taste.

Grace's lips were bloody amazing.

And he'd gone completely mad.

She opened her lips to tease him, tasting him, flirting with him. He couldn't control his arousal, his need for this woman.

No, it was a natural response. He'd be hard like this with any woman who lay across his chest, kissing and touching. She slipped her fingers into his hair, the touch so utterly sensual, erotic.

She's throwing herself at you because you're her protector and she's scared.

It wasn't like he hadn't been used before to pump up a woman's ego by making her feel desired. It had never mattered before. They'd both gotten what they needed: the woman got her ego stroked and Bobby enjoyed physical warmth for a few hours. But this time...

Holding her by the shoulders, he broke the kiss. "Stop."

Her cheeks reddened as she looked at him with confusion mixed with need. He didn't read either gratitude or fear in his eyes.

No, he read desire.

For him.

"Did I misread you?" she said. "Oh, my God, I did. I'm an idiot."

She got to her feet and ran her hands through her hair. Bobby sat up and watched her go through a range of emotions from panic to embarrassment to hurt.

He didn't mean to hurt her. It was a mistake; a misunderstanding.

She misunderstood the need in your eyes? Not likely.

"I hate lies, Bobby," she said, suddenly,

facing off at him. "My whole life seems like one big lie right now. Don't lie to me and tell me I misread the signals."

"You didn't." He stood and brushed off his jeans. "I'm attracted to you. You're a beautiful woman." He hesitated, hoping his next words would make her want to stay away from him—for her own good. "It's a normal reaction, especially with you throwing yourself at me."

"What?" She planted her hands on her hips. "I don't think so. You wanted to kiss me first."

How ridiculous, Bobby thought, the two of them acting like children arguing about who started a fight. Only there was a lot more at stake than who would stay after school for punishment.

Her safety was at stake. Her life.

And Bobby's heart.

What are you thinking about, mate? You can't act on your attraction if you want to keep her safe. It would be too distracting.

Not to mention complicated. When this case was finished, she'd fly back to her American boyfriend and Bobby would be…where? Alone, again, bedding scatty blondes.

As opposed to the blonde who stared him down, wanting him to admit his attraction to her.

"We need to go." He walked toward the car.

"You need to apologize," she said.

"For what?" He reached for the door and she blocked him.

"For being a jerk."

"I'm not going to apologize for who I am."

"And who is that exactly?" she said.

"I'm a ladies' man. I draw women like honey draws flies." He leaned forward, their faces merely touching. Her eyes widened. "I'm not your boyfriend, Grace. I'm the devil when it comes to women. Don't forget that."

He snapped the door open and her shoulders jerked, but she held his gaze. Tough little American girl. Good, she'd need that strength to protect herself.

From her pursuers.

And from Bobby. Because he wasn't sure how long he could be her companion without touching her blond waves, without losing himself inside her. Completely.

She broke their staring match and fully

pushed open the door, nearly hitting Bobby. Good, maybe he'd angered her enough that she'd stop looking at him with compassion in her eyes and stop speaking to him in that gentle, sweet voice.

She pulled her door shut before he could do the gentlemanly thing and shut it for her.

This is best, mate. For everyone.

He got behind the wheel and steered the car toward her mother's hometown. She leaned her head back against the seat rest, closed her eyes and turned her face away from him, her blond waves covering her beautiful pale skin.

He gripped the steering wheel and focused on the road, on getting them to Pitlochry.

Bugger, this was all wrong. Insanity. He should have put her on a plane to America.

Why hadn't he?

Because he knew she wouldn't go. Or was it something else? The longing he read in her eyes whenever she spoke of her mother?

Is that really it, Finn? Or is it your personal desire to spend time with her, bask in the warmth of her gentle energy? He thought about her mood before their shopping trip had gone terribly wrong. She'd been over the moon with everything she had purchased. He'd never known anyone generally happy with life, so open with her thoughts and feelings.

Bobby protected his feelings beneath an armor of smart-aleck comments and forced laughter. His feelings were ugly and sordid, not to be shared with anyone, ever.

Except for the one time he'd been arrested by Max. Bobby had fought by completely shutting down, and Max had poked and prodded until Bobby finally had exploded into a mass of pain, all the disappointments of his life tumbling out of his mouth; tears floating down his cheeks.

That was the second time in his life he'd cried. The first had been after Mum had left him with Uncle Thomas. Bobby had never felt more alone in his life.

It had been his own fault. He was a bad seed, a worthless big brother.

But he wasn't going to be a failure as a detective. Which meant he'd have to keep Grace safe.

He looked over at her. She'd opened her eyes and was leafing through her mum's diary.

"What's next?" he said.

She turned to him and her eyes seemed bloodshot. Bastard, had he made her cry?

He snapped his gaze back to the road.

"Next?" she questioned.

"We get to Pitlochry and then what?" he said.

"We find my family, or rather, Mom's family. I wouldn't mind stopping along the way first. Mom wrote about a place in her journal I'd like to see."

"Sightseeing," he muttered.

"I don't like this," she blurted out.

"Me, either."

"I'm referring to you acting like such a jerk."

"It's—"

"Don't say it. I don't believe it's who you are, Bobby. I think you act like a jerk to keep people away. I'm not going to hurt you. I have no reason to hurt you."

But you kissed me. And it wasn't a simple kiss, a one-nighter kiss. It got to me, shot panic through my nerves. You got through.

"Bobby?"

He didn't respond. What could he say?

They continued their drive in silence, until she pointed out a spot written about in her mother's diary. He pulled over and she got out.

"Are you coming?" she said.

"I'm fine right here." He stared out the front windshield.

She sighed, grabbed the diary and left. He watched her sit down and gaze across Loch Leven at a ruined castle on an island. With hands braced to the ground, she leaned back and soaked up the sunshine.

He wanted this assignment over, so he could get back to his real work: finding criminals.

There's no one I'd rather have watching Miss Fairmont.

Max might change his mind if he knew how Bobby was struggling to keep this a professional relationship.

Relationship? Is that what you called it?

After twenty minutes or so, Grace stood and walked back to the car. Good, they could move on. She got in and shut the door, clearing her throat.

"It's just as she'd described it," she whispered. "She came here with her grandmother once. Mary, Queen of Scots, was imprisoned in the castle. She escaped with help from her jailer's son who had fallen in love with her."

"Shall I drive on?"

"In a second. I want to savor the moment of being where Mom was. To breathe in the same air." She glanced at Bobby. "You wouldn't understand."

No? How many times had he wished for the chance to head out to sea, feel the sea air slapping his face as it did his father's nearly every day of his life?

"We can go," she said, readjusting herself to face forward.

He put the car in gear, a part of him wanting to tell her he *did* know how she felt, that he knew the ache of wanting to make a connection with someone so badly that you could barely breathe.

More silence. He couldn't stand it. He didn't want to be at odds with Grace. He just didn't want her getting too close.

"I think I do understand," he said.

"Yeah, then explain to me why I'm so scared."

"No one will hurt you, Grace. Not while I'm around."

"That's not what scares me," she said. "I'm scared to meet them."

"Your family?"

"What if they don't accept me?"

"Why wouldn't they?"

"I'm American, for one."

"That's not your fault," he joked. He pulled into town and looked for East Moulin Road.

"What if they don't know about me?"

"Highly unlikely."

"Or they don't..." she hesitated, "...like me."

"How could they not? You're a smart, witty, beautiful girl." He pulled up a long drive to a rather large bed-and-breakfast owned by her family.

"Yeah, you're paid to say things like that."

"I'd say them anyway," he let slip.

He found a parking spot outside the house.

"I don't know, Bobby." She eyed the house through the front window, nibbling at the side of her lip.

Bloody hell, he wanted to touch her, chase away whatever fears were making her nervous.

He got out of the car and opened her door. "It will be fine, Grace. I'm sure they'll love you." He smiled and extended his hand.

She took it and he pulled her out of the car. It was strange how she held on to it as he shut her door and stranger that when he let go she still stayed close.

He sensed her fear and he understood it. What would his father say to him if he saw him again after all these years? Bobby didn't want to think about that. He'd failed his family and didn't need his father's condemnations to pound that into his soul.

"I should have called," she whispered.

"No, but don't be alarmed if they're distant. You don't know if they know about you, how they felt about your mother's—" he hesitated and looked into her eyes "—possible involvement with the PIRA."

"I know that's not true. I know it in my heart."

"Good. Hold fast to that knowledge. In the meantime," he said, glancing back at the house, "it's time to meet your family."

"Stay close," she said.

"If you wish."

"I order. My dad's paying your salary, remember?" She shot him a nervous smile.

She started toward the house and he walked alongside her. She slowed as she reached the front door.

"Steady now," he whispered. "You're a brave girl. I know you can do this."

She reached out to knock and the door swung wide-open. A young couple breezed past, holding hands and nuzzling one another. Bobby encouraged her to forge ahead.

They went into the house, and Grace paused in the entryway. Looking around, taking it all in. Bobby assumed she was sensing her mother's presence here.

"Hello," a woman said, walking up to them.

"Hi, I'm Grace Fairmont. My mother was Mary Logan."

The woman narrowed her eyes at Grace and took a step closer. "If you know what's good for you, you'll turn around and fly back to America."

Chapter Eleven

Grace's heart plummeted. "Excuse me?"

"You heard me," the older woman hissed.

"Hold on there," Bobby said.

"Lydia!" a woman called, walking into the hallway. "Welcome," she said, turning her attention to Grace and Bobby. "Did you have a reservation?" She stepped in front of the older woman and gestured for her to leave.

The woman harrumphed and disappeared into the kitchen, but not without one last sneer. Great. This was a horrible mistake.

Bobby touched Grace's shoulder as if he'd read her trepidation, then turned to address the second woman, a redhead who looked to be in her mid-thirties.

"Miss Fairmont has come from the United

States to track down family. Her mother's last name was Logan?"

A look of surprise lit the woman's face. "Your mother? Your mother was Mary Logan? Mary Logan was my aunt. That's fantastic!" She gave Grace a hug, then stepped back. "I don't believe it! I never knew my aunt had a daughter. I'm Anne, your cousin. I'm so stunned."

Anne had reddish hair, like Mom had had, but other than that, Grace didn't notice much of a resemblance.

"Out of nowhere you show up?" Anne said. "How wonderful."

"I'm glad you think so." Grace glanced toward the kitchen.

"Oh, don't mind Lydia. She's a little touched in the head, but she makes delicious cakes. Who's this, your boyfriend?"

Grace started to correct her, but thought better of it. How would she explain Bobby's presence without alarming the family?

"This is Bobby Finn."

"Good to meet you," he said.

"Ah, that's an interesting accent," Anne commented.

"Originally from Ireland," he explained. "Moved to London as a boy."

"We met in London, actually," Grace said. "On business." Great, she'd just met her new family member and was already lying.

Bobby smiled at her. "Grace has been talking about visiting her mother's home town for months now."

"And I'm glad you came." She smiled. "I'm having a hard time wrapping my head around it. You'll have to forgive me."

"I should have warned you," Grace said.

"Well, let's get you two settled so you can rest up from your trip."

"May I ask," Grace started, following Anne to a small office off the main hallway, "are there other family members here? My grandparents?"

Anne's dark-green eyes met Grace's. "I'm sorry, they're gone. But your Aunt Rosie and Uncle Gerry live here, that's my mother and father. They run a shop in town and will be back for dinner. She's going to be so excited to see you."

"Thanks." Grace glanced at the artwork on the walls. "My mom lived here?"

"She did, yes. When she wasn't in Ireland."

Grace sensed something in the woman's voice.

Anne pulled a key from the top drawer of her desk. "We can catch up on all that later. I've got a cousin from America," Anne said, awe in her voice. "Let's get you settled. Have you got luggage?"

"I'll get it," Bobby offered.

"Meet us upstairs," Anne directed, then motioned for Grace to join her.

Grace started up the stairs and heard the door to the kitchen creak open. She spotted Lydia peeking through the doorway. The woman did not like her. Not one bit.

But she didn't even know Grace. Maybe it was resentment about Mom. She must have been a handful growing up.

"Your mother lived here until her twenty-second birthday, then she went to America to find the man of her dreams," Anne said.

"My father."

"We received a postcard periodically. Then nothing. Then we were notified of her death in London. It didn't make sense, why she was back in the country and we hadn't heard from her. Grandmother never quite got over that."

I haven't gotten over the fact I lost my mother, seemingly before she was killed.

"You have no idea why she came back?" Grace pushed.

"I'm not much for gossip."

"Gossip?"

"Here's your room." Anne paused at a door and stuck the key in the lock. She shot Grace a sympathetic smile. "There were rumours about your mum's involvement with a radical group. But your mother's gone. We should all move on."

If only Grace could.

Anne opened the door and Grace stepped inside a room decorated in Victorian style, with lace pillow covers and flowered curtains.

And one bed.

Luckily it had a private bath, so she wouldn't be stuck in a bathroom down the hall with the lights out again. No, she'd be stuck sharing a room with Bobby Finn.

"I'll leave you to rest up," Anne said. "I'd love to stay and chat but I have rooms to ready for today's new guests. I keep this one reserved for special friends." She smiled and gave Grace another hug. "I'll check back when I can. Supper isn't until seven, so why not take a walk down to the village, or drive out to the Pass of Killiecrankie? We'll catch up later. The family will be so excited to meet you."

"Thanks," Grace said, suddenly hating her midwestern accent.

Anne left and minutes later there was a knock.

"Room service," Bobby called through the door.

Graced opened the door and he stepped into the room carrying the luggage. "Nice room," he said.

"I guess you expect a tip?" she joked.

"No, just loan me a pillow from your bed, and maybe a blanket if you can spare one."

She went to the window and hugged herself. Glancing across the rolling countryside, she wondered which room Mom had slept in. Had she walked the green hills that seemed to stretch for miles? Grace loved being outside basking in sunshine. Was she like her mother in that respect?

"You can keep your pillows," Bobby said, walking up to her. "I'm sure they have extras."

She glanced at him. "No, it's fine. You can have whatever you need."

What Grace needed was to have Bobby's arms around her right now to absorb some of his strength. She could use a friend.

Bobby would quickly become more than that, she sensed. He'd already lit something inside her that had made her kiss him a few hours ago. If he got too close she was going to do it again.

"Stop looking at me like that," he said. His soft brown eyes grew dark, more intense.

"Like what?" she said.

"You know like what."

"I'm sorry." She ripped her gaze from his and hugged herself tighter. "I guess it's all these emotions flooding to the surface. Being in Mom's home."

He wrapped his arms around her and squeezed. She leaned into him, as she'd wanted to before, welcoming his strength to hold her up. Because, right now, she was dangerously close to dissolving into a puddle on the floor.

"What is it?" he asked.

"Everything."

"Your cousin seems nice."

"It still doesn't feel right."

"Maybe it never will," he said. "Maybe it's not meant to feel 'right.'"

"That's a depressing thought."

He stepped back and turned her to face him. "Things are rarely what you anticipate them being. They just are what they are, and you've got to make the best of it."

"A philosopher cop? Nice."

He smiled. "Since the rest of the family won't get back until later, we have all afternoon to go exploring. That will cheer you up."

"Mom wrote about the Pass of Killiecrankie in her journal."

"I'll take you there. We could both use the fresh air, then we'll head back for a nap.

You'll need a rest before meeting the entire family. Boyfriends know best." He winked.

"About that, sorry I didn't correct her."

"Quick thinking on your part. You're catching on."

"That's what worries me. I'm turning into a liar and a flirt."

"No, just a lost girl looking for answers."

A girl who wants you for more than protection.

Damn, she really was an emotional mess. She didn't like having to lean on Bobby Finn. He'd made it clear he had no feelings for her, that their kiss was a result of her "throwing herself at him."

The strange thing was, she'd never felt like that when kissing Steven or anyone else, for that matter.

"I'm going to wash up," he said. "You'll be okay?"

Sheesh, he was afraid she'd fall apart in the few minutes it took him to wash his hands?

"I'm fine." She turned and glanced out the window. He went to the bathroom and shut the door.

She was an emotional mess, sure, but worse, she was depending too heavily on a man again, and this time it was a man who'd be out of her life the moment they landed in the States.

She'd been a good girl her entire life, listened to Dad and followed his suggestions. Her relationship with Steven had fallen into the same pattern. Sure, she cared about him, but it was becoming apparent that she needed him as her touchstone, her stability.

From the window Grace watched Lydia toss garbage out back. The older woman glanced up at Grace, but Grace didn't step away or avoid her gaze. She would not be shamed by this woman. Whatever sins her mother had committed as a teenager didn't belong to Grace.

Lydia pursed her lips; her brows knit together in a sad, almost regretful expression. Then she started walking toward a barn on the far side of the property. About halfway, she turned and motioned with her hand for Grace to join her.

Did she dare?

She'd talk to anyone to get answers. Maybe then she could put the pieces together, figure out why Mom had left and what she was really like as a woman.

Maybe then Grace could find peace.

BOBBY SPLASHED cold water on his face, needing to shock himself back to reality. Studying his reflection in the mirror he noted the few day's growth of beard, rough to the touch.

Yet she'd kissed him anyway.

Splash. Splash. He tried to wash the memory out of his mind.

He could tell she'd wanted to kiss him again just now as they stood by the window overlooking the countryside. She'd wanted to kiss him and he'd barely held on to his self-control.

Not good. Need to get your perspective back, mate.

He had to get control of this thing.

"She has a boyfriend," he said to himself in the mirror.

A boyfriend and she's an emotional wreck. She'd be attracted to any male who offered a shoulder. *It's not like she wants you, Bobby Finn.*

No, she had a straight-up bloke waiting for her back home; a boring financial analyst with a daily routine of workouts at his club and fresh salads for lunch. He probably rotated his mattress regularly and bought a new toothbrush every few weeks.

Then there was Bobby, who lived in a constant state of chaos, not knowing where he'd be going next, which murderer he'd be tracking.

For a second he wondered what it would be like to wake up every morning to a fresh-faced girl like Grace, to go to a boring job and come home to share dinner with her.

The second passed.

"It's a bit fancy for a bloke like me," Bobby said, coming out of the hoity-toity bathroom.

The bedroom was empty. "Bloody Nora," he muttered.

They'd only been apart five minutes, couldn't have been more.

"Grace," he called, hoping she'd material-ize from under the bed.

He went into the hallway. "Grace!"

His voice echoed back at him. Racing downstairs, his mind rattled off possibilities. *She's gone down for tea with her cousin, mate. Nothing life-threatening.*

He tried to check the office but it was locked. He poked his head into the empty study, then went to the kitchen. He swung the door open and found Lydia kneading dough.

"Have you seen Grace?" he asked.

"I've seen her."

"Where has she gone?"

With an icy glare, she looked up at him. "She should have gone back to the States. If you really cared about her you'd take her back. This afternoon."

"I tried that already. She needs to find answers."

"She's going to find trouble is what she's going to find. Her mother was trouble and paid for it with her life. Tell the girl to go home and enjoy her nice, safe life. She won't like what she finds here."

"Where is she?"

"I sent her out to the barn." She went back

to wrestling with the dough. "She wants answers? She'll find them out there, in her mother's trunk."

"She's not like her mother," Bobby said. "Grace is a sweet girl."

"That will change when she finds out the truth."

Bobby went out the back door and raced to the barn.

That will change when she finds out the truth.

He wouldn't let that happen, wouldn't let her mother's past dim Grace's sparkling personality. She was a sweet, intelligent girl with a warm heart and no ulterior motives. Whatever her mother's sins, Bobby wouldn't let Grace take those on herself.

He pushed open the barn door. "Grace?"

"I'm here."

A shaft of sunlight streamed through a top window, lighting Grace as she sat on the floor. Photographs and papers filled her lap. A black trunk lay open in front of her.

He approached and she glanced up, a lost expression on her face. "Mom's stuff."

"Anything interesting?"

She didn't answer, but held up a newspaper clipping from 1972. The headline read, Bloody Sunday.

"That was a very bad day," he said.

"But why would she have this in her trunk?"

He knelt next to her. He could tell from the look in her eyes that the possibility of her mum being involved with the PIRA was starting to sink in.

"I don't believe it," she whispered.

"It's nice outside, Grace. Let's take a drive," he suggested, afraid of what else she would find.

"And there's this." She handed him a photograph of a group of young people.

"That's my mom." She pointed to a girl, her hair in a ponytail, wearing a big smile.

"She's almost as cute as you."

"Her friend, the boy on the right? He was arrested." She handed him another newspaper clipping featuring a mug shot of the same dark-haired boy.

"That doesn't mean anything, Grace."

"Thanks for trying." She glanced back at the pile of clippings and photographs.

He took her hands in his. "You can make up stories in your mind or you can wait to speak with your aunt and uncle tonight at dinner. They'll tell you the truth, good or bad. This—" he motioned to the trunk and its contents "—is just torturing yourself. Come on, luv, it's an excellent day for a hike."

He placed the photographs and clippings back in the trunk and shut it, then pulled her to her feet.

"I don't get you," she said.

"What, you don't think I'm the out-of-doors type?"

"You act like…"

"Like a bossy wanker? I know. It's a bad habit of mine, always ordering people around." He started walking, hanging on to her hand, taking pleasure in its warmth. Her warmth. He would not let this girl be destroyed by her mother's sins.

"You don't have to do this," she said, as they stepped out of the barn into the sunshine.

"I don't have to take you out to see the countryside? What else would you have us do? Sit in our room and read all afternoon? How bloody boring."

"I meant you don't have to keep trying to cheer me up," she clarified.

He squeezed her hand and kept walking. "Do you need anything from the room?"

"No," she said. "I could use something to eat, though."

"We'll grab lunch on the way out of town."

"Where are you taking me today, Mr. Finn?"

"Well, Miss Fairmont." He smiled at her. "I hear there's a spectacular place just north of town called the Pass of Killiecrankie."

They walked to the car and he opened the door for her. She hesitated and looked into his eyes. "I'm glad you're here." She smiled and slid into the passenger seat.

He shut the door, struggling with the thought of an entire afternoon walking the countryside with Grace beside him, because, truth was, he was more than *glad* to be with her.

He felt whole when helping her, as though all his past failings were washed away every bloody moment he looked into her crystal-blue eyes.

Don't look too much, Finn. It's only an illusion.

"It's AMAZING," she said, her eyes widening as they started up the trail, her camera bag over her shoulder.

They were surrounded by lush green forest. The sound of the River Garry rushing through a deep gorge below echoed through the pine and birch trees.

He was glad he'd brought her here. It seemed to have brightened her spirits a bit. She'd eaten little of her sandwich at lunch, even with his encouragement. There was too much going on, she'd said. Too much upheaval.

Like the upheaval in his chest whenever he let his gaze linger too long on her beautiful face?

They strolled along the trail, the sounds of nature making this a serene experience, surreal even. He couldn't remember the last time he'd been in a forest; his work always kept him in crowded, noisy cities.

"There's an attraction up ahead called Soldier's Leap," he said. "The story goes that a fleeing soldier leapt between two rocks and eluded his enemy."

She nodded, smiled. He wished she'd say something.

Now, there's a first. Bobby Finn actually wanting a woman to speak.

They walked a bit and reached The Pass.

"Wow," she said, standing on the very rock the soldier had jumped from. "It's so quiet out here."

He was thinking the same thing. Quiet and peaceful.

Actually perfect, with Grace standing slightly above him, the thick forest framing her face, the slight wind tossing her hair about her cheeks.

"What?" she said with a laugh.

"Nothing," he said, embarrassed that he'd been caught again so obviously admiring her. "There are other places like this close by, Blair Castle, for instance. Here, let me take your photograph."

She handed him her camera bag and he snapped a few shots. He wanted to ask for copies, but didn't.

She stared into the water below and took a deep breath. "It's so peaceful."

"I'm glad you like it."

"Does your job keep you in the city?"

"Mostly, but our last case took us to a small coastal town off the Pacific Ocean."

"What was it about?"

"A boy had gone missing. Authorities thought he'd drowned, but our team wanted to pursue the kidnapping angle."

"I'm almost afraid to ask, did it turn out okay?"

"Yes, actually. We found the boy, no thanks to me."

"Sore subject?"

"A bit. I looked right into the eyes of the man who was blackmailing the family and didn't have a clue he was the culprit. I hate being fooled like that."

"I know the feeling."

He eyed her. "Who fooled you?"

"My father, for one. He should have told me about Mom's dark past long before now."

"He was trying to protect you."

"He lied."

"He didn't lie exactly, he just withheld information. There's a difference."

"Sure, okay, if you say so." She turned to look across the river.

"I've made you cross," he said. "I'm sorry."

She had enough to deal with, poor girl. His job was to protect her and keep her happy.

Admit it, mate, keeping her happy has little to do with this job at this point.

A sound echoed from a mass of trees behind him. He jumped in front of Grace, shielding her.

"What was that?" she said.

"Probably a fox." He eyed the dense grove. "Ready to go back?"

"Sure," she said, as if she sensed danger beyond the trees.

He led her up the path to the rental.

"My camera," she said. "I left it back there."

"Get in the car. I'll go fetch it."

"But—"

"Stay in the car, Grace. I'll be right back."

"Bobby—"

He shut the door on her protest. Walking back to retrieve the camera, he scanned the woods looking for anything out of place: bright colors, something reflective.

Don't see danger where there isn't any, mate.

Yet Bobby could feel the threat, be it human or wild animal. He grabbed hold of the camera-bag strap and straightened.

A click echoed behind him. "Don't turn around."

Blast, he was right to trust his instincts. Bobby raised his hands.

"Good chap." A set of hands patted him down, searching, he presumed, for a weapon, while the barrel of a gun pressed against the back of his head.

"I'm not armed," Bobby said.

Someone affixed a blindfold to his eyes. They were terrorists, out to kidnap him? No, he couldn't be taken away from Grace. *They're probably going to take her, too, mate.*

He grabbed the bastard's wrist and spun around, but the gunman knocked Bobby across the back of the head and he went face-down to the wet earth.

He couldn't see, didn't know how close they were, where the barrel of the gun was pointed.

But he could guess.

Stupid, bloody fool. You never should have left her.

"Can we be gentlemen about this, Mr. Finn?"

"What do you want?" Bobby said.

"The girl, what does she know about her mother?" It was a woman's voice this time.

"You're with the PIRA?" Bobby said.

Someone kicked him in the gut. "Don't ask questions. Answer them," the man said.

"She doesn't know anything," Bobby coughed. "She didn't even know her mother."

"Then why is she here?" the woman asked.

"It's a bloody soul-searching mission."

Silence.

"She's trying to find herself, to find some sort of emotional peace before she moves on with her life," he continued.

"She's in danger," the woman said.

"No bloody kidding."

He thought he'd get another kick for that, but didn't.

"That smart-aleck attitude could get you killed."

"Bobby!" Grace called from the car.

"Don't answer her," the man ordered.

"Leave her alone," Bobby said. "She doesn't know anything."

The barrel of the gun pressed against his temple. "And neither do you. You didn't see us, this didn't happen."

"I understand."

"Smart chap. Now, if you're really that smart, you'll lie quite still and keep your eyes closed." The blindfold was ripped off. "If you move, we'll track you down and kill you both."

Chapter Twelve

Stay in the car, he'd ordered her.

Ordered. And Grace wasn't taking orders anymore. She could go back and get her own darned camera. She'd forgotten it. "He's just trying to be a gentleman," she whispered.

She headed back up the trail, pepper spray in hand. "Bobby?" He didn't answer. He surely had to hear her. "Bobby, answer me!"

She was getting angry, worried and a bit scared.

Her pulse raced as she forged farther up the trail, paying close attention to her surroundings; the birds chirping, the wind whistling through the trees. She heard a man and woman chatting up ahead. They were off in the distance, and she could only see their backs as they continued along the trail. Is that what she and Bobby had heard? Other tourists?

A few hundred feet down the trail she spotted something bright green in the woods. The shirt she'd bought Bobby as a joke. He'd put it on this morning.

"Bobby," she whispered and went to his side. She kneeled beside him and noticed a bump at the base of his skull. "My God, what happened?"

He opened his eyes, squinting at first. Then he sat up and glanced around. "I—" He looked at her, then to their surroundings. "I'm not sure."

"Let's get you up." Gripping his arm she helped him stand. His hair was mussed, his eyes glassy and his clothes were covered with mud. "Did you fall or—"

"I don't remember." Panic edged his voice. Now *he* seemed shaken, spooked.

"Let's go. I'll drive." She led him to the car.

With a deep, fortifying breath she focused on getting him back to the bed-and-breakfast and settling him down. But if he had a concussion, should he rest or be taken to a clinic?

"We'll find a doctor," she said.

"No, I'm fine."

She wasn't going to argue and upset him further, not now, anyway. They drove back to the house and she helped him to the room. He changed into fresh clothes.

"Lie down," she ordered.

"Don't leave," he said as she tucked the blanket over his fully clothed body.

She touched his forehead. He burned.

"I'm always hot, remember?" he explained with a smile.

"I'm worried about you," she admitted.

A second passed. Her hand still touched his face. She wished she could crawl into bed with him, but he'd object for sure.

"I'm going downstairs to get you some ice for the nasty bump on your head."

He didn't let go of her hand. "A cool cloth from the bathroom will be fine. Don't leave, please?"

She went to the bathroom and ran a washcloth under cold water. Glancing into the mirror, she realized she could probably use a rest herself. Her eyes were bloodshot and worry lines creased her forehead.

Walking back into the room, she noticed the clouds had masked the sun outside.

"I think I remember," he said.

She sat on the bed and pressed the cloth to base of his head.

"I lost my footing and slipped. Must have hit my head."

She eyed him. Something didn't feel right. He was lying to her. But why?

"I've got some aspirin," she offered.

"Maybe later. I need to rest. You...you can lie down, as well, if you'd like."

She stretched out beside him, staring at the plaster ceiling and wondering why this felt so comfortable, especially when she knew he was keeping something from her.

"Can I ask a favor?" she said.

"What kind of favor?"

"Please, don't lie to me. Ever. Can you do that?"

"No."

"No?" She turned and their faces nearly touched. "What do you mean, 'no'?"

"My first priority is to keep you safe. If I must lie to do that, then I will."

"But I need to be able to trust you."

"You can. Just know I'm always looking out for your best interest."

"My best interest is the truth," she said, her gaze drifting to his full lips.

"Your best interest is staying safe."

"I've been safe my whole life," she whispered. "But have I lived?"

He glanced back at the ceiling.

She reached out and guided his eyes to meet hers. "Why are you so afraid of me?"

He didn't answer, just stared at her with that lost expression. She pressed her cheek to his chest and closed her eyes.

BOBBY AWAKENED a few hours later. Something ached inside his chest as he felt Grace's body against his. He couldn't believe she'd snuggled up to him with such complete trust, especially since he sensed she knew he was hiding something.

No one had had that much faith in him. Well, no one besides, maybe, Max Templeton.

Not telling her about the assault by the mysterious couple was the right thing to do, at least until he determined who had attacked him, who had asked questions about Grace. Terrorists would have killed him for sure, which meant they were MI5 agents, didn't it? He needed more help from the Blackwell Group, more background information to help him piece this together.

But when could he call in? If he was to keep Grace safe by sticking with her every minute of the day, there wouldn't be much opportunity to call and ask Eddie for research specifics about Grace's mum, the PIRA and MI5. With any luck, Eddie would call Bobby with some news.

In the meantime they were safe here in bed.

At least Grace was safe. Bobby, on the other hand, was at high risk of losing his heart.

He lay there, wide awake, trying to make sense of things. It didn't tally: her mother's involvement with the PIRA, having Grace, leaving her behind. Unless it was because she loved Grace so much. Bobby didn't understand how that worked, but parents were known to do incredibly selfish things and claim love for their child motivated their actions.

He thought about that, thought about what would make her mum leave. No, he couldn't understand it, unless the child was bad, like Bobby, or in danger.

From the PIRA.

Blast, that's it. Her mum had left to protect her.

But why would the PIRA even care about Grace's mum, a woman who had died twenty years ago? It made no sense.

Unless her mum had had something on the group, something that could destroy them.

But they weren't active these days. They were more into discussions than bombings.

He thought about the man in the woods telling Bobby to take her back to the States. It almost seemed as if he cared about keeping Grace safe, not as if he wanted to harm her. Which meant?

Bobby's head ached the more he tried to puzzle through it.

Grace stretched across him, claiming his body with an arm over his chest. He couldn't move, could hardly breathe, the pressure of her arm seeping through his shirt to his skin and deeper still.

The clock on the dresser read six.

"Gracie?" he said.

"Hmm?"

"We've got an hour until supper. Maybe we should think about getting ready?"

"Okay." She didn't move.

"Or not," he whispered. Truth be told, he could lie here all night, content, with Grace leaning into him.

Someone knocked softly on the door. Grace didn't budge. Bobby slipped out from beneath her and cracked open the door.

Anne smiled at him. "Did you two have fun out at Killiecrankie?"

"Yes, thank you."

"We're getting ready for dinner. You may come early if you'd like. Mum was so excited to hear about Grace." Anne strained to peek in the room.

"She's asleep," Bobby said, not sure why he felt the need to protect her from her own family.

"Right, well, do come down soon. My parents are so anxious to speak with her."

"Thank you. We will."

She walked down the hallway, turning once to smile again before she disappeared down the stairs. He closed the door. Grace looked up from the bed to smile at him.

His world tipped a bit, and not because of the blow to his head.

"Thanks for the nap."

"Don't thank me." He went to the bed and sat down.

"I haven't slept that well in days," she said. "Having a live, warm teddy bear must have helped."

"Is that all I am to you? A cuddly toy?" he joked.

"You don't really want me to answer that." Her smile faded. "So, let's get ready." She jumped off the bed and raced to the bathroom.

"No fair!" he called.

She poked her head out the door. "We women take longer to make ourselves beautiful." Then she shut it.

Bugger, he wished she was making herself

beautiful for him, not to impress long-lost relations. He glanced at the bed, the rumpled spread and tossed pillows. It was going to be a long night if she expected a repeat of this afternoon, both of them sharing the bed, not touching as lovers, not kssing.

No, he'd take a spot on the floor and stretch out. It was safer that way.

He hoped this reunion with her family would be the end of it. Dinner tonight, maybe a day or two after that, Grace spending most of her time with the newly found relatives. *It will be over soon, mate. Then you can get away from temptation.*

THE EVENING went just as she'd imagined: Aunt Rosie and Uncle Gerry showering her with questions and advice. Grace could barely get a word in edgewise.

"And a teacher," Aunt Rosie said. "What a lovely profession."

"I enjoy the kids," Grace said. "But sometimes I think about doing something else."

"Like what?"

"I don't know, something a little more exciting."

"Excitement is highly overrated," Uncle Gerry said.

They were seated at the formal dining table: Aunt Rosie, Uncle Gerry and Bobby were seated across from her, and Cousin Anne and her brother Jimmy were beside her.

Bobby caught her eye every now and then, shooting her a smile of encouragement.

He seemed to be happy for her, happy that she'd reconnected with her family. She didn't read melancholy or sadness in his eyes for his own loss. She suddenly realized how painful this must be for him.

"I was wondering why the family moved here," Grace said.

The room grew silent.

Aunt Rosie forced a smile. "Your mum had some bad friends in Ireland. Our parents thought it best to move the family to another part of the U.K. They learned about this bed-and-breakfast, that it was up for sale and we moved. It's simple, really."

"Tell us about America, Grace," Jimmy said, forking up a boiled potato. "Is it exciting?"

"I guess that depends what you consider exciting," she said.

Jimmy seemed close to Grace's age, but looked younger with his youthful face and exuberant smile. He had narrow green eyes and full lips and didn't look like anyone in the family.

"Jimmy's into motorbikes and parasailing," his mother scoffed.

"Boy, you really are into excitement," Grace said.

The family chuckled. Laughter, teasing, conversation. All the things she'd never shared with a family, with blood relations. Sure her half-sisters were sweet, but they were ten years younger; Grace hardly shared a sense of humor with them.

They chatted all the way through the entrée and dessert. Uncle Gerry fired off questions about Grace's upbringing and her childhood. It was as if he was trying to piece together the years lost in not knowing his niece.

Did she remember her mother?

Did her father say where they met?

Did her father know why Mary had come back to the U.K.?

"Enough, Gerry," Aunt Rosie said.

Tea was being served when Grace felt the need to ask the question she'd been avoiding all night.

"Aunt Rosie, you said Mom was involved with a bad crowd. Is it true she was involved with the Provisional Irish Republican Army?"

"We're not sure." Aunt Rosie stood and started clearing dishes. "Help me, Gerry. I'll put the tea on."

Cousin Anne started to get up.

"No, you sit and talk to your cousin," Aunt Rosie said.

Grace glanced at Bobby, who watched her aunt and uncle clear dishes in silence. They went into the kitchen, the door swinging closed behind them.

Cousin Anne faced her. "She doesn't like talking about her sister's activities in the PIRA. It was very hard on the family, not knowing if she was alive or dead, worrying about her day and night. They didn't know where she went when she lived in the States."

"I have a hard time with all this," Grace said. "I always thought of Mom as being such a loving family woman. That is until I learned she abandoned Dad and me long before she died."

"You don't remember her, do you?"

"Not at all."

"She had a bright smile, like yours. I've seen pictures. Did she leave you any pictures to remember her by? Any keepsakes?"

"A locket. Her journal."

"How lovely. What did she write about?"

"Me, as a baby. This place. I mean, Scotland: the hills, the castles, the lochs."

"But nothing about her family? Or friends?"

"No, nothing like that."

"I'm going to help with the tea," Jimmy said.

Bobby narrowed his eyes and watched her cousin leave. Grace watched Bobby. She knew that look, that suspicious look. What was the deal?

"Grace, it would make my mother feel so much better if she knew she'd been remembered in her sister's diary. Was there nothing about her? Or her parents?"

"No, I'm sorry. She wrote exclusively about me, a little about my dad and a lot about Scotland. She loved this country."

"Yes, I'm sure." Anne's voice drifted off.

Aunt Rosie floated in with the tea, followed by Uncle Gerry with mini-cakes. They continued their conversation about Grace's life and potential future.

"What about a serious boyfriend?" Aunt Rosie said, winking at Bobby.

"No, we're not," Grace paused, "serious." Her gaze caught Bobby's. His brows furled together in question.

"I'm not ready," Grace admitted.

Not ready to marry Steven, the wrong man. It felt as if a weight had been lifted from her shoulders. Admitting the truth to herself was a huge relief.

"Well, don't wait too long," Rosie said. "Let's sit in the front room, shall we?" She stood and they all followed her into the delightful room with a fireplace centered on the far wall.

They chatted and told stories, mostly about Grace's mother as a child, but nothing about Mom after the age of seventeen, Grace noted. Were they all ashamed of her? Maybe, but they seemed to accept Grace unconditionally.

While Anne had said she was readying the rooms for guests earlier, Grace hadn't heard anyone enter or leave tonight. Maybe they had romantic couples checking in, wanting their privacy.

She glanced at Bobby, whose intense stare made her want to shift position in the highback chair. He was studying her, almost as if he was trying to read her mind. He jumped to his feet. "I'll be right back."

She looked at him in question, but he didn't make eye contact. Odd.

She and the ladies continued their storytelling, while Uncle Gerry smoked his pipe. Jimmy had been absent since dessert, probably fearing he'd be bored to tears by the conversation. He seemed the wild sort, but playful. A bit like Bobby Finn.

As she leaned back and enjoyed the camaraderie, she realized this was what she'd been looking for: this connection to relatives, the unconditional acceptance, maybe even love.

"You'll be staying with us for how long, then?" Aunt Rosie asked.

"I guess that depends on how long you'll have me."

Aunt Rosie gave her a strange look.

"Just kidding," Grace said. "I plan to stay a week in Scotland, maybe a few days in London before I return home."

"You're welcome to stay longer," Aunt Rosie offered.

Uncle Gerry shot her a look, probably dreading more nights of sitting around listening to women's chatter.

"Thanks, that's a nice thought," Grace said. "But I do have things to get back to." Like breaking up with my boyfriend. Yikes. How was she going to explain that? *You're a nice guy, Steven, but now that I've found some peace in my life, I no longer need to depend on men like you to make me feel whole?*

"It's been lovely to meet you," Aunt Rosie said.

"Same here." Grace smiled, feeling a new connection to her mother.

The door burst open. Grace turned to see Bobby marching into the room, his hands raised.

"Sit down," Cousin Jimmy said, shoving at Bobby from behind.

That's when Grace saw the gun. Her blood ran cold.

"Sorry, Gerry," Jimmy said to his father. "The bloke found me making a copy of her diary."

"Wait, what?" Grace demanded.

"This isn't real, Grace, it's a set-up," Bobby said. "My guess is they're British Intelligence. They're not your blood relations any more than I am."

Chapter Thirteen

Grace's heart split in two as she struggled to process Bobby's words.

"British Intelligence?" she repeated.

"Your mother was on our watch list," said Anne, the person who she'd formerly thought was her cousin. "She was a high-ranking member of the PIRA and a new, radical group has been formed in her honor. Your mother had stolen a list of MI5 agents. She died before we could get it back."

"You killed her?"

Anne glanced at Uncle Gerry. Or rather, not Uncle Gerry. He shook his head.

"You did, didn't you?" Grace pushed.

"We didn't have her killed," Gerry said. "That was her own doing."

"You bloody twit," Jimmy said to Bobby. "You've complicated everything because you're trying to be clever. I'll wipe that clever grin off your face." He raised his hand to hit Bobby.

Grace jumped to her feet. "Stop!"

"Enough!" Gerry commanded.

Jimmy's face turned red as he stared down at Bobby, who returned the man's gaze with cold, hard eyes.

"All lies," Grace said.

Bobby got up to go to her, but that bastard Jimmy pushed him back to his chair. Bobby couldn't stand the look of confusion in her eyes.

She glanced at each person in the room, one by one. "None of you are related to me, are you?"

"No," Anne said. "I'm sorry, but the truth is your boyfriend is with MI5, as well."

Grace leaned against the sofa. "Steven?"

"An agent assigned to befriend you," Rosie explained.

"No wonder I've been keeping an emotional distance," she whispered. "I felt something wasn't right."

Silence filled the room. Bobby wanted to comfort her but he sensed she needed space, time to process.

She looked at Gerry. "I haven't been imagining things. Steven's here, in Scotland."

"He's been keeping watch over you, yes."

Her gaze drifted to the floor. She seemed devastated. Bobby wanted to slug someone.

She pinned Gerry with a cold stare. "What happened to Mom's family?"

"No one knows."

"Ah, no one knows," Grace said, defeat coloring her eyes. "This, this was all a big game to you, manipulating my feelings and acting as though you cared about me."

"We needed information," Anne said. "We think the radicals are after it, as well. Your life may be in danger."

An odd chuckle escaped Grace's lips.

Bobby gripped the arms of his chair. Was she going to have a breakdown?

"Are you done? With me?" Grace looked Gerry directly in the eye.

"After we get a copy of the diary, yes."

"Fine." She walked toward the door, hesitated and turned. "So, you're with British Intelligence and you have no idea where my mother's family is?"

"I'm sorry," Rosie said.

"British Intelligence," Grace repeated. "Now there's an oxymoron if I've ever heard one." She left the room, seemingly in control, yet Bobby sensed the storm brewing. She'd been lied to, manipulated and played like a harp.

Bobby stood to follow her. Jimmy shoved the barrel of his gun in Bobby's face. "Where do you think you're going?"

"Listen, you wanker, you four just built her up and tore her down to pieces. I'm not going to sit here and watch her fall apart because of an old score you have with her mum. You're paid to be heartless, I'm paid to protect. Now get the hell out of my way before I rip your arm out of its socket."

"You really think you can do that, mate?" Jimmy taunted.

"Enough!" Gerry ordered. Jimmy lowered his gun. "There's more to this than her mother's involvement with PIRA," Gerry explained.

"Gerry, don't," Rosie warned.

"He needs to know if he's going to protect her." He looked at Bobby. "Grace Fairmont's mother was recruited by British Intelligence in the seventies for the purpose of infiltrating the PIRA."

"She was an MI5 agent?" Bobby couldn't believe it.

"Yes. As an undercover agent she'd told the PIRA about a list she had of MI5 agents. She was using this to work her way up the ranks. She died before they could get it from her, and now there's a new radical branch that's out to find the list and use it against England."

"But it was a fake list, yeah?" Bobby said.

"We gave her a list to use, but unbeknownst to us, a traitor in MI5 printed out the real names of agents. Once she discovered what she had, Mary couldn't pass the names. If she passed false names to PIRA, they could check with their insider and she'd be dead. She was compromised. She," he hesitated, "died in the bombing. PIRA never fully believed she died."

And Bobby wondered himself.

"Would you tell me if she were still alive?"

Gerry sighed. "She's not. But know this, everything Mary Logan did, she did because she loved her daughter and wanted to protect her."

"But why is PIRA interested in Grace?" Bobby said.

"They weren't. Until she came looking for her mother's past. The truth is, Mary Logan was a spy before she came to America. We sent her there on another mission. She fell in love, had a child and panicked that she'd be putting the girl in danger by being a part of her life. Mary left America and her daughter to break all ties, to keep the girl safe. She was an honorable woman."

"And a good agent," Rosie added.

"You were the ones on the path this afternoon," Bobby said.

"Yes," Gerry said. "We were hoping our threats to kill her would encourage you to take her back to the States."

"I would like nothing better. But you've seen how determined she is."

"You can't tell her about her mother being MI5," Anne said.

"Excuse me?"

"It will put her in even more danger. If she knows, Grace's questions will only bring things to the surface again."

"The radicals are hoping to find Mary Logan's list," Gerry explained. "They want to use it to raise money to revitalize their cause by selling it to our enemies."

"Good God."

"If we find the list there will be no reason for this new group to pursue Grace. We'll get our advantage back. And as long as you two are here with us you're safe."

Bobby struggled to make sense of it all. *The only thing that matters is keeping her safe.*

Bobby left to find Grace and he ran into Lydia in the hallway. "She's outside," she said, her voice softer, more compassionate than before.

"Where?"

"I gave her a cup of hot tea and a blanket and sent her to the barn to sit with her mother's things." Lydia touched his arm. "I'm not with the others," she said, then smiled. "Her family were good people."

He pushed through the back door into the cool night. Heading for the barn, his mind filled with confusion. Would she ever be safe? Or would protecting her be his job forever?

He could think of worse assignments.

He entered the barn. A small lantern lit the corner where she sat on a blanket.

She glanced up as he approached. "Lydia said…she said everything in here is for real. I'm not sure if that makes me feel better or worse."

"Grace," he started, then went blank. What could he say?

"What does it matter anymore?" She tossed a pearl-handled comb back into the trunk.

"I know what matters." He shifted to the ground beside her. She glanced up into his eyes with a lost, yet angry expression. "What matters is how you see yourself, love," he said, fingering her hair behind her ear.

"I don't know who I am, even less than I did when I started this trip." She pinned him with her sad blue eyes. "I feel disconnected from everything. My dad lied to me, my mom was not what I thought she was, these people—" she glanced at the house, "—used and manipulated me, for what? To get a look at my mother's journal because she was a terrorist. Nothing in my life feels real."

Then her eyes were on him again. "Except you. This." She leaned forward and kissed him. He held her shoulders and broke the kiss.

"Grace, this isn't right."

"Don't push me away."

"I have to."

"Why? Because…because I'm a fool, right? Because I'm such a stupid girl that I was fooled by my father, by those people in there, even by Steven? My God, would he have married me for his job?"

She stood and paced to the other side of the barn. "The way he pretended to care about me, the way he touched me." She shivered. "Yeah, you're right not to fall for a girl like me. A complete idiot."

"Stop it." He went to her.

"Why? It's true. You're probably snickering with the rest of them at the stupid American girl."

"Don't say that. You're bright, and witty and beautiful. I can't kiss you because I want you so badly I won't stop there. I want to drive myself into you, possess you in every way possible, and even then it won't be enough. I've never wanted to possess a woman like that." He caught his breath. "I don't want you to be hurt."

"You won't hurt me."

"You will be hurt. Those bloody terrorists will hurt you right in front of me because I'm distracted by how I feel about you. Let's get into the house where we'll be safe."

He took her hand and led her out of the barn, across the green grass to the house. They went upstairs to their room, seeing no sign of the others.

He couldn't believe he'd so completely lost it, had confessed how he felt about her and what he wanted to do to her. But she didn't seem put off by his outburst. He didn't read fear or apprehension in her eyes.

No, the reflection of desire sparkled back at him. Bloody hell.

He stood by the window, staring up at the

stars, when he heard Grace close the bathroom door behind her. He would do anything to ease her pain. The poor girl deserved so much more out of life than being lied to by the people around her. She deserved to be loved and respected. It seemed an easy assignment for Bobby. Too easy.

A few minutes later she came out of the bathroom wearing a nightshirt. She padded to the bed and climbed under the covers. He reached over, turned off the night lamp and went back to his spot by the window. He wasn't going to get any sleep tonight.

"Bobby?" she said.

"Yes?"

"Would you…would you mind lying with me?"

You wanted to know how to ease her pain, well, this is it, mate. All she wants is a warm body beside her in bed, not to feel so bloody alone. It's a small request.

He sat on the edge of the bed and took off his shoes. Arms behind his head, he stretched out beside her, on top of the covers.

They lay there, bodies touching through

the bedding, for a good five minutes. Then she turned over and pressed her cheek against his chest. He thought he'd break apart inside.

Suddenly she shifted up in bed and kissed him.

It started as a sweet kiss, a kiss of thanks, but he couldn't control himself and opened to her, wanting more, needing to taste her.

He broke the kiss. "I'm sorry."

"I'm not," she said, kissing him again, practically climbing on top of him.

He wanted to tell her to stop, that she was on the verge of falling apart and was turning to him not because she wanted Bobby, but because she wanted somebody.

Isn't that what his one-night affairs had always been? For the few hours he'd spent between the sheets with a woman, their bodies tangled and humming with sex, he'd forgotten how empty he felt inside.

Which is probably how Grace felt right now; empty.

And she was turning to Bobby to fill her up, with hope.

He'd do this one thing for her, tonight, and

never again. He'd surrender himself to whatever she needed of him. Completely.

NOTHING MADE SENSE anymore. Everyone had lied.

What *was* real?

This, she thought, kissing Bobby Finn. His lips were warm and soft and opening to her with such need.

What had he said? That he wanted to drive himself inside her and even then it would never be enough?

She suspected he hadn't meant to say it, but she knew exactly how he felt.

She'd been drawn to him from the first time they'd met on the train. There had been something tender and loving in his eyes: something genuine.

Pulling his shirt from the waistband of his jeans, she caught him watching her, his eyes half-closed, his lips curved in a subtle smile. She pulled his shirt up and over his head, admiring his firm, slightly hairy chest.

He could have taken the lead, but she suspected he'd had his share of women and knew exactly how to pleasure them. Instead, he lay with arms stretched to his sides, letting her have her way with him, being the gentleman.

Her life was in shambles, yet there was one thing she knew for certain: what she felt for Bobby Finn was real and it was more than simple lust. She'd made an emotional connection to him that first day he'd comforted her on the train. She'd recognized his tender nature beneath the jokes he'd used to cover his pain.

She slipped off her nightshirt, exposing herself to him. "Bobby," she whispered, as she pressed kisses against his chest and down to his stomach. She unsnapped his jeans and slid them off, his need obvious, exciting her. Heat pooled between her legs.

She touched him and he moaned, his right hand clenching the sheets as if he struggled not to lose control. Yet she wanted him to lose control. She wanted him stripped of pretense and politeness. She wanted to know that his intensity matched her own.

Sliding up his body, skin-to-skin, she nibbled and kissed her way to his lips, kissed him once, then broke the kiss and said, "Touch me."

It must have been the permission he'd been waiting for, because he rolled her onto her back and straddled her, his gaze taking in her breasts with a twinkle in his dark-brown eyes. He leaned forward and nuzzled her left nipple and she cried out, grabbing his silk boxer shorts and pulling them down, off his butt.

He eyed her and smiled. "Wild wench," he teased, then kissed her right breast, taking her nipple into his mouth, his tongue flirting with it, driving her completely insane.

If he didn't bury himself inside her soon, she was going to scream in agony. She gripped his buns with trembling fingers, pulling him closer, letting him know she needed him inside her, now.

But he resisted, the tip of his need teasing at her opening.

"Wait." He leaned across the bed and pulled a condom from his wallet in his jeans.

He tore the foil packet with his teeth. "Allow me," she said, taking it from him.

His eyes widened as she pulled the condom from the packet. She reached down to slide it in place and he clenched his jaw, barely able to control himself.

Yet there was no reason to hold back. They were safe in each other's arms, able to trust completely and love without condition.

"Bobby," she breathed. "Please."

He leaned forward and nuzzled her breast, then closed his mouth over hers, teasing and taunting with his tongue. She opened to him, spreading her legs for encouragement, then she gripped his buttocks and pushed him inside her, crying out as they joined together, the rhythm slow and steady, her body on fire.

He reached between them and gently stroked her sensitive nub. She arched, cried out, and he drove himself deep, just as he'd promised, her body absorbing him completely.

He collapsed against her, his heavy breath warming her skin, filling her heart.

This was real.

This was good.

This was love.

BOBBY HAD NEVER felt this way about another living soul.

He stroked the bare skin of her back, thinking they should get up soon. He glanced at the clock on the nightstand. It read twelve-fifteen.

She was probably exhausted from their marathon night of sex. No, it was more than that. Last night with Grace had been Bobby's first true experience of making love to a woman.

Love.

A complicated emotion, and one he'd never truly felt before.

Did Grace feel the same, or was this a case of finding comfort in a stranger's arms?

Stranger, mate? Is that what you are to her? Possibly. But Grace was no stranger to Bobby, not deep in his soul. She'd peeked into his ugly shadows and had seen his ghosts, yet still she wanted him inside of her.

She was just his job. It would all be over once he got her back to the States.

She stretched and opened her eyes, smiled at him.

"Hey, you," she said, kissing his cheek. Warmth floated across his skin and down his neck to settle around his heart. Nothing would make him feel like this ever again.

At least he'd felt it this once. At least he knew it was possible for him to experience this kind of love. But he didn't want it from anyone else.

He wanted it from Grace.

"What are you thinking?" she said, narrowing her eyes.

"What an amazing woman I have in my bed."

"I'll bet you say that to all your one-night stands." She smiled and placed her cheek to his chest.

His heart broke. Of course, that's what she considered last night. He wouldn't correct her. If that's how she wanted it, he'd go along.

"I hope you know I'm kidding," she whispered against his skin.

He didn't answer, not sure what to say.

Her head popped up and she fixed her eyes on him. "One night of that isn't nearly enough, you know that, right?"

"I couldn't agree more." He smiled, but still wasn't sure where that left him. Was he her sexual playmate or potential boyfriend?

She laid her head against his chest. "I guess this vacation has been a bust."

"A bust?"

"A failure. A disappointment."

"So sorry, Miss Fairmont."

Her head popped up again. "No, not the you-and-me part. I meant the whole soul-searching part. I guess I would have been better off not coming at all." She rested her chin on her upturned palm and glanced lovingly at him. "But then I never would have met you, would I?"

"Probably not."

"Then, it wasn't a complete bust." She blinked and got a faraway look in her eye. "I just can't believe Mom was a terrorist."

She wasn't! he wanted to shout. She was a government agent assigned to infiltrate the PIRA.

He knew the agents were right; if Grace knew the truth she'd start asking questions and put herself in danger. She needed to let this go; she needed to move on.

With or without Bobby. He had to be fine with her decision. Only, he wasn't sure how he was going to keep the secret about her mother from her. She sensed things about him; puzzled out his thoughts.

"You look awfully serious this morning," she said.

"Didn't get my proper night's rest, is all."

"Yeah? You blaming me for that, big guy?"

"Wouldn't think of it, Miss Fairmont."

She sighed. "What do I do now?"

"I'm sorry?"

"British Intelligence thinks PIRA might be after me, but why?"

"That list of agents was never found. PIRA thinks you could lead them to it."

"But I didn't even know my mother, and I surely don't condone her actions."

Bugger, he ached to tell her the truth, that her mother was not a terrorist, but an agent assigned to prevent terrorism.

"Yet, she was my mother." She glanced at him. "No matter what she did, or who she was, she loved me. I guess that's what matters most."

There was a knock at the door. Bobby got up, put on his shorts and jeans and answered it. "Cousin Anne" stood in the doorway.

"Here's the diary," she said. "If you two wouldn't mind, we'd like to talk to you downstairs."

Bobby nodded and shut the door. He handed Grace the diary.

A half hour later they went downstairs, holding hands, and found the two female agents in the kitchen, sitting at the counter drinking tea.

"I wouldn't mind some of that," Bobby said, searching through the tea bags for a breakfast blend. Grace stayed close to him, ignoring the agents.

Gerry came in through the back door and removed his boots. "Hope everyone slept well," he said.

"We did," Bobby said. Grace blushed and stared at Bobby's tea.

"We've had word from London. The radical group after the agent list is on their way to Pitlochry."

Bobby automatically put his arm around Grace and held her close.

"Which means?" she said, defiance in her voice.

"Which means they are determined. And so are we." He paced to the island opposite her. "We're determined to protect you as well as to find the list."

"I don't have the damn list," she said.

"No, but they don't know that." He glanced at the women. "We've been planning all night and have come up with a strategy."

Bobby clenched his fist. He sensed what was coming and didn't like it.

"Strategy for what?" Grace asked.

"For ending this," Anne said. "For making sure you're safe, even after you go back to America."

"And what would that be?" Bobby pushed.

"Grace meets with Harry Franklin to give him the list, one that we've provided. We'll take it from there."

"You mean, you eliminate him," Bobby clarified.

Gerry stared him down. "He runs a group of terrorists that could potentially kill thousands. We'll do what's necessary."

"It's dangerous," Bobby said. "She won't do it."

Grace glanced at him, then at Gerry. "Actually, I will. I won't live my life in the shadow of my mother's sins. Stopping these guys, saving lives, will make up for the ones that were lost. It's the right thing to do."

"I can't let you do this, Grace," Bobby said.

Grace turned to Gerry. "What time and where?"

Bobby glared at the bastard. He was going to use Grace's guilt to his advantage. Bobby wouldn't allow it.

"We've already sent a message from your e-mail address asking to meet Harry at Blair Castle this evening, nine o'clock," Gerry said.

"You bastard," Bobby said. "You weren't going to give her a choice."

"Not true. We knew she'd make the right choice."

"You call that the right choice? Hooking her up with a bloody terrorist?"

"She'll be safe. We'll be close by."

"I'll be closer," Bobby said.

"She should do this alone," Gerry said.

"Rubbish. I'm paid to protect her. I'm

going with her." He respected her need to do this and knew she could take care of herself, but he couldn't stand the thought of her being in danger.

"No, Bobby, it's okay." She turned to Gerry. "I hate what you've done, how you've lied and manipulated me. I'm ending it all at Blair Castle. What's the plan?"

"We'll take you up there for a dry run and show you the equipment," Anne said, walking toward her.

"Grace, listen to me—"

"Don't worry," she said, kissing Bobby on the cheek, her blue eyes brightened by their lovemaking.

"I'm coming with you. We've got to talk."

"I need to do this on my own, without leaning on anyone. I'll see you later."

She left the kitchen with Anne.

"No, Grace." He started after her, but Jimmy got him in some kind of fancy headlock.

"Let me go, you bloody beast."

Gerry walked around to face Bobby. "Can't do that, mate. Can't risk you telling her that her mum wasn't a terrorist. She might lose her motivation." Gerry reached over and stuck something into Bobby's arm. The room spun, then faded to black.

Chapter Fourteen

It was well past suppertime when she got back and found Bobby fast asleep. Boy, he must have been exhausted from their night of lovemaking.

She curled up next to him and watched him breathe, slow and steady. He looked so peaceful.

Her stomach was tied in knots. Even after all the preparation, all the explanation of listening devices and exact location of agents, Grace was nervous as hell about luring Harry Franklin in for the capture.

In truth, she now wished Bobby *would* come with her.

"Bobby," she whispered.

He didn't respond. She should try harder to wake him.

Then he'd be more determined to come with and she knew the agents didn't want Bobby messing up the plan. What had Bobby said? That his feelings for her would get in the way of him protecting her?

Her feelings for Bobby would surely distract her if he was with her tonight. No, doing this alone felt right and good.

It would finally put an end to her soul-searching about her mother.

She'd finally have peace.

"I'm going to make it right, Mom," she whispered, and closed her eyes.

She was starting to understand why Mom had left her and Dad—for their own safety. To a certain degree, that's why she was leaving Bobby behind.

To think that there were some sins you couldn't leave behind, no matter how much you wanted to. But Grace would end this chapter of Mom's history by repairing her honor. Then Grace would move on and build a new life, hopefully with the man sleeping beside her.

It was strange, but a rush of excitement filled her chest at the thought of helping track down terrorists. She felt she was doing something honorable for potential victims. She could see why Bobby had chosen the profession he had. He wanted to make a difference and keep people safe.

There was a soft knock and the door cracked open. "We're leaving in fifteen minutes," Anne whispered.

Grace nodded and placed her hand to Bobby's chest. "Be proud of me, Bobby."

HIDING IN CHAPEL RUINS on the property of Blair Castle, Grace anticipated the sound of footsteps. Nerves twisted her stomach into knots.

"Nothing yet," Gerry said through her earpiece.

She tapped her fingers against Mom's diary in her lap. It was a convincing move, to rip a page out of her diary with the false list of agents and hand it to Harry. That would explain why Harry hadn't found the list in her backpack, because her diary hadn't been in the backpack.

The agents had planned everything to the nth degree. She rubbed her thumb against the inside back cover, back and forth, as she'd done so many times when thinking or nervous. Back and forth.

She felt a rough spot, opened the journal and looked closer, using her miniflashlight. The seam had come loose. She peeled back the edge and felt something tucked behind the panel. She pulled out a slip of white paper and opened it.

"Oh, my God," she said, reading a list of names.

"Grace? What is it?" Gerry asked via her earpiece.

"The list."

"It's right there, in Mary's diary."

"No, I mean…" Her voice trailed off as she scanned the list, complete with photos of MI5 agents. She recognized Gerry and Rosie… and Mary Logan.

"She was with British Intelligence?" she whispered.

"Bloody hell, who's that?" Gerry said.

"Gerry, I have the list. Why is my mom on it?"

"Get out, now!" Crackling filled the line.

"Gerry?"

Nothing.

She suddenly felt all alone. And she had the list, a list of MI5 agents that included her mother. Those bastards had lied about that, too.

"Mom, what do I do?"

Mom had been an agent; not a terrorist. She had been a protector, a woman trying to save lives, not take them.

If the real list fell into the wrong hands Mom would be known as a failure, her work would have been for nothing. Abandoning Grace and Dad would have been pointless.

Grace stood, sensing she was on her own, that somehow the agents had been compromised. She wasn't going to sit here and wait for Harry Franklin to kill her.

She heard gravel crunch under a man's boots. Too late. He was here.

Tucking the list in her pocket and the diary at the back of her jeans, she waited, holding the pepper spray in a firm grip. She hoped it had enough power left to paralyze Harry, giving her time to escape.

Harry Franklin stepped into the chapel ruins.

"Harry?" she said.

He turned. She aimed and fired, hitting him square on. She ran, but he got hold of her jacket and jerked her back.

"You bloody bitch! Get back here!"

Do whatever it takes, Bobby had said.

She grabbed Harry's hair and yanked as hard as she could, smashing his face against the back of her head. It was enough to stun him, enough for her to get away. She stumbled and tripped, but managed to stay on her feet, racing across the grounds. The wind blew her hair across her face as she sprinted toward the woods.

What if they catch you? What will they do to you?

She couldn't think about that, now. Had to get away. Had to tell Dad about Mom, that she was a hero, not a terrorist, that she was—

She tripped on a tree root and went down. She hit the ground with a thud, the wind knocked from her lungs. She heard footsteps closing in. She tried to scramble away, but a hand grabbed her arm and jerked her to her feet. "Keep running," Bobby ordered.

"Bobby?"

Her protector. Her love.

They raced into the forest, Bobby pulling her across the uneven earth deeper into the woods. He squeezed her hand to comfort her.

"Are you hurt?" he said.

"No, I'm—"

A shot rang out and she went into Bobby's arms.

"You're dead if you don't come with me," Harry threatened from behind.

So it had come to this. Harry Franklin and his terrorists against Grace and Bobby.

"Thought you could outwit me?" he said with a cough, stepping closer, aiming the gun at them. "Stupid girl, I should have finished you on the train."

Bobby shielded her.

"Come out from behind him," Harry ordered.

"Don't move," Bobby said to Grace.

"You're going to die for this girl? Why, because she's good in bed?"

"She'll give you the list, then you'll let her go."

"No. We've got some questions about her mum."

"She didn't know her."

"I think she knows more than she's letting on, isn't that right, Gracie?"

Bobby lunged at Harry Franklin. "Run, Grace!" he cried.

She turned and raced into the woods, panic flooding her chest. A gun went off, twice. Tears streamed down her face. She'd just found Bobby, had just fallen in love with him.

And he was protecting her, giving his life to save hers.

She would not get caught by these bastards again.

She jumped behind a fallen tree and burrowed deep against it, hoping Harry would run right past. A few minutes later she heard footsteps crunch against the leaves.

"Grace?"

"Bobby?" She jumped out of hiding and went to him, hugging him.

"Easy now," he said.

She stepped back. Blood was smeared across his jacket and shirt.

"Oh, my God."

"Don't get hysterical. I'm fine," he said. "MI5 showed up. Rosie and Jimmy took Harry away. Let's get back."

He led her out of the woods.

"I can't believe you're here. Bobby, look, I found the real list." She pulled it from her pocket. "And you're not going to believe it but Mom's name is on there. She wasn't a terrorist, she was a British Intelligence agent."

"I know."

"You know?"

"They told me last night."

"You knew she wasn't a terrorist, but you let me believe she did those horrible things?"

"I was trying to protect you."

"I'm tired of people protecting me, always assuming I'm unable to take care of myself."

"They feared if you knew the truth you'd

ask more questions, and that would put you in further danger."

"I'm not stupid, Bobby. And believe it or not, I can take care of myself. You lied to me after I specifically asked you to be truthful. What about last night? You made love to me. Why?"

"You know I care about you."

"How do I know that? You lied about my mother. My God, you were the only person I thought hadn't lied, the only person I could trust. You've been playing me like all the rest: Steven, these spies. You're just like them, manipulate the naive Grace Fairmont so you can do your job and get a raise. Well, good job, Bobby Finn, you should get a big one." She spun around to find Anne and Gerry staring at her.

"What?" she said. "I want to go home."

She marched toward them and Anne led her to the surveillance van.

Bobby just stood there. Gerry walked up to him. "Need a hand, mate?"

"No." He gripped his side, where the bullet had grazed his skin. "I'm fine."

Grace glared at him before getting into the van.

Gerry's speculative gaze went between Grace and Bobby, then he said, "Ah, don't worry. She'll come around."

"Not likely." It was then Bobby realized he'd secretly been fantasizing about a future with her.

"What do you mean? You took a bullet for her."

"I also lied to her."

"To protect her."

"She's had people lying to her her whole life. She was depending on me to be truthful."

"Well, she's alive, thanks to you. I think that trumps a little white lie. But then lying is my business, so what do I know?" He winked.

Bobby got in the back of the van and they headed to the house. Grace sat up front, back straight, mouth shut.

"Sorry about the confusion back there," Gerry said. "Harry Franklin brought more members than we'd anticipated."

"Yeah, it's a good thing Bobby showed up," Anne said.

Grace didn't respond.

"This is finally over," Anne said to Grace.

"And it was all because Mom had this." Grace pulled out a piece of paper and handed it to Anne.

"Good God, you found it!" Anne exclaimed.

"If you're ever interested in becoming a spy—"

"No thanks, *Uncle* Gerry," Grace said. "I have this thing about lying and manipulation."

"Pity."

"Maybe we should drop Bobby at a clinic," Anne suggested.

"I'm fine." He noticed Grace didn't react to the suggestion. Of course not. He was the enemy, a heartless bastard who'd lied to her then bedded her.

As they drove back to the house, Bobby pieced together events of the last few days. The driver who had picked them up at Waverly Station was most likely MI5, along with the two officers who had arrested him. They must have drugged him to get information about Grace, to determine what she knew about her spy mother and if she could lead them to the agent list.

Twenty minutes later they pulled into the drive and got out. Grace walked ahead, aiming for the house, ignoring Bobby.

"Guess you're sleeping on the couch tonight," Gerry chuckled.

"I can't stay here."

"But we've got to patch you up," Anne said.

"Then I'm gone. Can you drive her back to Edinburgh and make sure she gets on a plane?" Bobby asked.

"Sure," Gerry said. "Where are you off to?"

"London to visit some friends. Then back to America."

But his heart would never be the same.

THE NEXT MORNING Grace packed and went in search of something to eat. Bobby had come upstairs last night only briefly to pack his things then he'd left, probably to sleep in a spare room. Good. She still hadn't gotten over his lying to her, but it was damn hard to be mad at him with his bullet wound reminding her he'd risked his life for her.

Of course he had. That was his job.

Well, fine. She was going to do her job and live her own life, surrounded by people she could trust.

She went into the kitchen to find Anne at the counter drinking tea.

"Good morning," she said, and went straight for the teakettle to fill it with water.

"Good thing your friend was there to help out last night," Anne commented.

"My bodyguard," she corrected.

"Yes, well, it's a good thing. He surely cares about you."

"He lies, too," she shot back. "I'm done with liars."

"He kept our secret to protect you."

"I've heard that line so many times these past few days. I'm tired of it." She put on the kettle and searched through boxes of tea.

"Do you know why Bobby was asleep when you left for the mission last night?"

"He was tired." She tried not to blush, thinking about their lovemaking that had tired him out.

"He was drugged."

"What?" She turned to Anne.

"We drugged him because he was going to tell you the truth about your mother being an agent. It would have ruined everything."

"He was going to tell me?"

"Yes, and to hell with national security, or the safety of that list of agents or innocent civilians. He did not want you to go to Blair Castle and risk your life because you felt guilty about your mum's activities. He put you first. We don't have that luxury."

"Whatever. Where is he? I need a ride back to Edinburgh."

"He's gone. Left this morning. We'll get you to the airport."

Bobby was gone. She'd never see him again. She should feel happy, relieved.

But she wasn't. She felt empty inside.

"Did you love Steven?" Anne asked.

Grace snapped her attention to the agent. "What?"

"Did you love him?"

"I…no," she admitted.

"Yet you said the words, didn't you?"

"Yes."

"You lied."

"I was being nice. I…" she hesitated "…didn't want to hurt his feelings."

"And Bobby Finn didn't want to see you hurt. We're all liars at one time or another. The important thing is we know how to love. I don't have the luxury of being in love, not in my line of work." She turned off the kettle, poured hot water into a cup and handed it to Grace. "Just let me know when you're ready and I'll drive you to the airport."

Grace stood there in shock, absorbing Anne's words.

It dawned on Grace that her mother had sacrificed everything because she loved Dad and their baby so much.

Love *was* a gift. But Grace had been so blinded by her pride that she couldn't see past it into Bobby's loving eyes. God, what had she done?

Chapter Fifteen

Bobby didn't waste much time getting back to work. He spent two days in London then flew back to Seattle.

He was off-kilter, jet-lagged and cranky.

Not to mention heartbroken.

"The best remedy is hard work," he said to himself as he took the bus to Blackwell headquarters in Pioneer Square.

He got off at Yesler and went to the office building, glad that his work was the kind that consumed a man's mind completely.

If only it could consume his heart, deaden it to the constant ache.

Grace. How the bloody hell had he let her sneak inside like that? He should have known it would fall apart. He wasn't meant to have a successful relationship with a woman.

He climbed the stairs to the second floor, took a deep breath and pushed open the door.

"Hey, Bobby boy!" Eddie called out. The bloke wore a colorful, collarless T-shirt and tie. "I dressed up for ya." He shook Bobby's hand.

"Thanks, mate."

Jeremy congratulated Bobby, followed by Spinelli and Ramos. It felt good to be back; he felt as if he belonged.

"Excellent job, mate," Max said. "You get bodyguard duty and end up taking on PIRA and MI5. And you kept the girl safe."

"Did my best, guv."

"Brilliant. Well, we've got a new client and I'm in the process of hiring a few new members to round out the team. I thought you might want to review a candidate for office assistant before I offer her the job."

"Guv, I don't know. I'm a detective, not human resources."

Max smiled. "Do it for me, mate."

Bobby glanced into Max's office at a blond girl who sat in front of his desk, shoulder-length waves touching her shoulders. Now Bobby was hallucinating.

In slow motion he went to Max's office and hovered in the doorway. "Hello. I'm Bobby Finn." She stood and turned to him.

Grace. She smiled.

The world went wonky again and he could have sworn there'd been a bloody earthquake.

"Grace, what are you doing here?"

"Come in and shut the door."

He did, but he didn't get close to her for fear she'd disappear.

"I'm here to clarify a few things," she said. "First, you know how I hate when people keep things from me."

"I know, Grace, I was trying to—"

"Wait, let me finish." She took a few steps toward him. She looked fetching this morning in her tight jeans and T-shirt, wearing her favorite denim jacket. "But, the thing is," she said, within inches of him. "I've done the same thing with the people I care about. I lied to Dad, always pretending to be happy and content. I lied to you when I acted brave about taking on Harry Franklin—I was scared, but I didn't want to put you at risk by involving you. Yet you showed up anyway."

She touched his cheek and he closed his eyes.

"And I think I'm going to have to lie again and tell you I'm going to walk out of here and I'll be just fine without you in my life."

He opened his eyes and tried to read her meaning.

"I can do that," she said. "Or I can tell the truth and say I've never felt this way before. That it should scare the hell out of me, but it doesn't because it feels right, and it's something I'd like to pursue."

He didn't know what to say. This was more than he'd imagined, more than he deserved.

"But I get the feeling serious relationships freak you out, so I can lie," she said. "I can do that for you because I love you. And as you've taught me, we sometimes lie to keep loved ones safe, right?"

Completely humbled by her confession, he took her in his arms and held on. "Grace, I don't know what to say. I'm afraid I'll muck it up."

She leaned back and looked up into his eyes. "Have a little faith, Bobby. You'd be surprised what love can do."

* * * * *

Turn the page for a sneak preview of
IF I'D NEVER KNOWN YOUR LOVE
by
Georgia Bockoven

From the brand-new series
Harlequin Everlasting Love
Every great love has a story to tell. ™

One year, five months and four days missing

There's no way for you to know this, Evan, but I haven't written to you for a few months. Actually, it's been almost a year. I had a hard time picking up a pen once more after we paid the second ransom and then received a letter saying it wasn't enough. I was so sure you were coming home that I took the kids along to Bogotá so they could fly home with you and me, something I swore I'd never do. I've fallen in love with Colombia and the people who've opened their hearts to me. But fear is a constant companion when I'm there. I won't ever expose our children to that kind of danger again.

I'm at a loss over what to do anymore, Evan. I've begged and pleaded and thrown temper tantrums with every official I can corner both here and at home. They've been incredibly tolerant and understanding, but in the end as ineffectual as the rest of us.

I try to imagine what your life is like now, what you do every day, what you're wearing, what you eat. I want to believe that the people who have you are misguided yet kind, that they treat you well. It's how I survive day to day. To think of you being mistreated hurts too much. If I picture you locked away somewhere and suffering, a weight descends on me that makes it almost impossible to get out of bed in the morning.

Your captors surely know you by now. They have to recognize what a good man you are. I imagine you working with their children, telling them that you have children, too, showing them the pictures you carry in your wallet. Can't the men who have you understand how much your children miss you? How can it not matter to them?

How can they keep you away from us all this time? Over and over, we've done what they asked. Are they oblivious to the depth of their cruelty? What kind of people are they that they don't care?

I used to keep a calendar beside our bed next to the peach rose you picked for me before you left. Every night I marked another day, counting how many you'd been gone. I don't do that any longer. I don't want to be reminded of all the days we'll never get back.

When I can't sleep at night, I tell you about my day. I imagine you hearing me and smiling over the details that make up my life now. I never tell you how defeated I feel at moments or how hard I work to hide it from everyone for fear they will see it as a reason to stop believing you are coming home to us.

And I couldn't tell you about the lump

I found in my breast and how difficult it was going through all the tests without you here to lean on. The lump was benign—the process reaching that diagnosis utterly terrifying. I couldn't stop thinking about what would happen to Shelly and Jason if something happened to me.

We need you to come home.

I'm worn down with missing you.

I'm going to read this tomorrow and will probably tear it up or burn it in the fireplace. I don't want you to get the idea I ever doubted what I was doing to free you or thought the work a burden. I would gladly spend the rest of my life at it, even if, in the end, we only had one day together.

You are my life, Evan.

I will love you forever.

* * * * *

Don't miss this deeply moving
Harlequin Everlasting Love story
about a woman's struggle to bring back
her kidnapped husband from Colombia
and her turmoil over whether to let go,
finally,
and welcome another man into her life.
IF I'D NEVER KNOWN YOUR LOVE
by Georgia Bockoven
is available March 27, 2007.

And also look for
THE NIGHT WE MET
by Tara Taylor Quinn,
a story about finding love
when you least expect it.

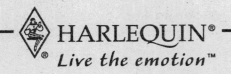

HARLEQUIN®
INTRIGUE®

BREATHTAKING ROMANTIC SUSPENSE

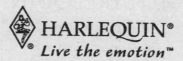

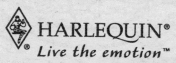

Harlequin® Historical
Historical Romantic Adventure!

Imagine a time of chivalrous knights and unconventional ladies, roguish rakes and impetuous heiresses, rugged cowboys and spirited frontierswomen— these rich and vivid tales will capture your imagination!

Harlequin Historical . . . they're too good to miss!

HHDIR06

Jess's First Impression Of Tad Was Of A Primitive Male, Powerful And Dangerous.

Tad's gaze swept the shadows, fixed upon her and drank in the sight of the shapely perfection of her female form clearly revealed by her transparent nightgown.

The blatant sensuality unnerved Jess. Her heart began to pound.

"Jess..." He came toward her.

Her arms went around Tad's muscled waist. The shock of contact with his body made her gasp. Arousal sizzled through her like an electric current.

She tried to move away, but he drew her inside the steel circle of his hands. Tad opened his mouth, inviting her kiss. Violent tremors of desire warmed her as her mouth lingered on his. She caught herself sharply, stunned by the intensity of her emotion. The way he held her, it was easy to pretend that he didn't really hate her.

"Don't go," he whispered raggedly.

"I must," she protested.

But Tad Jackson was a man used to getting his own way. A man who'd never learned to take no for an answer. She struggled no more....

It was the curse of her life that she'd always wanted him.

Dear Reader:

Happy Holidays from all of us at Silhouette Books. And since it *is* the holiday season, we've planned an extra special month at Silhouette Desire. Think of it as our present to you, the readers.

To start with, we have December's *Man of the Month*, who comes in the tantalizing form of Tad Jackson in Ann Major's *Wilderness Child*. This book ties into the Children of Destiny series, but Tad's story also stands on its own. Believe me, Tad's a man you'd *love* to find under your Christmas tree.

And what would December be without a Christmas book? We have a terrific one—*Christmas Stranger* by Joan Hohl. After you've read it, I'm sure you'll understand why I say this is a truly timeless love story.

Next, don't miss book one of Celeste Hamilton's trilogy, Aunt Eugenia's Treasures. *The Diamond's Sparkle* is just the first of three priceless love stories. Look for *Ruby Fire* and *Hidden Pearl* in February and April of 1990.

Finally, some wonderful news: the *Man of the Month* will be continued through 1990! We just couldn't resist bringing you one more year of these stunning men. In the upcoming months you'll be seeing brand-new *Man of the Month* books by Elizabeth Lowell, Annette Broadrick and Diana Palmer—just to name a few. Barbara Boswell will make her Silhouette Desire debut with her man. I'll be keeping you updated....

Before I go, I want to wish all of our readers a very Happy Holiday. See you next year!

Lucia Macro
Senior Editor

ANN
MAJOR
WILDERNESS CHILD

SILHOUETTE *Desire*
Published by Silhouette Books New York
America's Publisher of Contemporary Romance

To Ted...

SILHOUETTE BOOKS
300 East 42nd St., New York, N.Y. 10017

ISBN: 0-373-05535-8

First Silhouette Books printing December 1989

Printed in the U.S.A.

A Note From Ann Major:

When I was writing about the Jacksons and MacKays in my *Children of Destiny* series, I always knew I'd have to write more. *Wilderness Child* is the story of Tad Jackson, a stubborn male chauvinist, determined to seek his own destiny in the outback of Australia where he is pitted against the dark forces of greed, betrayal and murder.

Who should turn up to help him but the one woman he is most set against—Dr. Jessica Bancroft-Kent. She's a spirited, opinionated feminist with a quick mind and a quicker tongue. She's as bossy as Tad is stubborn, as determined to help Tad as he is determined not to be helped.

I had a lot of fun writing this book because I enjoyed working with these characters as they struggled to tame not only the rugged land but each other.

Books by Ann Major

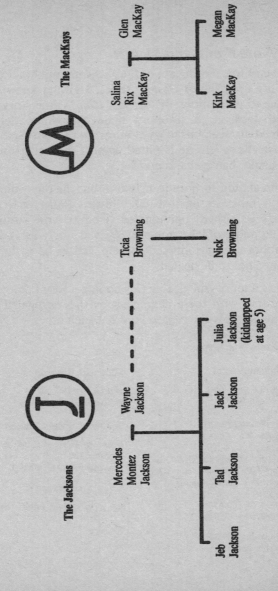

CHILDREN OF DESTINY

The Jacksons

Mercedes Montez Jackson — Wayne Jackson - - - - - Ticia Browning

Jeb Jackson | Tad Jackson | Jack Jackson | Julia Jackson (kidnapped at age 5)

Nick Browning

The MacKays

Salina Rix MacKay — Glen MacKay

Kirk MacKay | Megan MacKay

Prologue

The sun dipped below the broken battlements of the mountains. Half an hour later, the west wind, hot and fiery from its passage over a thousand miles of Australia's Never Never, died.

The pilot's glazed eyes were red-rimmed. His body movements were slow and deliberate because he had fought the heat and the head wind for hours.

The red sky was edged in opalescent colors. The mountains and gorges changed from scarlet to mauve to purple, and the wild night creatures that had been sheltering in caverns began to stir. No native creature ever traveled in the heat of the day.

Only the white man.

The plane was flying low, too low, following a north, northwesterly course home. The airborne Geiger counter went wild as the plane crossed the remote northern tip of Jackson Downs, forbidden territory. The pilot's pulse began to pound in his temples as he observed the high reading. He raised his hand and gnawed at his torn nails. Then he circled, flying even lower over the vast Jackson cattle station. Twice more he circled. Each time, the Geiger counter's readings soared. His hands were shaking. There had to be an immense deposit of uranium down there. There had to be.

The pilot looked down. Beneath the twin-engine plane stretched a million acres of baking-hot, blood-red desolation darkening in the twilight. And beyond those acres of eerie, undulating rock formations, were a million more. And beneath them—a fortune in uranium.

He could not wait to get back to the station and tell Noelle. At last she would see him as a man and not a boy.

Even though his brother had stupidly sold this hellish land and it no longer belonged to them, he could not contain his excitement.

For it would.

Again.

No matter what he had to do.

Just for a moment the pilot considered Tad Jackson, the owner. There was no man tougher, no man anywhere around this desolate emptiness who was more respected. Jackson, his wife, his kid, all of them would have to be crushed.

The pilot had started his climb when before him, out of nowhere, loomed a mountain, its violet razor edges higher than the rest. In his excitement, he'd failed to keep a sharp eye on his altimeter.

He pulled the yoke back to make a steep, climbing turn, but nothing happened.

Uranium!

He wasn't going to crash into a damned mountain. Not tonight.

The razor-red edges of the mountain rushed toward him.

Life had never been sweeter. Nor crueler.

The plane was like a dead weight hurtling through the sky.

In those last seconds, he wondered as he'd done so many times before—why was it always like this for him? Just when everything was beginning to go right for him, everything went wrong!

Noelle! Oh, God! Noelle!

The plane exploded against the wall of rock.

The man-boy inside was devoured in a billowing blossom of flame.

A flock of galahs rose screeching with doleful, disturbed cries from their nesting places in the cliffs. They soared and flapped wildly about like crazed bats above the petals of fire.

Then the flames died away, and the birds settled upon their gnarled perches in the casuarinas and stringy barks.

Flying foxes and euros, the small, gray mountain kangaroos, came out to forage and drink from a dark pool where cloyingly sweet applethorn was in flower.

There was a great quietness, and all became darkness except for the hard glister of a narrow moon that rose and swam through a sky that was as black as jet.

One

―――

"Why isn't that the Yank that killed..."

"It's hard to tell with his beard."

"I think you're right. That's him. That's the one! Jackson—bloody murderer."

The women's voices were high-pitched, curious, not in the least embarrassed, and they cut Tad Jackson to the quick. The hurt was immediately followed by fierce, murderous anger.

All eyes fastened upon the lean, golden-haired giant in the denim trousers and khaki shirt, that ubiquitous uniform of the Australian bushman. His skin had been burned and his hair bleached by too many hot, southern suns. Leather hat in his clenched hand, he was slouching negligently in the shadows while he waited for an elevator.

They had noticed him, of course. Right away. The moment he'd come into the building. Women always noticed him. Even now, despite his beard.

A look of quick, smoldering anger hardened his carved features, and his silvery blue eyes narrowed. His sensual mouth thinned. He moved his head slightly and a silken lock of gold swept across his forehead. There was a recklessness in his dark face, something intangible that was wild and dangerous, something hostile that exuded virile masculinity, and that special, barely tamed something had always been irresistible to women.

Once he'd considered all that an advantage, but for the past year it had been a curse. Why couldn't they leave him alone? Why did every man, woman and child in Australia want to nail him to a cross?

Wasn't it enough that he and his family and men had been terrorized for two years? Enough that his fences were routinely cut, his livestock shot, his stockmen ambushed, and the road trains carrying his cattle to market attacked? A year ago his wife had become so terrified she had taken their daughter Lizzie and run away. She'd come back, stolen money from him, and then run away again. He had loved his daughter, but not his wife. Then the rumors had begun to fly about that he'd killed them. But he hadn't. He wanted desperately to know where they were.

The women were staring at him in fascination and horror.

Heat stained his cheeks. Tad let his hot, blue gaze slide over them. Then his mouth curled as he strode past the pocket of women waiting for the elevator.

Maybe some day one of them would take a wrong step and learn what it was to be persecuted for a crime she hadn't committed.

As he pushed open the door to the stairwell, he stopped and turned. Forcing a bitter smile, he touched a tanned finger to his brow and muttered a savage, "G'day, ladies."

His greeting was Australian; the slurred drawl, Texan. But it was the white grin in the bitter, male face that brought startled little gasps of fear.

"He heard us!" There were more frightened titters.

He forced himself to keep smiling even though he felt as if the walls of the stairwell were closing in on him. God, was this nightmare never going to end? He had come to Australia because he'd wanted to be his own man, to stand alone. Because he'd never fit in with his own family back in Texas—at least, not with his older brother Jeb running things. Tad had brought Deirdre here, ruined her life. For what? He was ready to sell out, to pack up, to leave this country and go back to Texas. Even if it meant taking orders from Jeb again.

He could feel the women's eyes drilling into his back like the sharpest bits.

"The Yank killed his wife, they say. And probably his nipper, too. On one of them fancy resort islands off the Great Barrier Reef. There was something about it in *The Australian* again only last week."

"How horrible."

"He wasn't even charged. They never found her body."

"Poor little sheila. And they won't find her, either. Not with the sharks where she disappeared. And their child. The little lass disappeared without a trace. Good-looking devil, though, isn't he?"

Tad let the door bang behind him, and he raced up the stairs, his long legs taking them two at a time. He ran up eight flights. He ran till his heart felt like it was bursting in his chest. Then he stopped and leaned against the wall to run a shaking hand through his hair. He reached in his pocket for a cigarette, lit one, took a single drag and then, when his throat burned, he remembered his cold and that he wasn't supposed to smoke. The cigarette made the pain in his chest worse. He tossed the cigarette to the concrete and squashed it out with the heel of his boot.

He'd always been a loner. He'd thought he didn't give a damn what people thought of him, and he hadn't until now.

Ian better have a good reason for demanding that he leave the station and fly into Brisbane. Every time Tad came to town, it got worse. People stared at him, talked about him, actually accused him of killing his wife and his daughter. They were driving him from the country where he'd made his home for the past eight years. As if he could ever hurt a woman, or a child. His Lizzie...

Most of his friends had deserted him. Even Ian, his own lawyer, half believed he'd killed Deirdre. It was Ian who'd talked him into selling out and quitting Australia.

Tad walked up the last flight and barged into Ian's outer office and past Ian's receptionist who was carefully styling her billowing tufts of cotton-candy white hair. Her overblown, Kewpie-doll brand of beauty would have stopped most men dead in their tracks.

As Tad rushed past her, she dropped her brush. Her mouth formed a wide baffled O that would have made a perfect target for a blowie had she been in the bush. Then she jumped up, all flutters and big-eyed alarm. Just as his hand touched Ian's door, Tad heard the pit-a-pat of her heels behind him.

"Wait! Mr. Jackson, you can't go in there!"

He whirled, and she almost ran into him. Her neon-bright fingertips flailed wildly to avoid him. His narrowed gaze met the frightened baby-like brown dazzle of hers. As she shrank from him, he grinned bitterly. "You going to stop me, sweetheart?"

If he'd been a mulga snake towering twenty feet high and about to strike, the poor girl couldn't have looked more terrified. Tad's expression softened. "Why don't you go back to your desk, honey, and tackle something you can handle?'' He shoved open Ian's door.

The office was opulent and felt as safe and silent and as insulated from the real world as a bank vault. It was January, and the sun outside would bake a man alive. Inside this cell of urban splendor, blasts of icy air cooled the plush carpeting, rich, lustrous mahogany walls and floor-to-ceiling sheets of glass.

Ian was one of the richest men in Queensland. Unlike Tad, Ian had started with nothing. Nothing but greed and ambition, Tad thought bitterly, two of the most powerful forces in the world. Ian had grown up in Queensland on a cattle station, the son of a horse-breaker and a shepherd girl. At the age of six Ian could track a lizard across rock better than most Abos. At the age of ten the station had been sold to American investors and Ian's family had ended up destitute on the streets of Brisbane. Ian wasn't forty, but he'd done well.

On one wall were maps of Queensland and the Northern Territory where Ian had colored in the properties he owned. He owned stations that totaled in the millions of acres. He was into ore, salt, gypsum, cattle and wool. "You name it and I'll own it" was his motto. He was the best lawyer in Queensland, but despite his upper-class pretensions, he was a street fighter at heart. He'd been one of the first friends Tad had made upon coming to Australia to take over the management of his family's holdings.

Tad studied the maps rather than the magnificent views of Brisbane's sprawl, the famed Story Bridge over the wide, curving river, the moored yachts, the snarl of river traffic. Tad saw that Ian was expanding his operations, and the fact was like salt in the wound of his own failures.

One of Ian's cigars was smoking in an ashtray. Ian was on the phone, barking orders. He was short and heavyset, and he exuded the raw, animal power of a weight lifter. His eyes were as bright as twin dark coals and glittering with fierce intelligence. He had a hard, bluntly carved face, bushy black brows and a thick frizz of prematurely gray curls. He took one look into the wild blue eyes of his client, growled an abrupt goodbye and slammed the phone down.

"This had better be good, Ian."

Ian was as cool and serene as his client was irrational. The lawyer picked up his cigar and puffed great clouds into the air before replacing it in the ashtray. "Oh, it's better than good," he said slowly. "Sit down, and I'll tell you." Ian paused. "Coffee?"

"Coffee!" The single word was an explosion. "Hell, no." Tad sprawled violently into the leather chair across from Ian's desk. "Well?"

Ian grinned. He was never intimidated by Tad's outbursts. Tad thought he took a perverse delight in drawing out this moment of suspense.

"Jackson, can't you ever relax?"

Never, when he was closed in by walls, by people, by the city. Never, when his lawyer demanded he fly into town.

"I thought you'd feel better," Ian persisted, "once you decided to sell."

"Who decided? I was driven to sell. I don't like quitting, but I'm not running a station out there anymore. I'm fighting a war. My men are armed to the teeth. None of us dares leave the homestead alone. I just wish I knew who I was fighting. They come out of nowhere. It's always a strike in the dark when you least expect it. One week they cut fences; the next they blow up a bore. The other property owners have had their troubles, too. There's the drought. My cattle are dying, but every time I try to ship them the road trains get attacked. It hasn't rained a drop on Jackson Downs in months. I've been heavily in the red for the past three years. I just flew across a thousand miles of spinifex, scorched bush and dying cattle, and you say relax!"

"Things haven't eased up, then?"

"Eased up? Hell. Ever since Holt Martin's plane was sabotaged a couple of years back . . ."

Ian ran a hand through the gray frizz. "So you think it was sabotage?"

Tad's face darkened. "Who knows? The bush coppers, acting officious as hell, poked around the wreckage for a while, came by the station in their new Jeeps and wrote up a report. Then we never heard from them again. I didn't think it was sabotage then, but all I know now is that that was the beginning of it all. Holt was a harmless sort, poor bloke. A geologist. Always out poking around where he didn't belong, exploring for minerals. Never found much. I guess he never knew what hit him."

"You don't have any ideas who's behind this mess?"

"I have a few, but I can't prove anything. I don't trust any of the Martins. Not even their American cousin, Noelle."

"You've been down on women ever since I've known you."

"Ever since I stuck my head in the noose and married one of them. But I can't forget that we didn't have any trouble till Noelle turned up. Now it's brother against brother, property owner against property owner. We used to trust each other out there. With every property under attack, nobody trusts anybody anymore. Hell! Who knows? Anyway, I didn't come here to rehash my problems!"

"Well, I called you because I've got good news." Ian's grin broadened. "One of my men found Deirdre."

Tad sprang out of his seat and leaned across the desk. Forgotten were the killers that stalked him night and day. Forgotten were the Martins and the drought.

His fear was an icy, suffocating mist that seemed to mingle with the noxious curl of acrid cigar smoke, gagging him.

"What?" he rasped. "You mean her body? Where? It must have been badly decomposed. Lizzie..." He hardly dared breathe his daughter's name.

Ian leaned forward, too, his grin intact. His dark face was placid. Only his sharp black eyes belied his outward calm. "Not her body, you bloody bastard. Her." He seized Tad by the forearm and held it in a death grip. "She's alive. So's your kid."

"Alive..."

Ten thousand pins seemed to pierce him just beneath the surface of his skin. He couldn't believe it. Tad didn't want Deirdre dead, but he didn't want her back in his life, either. He just wanted Lizzie.

Deirdre had to be dead, or she would never have left Australia without the money. And he had found the money in the cottage.

Images of that nightmarish time nearly a year ago came back to him. The bush coppers had seized him and flown him to the island, to her cottage. He could still remember the way her suitcase had lain half open on the rumpled bed with her lacy garments dripping out of it. The rest of her things had been scattered untidily about on the rose-patterned carpet and couches. Meticulous about her person, Deirdre had always been messy when she traveled. They had told him she'd probably drowned.

He could almost hear the rush of the sea sounding through the windows, almost smell the salty dampness of it seeping inside. He had picked up her lavender silk blouse, which had fallen carelessly beneath the white wooden rocker. He had caught the faint, lingering fragrance of her scent. She had been wearing that blouse the last time he'd seen her alive, the afternoon three days before when she'd come back to the station on the pretext of discussing their problems and telling him where Lizzie was. Only what Deirdre had really been after was the operating cash he kept in his safe. She'd stolen the money—all $75,000 of it, and his plane—and run out on him again. She'd emptied their joint checking account in Brisbane. He hadn't had the vaguest idea where she'd gone until the coppers had come for him.

He remembered standing in that cottage. He had felt her presence everywhere. It was as if she had only gone out for a minute and would be back in a little while. Only there was an eeriness about her absence that had told him she would never come back. And she hadn't. Nor had his child been found.

He had told the police to look in the lining of Deirdre's suitcase because he'd known her to hide things there before. When they found the money, they'd considered that incriminating evidence against him.

Apparently she had gone diving alone, the police had said. Or someone had made it look like she had. Did he know why she'd come to the island, alone, with the money? Where had he been at the time of her disappearance? What was his alibi? They had found bits of what might have been her diving gear washed up on the beach. A battered yellow tank. A piece of black hose. They weren't sure. Like Lizzie, she had disappeared without a trace.

Then they had begun to torture him with questions about Lizzie. Where was she? All he could tell them was that he didn't know. Deirdre had taken her.

"It is no secret you and your wife didn't get along, Mr. Jackson. No secret that you hated her."

Hate. The single word was inadequate to describe the complex snarl of emotions he had felt toward his wife.

"You say she took your child. She took your money. Did you follow her here? Did you kill her?"

They'd crucified him on that last question.

Tad had hired professionals to look for Lizzie. When they'd failed to find her, he'd retreated to his homestead, into his own pain and silence for nearly a year. There'd been times he'd been grateful for attacks against his station because at least they'd distracted him from wondering about Lizzie.

"There's no way Deirdre's alive," Tad whispered to Ian.

No way he was taking her back if she was. He was through. Through with all women, for that matter.

Ian's expression was intense, odd. "So you don't think she could come back?"

"No. It's a trick of some sort. A lie."

"It's no lie. You're lucky as hell she turned up, mate. You can quit hiding out on your property, and you can shave off that damn beard." Ian thrust a series of photographs in front of Tad. "My man took these yesterday."

Tad stared wordlessly at the pictures. A beautiful woman—if it wasn't Deirdre, it was an exact duplicate of her—was standing on a beach in front of a towering rain forest. Except for her dark eyes, she was tall and golden like a Valkyrie; sleek, slim and yet amply endowed where a man most wanted a woman to be. Her long, blond hair was glued to her shapely neck and head. Sparkling rivulets of water slid down the curves of satin-gold legs. She was wearing a one-piece black bathing suit that fit her body like a second skin. She was comforting a wet and frightened Lizzie in her arms.

Usually Deirdre had found other things in life infinitely more diverting than her child.

"Oh, Lizzie..." Tad breathed. His hand began to tremble. For the first time he allowed himself to believe she was really alive.

"Lizzie." He ached to hold his daughter as the woman was holding her. To touch her soft red curls. To hear her quick, lilting bursts of laughter. To watch her dart about in her dinosaur suits. He would relish even the sound of her tears, even the hot outbursts of her temper so like his own.

In the picture Lizzie's hair was the same brilliant copper red, but she was older, six now. Her hair was longer, tied back with purple ribbons. Of course, purple, only purple. She'd always had a fixation about anything purple. And dinosaurs. He realized with a pang how long a year was to a little girl. Would she even remember him?

He devoured the pictures of her. In one she was holding a starfish and studying it. In another the woman was bending over her and lovingly examining a hurt baby toe. The look of trust and devotion between the woman and his child touched something deep and longed for in his own soul.

Jess...

The forbidden name sprang from some place deep within him.

Jess, Deirdre's identical twin.

Dear God. Quickly he closed the door on the treacherous emotion Jess alone could arouse in him.

The woman, whichever she was, had his child. She had deliberately kept his child from him for nearly a year.

The last shot was of Lizzie alone.

Tad stared at it until the familiar upturned nose and red curls blurred. The excitement, the relief of knowing she was alive was unbearable. He felt a vague reeling sensation. He tried to focus, but the image of his daughter swam before his eyes. He could no longer ignore the woman who held his child in her arms. Lizzie looked happier than she'd ever looked with Deirdre. He forced himself to concentrate.

He picked up the picture of the woman and stared at it hard. With avid dislike, his eyes ran down the slim yet deliciously curved body. *Jess*... He knew it was her.

Just as he knew how the long, blond hair would blow in the wind, just how silky it would feel if he were to run his fingers through it. Just how hot her skin would be to his touch, or how cool. Just how warmly those dark, gold-flecked eyes could sparkle when she laughed. Just how treacherously she could use such beauty to twist and manipulate a man. Once he'd been bewitched by this woman. Her touch alone had enflamed him.

His heart filled with a savage, dark anger. Never again.

He studied the beautiful face, the magnificent bust, the cinched-in waist, and his mouth twisted with pain as he remembered.

Deirdre's face.

The face that had launched his life on a collision course with disaster.

Only it wasn't Deirdre.

It was her twin. His sister-in-law. Dr. Jessica Bancroft Kent.

A muscle in his stomach pulled.

Even more than Deirdre, he detested her.

Because it was she whom he had loved.

Years ago when he'd been hardly more than a kid himself—when he'd been in school at the university back in Austin, Texas and before he'd married Deirdre, he'd been thoroughly tricked by Jessica Bancroft. Though Bancroft had posed as a do-gooding intellectual bent on becoming a doctor and saving the world, he'd discovered that she was every bit as much a liar as her sister.

For it was Bancroft who'd played the starring role in the trick that had induced him to make the worst mistake of his life. Her excuse had been that she had been helping her sister. The knowledge of her betrayal lay as heavy as stone in his stomach.

Help... That was the catchword that gave people like Jess the excuse they needed to meddle in others' lives. Tad had always believed that if people would just mind their own business, the world would run a lot more smoothly.

Although Jess and Deirdre had kept up through the years, Tad had avoided Jess. He had never given a damn how Bancroft might feel about him. All he knew was that she had helped Deirdre trap him into his hellish marriage. Then Jess had gotten married herself. Not that she'd ever acted like a wife should. She'd run all over the world doctoring the poor, leaving her husband and son to fend for themselves.

Three years ago Jess's husband and their only son had been killed in a car accident in Austin. Deirdre had gone and stayed with Jess, but it hadn't bothered Jess enough to keep her from taking off almost immediately on another of those ill-advised, medical-missionary sprees of hers. She wasn't a woman, with a real woman's heart.

Sure, Bancroft had a meddlesome, do-good facade. The truth was she was bossy as hell. She was just conceited. She liked inserting herself in poverty-ridden villages where no one knew nearly as much as she. There she could strut about, filled with self-importance, as she taught those wretched creatures to boil water and wash their hands, as she delivered their babies, as she bullied them to her heart's content until they recovered from cholera or whatever blight had made it necessary for them to endure Jess's ministrating presence in the first place.

Deirdre had come home after the funerals, and after that two-month absence the sense of isolation she'd always felt about living in Australia on a remote cattle station with him had worsened.

Tad hadn't minded Deirdre being away. As always when he had had the station and Lizzie to himself he'd felt relief. That absence had been a turning point, and after it their marriage had gone steadily downhill. It was as if they had both known it was over and they had given up.

Holt Martin had crashed into Mount Woolibarra. Deirdre had flown to Brisbane and begged Ian to convince Tad to leave Australia or consider a divorce. Then the war against himself and his property had begun, and the tensions in his marriage had increased.

Tad stared at the picture in his hand. If Deirdre was dead, this could only be Jess. After a long time, he set the picture down beside the others.

A chill ran down his spine. It was as if the ghost of something he wanted dead had fluttered willfully back into his life. He tried to tell himself that it didn't matter. All that mattered was that she had his daughter, that his Lizzie was still alive.

"It's amazing," Tad whispered. "Truly amazing . . . Lizzie . . . Deirdre . . ."

"So you think it's Deirdre?"

Tad didn't look up. "Who else could it be?"

There must have been something odd in his face because Ian was watching him, examining every nuance of his expression.

"It was so strange. I got this call. A woman talked to my secretary and told her that a client of ours, Tad Jackson, would be very interested in what she had to say. The woman was an American; the take-charge sort. Bossy as hell. You know the type—the kind who makes her presence felt wherever she is. She wouldn't hang up till she got me."

So it *was* Bancroft. Cut loose from her do-gooding mission and thereby free to meddle in his life.

Dear Lord! Oh, yes. He knew the type.

His jaw clenched. Just the memory of her still cut him to the quick.

But she had Lizzie! And it was obvious from the pictures they were getting along famously. Something in him that was fatherly and possessive glared at the redheaded six-year-old in the purple swimsuit as if she were a traitor.

Then his gaze returned to the blond who was to blame, and that was a mistake, because he couldn't stop himself from staring at the snug swimsuit where it clung to the soft swell of her breasts.

Those breasts! Damn her! They were magnificent! He had a weakness for the exquisite proportions of well-endowed women. He told himself it was a general thing. Still, a hot tingle of something he didn't want to feel tightened every muscle in his body as he remembered a night he'd vowed to forget.

A magical night when orange blossoms had bloomed on a verdant lawn that swept down to Town Lake in Austin. A night when moonlight was blue dazzle on rippling waters. An unforgettable night of unusual and tantalizing pleasure.

Jess Bancroft had been too damned good to forget.

Who would have thought a Puritanical do-gooder like Jess would be a wanton in the sack? He had been stunned by her primitive, abandoned passion.

She had made him think it was Deirdre he was making love to. For that, he could never forgive her.

Tad frowned uneasily.

Ian said, "She said I ought to come to a certain place. That I'd find something of interest. I thought it was some sort of hoax, but I sent a man down there just in case. And he took those snapshots."

Tad sank slowly back into his chair. He was numb with shock. His face was white, sick-looking. He could feel the violent thudding of his heart, the perspiration beading on his forehead. Was it his cold that was suddenly making him feel so ill or the murderous all-consuming fury anything that reminded him of his wife or her twin could arouse?

"Where were these pictures taken?"

"I really don't think you should see her," Ian replied coolly. "At least, not for a while. Not . . . not till you calm down. Your face is purple."

"Achoo!" A raspy curse vibrated behind Tad's sneeze.

"She's my . . . er . . . wife, damn it. She's put me through hell, and you really don't think I should see her! I'll strangle her with my bare hands, that's what I'll do." Tad was getting carried away, but he couldn't stop himself. "I'll strangle you, if you don't tell me."

"As your lawyer, I didn't hear that, and I advise you not to go around saying things like that to other people."

"Okay. Okay. But you're my lawyer, not my keeper. No one runs my life but me."

"You've sure done one hell of a job."

"Where is she?"

Ian hesitated. "Maybe she doesn't want to see you."

Fat chance. Jess Bancroft hadn't come to Australia to count legs on starfish or coo over Lizzie's injured baby toes. "She called you!"

Ian was regarding him coolly. "That's the odd thing I can't figure. Why did she call me . . . and not you?"

"Ian, for God's sake! She's got Lizzie! Have you never felt a single overpowering emotion in your well-ordered life?" Tad's hard gaze was riveted to the map with the colored pins on the wall. "Besides greed?"

Ian smiled grimly, "Not since I was young. Not since my home was sold out from under me to some Yanks, and my parents and I were out on the streets starving. Not since my sister died on those streets. I learned to channel my emotions, not to act on them. I married a woman who likes to stay home. A woman who understands that this is a man's world. She knows her place—and mine. While you . . . You married the most beautiful creature on earth. A goddess meant to dazzle and be admired. Then you buried her alive on Jackson Downs with nothing but cows and termite mounds and goanna lizards scuttling about for company. And then people started shooting at her. So she got a bit jumpy."

"If I had it to do over, I would run like hell from anyone who even remotely reminded me of Deirdre."

For a moment two pairs of male eyes were drawn to the voluptuous image of golden female beauty in the photograph. Then both men looked away—too quickly.

"I wonder..." Ian folded his hands beneath his blunt chin in that curious attitude of prayer that meant he was thinking.

"You've got to tell me where they are, Ian. What if she takes Lizzie away again?"

The world was full of wretched niches where a doctor of Bancroft's curious bent could hide indefinitely.

"They're on the island," Ian said.

"What?"

"They're staying at the cottage—alone."

"She's crazy to go there."

"It's almost like she's tempting fate, isn't it?" Ian mused.

Tempting fate was exactly the sort of sport Jess Bancroft liked best. Aloud, Tad said, "It's the last place I would have thought to look."

"You're as crazy as she is if you go there. What's going to happen to Jackson Downs with you gone?"

"My brother-in-law, Kirk Mackay, is there, and there's no man alive I'd trust more to see after things."

"You should meet her on neutral territory. This could be a setup of some sort."

Tad's icy blue stare went over the slim, golden woman in the top photograph one last time. He remembered the way her body had fitted his. Rage flamed in his heart, but he could not stop the memories of her. He could almost feel her rosebud nipples pressed into his chest. Despite those immense breasts, she had been slender, lovely, instilling in him a hot, pulsating urgency and then fulfilling him beyond all his wildest expectations. She had been so good, so sweet— that once. Taking her had been so easy. Forgetting her so impossible.

Because he had loved her.

He'd been looking for her that night. She had said she was looking for him. Only when she found him she deliberately pretended to be her twin, Deirdre.

Her twin, Deirdre, whom he'd married because of that one night of ecstasy.

His wife, Deirdre, who had been frigid, at least in his bed, for ten years.

His spoiled, selfish wife, who had married him only for his money, who had taken his child and run out on him at the first sign of trouble. He flinched as though his chest had been stabbed by a knife of ice.

Ten years ago his relationship with Deirdre had been over until Jess had deliberately seduced him, pretending she was Deirdre, and then Jess passed him back to her sister as though he had meant nothing.

Tad smiled grimly as he pocketed the pictures.

Oh, it was a setup all right.

Only this time . . .

Two

The scent of mimosas and oleander and hibiscus mingled with the perfume of the sea.

Everyone else on the island was relaxing.

Everyone except Dr. Jessica Bancroft Kent.

Everyone except the aboriginal child with the matted gold hair who was watching her from the rain forest canopy of giant bloodwoods and ironbarks.

The hordes of tourists from the resort hotel at the other end of the rocky island were either swimming, snorkeling, windsurfing or viewing the wonders of the Great Barrier Reef from glass-bottom boats. But Jess had not come to this thickly wooded paradise of dappled sunlight, with its flitting blue butterflies and magnificent beaches, as a tourist. She was a woman with a mission.

And the word relax was not in her vocabulary.

She almost wished it was. Her heart was pounding violently from her exertions, and she was so hot she felt she might explode.

Then the child peeped out of the jungle. Their eyes met—the woman's and the boy's. Jess smiled, and as always whenever Jess made any attempt to communicate he became frightened and ran away. Sturdy brown legs flew past her down the trail of white coral.

Alone once more, Jess felt like she was in a steam bath. It had just rained. The fierce summer sun beat down on the tropical island with deadly intensity. Even in the dense shade of the rain forest—the Australians called it scrub—that skirted the rocky road where she stood huffing and puffing as she leaned against the mower she'd been pushing uphill, the heat was stifling. The narrow path was made narrower because some untidy individual, no doubt male, had parked a bulldozer square in the middle of it.

Jess's hair had come loose from its pins, and great globs of it were glued to her neck and forehead. Her khaki shorts and blouse were as wet as if she'd showered in them, and the blouse clung disgustingly across her too-ample bosom.

Even now, all these many years since school, her playmate-of-the-month figure remained a secret embarrassment. It was something to be hidden beneath high-necked blouses or baggy clothes. It galled her that her breasts were the first thing men noticed about her, her brains the last.

"I've got brains of my own, honey," had been one boyfriend's crude gem.

She tugged at the clinging, sticky-wet fabric and then gave up the attempt to loosen it from her skin and fanned herself with her fingers. She had lost all enthusiasm for the prospect of mowing the overgrown lawn surrounding Deirdre's cottage. Jess could have gladly turned around and pushed the mower back down the hill except she was too stubborn to face Wally's boyish smirk of male triumph.

He had warned her, hadn't he? And like all men, even a green chauvinistic pup like himself, he would take great delight in being right.

She cringed as she remembered their conversation once she had lured him away from the contractors involved in the hotel's expansion.

"The motor mower's too heavy for a woman to push over that hill."

"For a woman..." How she detested superior, limiting, masculine phrases of that variety.

His eyes had fallen from her stern face to those two protruding, softer parts of her anatomy that always drew male eyes the way magnets attract iron filings.

"If you'll just wait till Hasiri comes back—" he said.

"Nonsense," she had replied crisply. "If I wasted my time waiting for all the Hasiris of the world to come back, I would have gotten very little done."

The handlebars of the mower had slid so easily from Wally's grasp into hers. He had managed to bring his gaze back to her face and keep it there.

Wally was a gentle soul. She almost wished now that he'd fought her a little harder. Not that it would have done either of them a particle of good. It was never difficult for a woman with even a bit of backbone to best the Wallys of this world, and Jessica had much more than a bit.

Not that she was a man-hater, despite the innuendos of more than one member of that sex over the years. She had found, however, starting with her handsome and dynamic father, that few persons of the male sex were to be trusted. Later experiences had merely confirmed her opinion.

She smeared the back of her arm across her damp brow. The rain forest was abuzz with insects—some of them huge, voracious, exotic-looking creatures that made her think she should carry a rolled newspaper at all times, especially when lifting toilet lids. Something horrendous flew past the tip of her nose, and she swatted at it. Suddenly she longed for a cool drink and a shower; she longed to be back at the cottage with Meeta and Lizzie.

Nearby in the dense tangle of bloodwoods and gum trees, a twig snapped. Every muscle in her body went rigid. For the first time it occurred to her how remote her end of the island was, how lonely this particular part of the trail was, how dark the shadows of the jungle had become.

She'd come to this island and asked a lot of questions, perhaps too many, about her sister who'd died violently.

Jess's stomach felt hollowed out, that overpowering indication of fear, of the hunted realizing she was hunted. She instinctively knew it wasn't the child. The boy crept stealthily through the jungle without making a sound. This was something bigger, something clumsier.

Jess swallowed. Normally she wasn't the shrinking, terrified sort of female her father had taught her to despise. Hadn't she fearlessly braved the slums of Calcutta for the past two years? But those garbage-strewn alleyways had been familiar territory. And those teeming slums, for all their filth, weren't nearly as dangerous as most downtown American streets after dark.

A brooding atmosphere hovered in the dark rain forest. The green-breasted parrots had stopped their raucous squawking. She was a stranger to this country, to this island, to jungles and their dangers. Obviously, she was not nearly so talented at playing detective as she'd naturally assumed she'd be. She peered warily into the darkness and listened to the eerie quiet.

An explosion of white burst from the jungle.

Jess screamed, jumping back as feathers brushed her cheek.

"Silly goose!" She chided herself shakily as she watched a cockatoo, its crest sulfur yellow, flutter gracefully down from the branches of a firewheel. "It was just a bird."

She had let go of the mower, and it began to roll backward toward the edge of a six-foot cliff.

"Be careful with it, love," Wally had said. "Believe it or not, this is the only working motor mower on the island."

"I always take excellent care of every item I borrow," she had promised faithfully.

She lunged after the borrowed item that she was taking such excellent care of, catching it just as it tilted precariously over the edge. Once her pulse had calmed, she began to tug on the mower with all her strength, but its wheel was jammed in the crevice between two rocks.

It was then that the unmistakable sound of a human sneeze issued forcefully from the jungle.

"Achoo!"

She nearly jumped out of her skin, and the mower lurched even more dangerously.

"Achoo!"

This second sneeze was followed by a man's quick, low, snarled curse. "Damn."

A ripple of fear raced up her spine.

There *was* someone! Someone who was deliberately hiding in the trees.

Paralyzed, she clung to the mower. "Who's—"

A dark cloud came out of nowhere and obliterated the sun.

She yanked at the mower but it wouldn't budge.

If she let go, it would fall. If she didn't . . .

More than once in the span of her twenty-nine years, her audacity had carried the day. "Come out of there, whoever you are," she called softly in what she had intended to be her I'm-not-afraid-of-anything tone, "and help me with this mower."

No answer. Not even a sneeze. There was only the thudding of her heart. Only the silence—thick and cloying like the heat, like her terror. Only the one motor mower on the island, heavy as lead, its wheel sliding out of the crevice and rolling downward over a large, slippery rock, pulling her with it toward that shadowy ravine.

She screamed as she felt a wheel go over the edge.

Something heavy jumped out of the rain forest behind her. Before she could turn around, an arm went around her waist like a steel band, pinning her arms to her side. She felt his fingers settle beneath her breasts.

That was the one place she didn't like men touching.

She let go of the mower with a yelp and watched in a horrified daze as it hurtled slow-motion past a strong brown hand over the edge of the cliff and smashed itself on the rocks below. Before she could scream, that same callused hand clamped firmly over her mouth.

Her body was arched against a solid wall of muscle and bone. Hard male fingers burned into her breasts.

"Stop fighting me, you silly fool. I'm not going to hurt you," a deep, vaguely familiar masculine tone growled.

She forced her panic to subside, and when it did she stopped struggling so frantically.

Her attacker gallantly relaxed his grip, and that was his mistake. Jessica was a student of the martial arts. From then on it was pure, delicious instinct.

Teeth into brown fingers. A deft twist. A knee in his groin. A sharp blow with her heel in his solar plexus.

He doubled over in a spasm of agony. She kicked at his shin. He lost his footing, and the great, bearded giant was tumbling over the rocky edge after the mower.

He bellowed like an injured bull all the way down.

Till he hit bottom with a sickening thump.

Though she hadn't heard Tad Jackson's voice in over four years—she'd thrown him out of her house on that last memorable occasion for a barrage of chauvinistic insults about busybody females galloping about the world like a herd of misguided mares, pretending to help others when all they were really doing was running away from their own personal problems—no other human alive could make that particular howl of frustration and fury except him.

There was an awful silence.

Then a parrot squawked. In the distance a lone wind-surfer streaked past on the glittering ocean.

She was shaking, but the pure horror of what had happened did not strike her until she stepped out onto the ledge and peered down at him.

In spite of his beard, she recognized him instantly.

Jackson!

Dear God!

His great, muscled body lay sprawled as still as death across the bleached coral beside the mower. A faint breeze blew the bright mass of gold back from his tanned brow, and she saw the blood.

Terror gripped her.

What had he growled into her ear? "Stop fighting me, you silly fool. I'm not going to hurt you." And she knew that despite all her brother-in-law's character defects—and they were too numerous to catalogue, not that she hadn't made the attempt on more than one occasion—he would never have physically hurt any woman. Not even her.

For four days she'd waited for him. He needed her help—desperately—but he was so stubborn it was the last thing he would ever willingly seek. For that matter, it was the last thing she would ever have willingly given him. For four days she'd expected him to barge into the cottage like a great giant roaring to the rooftops in one of his high rages, demanding his daughter and demanding Jess's own departure from his life.

Instead, like most men, he had taken the most unexpected, the most foolhardy and the most calamitous course of action. He had snuck up on her in an idiotic macho attempt to bully her. And she had bested him in physical combat.

If he lived he would add this to his lengthy list of unforgivable things she had done to him.

If he lived . . .

She scrambled down the cliff after him.

Three

Tad lay on the rocks in a blur of agony. Vaguely he was aware of his surroundings. The resort was expanding. Bulldozers had gouged great chunks out of the jungle, but they'd left the cliff with its famous Aboriginal rock art intact. Crudely painted crocodiles and kangaroos and other unknown animals that recalled the Aboriginal creation myth of the Dreamtime loomed above him. But he was not admiring this splendid example of rock art; he was concentrating on her.

Pain splintered through his battered body. He had hit his head when he fell, and it was a struggle to focus his eyes on the she-devil. He watched, though, as she climbed as nimbly as a goat down the rocks—no doubt, to finish him off.

He'd been following her all day, trying to figure out her game plan, trying to figure out when and where to confront her, how best to seize the advantage. Then he'd gotten soaked in that shower which hadn't helped his cold, and he'd sneezed and given himself away.

He'd only jumped her because she was so stubbornly determined to save that rattletrap mower—he'd been afraid she was going to let it drag her over the cliff. Instead, she'd shoved him off it.

Jess-of-the-jungle grabbed a spidery vine and with an agile jump made her final descent. She landed light as a feather. Was there nothing that woman couldn't do?

Through half shuttered eyes, he watched her sink to her knees beside him. Her immense breasts heaved beneath her damp shirt. He could make out the outline of taut nipples thrusting against wet cotton. He knew better than to watch those, so he gritted his teeth, fighting to concentrate on the danger of her proximity, fighting to ignore the fiery, pulsating pain in his leg and lower hip.

It would be so easy to grab her by the throat, to pull her down, to scare her witless and thereby make her pay for what she had done. He almost succumbed to this nearly irresistible temptation, but some part of him was curious as to what she planned to do next. Besides, to lie still was the easiest and least painful thing to do.

To his surprise, instead of picking up a rock or a stick to pound him with she gently lifted his hand, her practiced finger searching his wrist for a pulse. She mashed her magnificent breasts against his chest.

Her own hand felt as cool as springwater against his blazing skin. How could anything alive feel so cool and nice in this heat? Her cotton blouse was as wet as his own soaked shirt, her breasts soft and deliciously warm.

How could Jess . . . feel so nice?

Jess, whom he hated even more than he'd hated Deirdre.

Jess, who had betrayed him, who had tricked him into marrying Deirdre.

Jess, whom he had loved as he'd never loved Deirdre.

Jess, who had just pushed him over this damn cliff.

What the hell was Jess doing here anyway—besides trying to kill him?

The she-devil lowered her head to his chest and listened for his heart, and he was forced to endure the lustrous tangle of her soft, blond curls tickling his chin and nose.

When he thought he couldn't hold back the sneeze that threatened a second longer, she lifted her head and brought her face closer to his. He was aware of her lips hovering, lushly half opened, tantalizing, a scant inch above his. He could smell her, and her nearness stirred old, long-forgotten memories. No...

Not forgotten. Never forgotten; just repressed because they had hurt too much to remember. He could almost taste her.... He wanted to, and he loathed himself for that weakness.

She licked her lips, and he watched the curl of her pink darting tongue follow the lush curves of her perfectly shaped mouth. A fingertip dubiously touched his beard and then withdrew.

He caught the scent of something sweet, like orange blossoms. Her scent, enveloping him.

"Jackson," she whispered. The sound was ragged with fear. Through the dampness of their clothes, the points of her breasts shuddered delicately against his hard chest muscle. Her warm breath caressed his throat.

The jungle was a beastly sauna.

He could hear her labored breathing. Or was it his?

"Jackson, can you hear me?"

No use to answer. They'd quarrel, and he felt weak, too exhausted for one of their battles.

When he clung stubbornly to his silence, he heard her muted cry of remorse. "Dear God!" Her fingertips stroked his cheek. "You big, impossible lug, I never meant to hurt you."

She—who'd been the cause of all his hurt—had never meant to hurt him.

He studied her through the thick veil of his almost closed lashes, and he felt twisted with conflicting emotions. The sunlight was in her hair. Her wet blouse outlined her lush female shape. Even in a state of dishevelment, she was golden, lovely.

He didn't want his thoughts journeying down that fatal path, but a man's thoughts are not so easily whipped onto the path of his choice when the woman he doesn't want to think about is right there pressing her breasts into him, distracting him. So he kept looking at her, thinking about her.

Hell. Jess certainly wasn't her usual prim and proper Puritanical self. She was badly shaken, soft and vulnerable. Indeed, she looked exactly like she'd stepped out of the centerfold of a men's magazine and come to life.

She sat up, this tabloid fantasy that he knew from past experience was no tabloid fantasy, and he closed his eyes with a faint groan, but not before he'd gotten a good look at her beautiful, anguished, tear-streaked face.

He wanted to hate her. He was determined to.

But it was hard to hate a woman, no matter what she'd done, when she was crying over you.

Instead of hatred he felt the dangerous pull of that old indefinable power that had crawled inside him and eaten him alive—body and soul—until there had been nothing left. For years he had told himself he was glad she was out of his life, glad that whatever had been between them was finally over.

But memories of her had haunted him. Sometimes he'd dreamed of that night ten years ago, the one night he'd had her, the night that had made him want her forever—he'd dreamed hot, lascivious dreams in which Jess crawled all over him in wanton abandon.

He had married the wrong sister. Damnation! Was that why he hated Bancroft even more than Deirdre?

The jungle was hotter and more oppressive than ever. There was a smell in the heated air that was very Australian, a thin, subtle odor of the scrub, an unmistakable pungency of aromatic oils stealing out from the trees. Tad began to perspire, and the faint breeze trickling through the trees from the ocean made his skin feel like ice.

Her fingers sifted through his golden hair and probed the burgeoning lump and the hot stickiness surrounding it. He groaned aloud, and she drew her hand away as if burned.

"Don't be such a sissy," she whispered. "I don't want to hurt you. I have to do this."

Sissy! It was all he could do not to grab her and make her pay for that one.

The hand came back, gently probing his eyelid open so she could check the dilation of his pupil. She opened the other eye. Then she ran her hands over every part of his body, examining every bruise, every scratch. It was hard for him to remember she was a doctor and that it was the doctor touching him, not the woman. When she finished, she observed his still face thoughtfully.

"Jackson . . ."

Her low, melodious voice wasn't nearly so bossy as usual. Yes, she had clearly been shaken off her know-it-all pedestal.

He felt her fingers touch his cheek. "Jackson, if you can hear me, would you please . . ."

She took his hand and gripped it again. He felt her other hand push his hair from his brow and remain there. Her cool touch was gentle, infinitely sweet, comforting.

"Jackson, your pulse is strong. I don't think you're hurt too badly. You're going to be okay, but I'm going to have to leave you here for a little while. I'm going to the cottage to get someone to help me carry you."

Her voice went on, but the sound seemed to drift in and out. He could only hear snatches of it. He tried to open his eyes, but when he did, he couldn't see her anymore.

Suddenly he wished he hadn't been so obstinate. He wished he'd spoken to her when he'd been able to. He was afraid that he was bleeding internally and that he might never get the chance again.

He wanted more than this abrupt finality with her, more than one of those endings without a goodbye. Without even an I'm sorry. Suddenly he knew that he wanted much, much more than a goodbye with her.

But there was only a whirling blackness sucking him under. Only a numbing pain that seemed to engulf his whole being. Only her hand clutching his as she tried to pull him back.

"Jackson, you stubborn fool, why didn't you speak to me?" she screamed.

He could barely hear her, but he tried to make his lips form the words. "Because...because..."

Because he had wanted to so much.

When he came to again, he felt faint with agony. And yet relief.

He was still alive. He was in the cottage. Safe after an eternity of danger.

Here there were no guns. No one was stalking him. Only this woman.

It was night. The heat of the day had lessened. Moonlight slanted through the shutters. The air was dense and humid and smelled sweetly of rain and pungent, wet gum leaves. The jungle was alive with a riot of bird sounds. Above the bed, the blades of a ceiling fan stirred lazily and cast flickering shadows against the ceiling. Even in the darkness he could see that the room was neat, tidier than it had ever been when he'd stayed in it with Deirdre. Jess was a fanatic when it came to neatness.

From downstairs came the scent of something cooking, something that reminded him of sweet long-ago things when his life had been simpler—Texas, his mother, home. Of being a little boy. Of happiness. Of that pleasant time before his parents had separated, before all the loneliness, before Jeb had taken over and made him feel like an outcast among his own family.

Chicken soup.

Jess always knew how to get next to him. Deirdre had never cooked chicken soup. But Jess, for all her faults, had a couple of saving graces. Those breasts... He pushed that thought aside and concentrated on the delicate aroma of chicken soup. She could cook better than any woman he'd ever known. And he had a weakness for good cooking.

He watched the blades of the fan; he watched their shadows on the ceiling. He wished he didn't have a weakness for big breasts and good cooking. He tried to concentrate on the faint throb of music drifting from the hotel's bar at the far side of the island. Then he heard Lizzie's laughter downstairs mingling with Jess's stern voice.

Lizzie... He struggled to sit up, but he was too weak to manage it. Slowly he became aware of his circumstances. He was lying upstairs in the master bedroom, and he was naked between crisp white sheets.

Naked!

The she-devil had stripped him and robbed him of his clothes! At the thought of her hands going over him he went hot all over.

She had no right to touch him! But the memory alone made him rock hard.

Vague memories, like those from some barely remembered dream haunted him. Long, slim fingers, cool fingers, had slid over the hot skin of his body, touching him everywhere. He remembered scissors snipping away at his trousers. Cold points, needle sharp, had teased his burning skin. He remembered icy cloths being pressed against his forehead, against his neck and shoulders. He remembered a gentle Indian girl in a scarlet-and-gold sari. Most of all he remembered Jess's voice. She had talked to him in the darkness, talked to him until the gentle sound had lost its soothing quality and had become raspy with weariness.

Jess had managed to get him to the house, to carry him up the stairs, to undress him, to put him to bed. As always—when she put that very determined mind of hers to it—she was a whirlwind of efficient, competent energy.

That same whirlwind of energy had kicked him and sent him whirling over that cliff.

God, he needed a cigarette! But where were they? She had taken everything.

How long had he been here? Hours? Days?

He heard her footsteps on the stair, and a child's lighter, faster steps dashing in front of her.

The door burst open.

The doorknob banged against the wall.

He closed his eyes.

Jess's urgent whisper across the darkness. "Lizzie! Careful!"

Then a breathless silence.

A knot of suspense formed in his gut. He didn't know what to say to either of them.

He was a man used to the vast expanses of the outback, a man who could go for days sometimes without talking as he traveled from cow camp to cow camp, a man who did not mind such long silences.

Everyone in the room waited. There was only the whir of the ceiling fan rotating lazily.

Then a tiny, impatient hand with cold, sticky fingers curled tentatively, gently around his little finger.

The nightmare of the past year was over.

He opened his eyes, hardly daring to believe the angelic vision of bright red curls tied back in a lopsided purple bow. Big, dark eyes glowing with joy and yet mirroring his own uncertainty.

"Daddy!" The uncertainty was in her voice, as well.

This bright-eyed waif was wearing a crinkly green-and-yellow dinosaur raincoat and holding a half-eaten grape Popsicle that was melting all over her hand. She brought this dribbling delicacy to her lips and licked greedily.

His child.

He was not a sentimental man. His grip tightened on hers.

"He's awake," Lizzie squealed, jumping up and down.

"It's about time," Jess murmured drily. She, too, looked excited, pleased, proud that he was better, though she was attempting to appear stern.

"Aunt Jess!" Lizzie whirled, then turned back to her father. "Aunt Jess, he's crying." Lizzie's eyes were wide; her low tone awestruck.

"Nonsense, darling," came Jess's crisp, firm tone, removing the Popsicle and giving her charge a much needed tissue.

"Lizzie..." His voice was so deep and hoarse with emotion he hardly recognized it. His hand closed over the smaller one, careful not to crush it.

Very gently Jess lifted the child up so that she could put her arms around him and press her face against his grizzled cheek.

"Daddy, I missed you something awful." Green-and-yellow plastic crinkled as she squirmed closer. Jess stepped back.

His fingers tangled in her curls. "I missed you, too..."

Did those words convey the emptiness of the past year? The helplessness? The sick, gnawing fear? On top of it all, everything he'd loved had been under attack. "You look wonderful," was all he said.

Jess seemed to be staring out the window as if she, too, were deeply moved. He remembered she'd always tried to hide her sentimental nature.

"Daddy, I know why Mommy never came back. But why did she take me away? I wasn't scared of the bad men."

Jess's head pivoted sharply. "Not now, Lizzie darling," came Jess's voice, still raspy with exhaustion. "Remember what I told you about not upsetting him."

Lizzie lapsed into silence. As though bored, the child brushed a finger through his beard and pulled it back. "Sticky. I don't like it. You didn't have it before."

"Then I'll shave it," he muttered, unhappy that anything about him should displease his Lizzie.

Lizzie touched the bandages on his head. "How'd you get hurt, Daddy? Aunt Jess said..."

His eyes rose to Jess, who had become rigid behind Lizzie. Jess was prim and proper now, dressed in a white poplin blouse with a high collar. The blouse buttoned practically all the way to her nose. She wore navy slacks, and her hair was neatly bound at the nape of her neck. The hairstyle couldn't have been sleeker if every hair had been glued in place.

The schoolteacher look! He didn't like it. He'd liked her better in the clinging, wet blouse with her hair streaming down her neck. With her body hot and breathless against his. With tears of passionate concern for him streaming down her cheeks.

At Lizzie's question the look of excitement and shining pleasure in her aunt's eyes died. A guilty flush came into her face.

"What did your Aunt Jess tell you?" He kept staring at Jess until the color in Jess's cheeks deepened.

The line of Jess's mouth tightened. "Tell her whatever you want."

"Oh, I will." His voice was husky. "I will." His velvet tone went softer. "All in good time. But first, I'd like to hear your Aunt Jess's version."

Lizzie got down off the bed and eyed her aunt dubiously. Jess's cheeks remained as bright as a pair of beets.

"She said you fell off that cliff with the big pictures where she keeps telling me to be careful."

Tad's eyes slanted toward Jess, who seemed to be holding her breath as she looked past him out the window. A sliver of moonlight molded the lovely curve of her neck. He smiled crookedly.

"I fell, did I? What an interesting...er...interpretation of events."

More blood seemed to gush into Jess's face. She started to back away from the bed, but he lunged forward and seized her wrist.

They screamed together—she in surprise, he in agony. One glance at his white face, and she stopped fighting him.

Pain shot from his hips and thigh, but even as he sank back into the bed, he clung stubbornly to that tiny bit of female flesh and bone, pulling her closer.

The scent of orange blossoms and soap enveloped him. Her scent, treacherously pleasant. He fought to ignore it.

What he couldn't ignore were those two temptingly soft parts of her anatomy that spilled over his chest.

"Send Lizzie away," he croaked hoarsely into Jess's ear.

A golden tendril came loose from her stern hairdo and blew softly against her cheek.

"You need to lie still, Jackson," Jess murmured, not in the least intimidated by him. "You're too hurt and weak for this idiotic macho behavior—as if it hasn't already gotten you in enough trouble."

This reminder of how easily she'd bested him only served to make him madder.

"Get Lizzie out of here. I have to talk to you alone."

His eyes burned into Jess's for what seemed an eternity.

At last Jess averted her gaze and whispered softly, "Lizzie, darling, would you be a little angel and run down to the kitchen and tell Meeta to heat the soup I made for your Daddy? I'll come down for it in a minute. I need to check him first."

That sweet, hypocritical, ladylike voice that made him want to snap her head off! But it fooled Lizzie, who dashed out of the room.

When they were alone, his grip relaxed ever so slightly upon Jess's wrist, but he kept on holding her. "Bancroft, just what do you think you're doing?"

"For the last twenty-four hours—nursing you. Believe me, that was hardly a prize assignment. Like most men, you were no use in an emergency. You've been very difficult. First you refused to walk. We had to carry you. Uphill. You're heavy as lead."

"Good!" His blue eyes glinted with savage pleasure at having put her to trouble. "You probably broke both my damn legs when you pushed me."

"You're exaggerating—as always."

"All I know is that I was in perfect health until I met up with you."

She snorted. "Perfect health! Ha! Jackson, you had a case of walking pneumonia. A fly could have pushed you over that hill."

That stung. "I had a cold!"

"Pneumonia. You probably kept working and smoking—"

"Naturally I kept working and smoking."

"More of that idiotic machismo you take such absurd pride in! Even a fool such as yourself should have had better sense. Well, you won't smoke now. It was clear some-one had to take charge of you. It was equally clear there was no one but me to do so. I tore up both of the packs of cig-arettes you had in your pocket."

She was just like his older brother, Jeb, who was always telling him what to do.

He felt apoplectic. "You what?"

"They're the last thing you need in your weakened con-dition. You were on the verge of collapse."

Her smug superiority was more than he could endure. What did she know of his hardships? "No, *you're* the last thing I need." He yanked her closer so that her soft body fitted intimately to his. She felt cool to the touch—ah, too pleasantly cool; his body was racing with heat. "You tried to kill me, you witch!"

"A fate you brought on yourself when you attacked me!"

"I didn't attack you. I was trying to prevent you from going over the cliff with the mower."

"Well, it doesn't matter now," she said softly.

"Doesn't matter?" he exploded.

"For once, you might surprise me and try thinking ra-tionally," she continued in that cool know-it-all tone of hers that would have been a needle in any man's ego. "We can't alter what happened, can we? Besides, you're not hurt all that badly, despite the way you're carrying on about it. Like most men, you're a big baby when it comes to illness."

"A big baby!" He'd been fighting a guerrilla war all by himself for nearly two years. If he was sick, it was because he'd driven himself so hard.

"A few bruises, a slight bump on the head, and you carry on like it's the end of the world."

"A slight bump! I'm seeing two of you. Believe me, that's more than any man could stand!"

She went on. "A slight bump, a very mild concussion, a pulled muscle in the groin—that's all that's wrong with you."

"My groin!" This time it was he who was blushing. "For God's sake, I hope you didn't examine me there."

"Naturally I examined..."

The thought of her fingers probing around there made him go hot beneath his beard.

"Jackson, the reason you feel so rotten is because of the pneumonia, and you brought that on yourself. You've been burning up with fever. I had to pump drugs into you to get it down. I bathed you with cold cloths all afternoon and last night. Then this morning, your fever went back up and we had to do it all over again."

For the first time he saw the dark shadows beneath her eyes, the lines of weariness etched into her face. Somehow, this evidence of her dedication toward him made him want to attack her with an even greater ferocity.

"Don't expect gratitude or an apology from me," he jeered.

She pursed her lips.

So... She had felt at least a glimmer of doctorly compassion toward him because she'd nursed him through a crisis. He watched that sentiment die completely.

Her eyes were cinders. "Common courtesy, dear brother-in-law, is the last thing I'd ever expect from you," she replied coolly, in a miffed, hurt tone. "Not that you should feel you owe me anything. I would have done the same thing for a sick dog."

His fingers tightened around the slim wrist. "I want Lizzie, you man-hating witch. I want you out of my life. I have enemies enough without taking you on."

"I know." She lifted her chin and stared at him down the length of her nose. "For once we are in agreement," she answered, this time in that infuriatingly placid tone a schoolteacher might use with an upstart youngster.

As he watched her flatten one of the tucks in her blouse with her free hand, he felt a wild jubilation. Nothing had ever been this easy with her. Then he grew aware that something in her smug expression didn't fit with her words. He realized she had caught him off guard.

"What do you mean?"

She smiled sweetly. It was the smile he most distrusted.

"Only that this once we both want the same thing, Jackson." She pressed her fingertips beneath her chin in that cool, determined manner of hers.

She was finished with the tuck. But not with him.

"You see, Jackson, I want Lizzie, too. I'm here to help you."

Four

————

Tad's hand was a claw gripping Jess's wrist. He felt the warmth of her breasts spilling voluptuously against his chest. Her body was soft and inviting. Too bad her head and heart were as hard as flint.

"You see, Jackson, I want Lizzie, too."

Jess's velvet voice seemed like a living thing, a hateful sound lingering in the darkness.

Her mouth was set, and she was looking down the length of her shapely, upturned nose at him again. Dear God! Of all the ills in the world, surely there was none worse than an interfering female who's made up her mind to bully you.

The ceiling fan droned. The moonlight was a halo of silver in her hair.

Tad could not get her statement out of his mind.

Her face was pale, her eyes darkly glimmering pools. The wisp of her hair that had blown loose wrapped around her neck.

In the smoldering silence that fell between them, they studied one another warily. It was as though so much was at stake, neither dared say more. It was as if a bomb was about to go off, and they were both in such a state of shock all they could do was listen to the ticking.

"What do you mean, you want Lizzie?"

"The same thing you do, Jackson."

"Lizzie is my child."

"Your child. Not your possession," came that precise schoolteacher tone he so despised.

Despite her air of moral superiority, she was the one who had stolen his child! He wanted to scream, "Mine! Mine, you fool!" and be done with it. But that would never work with Jess. He had to progress logically. Logically—whatever that meant to her.

He began in what he hoped sounded like a calm tone. "Surely you don't think a person should just take a man's child and keep her for a year without even telling her father where she is."

Darkly defiant gold-flecked eyes met his. "For pity's sake, Jackson, that's deplorable—even from you. I didn't take Lizzie. Deirdre entrusted her to me because your station was a war zone and you weren't doing anything about it."

"Not doing anything! I was fighting back with all I had. Then my sweet wife just took Lizzie and vanished."

"I don't blame her. Like all men, you see only your side. Deirdre was scared witless, and you couldn't protect her. You were always an impossible husband—even in the best of times. Of course she ran."

He controlled his rage and continued, his voice bitter. "When she ran short of money, Deirdre came back to the station and stole my operating cash and one of my planes."

"She needed money to live on."

"She left me nothing. She emptied out our joint checking account, too. After that she came here and never returned."

"Because she was killed!"

"My child was gone, and the only person who knew where she was was dead. My station was a battlefield. Everyone thought I killed them both. My own child! There was no way I could defend myself. The only thing that stood between me and prison was Ian McBain, my lawyer. Believe me, his legal fees, on top of all my other expenses, have dealt the station a death blow."

Jess's expression was odd. "Deirdre mentioned Ian."

Tad's mouth thinned. "Do you know what it's like to be hated and despised for something you didn't do? What it's like to live with the terror that your child is somewhere hurt or dead and there's nothing you can do? To go to bed every night looking at her picture, wondering if you'll ever see her again? That ate at me more than living with the constant violence."

He felt Jess flinch. The moonlight seemed to bleach all color from her face.

Her voice was smooth and unemotional. "I'm sorry."

"You'll have to do better than that," he murmured tightly. "I'm sorry's have never cut any ice with me."

"I-I didn't know what to do," Jess said at last. "When Deirdre didn't come back for Lizzie I did make inquiries, and I found out you were in terrible trouble."

"Trouble?" He sneered. "I was in hell. You knew! And still you didn't bring Lizzie."

"You have never exactly been my favorite person."

"You didn't even write! Not a line to tell me she was alive."

"But then you would have known where we were."

"So you admit it—you deliberately kept her—knowing what I was going through?"

"What else could I do?"

"You could have brought her home!"

"How? I was working in Calcutta at a clinic. I couldn't just leave. I came as quickly as I could find a replacement."

"No, you were too busy saving the world to give a damn about the one man whose life you've been set on destroying ever since you first laid eyes on him."

"That's not true."

"It damn sure is."

"How could I bring Lizzie to you? Not after what Deirdre said about you. Not when she made me promise—"

"And I'll just bet she said plenty! My sweet wife had the habit of blackening my name to anyone who would sit still, and I'm sure you enjoyed listening when she aired all the dirty laundry of our marriage."

Jess's eyes grew huge, intent on his face. "Would you believe me if I said you're wrong about that?"

"Deirdre doesn't matter anymore. Whatever she told you doesn't matter."

"It does to me. A year ago, to help her when she came to me and said you both were in trouble, I accepted responsibility for her child. Lizzie's been through a rough year."

"Tell me about it," he said caustically.

"It wasn't easy for me, either. I was in India working fourteen hours a day in a clinic. I-I was trying to forget about . . . the accident. Deirdre left a five-year-old child and never came back. And Lizzie, who just happens to take her willful disposition after you, is hardly the most easily managed child. My life was turned upside down, and I had to make changes. Lizzie was separated from her home, from everyone she loved, everything familiar. I understood her loss. For several months I thought Deirdre was coming back. Then I found out that Deirdre was dead, that there were rumors about you having had a part in her death."

Jess stopped, and the tortured look on her face that he read as disgust and fear made him writhe inside.

"So you, too, think I killed her?"

When Jess didn't answer, he yanked her closer to the bed, so close he could feel the heat of her body, the intoxicating scent of her perfume. Her haunted eyes were filled with some emotion he did not understand.

"Answer me," he demanded.

"No, I don't." She lowered her lashes.

He could not stand her cool remoteness. "You do!"

She forced herself to look at him again. "I never lie," she whispered.

"That's not true."

Her face went blank. Her eyes glittered darkly in the queer light of the moon.

"You did. That once," he said, "ten years ago."

She shook her head in denial, but he kept glaring at her until she flushed guiltily.

"All right. Yes. Back then maybe, but not now. I don't know what happened to Deirdre. Except I know...I know you didn't kill her."

"Then why are you looking at me like that?"

"B-because I know what it's like to take the blame for something terrible like that. You see when Jonathan and little Benjamin were killed...I was driving."

His grip tightened. "It wasn't your fault."

"I wish I could be so sure. All I know is that if I could undo what happened that night I would. But we make mistakes, and sometimes there are no second chances."

He felt a strange pull from her, a crazy desire to drag her into his arms, to touch her, to caress her, to comfort her. Unknowingly she caught her lower lip with her teeth and a sudden tremor shook him.

He stared at her. She believed him! When everyone else doubted him. She had known what it was to suffer, to be blamed for something she hadn't done.

A wild elation filled him that someone understood, even if it was only Bancroft, who was his enemy. It pleased him that she didn't think he'd killed Deirdre. For the first time in a year, some of his loneliness left him.

He wanted to seize Jess and kiss her. Immediately he realized how absurd such an impulse was. This gorgeous blonde whose voluptuous curves fitted him so enticingly was none other than his conniving, bullying sister-in-law.

He wanted to throw her out of the room and never lay eyes on her again. The last thing he wanted from her was kindness. And yet there was an ache in his gut that told him it *was* the one thing he wanted.

He remembered how she hated sentimental fools. He hated them himself.

"So you see, I know you'd never hurt anyone . . . not like that anyway. Still, I can't just turn Lizzie over to someone who . . ." Her voice caught. "I can't send her to Jackson Downs with all the violence, back to you, when I know you won't see after her properly."

"I'm her father," he said roughly. "I'll be there, damn it. She's my responsibility, not yours."

He could feel Jess's hand trembling in his. She was as deeply upset as he.

"Then we're at odds," she said firmly. "As usual. Because I consider her my responsibility, too."

"And you take all your responsibilities seriously."

"You know I do." She hesitated. "Especially this one. Jackson, I don't want to fight you."

He studied Jess's still, white face, and he knew that his sister-in-law was just as determined as he. And just as stubborn.

"I don't want you in my life," he said. But he gripped her hand like it was a lifeline.

"I didn't ask Deirdre to make Lizzie part of my life, but Deirdre did it anyway. I-I never wanted to love another child again. Not after..." Her voice broke. "And especially your child. B-but I do. I won't let you take her and ruin her the way my father..."

A cloud passed in front of the moon, and Jess's face was lost in darkness for a few seconds. Then the moonlight shone through the shutters once more, brighter than before, and he saw the terrible vulnerability in her eyes again.

He was not the only one who had lived in hell.

With his free hand he reached up and traced a finger against her jaw, along the sensitive skin beneath her chin and neck. He felt her pulse leap in response. He saw her lower lip quiver. Then she fought to control it.

His own pulse started to throb, and he tore his finger away from the tantalizing softness of her throat.

She took a breath and then lost it. He felt her stiffen. The wrist he held had stopped trembling and was again cold and rigid with tension. He struggled to control his own emotions.

There was going to be a battle. The fiercest he'd ever fought.

"You kept my child," he said, "for a year, without ever letting me know where she was."

"Someone had to look after her. It was obvious that her parents were too wrapped up in their own problems to do so."

He'd been ambushed more times than he could count. "You dare imply that I was not a good father?"

"Let me go, Jackson," she whispered. "We'll talk about this tomorrow."

"I want to finish it now."

"You're as weak as a cat." She twisted her wrist and broke free of his grip. "See!"

It was humiliating how easily she had freed herself.

"Tomorrow," she insisted, backing into the shadows. "You must go to sleep now."

Then she was gone.

All through the night Jess's words thrummed like staccato heartbeats in Tad's fevered brain.

I want Lizzie, too. I want Lizzie, too. The words mingled with the raucous thunder of parrot sounds outside and drummed even louder.

Another, more dangerous sensation thrummed in his blood like the rain that pattered for a time against the roof and thick clusters of broad banana leaves.

She had commanded him to sleep. Even if he'd been the kind of man to let a she-devil boss him, how could he sleep with her words whirling in his head? How could he sleep when the scent of orange blossoms lingered in his bed, when she'd left behind her an aura of sensuality that stirred forbidden memories? But it wasn't only her beauty that haunted him, it was the sadness he'd seen in her eyes, the terrible longing in her soft voice, the way her skin had been like hot silk beneath his fingertips.

All he wanted to feel for her was a cold, hard anger, and an even colder satisfaction that her life had gone as badly wrong as his. But something stronger than hate was in his heart, something that filled him with fear.

He told himself that it was the stifling heat that made the bedroom so unbearable, and not this new unwanted emotion. It was the moonlight, slanting across the bed, right in his eyes that made it impossible to sleep.

Restlessly, he threw off his sheet and lay sweltering on top of the narrow bed, fighting not to think of her.

He could think of nothing else. He hadn't had a woman in over a year. Maybe that's why he kept remembering how beautiful Jess was, with her pale hair shining in the darkness, with those flyaway wisps blowing against her face. He couldn't get her out of his mind. He remembered the way the poplin material had stretched across her breasts and pulled at the row of buttons, and a fever throbbed in his blood. He clenched his fists and willed himself to forget. He hated her. He hated that stubborn, willful streak in her that refused to bend. At the same time he ached to take her in his arms and hold her all through the night. He wanted to comfort her. He wanted to make her forget Jonathan and Benjamin. Never again did he want to see that terrible look of anguish on her face. He knew too well the pain she must have suffered.

The fan blew across his skin, and he started to feel cold. So he pulled the covers over him again. No sooner than he got warm, he was too warm.

Some time in the night he got up, bundling the sheet around his waist. He tore open the shutters and opened the doors that led out onto the veranda. There was no breeze. Only the thick, wet heat seeping out of the jungle. He felt faint, sick, drugged. The black trees seemed to whirl like towering giants.

It was Bancroft's fault! She had plunged him into this hell. She'd taken his child. She'd pushed him over that cliff. She'd given him all that medicine.

He almost fell down. He lunged wildly to save himself, and crashed into the shutters instead.

Wood splintered. One of the shutters drooped crazily.

He knew he should go back to bed.

He stumbled outside anyway.

Five

────

It was after midnight. Jess lay awake, absently twirling a strand of her hair as she glared at a ribbon of moonlight on the wall. She'd been awake for hours, her mind stewing endlessly about Jackson. From where she lay, she could see the dark rain forest clearly.

She had known when she came to Australia that Jackson would behave in his inimitable deplorable fashion. She had never expected him to willingly cooperate with her.

Blast him! Why did he have to be so impossibly macho and stuffed to the core with his own pride? Despite all his ferocious strutting and chest-thumping, he was only a man. But what a man. She smiled weakly, and not the usual sweet, superior smile that Jackson hated. Her lips felt hot and fluttery as she thought of his long, dark fingers, holding her prisoner, of his immense bronzed body coiled into hers, of how deliciously small she'd felt as she'd lain on top of him. Her stomach felt hollow and clammy.

Dear God, what was happening to her? How could this perverse man still affect her in the same way he had when she was a girl? For all her blustering determination when she'd been with him, the truth was she was actually afraid to go to Jackson Downs with him.

Why did he have to be so excessively masculine? So disturbingly male that even a woman with a character as strong as her own still found him exciting? She lay in her empty, cold bed and wadded her top sheet restlessly as she thought of him alone in his. Her heart throbbed dully as she remembered his tight fingers gripping her wrist, his hard body beneath hers.

Why him? Why did he alone have this power over her? He was a hunk of muscle and conceit—strong-willed, grouchy, selfish, stubborn, spoiled. The list was endless. He didn't care a whit for the world or its problems. Only his own. She'd grown up abroad, seen the world and its problems; she'd wanted to make a difference.

But she had to help him—because of Lizzie. It wasn't going to be easy. Like all men, of all colors and all nations, he was unable to accept the unpalatable possibility that an intelligent woman might be able to put his affairs in order more capably than he.

For all his strutting and chest-thumping, he had certainly made a mess of things. His station was under siege. He was suspected of murdering his own wife. He'd had a year to clear his name, a year to resolve the conflict at Jackson Downs, and what had he accomplished? The violence was accelerating. He was living under this terrible shadow and he expected Lizzie to live under it, as well. Did he intend to hide out on his station forever in the hope that the sordid rumors would die down? She'd heard he might sell out if things didn't improve. That was no way for a child to grow up. At least not for her own, darling Lizzie.

Jess traced the heavy thread of stitching along the sheet's edge. Her Lizzie. His Lizzie. Whether he liked it or not, they were all in this together.

There was, no doubt, a simple solution to this whole affair. Someone had to ask questions, investigate, think. Men always used force when sometimes a fresh insight, a different tack, would make all the difference. More guns! was their cry when usually what they needed was more brains. There wasn't a man alive who could do much without a woman behind him. Nor a country that could be a great nation without allowing women to realize their full potential. Through the centuries men had warred and strutted, while women had quietly done the really important work— taming and civilizing and promoting culture. Not that men or the history books written by men had ever given them due credit.

Something small and dark moved beneath the spreading branches of the flame tree. The child was at his post again, like a silent sentinel, watching her. Moonlight shone upon the bright thatch of matted curls.

Jess had talked to Wally and to everyone else on the island and learned nothing. This child had followed her everywhere. Why? Did he know something? Why was he so afraid of her?

Jess determined to take him something, a present of some sort, in an attempt to win his trust.

She went out onto the landing. On the stairs lay several of Lizzie's toys. Lizzie had so many.

Jess picked up a small, stuffed pink brontosaurus with a purple ribbon around its neck and carried it down to the flame tree. As always the boy disappeared at her approach, but Jess was sure he couldn't have gone far. She laid the dinosaur down in a nest of tall, damp grasses and then ran back inside the house and up to her room.

No sooner was she inside than there was a crashing sound against her bedroom door. She flew to the window, thinking it was the child. At first she saw nothing but night and stars. Nothing but the Southern Cross blazing overhead like a great brooch on a black velvet canopy.

She opened the door out onto the veranda. The floor planking creaked, and suddenly a huge, ghostly apparition loomed out of nowhere, filling the darkness. She heard the dry rustle of the creature's white gown as it was dragged behind him. She almost screamed before she realized it was Jackson sleepwalking on the veranda. Because of the white sheet wrapped at his waist like a flowing skirt, he towered darker, bigger. Jess's first impression was of a primitive male, powerful and dangerous, sinewy muscles rippling in the moonlight. Then he wobbled against the railing and she was terrified he was going to fall.

The child was forgotten.

"Jackson."

It was a cry, and yet it was softer than velvet in the darkness. She did not recognize it as her own.

His unseeing gaze swept the shadows, fixed upon her, and drank in the sight of the shapely perfection of her female form clearly revealed by her transparent nightgown. The blatant sensuality of the look unnerved Jess.

Her heart froze and then began to pound more violently.

"Jess . . ." He tumbled toward her.

Her outstretched arms went around his muscled waist. The shock of unexpected contact with his virile body made her gasp. A tremor went through her and through him, as well. The sheet fell away, and cool fingers touched hot, naked male skin. Yet even though her pulse was racing, she did not shrink from touching him. He was burning up.

She was afraid as she'd never been afraid before.

"I thought I heard something," she said, alarmed. "You should be in bed."

"I'm not going to give Lizzie to you!" he roared.

"Dear God," she moaned, "you're delirious again."

He staggered, and they both nearly fell.

"I've got to get you to bed," she said.

His room was too far. She led him to her own and helped him into her bed. To get him onto it, she collapsed on top of him. When he kept holding her, she could not get up.

In the struggle her corn-silk hair came loose and fell in a mass against his throat, where it was glued against his hot brown skin. She wore only a thin nightgown, and the filmy thing rode up to her thighs. Her legs were spread open across his, and she was straddling him provocatively.

The coarse hair of his muscular legs scratched the satin smoothness of her thighs. Her senses catapulted in alarm as she felt the force of his earthy, pagan attraction. She remembered another night when she'd lain on top of him writhing with ecstasy. That terrible night when she'd betrayed her sister and in doing so had destroyed them all.

He was sick, she fought to remind herself, attempting to break the spell. She struggled, but he merely tightened his grip and aligned her body more closely to his.

Arousal sizzled through her like an electric current, but fortunately his mind seemed on something else.

"Lizzie... Don't take her away from me again," he pleaded desperately.

He was so helpless, so sick. Deirdre had obviously put him through hell. The past year, when he'd been accused of her murder, had not been easy.

Despite her stubborn will to resist his appeal, a great tenderness welled in Jess. Gently she brushed his cheek, his lips. "I'm not going to take Lizzie away from you."

"No?"

"No," she whispered.

He breathed more easily.

Again she tried to rise, but he drew her inside the steel circle of his hands, flattening her once more against his chest. "Don't go," he said. She felt his warm breath waft against her throat. "I need you—now. I've been alone so long."

She knew all about being alone. For years, even when she'd been married, she'd felt alone. Jackson seemed so lost, so vulnerable. So hot and ill.

Another involuntary impulse of exquisite tenderness toward him seized her. She wanted to help him, more than she'd ever wanted to help anyone. He was much more charming and trustful delirious than he ever was when he was feeling well. She bent closer to him, meaning only to trace her fingertip across his brow. Instead she found she could not resist kissing his dark lashes. Then her mouth grazed his bearded cheek and last of all his lips, lingering for a timeless moment on their hot sensual fullness.

He opened his mouth, inviting her to deepen her kiss.

Violent tremors of fresh desire warmed Jess's melting flesh as her mouth lingered on his. She felt his fingers stroke her hips. Her heart fluttered with a strange, thrilled wildness. She caught herself sharply, stunned by the intensity of her emotion. The way she lay against him, it was easy to pretend he didn't really hate her. It was difficult to remember how impossible he would be when he was himself again. He was so sweet, like a sick child.

She felt the hard, muscled contours of his shape burning against her body.

He was no child; he was all man. It was the curse of her life that she had always wanted him.

His fingers wound in her hair. "Don't go," he whispered raggedly again.

Nothing seemed to matter at the moment. The only reality was his touch, his caress, his burning mouth beneath hers tasting faintly of the sugared medicines she'd forced down him.

"Don't leave me."

"You needn't worry about that," she murmured, loosening his hand, making her voice light even though she was more shaken than she would have ever admitted. "Tonight I'm going to take care of you, and when you're better I'm going with you to your property and help you make Jackson Downs safe for Lizzie." She stroked his forehead.

"Dangerous," he muttered thickly. "It's too dangerous."

"Nonsense! Why should you men have all the fun?"

"You're the most meddlesome..." His voice died away.

Jess knew he was too delirious to remember anything, but she kept talking to him because she always talked to patients in his state as if they were perfectly rational. "She needs both of us right now. I know you dislike me."

"I don't dislike you," he muttered passionately.

If only he didn't. If only she didn't long to feverishly draw him closer. If only she didn't enjoy quite so much the press of her warm, soft flesh against his.

"Well, even if you do, your property is so enormous—nearly a million acres? When we aren't actually battling, we shouldn't have to be with one another too often. You see, Jackson, I'm writing a book, from the journals I kept in India. And I've got a recertification exam to study for. So during the lulls, I'll have plenty to do. As you know, I don't believe in wasting anything so precious as time."

"Then why did you let us waste the past ten years?"

You were the one who married first, she wanted to say. The one who always belonged to someone else. Instead, she whispered, "We'll take care of Lizzie together."

"Together," he groaned.

Whether this was a groan of affirmation or misery Jess couldn't quite tell, but she thought he'd agreed. His single word was deep and long and husky before it died away.

His body went limp.

He lay so still that for a moment horror gripped her. She took his pulse. It was rapid but steady. Then she loosened her body from his and stumbled downstairs to get his medicine, water and some towels.

She chopped his pills, put them into a spoon filled with sugar and water just as she would have done for Lizzie and forced his mouth open. He knocked Jess's hand aside and sent the spoon and medicine clattering to the floor.

Jess thought of how docilely the hyperactive Lizzie took her pills. Like all men when ill, Jackson was more difficult to manage than the most obstreperous child. As always, such resistance increased her determination. She commanded Meeta to come up, sit on one of his arms and squeeze his nose tightly shut. Jess tied his other hand to the bed, pried the spoon between his clamped teeth and made him swallow the second dose. Although he twisted his head and coughed and sputtered and growled like an angry bear, she succeeded in getting it down him.

"Madame doctor," Meeta whispered in her perfect English as Jess was untying him, "he seems very sick again."

"He made himself sicker by trying to bully me. There's no real danger. He's as strong as an ox. Besides, though I deplore a certain tendency I have to brag, I'm on the job."

The worry went out of Meeta's dark, pretty face, and the flash of her sudden white smile was luminous as she looked up at Jess in that awestruck manner that Jess found so engaging. "You do not brag. I have seen you save so many who were not so strong. My brother..."

Images of frail brown bodies, young and old, lying outside on the pavement of her clinic flashed in Jess's mind's eye before she suppressed the pain of those memories.

"Hush," Jess whispered. Effusive sentimentality always embarrassed her.

All through the night the two women sponged the man with the hard, beautiful body that seemed to have been cast from bronze. Jess tried to ignore how muscular he was, how shapely. But as always when she touched him, even now when he was so sick, something outside herself took hold. She was aware of a ripple of excitement in the center of her being, of a treacherous softening toward him. Even when he was in the middle of one of his childish tantrums, she sometimes experienced this same keen excitement. Indeed, never except when in his presence did she ever feel so vitally alive.

She had spent her life chasing restlessly about the globe searching for something that was always just out of reach. Only when she was with him did she feel some sense of being where she really belonged. Now he was in trouble, and she was determined to help him.

It was almost morning when his fever broke. Jess sent Meeta downstairs, and because Jackson was holding onto her hand she allowed herself to collapse beside him.

He flung his arms across her waist and drew her close. She was supremely conscious of the feel of his large body all around her as he held her enfolded against him.

"No-no," she protested wearily.

But he was a man, used to getting his way. A man who had never learned to take no for an answer.

And he was stronger than she.

Deep within her was the desire to lie beside him and never leave the contentment she would know there with him in that soft, warm bed.

His arms locked around her silken body and she could feel the moist heat of his bare chest burning through her gown to the skin of her breasts.

She couldn't move even if she'd wanted to.

She struggled no more.

The cotton sheets were cool against her body as Jess dreamed of Jackson. She was back in her college days at the University of Texas when she'd been young and naive, sure that all the world needed was Jessica Bancroft to solve its problems.

It was a bustling Saturday morning in October. There was the hint of fall in the air, and the tennis courts were crowded with students who had no Saturday classes and were killing time until the football game and fraternity dances that night. The U T tower chimed the quarter hour.

Jess was sagging against the net while she waited for her twin to return. Deirdre had said she wanted a Coke. In reality she'd stomped off the court, mad about a line call.

The clay court burned through the rubber soles of Jess's tennis shoes to her toes. Impatiently she glanced at her watch. Her own temper was rapidly becoming as fiery as her feet. Then Jess heard someone on the court behind her. Thinking that it was Deirdre, Jess had squared her shoulders and prepared herself for battle.

Without warning a golden giant of a man in faded jeans and scarred boots loped across the court and swatted her affectionately on her behind. Furious, she whirled. He took one look at her scowl, laughed, threw his cowboy hat to the ground and pulled her into his arms, crushing her against the granite wall of his chest.

Never in all her life had Jess felt anyone who was so lean and rangy, whose skin was so hot, whose body was so brick hard. He was not the usual UT sort, but a kicker, a man used to the open ranch lands of Texas. His hands were callused but his touch was gentle.

"This court's taken," she hissed.

"I don't want the court. I want the woman," he drawled cowboy-style, smiling down at her.

His smile lit up a pair of beautiful blue male eyes. She couldn't think for the bewildering waves of warmth that heated her trembling body.

His features—the wide forehead, the carved cheek and jaw, the strong chin and straight nose—seemed chiseled from dark stone. He was blond, and he kept smiling. Cowboy or no, he was gorgeous, too gorgeous to smile in such a crooked, sexy way.

He wore a washed-out blue cotton shirt that stretched tautly across powerfully muscled shoulders. She felt mesmerized, frightened. She wanted to look away. To catch her breath. But when he didn't release her from his level gaze, she found herself gaping at him instead.

"Darling," the charismatic stranger drawled. "Don't get so riled."

Her face flamed. "Darling?"

She echoed his endearment in a dumbstruck tone, but apparently he thought she was using it in the same seductive manner he had.

"God, you're beautiful," he murmured in that deep voice that made shivers crawl up and down her spine. "What do you say we kiss and make up?"

"Y-you're crazy."

A lazy look of wickedness and delight stole over his face. "Only about you."

She shoved at him, but it was like trying to move a mountain of rock.

"One kiss," he whispered, grinning down at her in a manner she found absurdly engaging.

His long fingers wound into her thick hair, gently pulling her head back so that the curve of her slender neck all the way down to the provocative swell of her breasts was exposed. He lowered his mouth to hers.

She caught the heady scent of his after-shave, and it worked on her shattered senses like an aphrodisiac.

She swayed closer. Why wasn't she doing anything to stop him? Why was she just standing there with her lips pursed in readiness?

Like one hypnotized, Jess watched the tantalizing descent of his beautifully sculptured lips. At the last second, in a frenzy she tried to twist away but that had only made him more determined. His lips ruthlessly zeroed in on hers.

She opened her mouth to scream, but his tongue merely slid inside it. He tasted faintly of cigarettes. She could smell his hot, masculine scent, and the odor was warmly erotic. She felt the heated dampness of his skin under her fingertips. His wide brown hands shaped her against him, and every bone in her skeleton turned to wax.

She felt a quickening deep inside her, a longing so intense that she felt faint. He was breathing unevenly himself.

One kiss with this brash, blond, suntanned cowboy, and she was dissolving into him. One kiss was merely the appetizer that whetted her appetite for the whole meal.

Alarm bells were ringing in her ears. But she ignored them. Her arms circled his neck with a moan.

She felt him shudder and her heart leaped as she realized he felt it, too.

Suddenly he released her.

He had that lopsided grin plastered on his gorgeous cocky face again. His golden hair fell in sexy tangles across his brow.

"God, you're hot," he whispered, his low tone huskily pitched. "We shouldn't waste this on tennis. Your place or mine?"

His insolence snapped her out of her hypnotized state. She had no idea who this impertinent sex maniac was and why he might be kissing her, nor why she was so crazed by his kiss that her mind refused to work logically.

The most appalling thing of all was that she was actually tempted!

His place? Dear God!

Utterly shaken, her reaction was pure instinct. Her hand slammed into his brown cheek with all the force she was capable of. "Just who do you think you are, you lunatic?"

That got his attention.

His sheepish, charming look died instantly. He stared at her for a long moment as he rubbed the red mark on his face, his blue eyes smoldering with a rage equal to hers. "What the hell's the matter with you?"

"What the hell's the matter with you?" she snapped back.

"Darlings!" Deirdre popped out of the cabana with two iced colas. "Hey, great! Tad! I see you've decided to forgive me."

Jess and Tad glowered at one another, stunned, as the truth dawned on them both.

Whoever he was, he'd mistaken her for Deirdre.

And that kiss, that incredible, melting explosion of body and soul had been Deirdre's kiss! Not hers! For some idiotic reason, Jess felt like weeping.

Deirdre looked trim and cool in her white tennis shorts. She had brushed her hair, and it shone like puffs of gold. She handed Jess a Coke, sharing her own with Mr. Beautiful. "You two getting acquainted?"

"You could call it that," Jess replied coolly.

"Tad, meet my twin, Jessica Bancroft. Jess, my new boyfriend, Tad Jackson. He's on loan from A & M University for a semester."

The man and woman who'd just tasted each other's mouths inside and out stood as still as statues, glaring at one another under that hot October sun.

"An Aggie," Jess wailed with fresh despair.

There was an ancient pseudo-friendly rivalry between UT and A&M.

"And proud of it," Tad murmured drily. To Deirdre he said, "We already introduced ourselves."

"Is that what you call it?" Jess grumbled.

"Great!" said Deirdre.

"Why the hell didn't you tell me you had a twin?"

"Why didn't you tell me you had another boyfriend?"

These two questions were blurted by both injured parties at once.

"Because Jess always hates my boyfriends," Deirdre explained.

Jess felt the man's blue eyes assess her from that hard, sun-dark face with a sweeping, superior coolness.

"This once I wanted the man in my life to make a good impression on Jess," Deirdre explained.

"Well, you damn sure made one," Jess said slowly and distinctly.

"Did I?" He met Jess's boldly inspecting stare and returned it with a mirthless quirk to his mouth.

"Don't mind Jess. All she does is study. She thinks she hates men. Especially Aggies."

Tad's hand went back to his cheek. "I can tell," he murmured. "Still, the women who protest the most are usually the most susceptible to us."

"Men take up too much time," Jess said stiffly. "I'm going to be a doctor."

"All I want is to get married, but our Jess is going to save the world," Deirdre said laughingly, sipping her Coke.

Tad set his hot, insolent gaze upon Jess until she blushed. "Well, the world certainly needs someone to save it. But my personal motto is every man for himself."

His gorgeous voice was low and disturbing, and the vaguely possessive note in it sent quivers down Jess's spine, especially since he kept looking at her.

Jess's face felt warm, too warm, and not entirely from the sun. "I could tell that the first minute I met you," she said, feeling as if she were on treacherous footing as she baited him. "But it's not a very original motto, Mr. Jackson. It happens to be what nearly every human who has ever lived has thought also. Which is exactly why the world is in such a deplorable state."

Jess would never have insulted him had she known that there was no surer way to inflame his interest.

Tad forgot Deirdre and loomed nearer Jess, his mouth tight. "So you're blaming me for the mess we're in?"

"In a way."

His dark brows shot up. "And you're going to change it all?"

"Is it so wrong to want to make a difference?"

"No. But maybe it's just a little hypocritical of you. What can one person do? One... woman?"

She shook with temper and reaction. "How dare—"

He moved nearer. "You see, I could tell—the first minute I met you—that you were a woman with selfish impulses of your own. It's just that you're not as honest about them as I am." Again he let his hot, liquid blue eyes wander boldly over her body. "I know what I want." His gaze lingered on her breasts. "You don't."

"Not so honest," she'd sputtered, furious. She whirled on her twin. "Deirdre, th-this conceited... individual is the worst boyfriend you've ever had."

His smile broadened. "I take that as a compliment," the conceited individual whispered so close to Jess's ear that his warm breath tingled on her neck. "There's nothing I like better than standing apart from the crowd."

His gaze slid to her lips, and Jess had to fight the impulse to moisten them. She remembered his kiss, and the memory caused a curling sensation in the pit of her stomach.

She was hungry. But not for food. For him.

He was watching her. There was a musing curiosity about the look he gave her, oddly warm and gentle.

Deirdre put her arms possessively around him. "Please, Jess, please quit picking on him!"

Picking on him!

He laughed and lowered his golden head toward Deirdre's so that she could pet him more easily. But his blue, amused gaze was on Jess.

He was horrid! But as she watched the manicured fingers stroking his brown neck, caressing the strong jawline, Jess wanted nothing more than to have the right to touch the smirking devil like that herself.

The sunlight made his hair gleam silvery gold. His dazzling eyes blazed at her, mocking her. His white smile was equally dazzling and equally mocking. Aggie or no, she caught her breath at the masculine beauty of him.

Never in all her life had Jess felt more rawly vulnerable.

She spun on her heel and stomped toward the chain-link gate.

But their voices followed her.

"Oh, dear! I so wanted you two to get off to a great start," Deirdre moaned.

"Well, at least it was memorable," he replied huskily, unperturbed.

"But I don't think she even likes you."

"I think she does," came that silken, know-it-all tone.

Anger boiled up so violently it practically choked Jess. She wished the earth would open up and swallow her because the galling reality was that he was right. On that hot, miserable morning Jess had met and fallen irrevocably in love with the exact sort of scoundrel she'd always told herself she despised. And if that wasn't bad enough, he was an Aggie who belonged to her twin.

Forbidden fruit. Was that why his kiss had been sweeter than candy? And hotter than fire?

Was that why even as Jess quickened her steps across those white-lined, baking green rectangles of clay, deep in her bones, she already craved the sweet hot taste of him again?

Lying in one corner of the court was a brown, crisply creased Stetson with two jaunty turkey feathers sewn into the headband.

His hat!

Suddenly all Jess's frustrations were focused on that wide-brimmed hat with its saucy feathers. She took a sharp detour and made a flying leap right in the center of it and jumped up and down on the crown until it was as flat as a pancake and the quills of the feathers lay limp and broken.

"Jess!" Deirdre yelled.

Jess just dashed toward the gate like a naughty child.

"I can't believe she mashed your hat," Deirdre cooed. "And look what she did to your feathers!"

His laughter was a deep, reverberating bass. "What's one ornery tea-sipping girl to a hat that survived a stampede of ornery bulls?" He shoved a fist into the crown to straighten it. "But I will have to pick up a couple of feathers somewhere. Deirdre, darling," Jess heard him say. "How many boyfriends have there been—I mean—before me?"

So that dart had found its mark, Jess thought with grim satisfaction.

"None that counted, darling," Deirdre purred. "She just said that to stir you up and make you mad."

He placed his crumpled hat with the broken turkey feathers on his head at a jaunty angle. "Well, I don't know about mad, but she damn sure stirred me up."

Jess slammed her car door.

All the way home Jess told herself that she hated him.

But why, oh why, did she keep picturing him in her mind's eye? Why did she keep remembering the piercing quality of his shattering blue eyes? Why did she keep remembering the way his hair had slid like silk through her fingers? Why did she keep shivering every time she remembered his lips on hers, his hands roaming her body?

She clutched the steering wheel and groaned. "Why him? Dear God! Why him?"

Tad Jackson did not even remotely resemble the kind of person she had intended to choose for the role of her leading man. Hadn't she always dreamed of someone tall and dark, a paragon of easygoing affability and charm? Someone who cared about the poor? Someone sensitive and kind who would court her gently? Someone who shared her views, or at least someone who could be persuaded to share them? Someone, although she did not admit this to herself, with a tractable disposition whom she could easily bend to her will? Only recently she had begun to date such a man—Jonathan Kent.

Tad Jackson was the epitome of everything she hated.

But he was tall, whispered a treacherous little voice in the back of her mind. And quite handsome.

But he was blond, and Jess had never had any luck with blonds.

He has the most devastating smile, said the voice. And he knew how to kiss.

But he was a smart aleck. He was also irascible, arrogant and selfish—the conceited sort of male chauvinist who was used to bending women to his will. An Aggie with tunnel vision.

But Tad Jackson had stormed onto that tennis court and taught her that most unforgivable lesson of all.

The truth.

With one kiss that had burned all the way through her to her soul.

With one kiss that had taught her that she did not know herself at all.

With one kiss that had made her betray her only sister.

After that day, Jess had pretended she hated him, but every insult she'd hurled at him had been a lie. Jess had wanted him, and because she had she had ruined all their lives. For that, she had never forgiven herself.

And neither had he.

Six

Tad thought he was dreaming when he awoke in a shimmer of moonlight and felt his hard body nestled into the softness of a woman's. Long strands of glimmering golden hair lay across his arm. In the darkness his fingers had tangled in the gleaming lengths of silk.

Jess. The one woman he hated. Her arms were around him. He lay beside her on a narrow bed. Hers, he realized. In her sleep she had cuddled trustingly against him.

What were they doing here together? Vaguely he remembered her nursing him long into the night. She must be exhausted.

He hardly dared breathe for fear of awakening her. Carefully he slipped his arm beneath her head to hold her to him and then he lay there, savoring the warmth of her nearness, thinking he was crazy to do so.

The sheet was drawn back, and the strap of her gown had fallen down her arm. He could see the movement of her breasts through her thin nightgown; he could see the darker circle of her nipples, their beaded tips pressing against the gauzy fabric every time she breathed.

He inhaled the dizzying sweetness of orange blossoms. And even though he knew the scent and her beauty were a fatal trap, his arm slid beneath her neck and drew her closer.

She moaned softly, and her mouth brushed his temple in an attempt to fight him. "Jackson . . ."

He liked hearing his name, even his last name, from her lips. Dear God! What was happening to him? That he could feel such tenderness toward this woman who had betrayed him into a marriage that had nearly destroyed him. A phony do-gooder. A woman who'd deliberately kept his child from him for a year.

He hated her. But that didn't stop him from wanting her warmth and nearness now.

Jess opened her eyes and stared at him in sleepy bewilderment. Her muscles tightened and she began to withdraw from the encircling fold of his arms and body. She started to say something. If he gave her half a chance there would be a lecture. He could feel her beginning to struggle. He grabbed her wrists and held her fast.

The velvet moonlit darkness cast a magic spell. The soft night breezes blew through the window and caressed their bodies. Tonight, this moment, there was no hate between them. He did not mind so much that she was meddlesome and determined. Still, if she talked, they would quarrel.

He felt a quickening emotion. Something deep inside him, something he did not understand at all wanted her with him as she had been in her sleep, silent and trusting. She was the wrong woman. He knew this in his bones. But he needed her, as he hadn't ever needed anyone else.

Like an animal following some primitive instinct, he brought a callused fingertip to her mouth, gently shushing her before she spoiled the mood with some tart comment.

He no longer held her by force but by the terrible strength of his will. He kissed her brow tenderly. Then her eyelids. His hand lightly caressed her cheek.

She tried to pull away, but he dragged her back. For a long moment they stared into one another's eyes. With a drowsy sigh of defeat, she closed hers.

They slept again.

When Jess awoke, she could not imagine where she was. She was tangled in Tad's brown arms and legs, her head resting on his shoulder. His beard was tickling her cheek. One of her arms was thrown across his waist; his legs were sprawled on top of hers.

Dear Lord! He looked so dark and virile against the white sheets. Against her paler body. She flushed as she became shudderingly aware of his nakedness and maleness.

He was sound asleep, his skin cool, his breathing even.

Thank God for that. But she couldn't let him find her like this. He was so abominably conceited, he would brag most obnoxiously about how she'd nestled up so close to him. He would never believe that he'd been such an impossible patient, she'd been exhausted from nursing him and had simply collapsed beside him.

Funny, how warm and safe she felt in his arms. It would never do to dwell on that! Cautiously she slid her legs from under his. Once safely out of the bed, she couldn't resist hovering above him for a moment.

How tired he looked, even in sleep. He didn't seem quite so arrogant. The agony of the past year was etched into his lean, dark face. There were new lines beneath his eyes; his tanned skin was stretched across his cheek bones. His hands were callused from hard labor, his skin peeling in places on his palms. She fought against some idiotic instinct to brush the golden hair away from his forehead, to smooth the lines with her fingertips. He drove himself—and everyone else—too hard.

Only minutes before she had felt so safe and contented in his arms. Now she wanted to protect him from the world, from the lies, the betrayal, from everything that had destroyed his life.

"You sentimental fool!" an inward voice scolded. "He hates you."

He must never never know how profoundly he stirred her.

She bolted from the room and from the house as soon as it was daylight, determined to face Wally about the mower.

In the gloom of the gum-scented rain forest, she stared at the shattered mower. It was ten o'clock in the morning and although she'd only gotten a few hours' sleep, Jess felt unusually vital and alive. Behind her, watching her from the cliff was the silent child, with the stuffed brontosaurus clutched in his hand.

The bulldozer had excavated more deeply since she'd been here last. Her gaze ran up the height of the jagged coral cliff where sunlight flickered across the path of torn vines and rock art. Jackson was luckier than he deserved. Any other man of a less stubborn will and constitution would have died from such a fall.

Unfortunately, the mower had not fared nearly so well. The housing was cracked; the blade and the crankshaft were bent. She picked up a wheel and tossed it back down beside the broken aluminum carburetor.

There was nothing for it but to confess to Wally and pay for the mower. Nothing for it but to scramble back up the cliff and head to the hotel. She grabbed hold of a thick vine to pull herself up.

Without warning the sky darkened, and the birds stilled. A sudden eerie silence charged the atmosphere. Normally Jess was not superstitious, yet she sensed something.

A warning.

It was ridiculous. Unscientific. Illogical. The type of superstition or paganism that might lie dormant in the palpitating breasts of other ninnies but never in hers!

A sudden gust of wind stirred the hot, humid air.

The child vanished into the scrub.

Jess felt Deirdre's presence—warning her. Her twin had been here. Something terrible had happened to her here.

Jess's heart beat faster. Her trembling fingers tightened with determination on the vine.

Ninnyville! Poppycock!

For an instant the powerful tug of some dark force battled with her equally powerful will. With a cry Jess flung the vine and its snarl of emerald leaves aside and clambered ungracefully up the cliff. Branches tore at her clothes and skin. The roughened edge of a tree limb nicked her cheek, bloodying it, but she struggled upward.

Above her, Jess heard a footfall. It stopped cautiously. A tiny rock tumbled downward through the vines. There was only silence.

"Hello there," she called out. Then she parted the vines and pulled herself the rest of the way to the top.

There was no one there.

And yet she knew there had been someone. Someone who had not wanted to be caught watching her.

Tad sat at a wicker table in a high-backed wicker chair. Where was Jess, damn it?

The tropical sunlight streaming across the veranda was bold and hot, and yet without Jess to battle, the morning lacked sparkle.

Her presence was everywhere. The gray painted floor had been mopped with something that made it gleam. No cobweb dangled from the eaves or from the shaded corners. Tad noted these details with amused respect. Jess, and her Dutch-housewife mania for housekeeping. In the past he had loathed this nit-picking trait of hers. A bit of dirt never hurt anything. For an instant he reflected on Mrs. B., his housekeeper, who preferred complaining about all the housework she had to do instead of doing it. What would Jess make of the shambles he'd allowed his homestead to fall into in the past year? Not that he'd ever allow her to set foot on his place, of course.

Jess. Where was she? He had felt out of sorts ever since he'd awakened and found her gone.

Tad sprawled in the wicker chair and rubbed his clean-shaven chin. Lizzie had watched him shave—fascinated. The skin was paler there than the rest of his face, but it felt good to be almost himself again.

Around him a profusion of begonias, spider lilies, cunjevoi and orchids bloomed beneath ten-foot-tall tree ferns. The flower beds near the house had been recently turned, and not a single weed grew among the blooms. Jess had doubtless been busy there, too, after she'd finished with the porch. A high weed-infested, emerald green lawn stretched to the dense scrub where the parrots were conducting a symphony—the lawn that she had meant to mow.

Tad's fever was gone. He was miraculously better. Naturally, he took full credit. His well-being owed nothing to Jess's nursing. He refused to dwell on the memories of how she had hovered at his bedside.

He told himself that he had the constitution of a horse. It took more than pneumonia (he still didn't believe that diagnosis from Dr. Know-it-all) and a kick off a cliff from a she-devil to get him down. Except for being a little sore, he felt invigorated from a night of rest, from a hearty breakfast of eggs, toast, butter, jam and purple passion fruit.

He sipped his coffee and felt bursting with energy.

He was a new man—ready for a cigarette. He fumbled defiantly in his pocket and then remembered that there were none.

A new man, more defiant than before, after that empty pocket, ready for battle with the she-devil.

If only there had been a she-devil to battle. He was almost in the mood for one of her lectures.

Grumpily he eyed the vacant wicker chair across the table. Where was she, damn it? Messing around in someone else's business, no doubt. With her gone, there was no one to fight. And that bothered him even more than the nagging urge he felt for a cigarette.

What did Jess have? The minute he was around her she crawled inside him and took him over until his every thought, his every emotion, centered upon her.

He hadn't seen her since that last hour before dawn when he'd awakened in the moonlight and discovered her nestled in his arms. Vaguely he'd been aware of her getting up some time later, after the sun had risen above the trees. She had crept stealthily out of the room as though she were ashamed of having slept beside him. She had cooked his breakfast, but Meeta and Lizzie had served it.

"Madame doctor went to the hotel to tell about mower you broke," Meeta had explained in her curiously precise English, when Tad had demanded to know where Jess was.

So, now it was the lawn mower *he* broke! Well, when was she coming back? How long did it take to walk two miles to the hotel, fabricate this half-truth, pay for the blasted thing and return? Usually she was efficient as hell.

Though he felt bored and irritable, he decided to waste no more time while she was away. If he was going to wrest control of his daughter from Jess, he needed their passports. That way Jess couldn't disappear with Lizzie the minute she decided to.

He hobbled to Jess's room and began going through her suitcases and briefcases. While he searched, he discovered several journals in which she'd made notes about her experiences in India. Vaguely he remembered her saying she was writing a book.

He found letters from the Indian government warning Jess that she had been admitted as a tourist to India and not as a missionary, that she had no right to operate her clinic even though the neighborhood wanted her to. As if legalities would stop Bancroft!

At last he located Lizzie and Jess's passports in the side compartment of one of her briefcases. Just as he pocketed them he heard a sound outside.

Lizzie bounded into the room, then came to an abrupt standstill when she caught him rummaging through Jess's papers. Two untied purple ribbons dangled from her hair.

"What are you doing in Aunt Jess's room, Daddy? She told me never to..."

He started guiltily, but he couldn't help feeling more secure since it was he who now possessed Lizzie's passport.

"Aunt Jess came to Australia to help us."

"That's what I'm afraid of," he muttered.

"She better not catch you! Come on, Daddy, I don't want you to get into trouble."

"I'm not afraid of her," he roared. Nevertheless, when Lizzie took his hand and pulled him firmly away, he let her lead him downstairs to his wicker chair.

He lifted her onto his lap. "All I want to do is take you home, Lizzie. Is that so wrong?"

"I heard you fighting with Aunt Jess last night. Daddy, you were so mean to her!"

"I wasn't mean. It was your Aunt Jess! She kicked—"

"You were too mean!" Lizzie gave him a long, searching look. Then she jumped off his lap and went to watch a weird bug inch its way across a fern. "Why don't you want Aunt Jess to come? She can take care of me. She can write her book."

The last thing he needed was Dr. Know-it-all setting up a command post at his station.

"I'm going to take care of you," he stated emphatically.

"I want her, too! I'll be scared when you're gone. I need her."

There was no way around the fact that Jess had been the only mother Lizzie had known for the past year. Tad remembered Deirdre's neglect. The only mother ever! No wonder Jess held his daughter's heart in a stranglehold.

Lizzie's childish mouth trembled. "Will you go away and leave me alone all the time, the way you used to? What if the bad men come while you're gone?"

He knew too well from his own childhood what abandonment felt like. He thought of how lonely he'd been the year Lizzie had been away. A vertical crease of worry formed between his brows. He'd been thinking of sending Lizzie to school until the station was safer.

"Aunt Jess pays attention . . . just to me. You never did that."

"Jess has her clinic in India," he said lamely. "What would all those sick people do without her?"

"She got another doctor to come for a while and take her place. Daddy, you don't know her like I do! She'll be sad and cry if I go away and leave her."

"Somehow I can't imagine your Aunt Jess crying."

"But she does. When it's dark and she can't fall asleep, when she thinks nobody knows. I saw her one night when I sneaked up to tell her I wanted a glass of water and I couldn't find my purple cup. She was in her bed looking real sad and holding Benjamin's picture. She showed it to me and let me climb in bed with her. Then she told me about him. He was her little boy, but he was killed. She'll never see him again. That's why we can't go away without her. She'll be all alone."

At the thought of Jess crying over Ben's picture, a strange feeling gripped Tad. He'd known long, sleepless nights the year Lizzie had been gone. He remembered the shimmer of desperate loneliness he'd seen in Jess's eyes.

There were quick, brisk footsteps on the stairs. The light patter of sound grew louder.

Bancroft.

He had learned the sound of her years ago and he felt cheered, much more than he wanted to. She was back. Safe. For the first time he realized how worried he'd been.

Behind him the footsteps stopped. She had seen him.

He inhaled the scent of orange blossoms. Jess's presence hovered in the air, electrifying him. He had difficulty trying to breathe and there was an odd tightening in the pit of his stomach.

"Bancroft?"

"You're better, I see," came her crispest, no-nonsense voice.

He turned and saw her. The expression in his eyes grew momentarily soft.

She was standing in a shower of sunlight. Her hair in its prim knot was as bright as gold. Her cheeks were radiantly flushed. As always she wore a white poplin blouse buttoned all the way to her throat. Only this one had a torn sleeve. He saw a tiny scratch across her cheek.

"Did you hurt yourself?" he began, his voice filled with concern.

"I-I tripped," she said. "I-I'm okay."

In his mind's eye he saw the broken bits of rubber hose, Deirdre's diving gear scattered upon the sand. "Where were you?" he demanded.

"Paying for the mower that you—"

"That *you* broke," he finished. "It damn sure took you long enough."

"Wally got to talking about the hotel expansion."

"And no doubt you insisted on seeing the plans and sharing a few of your own ideas."

"As a matter of fact I do know a thing or two about building. I couldn't resist helping the poor, befuddled—"

"I knew it!" This was a roar. "You are the bossiest! The most impossible—! Poor Wally!"

Jess's face darkened.

"Aunt Jess, please don't mind if Daddy gets grumpy and picks quarrels with you. He's been sick, and he always gets like this when he sits around by himself and starts feeling lonesome."

"Grumpy?" Tad almost snarled the word. "Lonesome? I was as happy as a lark while she was gone!"

Lizzie bounded into her aunt's arms to protect her.

"You're right, darling," Jess agreed in her sweetest, most galling tone, petting her niece and retying the purple ribbons as she ignored Tad. "He's impossible now." Jess hesitated. "The pity of it is that he's even worse when he's well."

"Worse!"

Lizzie snuggled even more tightly into her aunt's arms, and Tad reined in his fierce desire to rant endlessly as he observed the easy affection and trust between the two of them. With a pang of something that felt almost like—like jealousy—he watched Jess stroke the bright red curls tenderly, her face softening.

"Look, Aunt Jess! He shaved it off!"

"So I see."

Jess's expression was an attempt at sternness, as she studied him. Suddenly she smiled, that charming smile that lit up her eyes. His own anger and jealousy vanished. He stared at her, dazzled.

"I'm glad to see that you haven't acquired a double chin since I saw you last, Jackson," she murmured drily, com-

ing nearer, inspecting the hard line of his clean-shaven jaw
with disturbing intensity. "Or a scar."

"What?"

"In fact, I'm surprised." She squinted, studying every
detail of the hard jawline, the stubborn, clenched male
mouth. "I was afraid you must be hiding some new defect.
Why else would a man as vain and cocky about being
handsome as you are cover your face with those beastly
whiskers?"

He dismissed vain and cocky and beastly.

Handsome. He felt inordinately pleased by her back-
handed compliment. In spite of himself, he grinned at her.
"I'm glad that you... approve of my face."

There was a brief silence. Lizzie, who had tired of being
hugged, bounded exuberantly outside to chase blue butterflies across the lawn. For a moment Jess's gaze followed the
child. Then she turned back to the man.

"I'm sure most women who do not know you as well as I
do approve of your face, Jackson."

"Ah, but you who do know me, and quite well..." He let
his eyes flash with delicious, joyous insolence. "You approve, too."

"That would not be my choice of term. I heartily disap-
prove of your conceit, of your arrogance... In short, of the
multiple defects in your character. And character is what
really matters in a man."

"Well, at least there's something about me you like." He
grinned at her. "That's a start."

"A start?"

The most horrendous, the most outrageous idea had
popped into his head. He was remembering the way Jess's
eyes shone every time they touched Lizzie. He was thinking
of his own excitement every time he found himself in this
impossible woman's presence. He was remembering how the
station had been this past year. He was bored with the

dreary sameness of his lonely existence. And sometimes when he was bored he did crazy, crazy things.

"A start in the right direction," he replied casually. Tad's heavy-lidded eyes swiftly appraised the slim, full-breasted woman standing before him. She was wearing her khaki shorts again, and a great deal of honey-toned leg was exposed. But he wasn't looking at her shapely legs. He was studying the stretch of starched white poplin across her breasts.

He remembered those breasts, those ripe, lush breasts with their enchanting strawberry tips, rising and falling against the hot skin of his chest last night. He thought of her narrow waist, her curving hips, the long, luscious legs and he became uncomfortably warm as he remembered how marvelous she was in bed. Despite all the reasons he had for hating her, despite her contrary disposition, she excited him as no other woman ever had.

He had always wanted her.

He had just been tricked into taking the sister instead.

Jess's lashes fell before his bold, deliberate scrutiny, and she held her breath in an agony of embarrassment and irritation. He lowered his gaze—not a second before she would have blasted him with a barrage of temper.

He was insane—to even think of it. But at the mere thought of it, his blood tingled through his veins, setting every nerve alert.

His eyes rose to her breasts again.

He thought of the danger.

But there would also be the opportunity for revenge. She had betrayed him. She had made love to him, made him love her, and then... He remembered the years of bitter, soul-destroying pain with Deirdre.

Quickly he looked away, but he had made up his mind in that instant.

He was going to take Bancroft to the station with him. What were bullets and bandits to someone like Jess? It was time he took the upper hand with her and used her for his pleasure in the same way she had used him.

He wasn't going to fight her about it, after all. He was going to placidly agree to her plan. Of course, they wouldn't get along. He would have to endure her busybody presence. She'd insist on running things. So would he. They would fight like tigers.

But that's what tigers were meant to do.

He smiled back at her. He was drowning in the inky, gold-flecked darkness of her sparkling eyes. Long ago she'd looked at him in that same way when he'd made love to her, the night she had betrayed him.

"I see my medicines and my nursing have done the trick," she said, congratulating herself immodestly in that manner of hers that usually annoyed him.

Naturally, like any man with a dash of conceit in his nature, he felt it his duty to eradicate such an abominable trait when he found it in a woman.

"I wasn't very sick," he said huskily, deliberately goading her. "I'm healthy by nature."

She frowned slightly. "Oh, really?"

"Really. I didn't even need a doctor."

Her eyebrows arched. She pursed her lips at his conceit and ingratitude. "Yesterday you thought you did."

"You may be interested to know that I've decided to let you come with me to Jackson Downs," he said magnanimously.

"You already agreed to that last night."

"What?"

"When you were delirious. You practically begged me."

"When we were in bed," he amended. "At such times, a man will say anything."

Her narrowed eyes went from deepest black to fiery gold—her haughty-empress look. And yet beneath the look, he sensed a profound pain.

She moved jerkily, turning her back to him and crossing the veranda to the side door.

"I'm sorry if I embarrassed you," he pursued softly. He said that only to prevent her leaving.

She stopped.

"No you're not, Jackson. You're used to treating every woman as if it's your intention to seduce her."

"Not every woman," he said thickly. "I already succeeded with you—once before."

She sucked in a quick breath. Her fingers trembled as she struggled to open the door.

He jumped out of his chair and sprang toward her. She backed against the wall.

"Y-you're just saying this so I won't come," she said.

"Am I?" He towered over her, laughing, conscious of a hot male excitement. Once she had made him want her, and she had used his desire for her to destroy him. "Maybe I'm saying it so you will."

Scant inches separated them. She was so beautiful, like a goddess, with the sunlight turning her hair to glowing gold, with the color high in her cheeks. He longed to trace a fingertip gently across the jagged cut on her cheek. She turned from him and struggled with the door.

Dimly Tad heard the doorknob rattling furiously, but he was overwhelmed by an urge to touch her. Instead of doing so, his brown fingers clasped the brass doorknob, and twisted it. "Here, let me help you."

She yanked her fingers away, but not before his had touched them. Her face was as vividly red as a bush fire. He was afraid she might pop a blood vessel if he delayed her exit a second longer. Still, under the circumstances, a parting shot was irresistible.

"You know what they say?" he whispered silkily.

"No. And I don't want to know, either!"

He studied the curve of her full, lush lips. He longed to kiss her. It would be so easy to pull her into his arms. So easy to see if he could turn her blazing anger into blazing passion.

"I'm going to tell you anyway," he said. "They say the second seduction is usually easier—the philosophy being that a fallen temple is more easily plundered. Anyway...I'm looking forward to your stay at Jackson Downs. You said you were writing a book. When you're not doing that and I'm not fighting thieves and murderers, I'll have more than enough time..." The passion in his dark, hot look mesmerized her, and she swayed toward him. His voice was low and charged with emotion as he finished his taunt. "More than enough time to take a tour of the temple...and explore all its charms before conquering it completely and making it mine."

Her face went as white as the painted boards behind her. Her mouth was trembling with rage.

He was filled with an overpowering urge to seize her, to taste her. Would she melt in his arms? Or would she fight? Either activity would have been most enjoyable.

"You look faint," he murmured solicitously, staring sympathetically at her.

"I've never fainted in my life!"

"Still, you'd better get out of the heat." He opened the door.

She stormed inside.

He heard her brisk footsteps leaping up the stairs, taking them two at a time, and he obligingly slammed the door after her.

Then he sank down in his wicker chair and chuckled softly.

She would be his.

Correction. She already was.

She was just too stubborn to admit it.

And when he was through with her, he would force himself to turn his back on her, as once she had rejected him. He imagined himself in that pleasant moment—satisfied, proud, thoroughly finished with her. In control.

Then a cool wind whispered across the veranda, and the shadows from the rain forest crept across the lawn.

Now that she had gone inside he felt alone, and the same dismal darkness that had filled his heart for the past ten years filled it now—jealousy, rage, love and betrayal. Most of all there was an all-engulfing sensation of hopelessness.

He told himself it was time she paid for what she had done.

Seven

Damn her. It was time he seized control.

For two days Jess had sulked. For two days Tad had endured nothing except stony silence from her, nothing except dark, closed looks of deep animosity every time he attempted to break through the barrier of her tenacious will and tease her. When he addressed her, Jess would answer him only if Meeta was nearby. Then Jess would point her pretty chin high in the air and say in her sternest, bossiest tone to Meeta, "Tell Mr. Jackson thus-and-so." Before he could reply, Jess would turn on her heel and huffily march away to some safer quarter.

For two days Jess had clung stubbornly to her anger.

Despite his frustration, Tad had never admired her more.

He was also pleased by her reaction. For he was sure that no woman could stay mad so long over so little if she were not deeply involved with the man she was mad at. Every time he was with her he had felt a new and furious tension in her.

The trouble with her was that she was mortally afraid of having her temple sacked. Or maybe she wanted it sacked and hated herself for wanting it. This second analysis was just the sort of conceited idea that appealed to him most, and he chuckled at the delicious thought.

But enough was enough. He was tired of her sulking and her pointed chin. Tired of getting nowhere when he baited her. On that third morning he stomped through the house looking for Jess.

Instead he found Meeta in an emerald-and-gold sari feeding a mulish Lizzie in the kitchen. Lizzie always bounded out of bed before dawn, only to pout and be difficult. "Purple!" Lizzie screamed. Only when Meeta smeared grape jelly on her eggs would Lizzie touch them.

Sugar and eggs. It was disgusting.

"Where is Bancroft?" he thundered, his deep voice unusually resonant in the quiet house.

Lizzie dropped her spoon, and grape-spattered egg hit the floor. At this sudden eruption of sound in her peaceful kitchen, Meeta's liquid dark eyes rose swiftly to his. "Madame Doctor has gone swimming," Meeta replied in her gentle, soothing tone. She looked slightly frightened.

It was impossible to shout at such a woman. He softened his voice. "Swimming? You let her go alone?"

Meeta nodded meekly. "I can't stop Madame Doctor."

Like most bullies, Jess always surrounded herself with human doormats who were too afraid of her to oppose whatever outrageous behavior she might dream up.

"Daddy, don't you be mean to Aunt Jess!"

"Mean?" He was all innocence. "Me? I'm never mean."

"You are to her!"

Bancroft had turned his own daughter against him!

"You eat your eggs, young lady!" He grabbed the jelly jar. "Without this!"

Lizzie was screaming the frantic word "purple" as Tad stormed out of the house and ran down to the beach. An endless expanse of glimmering turquoise stretched toward the horizon where a red sun hung low.

Jess was nowhere to be seen. The sun was turning the water a vivid red. A tremor of anxiety traced through him. He was remembering another time, another woman who had gone swimming alone, a woman who had never returned. If he had to stalk the whole island looking for Bancroft, he would. And when he found her . . .

He began to stomp through the thick sand, mindless of it until the coarse stuff practically filled his boat shoes and ground painfully against his bare toes. Half an hour later he was drenched with perspiration.

He was about to give up when he found her, dripping wet, kneeling in a spot of dappled sunlight where thick jungle and a jewel-red hibiscus grew to the beach.

He frowned fiercely, feeling so annoyed he fairly radiated grumpiness. She had already been swimming! He felt a sick sensation in the pit of his stomach.

Bancroft's thick, lustrous gold hair was wet and lay glued against her neck. Water glistened on her golden arms. She wore a plain black suit. This scrap of thin, wet stretch fabric was plastered to her well-endowed curves so snugly almost nothing was left to his imagination.

He was struck anew by how lovely she was despite her bossy, hell-on-wheels feminism. She looked deliciously damp and flushed from her swim. She couldn't have been sexier if she were nude. He didn't know what he really wanted to do most—to throttle her or to enfold her in his arms and kiss her good morning.

Her fingers were sifting the sand that wasn't sand at all, but tiny pieces of coral. She held her hand to the sun and looked at all the strange patterns and shapes of the tiny broken pieces. Her snorkel and fins lay half buried beside her.

He moved toward her until his shadow fell across her, and she looked up to see him looming tensely over her, his mouth tight, his face dark.

The sand trickled through her fingers, some of the grains sticking to her wet skin.

His gaze flickered briefly across her lips, which were as full and luscious as a fresh rose. God, she was a beauty. Some day, when he was in the mood for that particular battle, he would tell her that it had always been his opinion that she'd make a perfect centerfold.

Her eyes were wide and dark and frankly curious.

"Hello, Jackson," she said. Those were the first words she had deliberately addressed to him in three days.

He felt a fresh surge of anger that she had been swimming alone. "What the hell do you think you're doing?"

She glanced at him without even a trace of her sulky attitude. "Swimming."

"Do you think I'm blind?"

"You asked."

"Don't you know anything, Bancroft? You shouldn't swim alone. Especially since you're a woman."

Usually she would have bristled at such a tyrannical tone. Usually she would have jumped at the chance to defend an attack against her sex, but she seemed in an odd mood.

"I wouldn't think you'd care, Jackson."

He shouldn't, and the realization that he did terrified him.

She seemed worried about something. "You know I—I usually don't have a superstitious bone in my body."

"I know."

"So this is going to sound ridiculous—coming from me."

"Well?"

"Something drew me to this place."

"Something drew you..." He started to shake like an engine about to explode. "You little fool, this is where—" He stopped himself. Behind her he saw a small black face in the rain forest. Then the child darted away.

"I didn't go far," Jess said. "I stayed in shallow water. Just a few feet away in that clear water there are the most wonderful fish. They are beautiful colors and they all play around like friends."

"Friends?" He snarled the word. He remembered that other morning when he'd come to this same beach and the coppers had shown him the bits of rubber diving hose, all that had been left of his wife.

A shadow must have crossed his face because Jess got up slowly and came to him. "Where did Deirdre die?"

For a long moment he stared at the sand, at the way bits of it were stuck to Jess's slim wet ankles, at the way her thighs glistened.

"Here?" she whispered.

He looked up at her, into her solemn, dark eyes. "Yes."

She came to him and touched him gently on his arm, and he shuddered at even this light brush of her fingers. He sprang back from her.

He wanted revenge, power over her. Not the opposite.

"I sensed something," she said softly. "I don't know how, but I did."

"She was scuba diving not far from here," he muttered.

"Alone?"

He nodded. "She did it often."

"You're sure? Did she have...a friend...on the island? Anyone she might have gone with?"

"Not that I know of."

She was regarding him thoughtfully. He didn't think she quite accepted his answer. "It's a dangerous sport even when you go with someone else. Why would she come here? Why would she risk—"

"Didn't you know your twin, at all, Bancroft? She always did what she wanted, without regard for the consequences." He stopped himself and wearily raked his hand through his hair. "Hell. What am I saying? I never understood her. I only married her."

"Maybe you should have tried harder."

His mouth thinned. He turned away abruptly, not liking the sharp note of accusation in Jess's voice. He was uncomfortable talking about his marriage with anyone, especially Jess, the one woman who'd deliberately set his life on the wrong course. But Deirdre had talked too much, and to Jess. For the first time in a year he felt the need to say something in his own defense. So instead of walking away and repressing his feelings as he usually did, he squared his shoulders and turned back to her.

"Look, I'm not in the habit of talking about my marriage. Not to anyone."

"I know that," she whispered.

"So I don't know why I'm talking to you—of all people!" He stopped and clenched his jaw so tightly he could feel the muscles of his cheek jumping. "Whether you believe me or not, I swear I wanted to make her happy. I tried as hard as I knew how. Nothing worked. We both tried, but we never really touched each other as people. Not even in the beginning . . . before all the trouble."

"And I always thought you two were so happy back then."

"Happy?" Low, harsh laughter came from his throat. "We were in hell."

"But Deirdre told me—"

"Damn it! Forget what she said! She only wanted everyone to think we were happy. Especially you. Because of . . ."

Because of that night, he'd almost said, remembering the night when he'd made love to Jess.

He struggled to go on. "I wanted people to think we were happy, too. We had everything money could buy—rich friends, parties. At first Deirdre was insatiable for all the things she'd grown up without. But eventually she wanted more than just the trappings of a successful marriage, and I couldn't give her that. There was an emptiness between us, a coldness."

His gaze was tortured. He stared past Jess as if he were looking back into the misery of that time. "She had other men. She kept a place in Brisbane. Despite its vast size, Australia is a small country in a sense. Rumors got back to me. Sometimes she would stay away for weeks. Then she would come back and things would be better for a while. But the inevitable dissatisfactions always returned. I was the wrong man. Our life was the wrong life. I got so I wanted to bury myself in my work and never leave the station. Lizzie was caught in the middle. Then when the trouble started—" He stopped himself. "If you want to know the truth, the amazing thing about our marriage was that we stayed together ten years."

His mouth was compressed grimly with the memory of that time.

Jess took hold of his wrist and laid her other hand palm-to-palm over his large brown hand. He felt her gentle warmth seeping into his skin.

"I—I'm sorry," she said. "I always thought . . ."

"Jess—" he began, his head moving to the side in a hopeless gesture. "I know there's no way you could possibly understand."

"But I do."

He saw her loneliness. He sensed that she had known deep unhappiness in her own marriage, as well.

He felt the pull of that special something between them. He wanted to take her in his arms. He wanted to bury his lips against her throat where her pulse throbbed unevenly.

She held her breath. So did he. They both felt themselves inexorably drawn against their wills. Silence crashed around them, and for one long, self-conscious minute they both stared longingly at one another.

Abruptly she pushed him away, her fear of sharing any intimacy with him as great as his. Her brows knitted. Firmly she clasped her hands together and tamped down her feelings. In her most matter-of-fact voice she said, "Jackson, you two stayed together because you were both too cussed and stubborn to quit. There's not anything amazing about it. Not when you consider that you're about the most ornery, the most mule-headed person I've ever known."

His eyes flashed. "Oh, really?"

A gust of wind blew across the beach, and she shivered. He leaned down and picked up her towel, unfolded it and drew it gently around her shoulders. Her skin was icy cool beneath his hot fingertips.

He felt a rush of excitement. He wanted to draw her into his arms and warm her with his body heat.

"I hope you don't mind if I return the compliment and say that you are the most ornery and the most mule-headed person I've ever known," he said lazily, gently.

She smiled at him. "I know all about trying to make my life and myself into something they can never be."

"Truce?" he whispered.

There was a momentary silence as his eyes ran over her from the top of her golden head, down the thick, concealing drape of towel to her shapely calves and ankles. She had long slim feet. Elegant feet. He watched one of her bare toes curl and uncurl in the sand. Even her toes seemed sexy to him.

"Truce." She nodded in agreement. "For now. Until you misbehave again."

He watched the sexy toe bury and unbury itself in the soft, warm sand. It was a good thing she couldn't read his mind.

A good thing the thick cotton towel he'd covered her with hid those parts of her anatomy that so tempted him and so embarrassed her.

"Knowing me that won't be long," he said. "Only this time, you're going to misbehave, too."

"Not me. I always behave myself."

She shifted from one foot to the other, and the towel dropped a couple of crucial inches. He saw the erect button tips of her nipples straining against her thin black suit.

With shaking fingertips he jerked the towel upward so that she was completely covered once more. Again his hands brushed her body. Again he felt her cool skin, hotter now, beneath his unsteady touch.

It was getting harder and harder to remember how she had wronged him. Abruptly he drew his hand away. She was watching his clumsy movements warily.

She repeated, and more emphatically. "Jackson, I'm determined to behave myself."

His gaze traveled over the soft roundness of a breast. "That's something I'm about to change," he muttered hoarsely.

Her eyes shot sparks. Then she picked up a great lump of sand and threw it at him. That sent him half skipping, half hobbling out of her range toward the cottage.

"Don't run," she shouted after him bossily. "You'll just get sick again. The last thing I want is to have you lying in your bed again and me doing your bidding."

That stopped him. He turned back with a smile. His look was long and hard, but there was laughter in his voice.

"Honey, you should never have put an idea like that in my head—me in bed, you doing what I say for once."

She was scowling. "And don't call me honey! You know I hate it."

"That's only because you haven't heard it often enough."

"I have no intention—"

"Honey," he drawled huskily, "you're going to do a lot that you have no intention of doing. And soon, my love. Soon..."

Later, as Tad was servicing his Cessna, he was coldly furious with himself. Every second he spent with Bancroft increased the level of intimacy between them.

Dammit to hell, anyway! It wasn't as if he didn't know how treacherous she was. Why couldn't he leave her alone? Why couldn't he just pack his bags and take Lizzie and return to Jackson Downs?

He knew too well all the complications a woman of Bancroft's infuriating inclinations could cause in his life if he let her. But even as he told himself this, he remembered the feel of that soft, silky body clinging to his when she'd slept with him in her bed. He remembered how she'd nursed him so carefully.

And more than anything he wanted to banish that glazed look of haunted sadness he saw so often in her eyes.

Eight

Ouch!" Tad shouted, strangling. "Take it easy! I'm a convalescent, you know."

Jess jammed the cold metal spoon into his mouth, and a bitter glob of medicine burned all the way down his throat.

"Really?"

Tad was sprawled across the bed, on top of a pile of plumped pillows. He swallowed the last bit of medicine and wrinkled his nose. This nasty grimace was so overdone that even she laughed, flushing prettily.

Her face lost all its primness, and when she started to move away he grabbed her hand. "I know something you could do, if you really want to make me feel better," he whispered.

The pulse in her wrist quickened beneath his thumb. Then she stiffened and tried to pull away. He just held on, grinning.

When she saw that there was no way to escape until he let her go, she sank down on the edge of the bed.

"All right," she said. "Since you're set on being stubborn I guess this is as good a time as any to talk about Deirdre."

"Again?" he thundered, letting her go. "Hell! More than anything, I want to forget her! Bancroft, why are you so obsessed with her and the way she died?"

"I'm going to swim there again," Jess confided. "Only this time I want to go all the way to the reef."

"What? There are great whites out there."

"There's something about that place that bothers me."

"Something bothers me, too! Deirdre died out there," he growled.

"I'm not so sure about that. Besides, just because you're a man, you have no right to boss me."

He gritted his teeth and sat up amidst the tangle of pillows on the bed. "Does everything always come down to that—man against woman—who's bossing who?"

"With a male chauvinist such as yourself—yes."

He struggled for control.

"Like most men, you think you know more. Just as you think you should be obeyed."

Beneath the sheets he clenched his hands into fists. His mouth twisted into an unpleasant scowl. Dear God, she was impossible! How had he ever imagined for a minute he could keep her safe on Jackson Downs if trouble started?

She leaned over him to straighten a pillow.

"I learned long ago that I was perfectly capable of running my own affairs," continued Dr. Impossible.

She bent lower, and her breasts accidentally grazed his bare arm as she put her hand to his forehead. His skin flamed to her touch.

And he was supposed to be conquering her.

With the dizzying smell of her so close, it was difficult for him to concentrate on her inane arguments, but he managed. "As well as running the affairs of everyone else you happen to encounter."

She drew her hand back from the pillow. "The world could do with a smart woman to run it. You men have had your chance. That's why it's in such a deplorable state! I'll bet it won't take me a week to set things straight at Jackson Downs."

His dark face turned a bright tomato-red. Just as he was about to shout his rebuttal, she returned to their original topic—her swimming.

"It'll be all right, Jackson, if I swim there again."

"I said no!"

"I've got to find out what really happened to her."

His hand closed roughly over her arm. "And I don't want what happened to her to happen to you!"

"It won't."

"If this is a battle to see which one of us is the more thick-headed, it's me!" he yelled.

"I never doubted it for a moment."

He ignored that. "I'm going, too." He shoved sheets and medicines aside and leapt from his bed.

He never wore much to bed, and he was suddenly conscious of her gaze raking his broad shoulders, of her gaze running lower, following the ripple of muscle-ridged abdomen even lower to the white elastic band of his jockey shorts. He felt hot blood crawl up his neck to his cheeks. Damn, he was blushing! Like a high-school kid. He grabbed the sheet and covered himself.

She watched this evidence of modesty on his part with suppressed amusement.

Damn her for being a doctor.

She said only, "This is just the sort of macho nonsense I'd expect from you, Jackson. If you go swimming, you'll have a real relapse in an hour."

He was hopping around in the sheet, still blushing like a boy, looking for his clothes—which she had hidden. "What do you mean—real?"

"You know what I mean, you big malingerer."

He smiled sheepishly. Then his gaze darkened as he took in the sensual beauty of her. Her golden hair fell about her shoulders in silky disarray. He decided it was time to show her who the boss was. "Can I help it if—for some quirky reason—I don't want you gobbled alive by sharks? If I want you near me?" he whispered huskily. He let his sheet drop a little.

Jess's eyes fell from his face to his brown chest again. She caught her breath. "I know too well what you want. You told me, remember? I'm a temple and you're the barbarian who wants to sack me."

"And you sulked over that for two days." The soft sound of his laughter taunted her.

He came closer. His sheet fell lower. He was as hot as fire. As hard as stone.

She backed away. He had her on the run. Now it was she who was blushing.

God, she was beautiful. So beautiful, he was almost tempted to drop his sheet and let her see how much she aroused him.

"If I was sulking," she said in a prim but slightly breathy tone, "it was because you were so obstinate there was no other way to communicate with you."

"Never mind!" he rasped. "All that matters is what I want now."

Involuntarily her hands came to rest on her hips. Her gaze drifted sensuously up and down his seminude body. "What do you want . . . now?" she whispered.

The air between them was charged.

"The same thing you do, honey."

Like one spellbound, she came a step closer.

Her mouth was a lush, pearl-flushed pink. Her silver-gold hair fell wildly about her neck.

What he wanted, what he ached for, was to kiss her. To feel her lips quiver beneath his, her arms tighten around him, to feel the press of her soft breasts against his solid chest. He almost groaned aloud, so acute was his torment.

She expelled a sharp breath. "What I want is to go swimming. By myself!"

He had followed her into a dark corner. Her eyes widened as he placed one hand on the wall behind her with studied casualness and leaned forward so that his great body towered over hers. Less than an inch separated them. They were so close he could feel her body heat. So close the scent of orange blossoms invaded every cell in his system. So close the dark intensity of her gaze mesmerized him.

He lifted aside the molten gold of her hair, pushing it away from her neck. "Jess…" He said her name in a gentle tone, reaching for her, lowering his lips.

She swallowed and stood very still. Gently he tilted her chin back. His unerring mouth found the sensitive place at the base of her throat, and he kissed the fiercely quivering pulsebeat there.

She gasped as she felt his wildness. Heat spiraled crazily inside him. Then she drew away.

Desire for her was melting his bones. With a low groan he let her escape.

"I'm going to swim alone, Jackson."

His features hardened. He shrugged. "Okay! Heaven help the sharks!"

Nevertheless, he wasn't nearly so indifferent as he pretended. With sulky misgiving he followed her about the house. He stomped, slammed doors, and made every remark he could think of to goad her as she got ready.

She ignored him. All too soon she was in her sexy, glove-tight black suit and marching officiously out the door carrying her snorkeling gear. Quickly he went to his bedroom, gathered his own gear, put on his suit and raced after her.

When he got to the beach she was already walking knee-deep into the waves. Her smile triumphant, she waved to him as he hopped about on the hot sand. He was furious as he struggled into his own flippers. He watched her disappear beneath the smooth, placid surface.

Then he waded into the shallow water. She swam farther and farther away, with him snorkeling behind her at a grudging distance. It took them a quarter of an hour to reach the reef. They swam amongst a school of fish that cavorted so enthusiastically they roughened the surface of the ocean.

A nagging worry plagued him—hordes of small fish brought bigger fish.

It was difficult to keep his eye on her in the rough water. He watched the school of fish stir the water. She kept swimming onward.

Just as they reached the reef, he saw the elongated dark body of something huge roll beneath them in the water. Another immense sea creature slid by him. A shark! Doubtless, there were more he couldn't see.

A pair of dolphins cavorted in the distance. Dolphins or no, he didn't like swimming with big things.

At just that moment Bancroft dove. Her black fins flipped water and then disappeared beneath the turquoise waves. Something immense brushed his leg. What was it? Where was Jess?

Hell!

What kind of wimp was he to let her run things? Rage strangled all his other emotions. He quickened his speed to catch her, using long, hard strokes to cut the water.

He waited for her to surface. Then he grabbed her by the hair.

She thrashed wildly in his arms.

He let her go. He ripped his mask off his face. "Swim back to shore," he yelled.

She pulled her snorkel out of her mouth and lifted her mask. "What?"

"Sharks!"

"I'm not afraid . . ."

"Swim back or I'll drag you back. If we splash a lot that attracts them."

"I know that! What do you think I am—some idiot?"

"Honey, you just read my mind."

If they'd been on shore, she might have slapped him. Instead all she could do to show her anger was to narrow her eyes and tread water mulishly.

"Swim or I drag you. It's your choice," he growled.

"Some choice." But something in his fiercely determined expression startled her into obedience. She swam toward shore. He followed her, keeping a wary eye on those large, dark shapes darting about making a meal of the teaming fish.

When they reached shallow water and Jess was trying to race ahead of him, Tad caught her and yanked her into his arms. The heat of his body burned into hers.

"You could have gotten us both killed!" he bellowed. "Those sharks—"

"Shark," she hissed nastily. "I just saw one, and he was only a baby. The rest were dolphins. If you're so scared why didn't you just stay on the beach?"

His blue eyes flamed as they swept over her flawless womanly form. He wanted to hate her, but his hatred had blurred and changed into a new, more powerful emotion that he could not recognize. All he knew was that she was Jess. His Jess. Infuriating, stubborn, impossible...and yet his stomach felt hollowed out at the thought of something happening to her.

His grip was making reddish marks on her arms. "I came after you because I didn't want you to die...the way Deirdre died," he muttered roughly.

His words fell away, fading into the silence of the glimmering afternoon, and yet the low, throbbing emotion that had governed them remained.

Her face was soft, sad, hauntingly lovely.

The familiar gnawing ache her nearness always aroused was back in his gut, only stronger than ever before. There was a wildness in him.

An answering wildness was shining in her eyes.

He jerked her closer, his large hands spanning her waist, their imprint burning through the wetness of her suit. For once, she did not resist him. His skin was mahogany dark against her paler body; his muscles sinewy and dangerous, her curves soft and feminine, molding him.

The sensation of her body pressed into his inflamed him. The creamy mounds of her full breasts pushed against the hard wall of his chest. Every muscle in his body tightened, and slowly his gaze lifted to her face. She began to tremble as the full force of his passion jolted through her.

Her dark, glowing eyes met his, and he felt her soul reaching out to him even as she fought an inward battle against the arousal of her senses. The wildness was drumming in his own pulse.

He knotted his fingers into the tangled masses of her hair. He pulled her closer until he felt the taut, quivering warmth of her body responding to his.

It was as if every moment of his life had been leading to this moment. Waves crashed against white coral. It was all he could do not to resist pulling her down in those warm, roiling waters and taking her. But anyone could see them. He had to take her somewhere where they could be alone.

Her fingertips came up tentatively and brushed the wiry vee of wet curls that grew on his chest, and she pushed at him to disengage the arms that locked her body to his.

Her touch set him on fire. He tightened his grip and drew her even closer.

Her eyes widened as she felt beneath her fingertips the flexing of his muscles, smooth as hammered steel, latent in their sexuality.

He could feel her heart racing; her breath quickening. Her fierce excitement mingled with his own.

Their eyes met and held. He felt the power of her stubborn will battling against her desire.

Her body stiffened.

"Don't," she whispered. "You don't really want me! You never did. You were hers! Always hers! Never mine! You blamed me for ruining your life! Well, what do you think you did to mine? You used me! I never loved Jonathan. And I ruined his life because I couldn't."

His hands bit into the soft flesh of her upper arms as she tried to pull away. "No."

"I—I want to talk about Deirdre right now. Not us. Or at least I want to think about her."

"Deirdre!" Damnation! "Now?"

Jess's big, grave eyes implored him. "Now."

Every male nerve in his body was aroused. He felt enflamed, enraged. He was so frustrated he wanted to smash something to bits if he couldn't have her. Instead he watched the surf breaking on the reef.

Reluctantly, gently, he let her go.

For a long moment she looked at him. Then she walked slowly toward the beach.

He felt like a bottled-up volcano.

He bit his lip until he tasted blood. Until pain brought back his self-control. Then he went after her, throwing his snorkeling gear in the sand beside hers.

Their eyes met again, and they both felt the new awkwardness between them.

"It's gorgeous down there, but eerie," she said in a strange, unsteady tone.

"Hell."

"I could almost hear things breathing, sucking in and out like a respirator. I mean everything under there is eating everything else, and when you watch it for a while, the beauty turns into ugliness. It's sinister. Something beautiful will lure something equally beautiful to its death."

"It's the cycle of life and death," he said. "Deirdre loved it here. She loved the reef."

Jess's mood was pensive. "Why did she take the money and then come here? Why? I have so many unanswered questions. I don't think she died in the water. I wish now that I'd known her better. But I never really could because except for a few summers and college we grew up apart. She and Mother always had so little money that they had to live with my uncle in New Orleans. I stayed with my father and grew up in oil camps and lived all over the world."

Damn. Tad didn't want to talk about this. Aloud he said, "I know. She envied you and what she imagined as your exciting life."

"Exciting! Ha!"

As always Jess's haunted, lonely eyes touched some deep chord within him. He knew too well what it was to feel starved for affection.

"You survived," he said.

"Yes, but I dreamed of being part of a real family."

"I was part of a real family. It only makes it worse when your own marriage fails."

"Maybe. All I know is I always wanted to feel close to Deirdre. But I just couldn't somehow. Maybe it was a mistake the way our parents split everything, even their daughters, equally when they divorced. Dad believed in clean breaks. Anyway, my only chance to get close to her was when we were in college, but she always resented the fact that Dad and I had so much more money than she and Mother. She knew nothing about the loneliness of my childhood, of the sadness and guilt I felt about the poverty I saw in all those countries where we lived. Deirdre thought I had everything. But she was wrong. And now she's gone. So utterly gone."

A single tear trickled down Jess's cheek and she tried stubbornly to brush it away with the back of her hand before Tad could see.

But he saw. "Hey, it's okay to cry," he murmured.

"I—I don't know why I'm acting like a sentimental fool when I didn't shed a tear when I found out she was dead." Jess was weeping in earnest now. An incoherent torrent of words mingled with her sobs.

His fingers curled and entwined with hers. "We both lost her long before she died," he said gently.

"I think that's what hurts the most."

"It always hurts when you can't love a person you want to love," he said huskily, taking her in his arms. He smoothed her damp hair out of her eyes.

"But you, of all people! To think that you should see me like this, that I should actually seek comfort from you," she wailed piteously, unable to stop the tears.

"Really, Bancroft, your manners are every bit as atrocious as mine," he admonished gently. "And as for gratitude that I'm here to wipe away your tears—"

"Oh, do shut up." She tilted her head back, but her attempt at a watery scowl disintegrated into fresh sobs.

Again she made no objection to being folded more closely in his arms. Indeed she clung to him, and he could not ignore how delicious and hot her body felt pressed into his.

The light was fading. The jungle was deep and dark. The child had not returned. The hushed, silent atmosphere was charged with emotion. Tad knew Jess was vulnerable. Just as he knew that he was probably taking advantage of that vulnerability.

But such a moment might not come again.

Jess—soft and gentle seeking his comfort. He might wait for years for another such moment.

He wanted her. He had wanted her for years, and because he had, his marriage had been a double torment. He had been forced to endure the presence of a woman who resembled Jess so exactly, he had never been able to forget her.

Jess's sobs were subsiding. In another moment she would regain her composure and her independence and push him away.

He locked his arms more tightly about her. He felt the lush, overflowing fullness of her magnificent breasts against his chest.

He was a healthy, red-blooded male.

He had never been a man to waste his opportunities.

It was time he taught her she was his.

Without a word, he lowered his hard mouth to hers and kissed her. She fought him, but he kissed her until she began to tremble again. He kissed her until she was breathless, until she was limp and dizzy and clinging to him. Until her fingers were curling weakly against his neck and into the thick wetness of the golden curls at the nape of his neck.

Then he lifted her in his arms and carried what was surely the most stubborn bundle of femininity in all the world into the jungle.

It was the golden hour of his revenge.

No hour had ever seemed sweeter.

Nine

The sun sank like a ball of flame behind the coral hills, and the moon came up to fill the velvet darkness with silver-spangled fire.

The jungle was hot and silent. Tad was burning with a strange heat that centered in his loins.

His blue eyes fixed Jess like piercing shards of glass. Her own dark gaze widened uncertainly. Without a word, he carried her deeper and deeper into the thick, blackening shadows.

He knew his life was plunging down a fatal course. This woman was all wrong for him. But all he saw was her brilliant eyes, her mouth, soft and inviting. He slid his hands along the velvet heat of her body. A soft sigh escaped her moist half-opened lips. He trembled from the intense shock of his ravening need.

"We shouldn't," Jess protested as he lowered her to the towel that he'd thrown down to cover the soft sand.

She was so right.

"Don't you ever give up, Bancroft?" he whispered, nuzzling her throat hungrily, his mouth hot against her skin while his hands cupped her breasts.

"Give up? Never!"

But he felt her convulsive movement, when the palms of his hands grazed her nipples.

"So you intend to defend the temple to the last?"

"Yes, indeed." But her arms wrapped around his neck as if she would never let him go.

"The hell you say," he whispered, crushing her to him.

"The hell I say," she murmured with a languid sigh of defeat.

He kissed her throat more fervently.

"After this, I'll be the boss," he murmured.

"That's what you think." She flung her words at him hotly. "Jackson, tomorrow you'll pay—"

His long, strong fingers with their faintly callused tips ran possessively over the crests of her breasts in the wet bathing suit. He felt her quiver.

"I'm willing to face the consequences, honey."

His mouth hovered above hers. The fight was gone from her. And from him. For the moment.

She opened her mouth to him endlessly and let his tongue slide inside. She was hot and honey-sweet. He felt the savage building fire of her response.

"I've wanted you," he whispered, "for years. No one but you. Although Deirdre looked exactly like you, she could never take your place. Not in my bed. Never in my heart." What traitor made him say such things? He didn't know. He didn't care.

His fingers closed over the black spaghetti straps of Jess's bathing suit. Her breath caught when his knuckles brushed the smoothness of her shoulders as he lowered the straps. She grabbed his hand, stopping him when the top half of her breasts were revealed. Her breathing was coming in tiny gasps and her pulse was racing out of control.

"No," she whispered bossily.

"Your body's nothing to be ashamed of, Bancroft," he murmured. "You're lovely. Lovely. Your breasts..."

"They're too big. Vulgar."

"Sexy," he argued. He pulled the bathing suit lower.

"They make me feel...dirty, somehow. Men always..."

"They're beautiful. Magnificent. You're beautiful. I want to love them. I want to love you. All of you."

"If I could have had a say in the creation of my shape, I would have asked to be made as flat as two pancakes."

"Thank goodness, then, that for once you weren't around to give your bossy opinion."

She had many faults, but her breasts were all his torrid adolescent fantasies come true. Somehow he controlled his pulsing male instinct to hurry. He touched her, his hands trembling.

Easy. He had to go easy.

And his tender caresses, his hands, his lingering kisses, his sweet murmured endearments—all served their purpose. He took a nipple in his mouth and she gasped. At her response, fire shot from his belly to his thigh. He buried his lips against her tender, voluptuous flesh and suckled her like a babe until she gave out whimpering sounds of ecstasy.

Tad felt so full with male need he strained against his swimming trunks. Still, his shaking hands were gentle as he lowered the straps and removed the clinging wet black cloth. Shifting, he yanked his suit off while she lay back, watching him with deep, dark, languorous eyes as he undressed. Moaning, she pulled him back until he felt himself hard and hot and naked, pulsing against her thigh.

At last she sighed again, softly in surrender.

And so began a long hour of bittersweet delirium for them both. In no time their stubborn wills were swept aside before the power of an inexplicable bond. All their differences became nothing. She was sweet; he was tender. For a timeless, unforgettable moment they were one.

He made love to her in a fever. They came together, flesh to flesh, gasping, sighing, clinging to each other as if to life itself, making each other whole, her response as searingly white-hot as his.

Their hellish private lonelinesses fell away. Never before had either of them felt anything remotely like it. It was as if some vital part of them had been dead and was now brought to life. That other time, ten years ago, had been a dream to them both, something they hadn't let themselves believe in.

With bruising kisses, he tasted the salt tang of her skin. Gently he kissed her slender throat, her trembling breasts. His tongue dipped deeply into her navel. She opened her legs, and his lips moved lower to devour that sacred dewy, musky essence that was hers alone. She was a fire in his blood, a steaming, pulsating part of him, completely his.

Then she kissed him back, tentatively at first, on his lips, then everywhere just as he had kissed her. She trailed light kisses down his belly. There was no part of him which that succulent, feminine mouth did not lick and nuzzle. Soft lips, the tongue darting out, traced the back of his earlobe, curved into the hollow of his throat, traced a tingling path down his chest to his stomach and lower. Soft lips, hotter than fire, tickled him until he was wild for her.

Suddenly he could contain himself no longer. He rolled over, pulled her snugly under him and thrust deeply.

That first moment, inside her, was ecstasy. She was tight and small. Woman. His woman. Velvet warmth and soul-destroying sweetness.

His salvation.

His damnation.

God, she felt good—tight and all-enveloping, her nipples pressing into his chest, her satin skin, smooth beneath his fingertips.

Then he began to move, too fast.

She cried out. He forced himself to stop and be more gentle even though every nerve in his body throbbed with urgency. Their hearts beat as one. Her hands stroked the damp curls that fell over his forehead. He opened his eyes and lost himself in the blazing darkness of hers.

"Bancroft..." he whispered in a voice so tender he did not recognize it as his own.

All of her primness and bossiness were gone. She was blushing and shy and yet a wanton.

His wanton.

"Jess..." she corrected. A fingertip toyed with his hair.

"You are mine.... Darling Jess."

"Mine," she said with those glowing, earnest eyes.

Whether this was in agreement or a possessive statement of her own, he did not know. Or think to care.

He began to move slowly again inside her sensuous warmth. He was careful, matching his rhythm to hers, until passionate waves swept away all restraint and his control broke. Then they were two beings, caught in a cataclysmic swirl of flame and darkness and unwanted passion that carried them out of themselves to a place of exploding ecstasy.

When it was over, they were left shaken and clinging. Vaguely he grew aware of her whimpering softly beneath him, of her body shuddering delicately, of her nail tips pressing lightly into his back. His body felt unbearably heavy and wet with sweat. She lay in his arms, her eyes closed as if she were in a torpid state of insensibility.

There was no strength in any of his muscles. He felt drained, content, unable to move, wishing never to let her go, never to leave this moonlit bower.

And in that moment he knew he was doomed. Dimly it occurred to him that he who had thought to possess was himself utterly possessed.

He shrugged his misgivings aside, and stretched his lean, muscled frame out next to hers. Gradually his body cooled and he drifted to sleep, holding her warm body.

He awoke to a lovely dew-moistened morning. The leaves and branches of the ironbark were black filigree against the red dawn of a brightening sky. He felt balmy, at peace, more self-confident, happier than he had in years.

That was before he reached for her and found that she was gone.

She had done it again!

He jumped up, an angered, naked, abandoned giant. He was alone in the long shadows of the thickly wooded rain forest. She had left him. Without a word. Just like she had before. Why? Damn it!

He had been a fool to have had anything to do with her. He saw his involvement with Jess Bancroft like catching some dreaded disease; once you got it, it never went away. It just kept getting worse.

Where the hell was she?

He grabbed his bathing suit. It was gritty and cold, but no colder than the fury filling his heart as he slapped the suit hard against a gum tree so that zillions of particles of silvery sand rained down onto the beach towel. Then he yanked it on.

He felt the same total despair and rage she'd plunged him into ten years ago when she'd made love to him and then run off and served him up on a silver platter to her sister.

It didn't matter that Jess had given herself to him. All that mattered was that she'd left him. Again.

He should have taken Lizzie and thrown Jess out the first chance he'd gotten. That's what he would do now, as soon as he found her.

Quickly he raced up the trail that skirted the cliff. Halfway to the cottage, he came to the place where she'd shoved him off the cliff. The bulldozer hovered precariously beside the cliff's edge. He was about to hurry onward when he was startled by two things. First he saw a man stealthily climb out of the bulldozer and sneak down the shadowy trail.

Tad was about to yell at him, when he heard the secretive sound of Jess's voice coming from below.

Tad peered through the vines but could see nothing. Then he pulled himself into the bulldozer which commanded a better view. He could see Jess bending over a child. Had the man in the bulldozer been watching Jess, listening to her? With what intention?

A key dangled from the ignition.

The bulldozer was parked on the very edge of the cliff.

The bloody bastard!

An ice-like throbbing started in Tad's stomach. He sucked in a hard breath. All it would take was a flick of the wrist, and the thing could be started, put in gear, and it would have driven itself over the cliff and smashed whomever was down there. In his mind's eye, Tad saw Jess, still and white, crushed beneath the bulldozer.

He thought of his road train, which had been blown up on Jackson Downs. The cattle had all died. The driver had been severely injured.

In an instant Tad's fury toward Jess died, and he knew that he wanted to protect her at all costs. Even at the risk of his own life.

The bastards! Had they followed him here? Were they after her, too?

Tad wished he'd chased the man and beaten him until he found out who he was and what he wanted—who had sent him here. And why.

With a shaking hand he parted the thick green vines. Jess was kneeling beside the wall of rock art, looking as prim as always in her baggy shorts and white poplin blouse. Her face was serenely unaware of the slightest danger. For all her courage and stubborn will, she was a fragile woman. He was determined to protect her.

With one hand she picked up a thick bouquet of wild flowers. In the other she was fingering a tiny, shiny object that gleamed in her open palm. A child with matted yellow hair hovered at the edge of the trees. He was clutching a stuffed toy with a tattered purple ribbon against his bony chest as if it were very dear to him.

"So you thought I was a ghost?" Jess asked gently.

The child nodded. "I'm glad you're not her. I didn't like her. You gave me..." The dark hand tightened on the animal pressed close to his heart.

"And you gave me this." Jess took one last look at the bright object she was holding and then carefully pocketed it. "Thank you. She was my sister. Do you know what happened to her?"

The big liquid-black eyes rolled in terror.

"Tell me," Jess pleaded. "Don't be afraid."

"He come back, too," the boy whispered.

"There are no such things as ghosts." The boy merely listened. "She didn't go swimming, did she? Not that last day. She came here to meet a man. A man who..."

"He come back, too."

"What happened to her?" Jess pleaded. "Please tell me."

"She fell down. He hit her with rock."

"Where?"

The boy caught sight of Tad through the vines and pointed at him, screaming incoherently.

Jess turned. Tad sucked in a deep breath. Damn! Was that brat trying to frame him for Deirdre's murder? Was Jess encouraging him?

Tad grabbed the vine and crashed down beside them. The child took one look at the flying male figure. The whites of the boy's eyes rolled. Then his high-pitched wails began again. "He come back, too! He come back, too!"

Tad lunged for the child, but the boy made an agile side-step and ran. Tad raced after him through the rain forest, crashing against trees, stumbling over roots, but the boy was faster and nimbler. He slipped between a crack in the forest wall and disappeared soundlessly into the gloom. In his panic he had dropped his stuffed dinosaur.

Panting and breathless, Tad leaned down and picked up the dinosaur. "The little lying thief! This is Lizzie's."

Jess was right behind him, panting and breathless, too. "I gave it to him, you big idiot!" Jess snatched the animal from him. "What do you think you're doing?" She placed it back on the ground so the child would find it when he returned.

Tad was equally enraged. He yanked her into his arms. "What's going on here? 'He come back!' What's that supposed to mean—that I killed her?"

Jess caught the wrenching agony in his low tone.

"No, you dope. The kid was so scared, there's no telling who he thought you were! But I might know if you'd kept quiet and let me play detective a bit longer. As it is... Oh, Jackson, why must you always be so difficult?"

"Me?" His tone was offended. She was the one who'd abandoned him! If he hadn't come along, she and the boy might have been crushed under that bulldozer. His hand dug bruisingly into her arms.

"These things take subtlety, not Tarzan machismo coupled with one of your childish temper tantrums," she hissed. "I was trying to help you."

Her dainty chin was thrust out. Her offer to help was the most provocative remark she could have made.

"Damn your help! I don't want it! I'm not some poor, starving, diseased native. What on earth makes you so conceited that you think you can manage my affairs better than I can? You who know nothing of Australia?"

"I have lived all over the world. People are the same everywhere."

"These people are dangerous."

"I've dealt with dangerous people before."

"Damn! Why did you run away without telling me?" All this was a muted roar. He did not tell her of the man who'd been watching her.

She smiled sweetly, having regained control of her temper. "I couldn't sleep, and you looked so tired I didn't want to disturb you."

He didn't believe her. Not for a moment. But he let her go on.

"So I got up. When I got to the cottage, the boy was there. I dressed and followed him here because I think he knows what happened to Deirdre. I was on the verge of something important, if only you hadn't decided to be Rambo."

"Deirdre." Tad ground out the name. "It's always Deirdre. She's dead. Why can't we just forget her?"

He held Jess close. He should have cast her aside and walked away. If he were smart he would never see her again. But his eyes were drawn like magnets to the luminous pain he saw in her dark gaze.

He buried his face against her throat with the profound despair of one totally lost. "Dear God, I want to forget her." Dear God, no matter what Jess had done, no matter what she would do to him in the future, he didn't want to lose her, too.

"I can't, till I know what happened to her."

"It's too dangerous, you fool." His mouth came down on Jess's, kissing her fiercely.

Her hand caressed the sandpaper roughness of his cheek.

"Damnation!" he growled. "You're the sexiest, stubbornest . . . You're driving me crazy. I can't live with you. I can't live without you."

"We can't shut out the world and pretend it doesn't exist, Jackson."

"Damn it, I don't care how she died anymore. I don't care if my station goes up in flames."

"I care."

"Damn. Why can't you understand it's too dangerous for you to get involved?"

Ten

Don't give me another one of your bossy lectures!'' Tad yelled.

For once she obeyed him and stopped talking. Jess stood on the other side of the white-sheeted bed and smiled at him.

She was so damn beautiful it hurt.

The thought of anything happening to her...

Tad's fear was a knife severing every vital organ in his gut. Why was she always so set against what he was for?

The rosy morning sunlight was like flame in her tousled hair. A pink stream of light sifted through the bedroom shutters behind her, revealing the outlines of her body.

Tad clenched his fists to keep from grabbing her and pulling her toward the bed. He could still taste her deep inside his mouth. The scent of her still lingered on his skin.

Why her, dear God? He hadn't wanted any woman in his life. Ever again. Why her?

He opened his eyes once more and began to perspire as he studied her. The glimmering backlight gave her the appearance of a voluptuous angel.

He was still furious, but more than that he was scared. In the jungle he had begun to realize he was beginning to care for her more deeply than he had ever intended.

Hell.

He was scared of caring, scared she would do to him what she had done before. Scared that she would stay with him only for a little while, just long enough to ensnarl every emotion in his heart. Then she would flit off and leave him to try to put together the shattered pieces of his life again.

What a fool he was. He'd thought he could have sex with her and be done with it. Never with any other woman had sex come with such an emotional price tag.

One taste of her, and he wanted her completely—not only for her body but for her stubborn mind and soul.

And she knew it.

He kept staring at her. Inside the bedroom it was as silent as a tomb. The only sound came from the breeze outside rustling in the rain forest.

Then Jess spoke. "You are the most stubborn man on earth. Why can't you understand that I came to Australia for the sole purpose of helping you and Lizzie? That's not such an awful thing."

The muscles in his throat tightened. At last he rasped, "I don't want your help!"

"I don't care. I'm here to stay."

"Deirdre was my wife. What happened to her is my problem."

"She was my sister, and she came to me for help. She told me something—"

"I won't have you interfering."

"You can't stop me," she whispered.

"I'm trying to protect you, you little fool."

"I've managed very nicely all these years without you around to protect me."

"Forget Deirdre."

"Okay. For now." Jess kicked her damp leather sandals off, arched her feet and wiggled her toes against the bare wood floor. "You want me around more than you'll admit."

"What?"

Her luscious mouth quirked in a seductive smile. "You do. I can tell."

"The hell I do!"

She just stared at him and wiggled her naked feet. Then she lifted her fingers to her hair and shook it so that it fell in a heavy, silken mass over her shoulders. Slowly, sensuously she combed her fingers through it. It was gold and silver, alive, on fire.

His heart began to pound, and he could think of nothing but his desire to shove his hands into her hair. He stood stock-still, looking at her.

Her eyes were half closed, her skin flushed a glowing rose. She pulled her hand from her hair and let it trail down her bare throat to the shadowy place between her breasts. She unbuttoned the first button of her blouse.

He wanted to rip the rest of the buttons apart. To shred her blouse. To clasp her to him. To feel her naked body beneath his again.

"What are you doing?" His voice was harsh. "Damn you! Do you really think you can get around me with sex?"

That quirky smile again. "Probably."

He was intoxicated by the sight of her, even though he could feel the danger, close, too close, swirling around them like a treacherous mist. Somehow the bastards had figured out that she mattered to him, and they would use her—to get to him.

He was on the verge of yelling, of smashing something, of doing anything to distract himself from the hot, sensual tension between them, but the narrow bed at the center of the room made him remember the night they'd slept together there, her body pressing into the heat of his.

He knew why she had brought him here. She knew his weaknesses.

"Quiet," she whispered, touching a vertical fingertip to her lips and then blowing him a wanton kiss. "No more of your pompous shouting. You'll wake Lizzie."

Pompous! His eyes traveled up the curved length of naked, honey-toned legs to the cuffs of her baggy shorts, and he forgot the insult.

He should never have followed her to her bedroom.

It was too late now.

She softly crept toward the bed and leaned back against a bedpost, watching him with her dark eyes as she began to unbutton the rest of the buttons of her blouse.

She arched her spine, stretched. Her breasts jutted towards him. White cotton peeled away to reveal the lush honey-gold fruit of her silken body.

Inch by inch, the poplin shirt was coming off. He watched cool ivory cloth slide slowly against fiery hot, womanly skin as she pushed the fabric down her shoulder. Carelessly she tossed it away into a pool of darkness. Her breasts were covered by wisps of beige silk and lace. He could see the outline of her nipples, delicate and dusky pink pushing against the silk cups.

An unwanted thrill coursed through him. He muttered a low, strangled curse.

"And you don't want to wake Lizzie, do you?" Jess murmured. "Not till we..." The sensual promise of her unfinished sentence hung in the hushed room.

He made no further sound. Their eyes met. Hers were blazing, and they lit a fire in him. If she was trying to break him, she was succeeding.

With a lingering fingertip she slowly traced the swollen roundness of a breast. The movement was intended to arouse, to primitively provoke his male mating instinct.

And it did.

Normally she was so shy about her breasts. This about-face held the tantalizing allure of the forbidden.

"Touch me," she pleaded.

He wanted to so badly he hurt. His senses reeled with his longing. A muscle ticked savagely along his jawline as he struggled to withstand her. He balled his fingers into fists until he felt hard bone bite through flesh to bruise bone. His chest swelled with a deep, hard breath. He let it out with a groan. His mouth felt as dry as dust. It was no use.

Her striptease had him mesmerized. His eyes were riveted on her long, graceful fingers unhooking the dainty catch of her bra between her breasts.

She stepped forward, her movements slow and seductive, just enough to make her breasts bounce lightly. She came out of the darkness, into a shower of rose light that touched her hair, splashed down the length of her golden arm, spilled over the voluptuous softness of her breasts.

Everything in the room blurred and dulled and darkened except her. She was at the center of a brilliant fire, and the heat of her was filling him, too.

He was full and hot, ready.

His gaze was drawn to her breasts, to her narrow waist, to the curve of hip and thigh. She was radiant, lovely, and his body was racked with pain from his desire.

She had him right where she wanted him.

Her fingers on the tiny clasp moved; her breasts jutted free of restraining lace. Slowly, tantalizingly she removed her bra all the way, letting the filmy object dangle from her hand for a long second before she tossed it aside.

She wore only her baggy shorts. It was the sexiest outfit he'd ever seen on any female.

He was caught in her spell; furious, yet totally aroused.

It wasn't supposed to be this way. She wasn't playing by his rules. She was playing by her own, using the splendid beauty of her body to captivate him. He felt his will, his intractable, stubborn will, dissolving in the heated mist of his desire. It galled him that she could so easily provoke in him white-hot adolescent emotions and use them to control him.

She laughed softly, touching his chest with hot, featherlight fingertips that traced a ridge of muscle until she made him groan.

"You've got a lot to learn about women," she whispered. "It's time for you to abandon all your outdated notions." Her hand explored the athletic hardness of his muscled shoulder. Her gentle voice went on. "Love is more than sex, more than words."

"Who said anything about love?"

"Me. It's two people sharing, trusting, working together to accomplish common goals. It's commitment."

So expert were those hot feminine fingertips, he could hardly think, much less talk.

"Damn. Why are you so determined to complicate everything? I don't believe in love. All I want to do is protect you."

"Right." Jess lifted her long-lashed eyes mockingly to his. Her fingernails lightly raked the length of his spine. The hunger that filled him was a fierce stirring in his vitals.

Her creamy skin glowed rose from his look.

She was so beautiful, he hurt all over.

Tad closed his eyes to shut out the hot, dazzling vision of her.

But that was his mistake.

He smelled the beguiling sweetness of orange blossoms. He felt her fingernails dig into him lightly with that faint promise of passion to come. Then she kissed him. He felt her tongue move across his chest; her mouth sucked his nipple. A bolt of electric excitement coursed through every nerve ending.

He felt her fingertips again, gliding over his taut stomach and narrow hips. Then she pressed herself into him. She was molten satin against him. There was no escape.

He lowered his lips to hers. His tongue plunged into her mouth, tasted her, and she began to tremble.

His hands were in her hair, combing through the silken tresses. Loose pins rained onto the floor and waves of sweet-smelling gold flowed through his fingers.

He kissed her mouth, ate it with his lips and tongue; kissed her face, her ears, her throat. He bent low and softly kissed one shell-pink nipple. He picked her up and carried her to the bed. Then he pushed her down on cool cotton sheets and covered her body with his.

Her cheeks were rose-colored like the dawn. Tousled gold curls lay in a riot of glimmering waves on the pillow. Her gaze was deep, dark, intense.

A vast silence seemed to envelop them.

Possessively she circled him with her hand and guided him toward her.

Then it began—the throbbing urgency that blocked rational thought. The hot, insistent craving that possessed every nerve in his body.

There was only woman. Only this woman. Only his fierce, raging need. It no longer mattered that she refused to behave the way he thought she should. He wanted her exactly as she was.

His hands were eager, trembling. He kissed her, roughly, softly, with a keen, seeking urgency, fusing their two naked bodies together.

He moved over her.

Her hands came together in an urgent knot at the base of his spine. She opened her body endlessly to his.

And he felt the world slip away.

She touched him everywhere.

The room whitened and exploded in a sudden and all-consuming, soul-filling lava fire.

And two wary, stubborn spirits were molded into one—for that brief instant.

A damp sheen of perspiration covered them both.

Tad wanted to own her, but he knew he never could.

He clasped her tightly, burying his face in her hair, inhaling the smell of her, the scent and feel of clean, silken hair and sweet, voluptuous woman flesh, the exquisite sensation of her sated body against his.

She began to laugh softly, a bit too conceitedly he thought. "That was really something," she purred. "I..."

"Yes. You're quite something. I know you just did that to throw me off balance."

"You were screaming and ranting the whole way back from the jungle. You refused to listen to my very logical lecture. I had to get your attention."

"You damn sure got it."

"You wouldn't listen to reason."

"Neither would you," he whispered against her ear.

"I wanted to show you that we are partners. We belong together."

"I always knew that."

"But I mean together—in everything. Not just in bed. We will be equals."

"A woman can never be equal to a man."

"Nor a man to a woman—literally, but I want to help you raise Lizzie. I will always have my career, my work outside our relationship that is as important to me as yours is to you.

But first, I want to help you find out what's going on at the station, what happened to Deirdre..."

He had bedded Jess twice. So she thought she had him.

He sat bolt upright, his body tense. "Why can't you understand that this is my battle? This is Australia."

"The male chauvinist's last domain," she murmured with gentle sarcasm. "But don't you see, Australia's no different than any other place. It's you and I who matter. If we love each other, your battle is my battle. And vice versa. I love you, and that means there is nothing, nothing I wouldn't do for you."

She said this sweetly with her warm eyes caressing him. But he knew that honeyed tone and that velvet gaze were like the sugar she used to coat her bitter medicines. Beneath the feminine wiles she meant business.

Our battle. Hell! She was so strong, so certain. But she knew nothing of what she was getting herself into.

He felt strange, unsure, not himself at all. He was possessive, jealous, protective, sick at the thought of something happening to her. He hadn't wanted another woman in his life, ever again. Especially not one like her. He was fiercely independent. He didn't want her meddling in his life, but he didn't want her out of it, either.

They were at an impasse. Each eyed the other warily, and while they did they lapsed into an uneasy silence.

A long time later she said, "I know it's probably hard for you to trust...a woman...after your marriage to Deirdre. Especially to trust me. But don't you see, trusting you is not so easy for me, either. You ruined my life, too. Only I'm not the sort to cling to a grudge the way you do."

As always it galled him the way she saw herself in a superior light to him. "I ruined your life?" His eyes darkened to midnight blue. "That's a joke."

"When we were all in college, you used me to get Deirdre."

"What?"

"You wanted to make her jealous so she'd marry you."

He laughed harshly in disbelief. Gently, roughly, he gathered Jess into his arms. "I never used you. And I never lied. It was the other way around."

"No!"

"Then explain why you went to bed with me, pretending you were Deirdre."

"Jackson, you knew who I was all the time."

"No I didn't. Not until after I married Deirdre."

"She told me you did...after..."

"I don't give a damn what she told you!" He was silent, his face dark and tensed.

Jess wrenched herself free and escaped to the farthest edge of the bed. "I remember that night like it was yesterday. I loved you. I thought you loved her."

"That sounds about normal for our relationship."

"Don't be sarcastic, Jackson."

He nodded grimly for her to go on.

"Well, that night I was in my lab studying. Deirdre stormed in, sobbing out some nonsense about you having broken up with her because you loved me. I was stunned. You and I always quarreled. You had never even hinted you loved me in any way. I decided it was just some trick of yours to make Deirdre jealous. I swore it wasn't true. Then I went looking for you to have it out with you for using me in one of your lovers' quarrels. I didn't realize until later that I had accidentally picked up her sweater instead of mine."

"It was dark," he muttered. "So when I ran into you outside your dorm in her sweater, I assumed you were her. The way I did that first day on the tennis court. Why the hell didn't you tell me who you were?"

"I don't know. I always acted crazy when I got around you. Maybe because I thought I could get to the bottom of what was wrong between Deirdre and you better if you thought I was her. Maybe because I was mad. I just asked you if you really meant it when you said you were in love with Jess.''

"And I said I did.''

"That made me even madder. I thought you were trying to make her jealous. I started to cry and begged you to stop tormenting me. You took me in your arms. You thought you were comforting Deirdre. Things got pretty hot between us very quickly.''

"They always do. I don't know why that didn't tip me off.''

"We made love,'' she whispered.

"And all the time I could hardly believe it was the same Deirdre I'd jilted. Always before she'd turned to ice when I touched her. The Jackson money was the only thing about me that ever turned her on,'' he said bitterly.

"Yes, but you see, I didn't know that then. Just as I was about to tell you who I was, you stopped me, and said, 'Marry me, Deirdre. I only said those things about Jess to make you jealous.' Jackson, in that instant my heart froze. It was like death.''

"All I knew was I had to have the woman who set me on fire. I really did think you were Deirdre.''

"Don't lie to me!'' Jess cried.

"I'm not.'' His hand clamped savagely around her wrist. "I didn't know till the honeymoon that I'd married the wrong twin. And then I hated you because I thought you'd slept with me to trick me into marrying her.''

"Dear God. Oh, Jackson. I loved you so much. After you asked me to marry you, thinking I was Deirdre, I was so hurt. You loved her, wanted to marry her, but I'd slept with you. That's why I ran away.

"All I could think of was Deirdre. How was I going to face her with what I'd done? I couldn't at first, so I just sat in a café drinking one coffee after another. Finally I realized there was nothing I could say. I just had to face her. But when I got back to our room, Deirdre was gone.''

Jess's voice became desolate. "She'd left me a note thanking me for fixing everything. The note said that you'd just said you loved me to make her jealous. That I'd seduced you, and you'd known all along who I was.''

"Damn her.'' He slammed his fist against a bedpost.

"I felt so cheap, so used. She told me she and you had run away to get married. She and you...together... I—I didn't know what to do. For days I was filled with the most bitter despair. After that, nothing mattered any more. I tried to tell myself that you were the wrong kind of man for me, that we were both better off. Eventually I married Jonathan. But, it's never any good—fooling yourself. My marriage didn't work out. I began my career, had a child. You know the rest. Deirdre finally told me most of the truth last year in Calcutta.''

"Deirdre...'' Tad's features twisted with bitterness. The memory of her filled him with black emotion. "All the time I blamed you for ruining my life, when it was her. I should have known.''

"The past is behind us,'' Jess whispered, but her voice was haunted. "You really loved me?''

Her pale, distraught face touched Tad, and the layer of icy distrust in his heart began to melt.

"Yes, I loved you. Only you,'' he whispered. "Always. Only you. Even when I was married to her. Even when I hated you.''

Her face remained bloodless.

He took her cold hand in his. "We were both such fools. But it's over,'' he said gently. He brought her fingers to his warm lips. "All that matters now is our future.''

"Yes,'' she said, "our future.''

"You will leave Australia, take Lizzie, and I will follow after I've taken care of things here.''

Her hand tensed, and although it was small and delicate in his larger one he felt her strength. Her warm, resolute gaze moved over him lovingly.

"You still don't get it, do you? I mean how it's going to be with us?" she asked quietly. "I stay. Beside you. Always. I could never feel safe anywhere if I were afraid for you."

He felt vaguely alarmed. "You talk like a man," he muttered uneasily.

"No, you're just a male chauvinist clinging to the dark ages." She lifted her arms high above her head and stretched languorously. "You're a man, but that doesn't make you my superior or my boss. And thinking that you aren't doesn't make me any less of a woman." The brilliant morning rays shining through the shutters bathed her body in a soft, golden, iridescent glow. "Or haven't you noticed?"

His eyes ran boldly over her. He kept watching her. She moved, smiling knowingly up at him, and the morning sun gilded her soft, lush curves, warmed creamy, pale flesh.

"I love you," she said, "and that makes us one."

Did it? Could he accept her on her terms? Had they in reality always been his terms, too? Did she know him better than he knew himself? All his life he'd been alone. Until now. With her.

But could he risk her safety?

He could feel the danger, all-enveloping, a menacing presence in the bedroom. She might think she was tough, but the bastards would kill her in a second, if he gave them the chance.

He was about to argue, but she melted against him, nestling her body between his thighs. As always she was a perfect fit.

She caressed his powerful, muscular chest with light fingertips.

He couldn't think.

"We are one," she said. "Partners."

"But..."

She began to stroke him. His body turned to flame.

"Partners for life," she said. "In everything."

She lowered her hand and touched that one part of him that electrified every cell in his body.

"It won't work," he growled weakly.

She bent her face to his cheek. "Wanta make a bet?"

He felt that moist, feminine tongue, seeking and searching near the sensitive spot beneath his earlobe, turning his blood to rivers of fire.

Even as he was protesting, he rolled her beneath him.

Sun-darkened skin covered her paler, silkier flesh.

"No." He whispered. "No."

But his body said yes.

Eleven

A mist rose from the damp earth of the rain forest, and under the flame of a new sun the trees wore a mantle of glowing wet.

Tad sprinted soundlessly down the narrow trail. It was still and hot. Muggy. His cotton shirt was glued to his body from his long run. But he didn't care. The weather forecast was perfect for flying.

He was leaving Jess! There would be hell to pay!

Tad remembered all her fierce arguments about her determination to help him fight his battles. He felt like a heel, running away from her, pretending he was going fishing with Wally when in reality he was flying back to Jackson Downs. But late yesterday afternoon, he'd gotten a message through Wally from Kirk that things were heating up on Jackson Downs. The Martin homestead had been attacked, and Noelle and Granger were on guard against the threat of another. Tad had called Ian McBain, and Ian was flying to Jackson Downs to assist in the signing of all the legal documents in regard to the sale of the station.

Tad was determined to keep Jess from meddling in his dangerous affairs. It was time she learned she could only push him so far.

Tad didn't trust the Martins, even though they were the prospective buyers for Jackson Downs. It was odd that Granger was buying him out. Granger had always had a weak stomach for violence. Odd how his determination had never wavered despite all the trouble. Odder still, when not so long ago it had been Granger selling out to him. And yet, if Granger were behind it all, why would he attack his own homestead?

Tad heard his Cessna even before he saw it. That was the first inkling that something was wrong.

His heart raced with panic as he slung his duffel bag over his shoulder and began to run even faster down the narrow path through the rain forest. He broke through the trees and saw his white, orange-trimmed plane.

The propeller was a big fan. The blades blurred, turning, thinner and faster as the engine sound grew stronger and deeper.

Who the hell had dared . . .

Tad remembered the man in the bulldozer. Was he back, sabotaging the Cessna?

Then Tad saw her.

He should have known.

Jess waved jauntily to him from the cockpit. A pale-faced Meeta and an excited Lizzie were bundled into the seats behind her.

Rage filled him. He should have realized getting away from her had been too easy.

How sleepily she'd lain against the pillow this morning. The smell of orange blossoms had been dulled by the warm, male scent of him still clinging to her skin. How docilely she had allowed him to kiss her goodbye before he'd left, jogging the long way to the resort as a safety precaution, and thereby giving her enough time to dress and beat him to the plane. He had planned to leave her on the island in Wally's care because Wally had assured him there wouldn't be a boat or plane to or from the island for three days. Somehow she'd gotten around Wally.

Jess opened the cockpit door and smiled down at him brightly. And her smile made him volcanic.

Bancroft was in his plane, disobeying him, having done God alone knew what to a delicate piece of machinery he'd babied for years. She stuck a denim-clad leg out of the door and he grabbed her by the thigh and pulled her, kicking all the way down, to the ground.

She threw him off balance, toppling him and sending him sprawling so that he lay flat on his back beside the chock. She fell on top of him, straddling him. He had a fleeting sensation of her softness fitting his tight, straining male muscles. He seized her wrists and held them fast so that she couldn't escape.

"What do you think you're doing?" he yelled over the roar of the engine.

"Going with you, you low-down sneak," she yelled back.

"I told you yesterday, you were to take Lizzie to Calcutta while I went back to the station."

His jeans were skintight. He could feel the warmth of her seeping inside him.

"But I never agreed," she began.

"That's why I was leaving without—"

"I'm not letting you sell out. What will that settle?"

"Everything! I've been losing money for three years. People are getting killed."

"No."

"What do you mean *no*? We're talking about my property!"

"I mean we're not leaving till we know what's going on!"

"I'm tired of fighting everybody in this country all alone." A muscle ticked in his hard jawline.

Her expression softened. "You're not alone—not anymore."

His eyes moved slowly over her with insulting deliberation. His hard mouth thinned as he regarded her usually sleek hair tumbling about her shoulders. His gaze fell to her heaving breasts beneath her tight cotton shirt. He thought of the dirty bastards getting to her in some way, touching her, hurting her. Damnation! For all her courage and heart, she was only a woman.

"And that terrifies me more than anything," he said, not ungently. "Don't you see, I can't stand it if they use you. If you and Lizzie are there, I won't be able to think."

"We're in this together."

"No."

"Deirdre was my sister. She was probably killed because of what was going on at Jackson Downs."

"And I don't want you to die the way she did."

"If you think I'm the kind of woman you can safely jettison like an unwanted bundle of cargo behind the lines of battle, you're crazy."

"If you give a damn about me or Lizzie, for once you'll do what you're told."

"I'm not a coward—even if you are."

"What?"

"Who's the brave boy that's selling everything he and his family owns and clearing out?"

"It isn't like that."

"Oh, it isn't? Then tell me how it is."

"It's none of your damned business."

"You can't shut me out, the way you always shut Deirdre out. I'm making it my business. I love Lizzie like she was my own."

"Sweet Jesus. I won't have you meddling in my life."

"You and Lizzie are my life, so it's my life, too."

"If we're ever to have a future together..."

"Don't threaten me with that, you low-down bully."

He continued. "You're not coming to Jackson Downs, and that's final. I won't have a woman running my show. What I'm saying is that if you do, we're finished. Do you understand me? Finished!"

A string of violently muttered curses burst forth from the pilot. This fresh outburst made Jess's heart grip with pain. She tilted her head just a little and caught a sideways glance of the irascible Jackson, who sat stiffly beside her at the controls wearing a look of sour gloom. He was doing everything he could to inflict his dark mood on her and make the journey as abominable as possible.

He really did look like he hated her. She turned away before he could see how nervous her forced smile really was.

The four of them were in the plane high over the flat red parched endlessness of Queensland's center, having left the dazzling aqua waters and all greenery behind hours ago.

In the back Lizzie and Meeta were as quiet as mice. Poor Meeta was probably terrified. She was too kind and too obedient. Inconvenient character traits when it came to dealing with a man of Jackson's stubborn temperament.

There were times when a woman had to assert herself. Jess had done the only sensible thing. There was a crisis at the station. Jackson had been too caught up in his chauvinistic views of gallantry to be reasonable. Clearly someone needed to take charge; clearly she was the one to do it.

He would have to forgive her eventually. But every time she looked at him and saw his black expression of fury, she paled as she considered the faint possibility that he would not.

Jess had to fight to maintain a triumphant attitude, a pretended eagerness for every detail of the monotonous scenery. She and Jackson had flown in tense silence most of the way. Like all men, Jackson was able to sulk ferociously when he didn't get his way. Well, that was just fine—even if his sulking was a constant oppressive force. Even if his doing so was ruining what might have been her first exhilarating view of Australia. Even if it took all of her considerable willpower to act like she was happy despite him.

His black mood and her determined cheerfulness were each weapons in a fierce battle between two stubborn wills.

They were flying over sparsely covered ridges of stringy-bark tress.

"Down there!" Tad pointed grimly, breaking the silence. "That's where Martin Reach ends and Jackson Downs begins."

She nodded, glad that he'd decided to speak to her at last.

"At the turn of the century that used to be lush home paddock," he said. "Now it's desert. The sheet erosion has stripped the topsoil from the underlying clay and degraded the rich pastures of Mitchell and Kangaroo grass."

The landscape beneath them was indeed forlorn: five-thousand acres of bare pans dusted with salt and ringed by yellow samphire. The illusion of limitless space in the small, manmade desert was at once fascinating and daunting.

His voice was cold. Her own heart fluttered painfully. But she kept her chin as high and proudly defiant as his.

Everywhere there was the sad evidence of the drought. The sky was a pitiless copper-blue, and the few clouds seemed to scoff at the dry, cracked earth with their dry, cotton puffiness. Tad flew low over his dams, which only had a little water in the center of them. The creek was a string of muddy water holes.

Again his frosty, toneless voice broke the silence.

"We have twenty bores, pumps, windmills, but when it gets like this, water alone will not sustain cattle because they can't find forage. We've got to provide feed, but when it doesn't rain, feed's too high to buy. The cattle die. Out here the distances to market are enormous. This is a heartbreaking business in a heartbreaking country. A few years ago a lot of Aussies began selling out to Americans. Now the Americans are selling. Six years ago I was buying land from the Martins. Now they're buying mine."

"Surely there must be something else you could do."

Tad just looked at her, his expression so dark and hard and cynical that she glanced out the window, chagrined.

The land did seem big. Ruthlessly big. Bigger than any one man. Bigger than any group of men. The kind of land that had broken the backs and the hearts of the grittiest of adventurers. There was a reason why most Australians chose to cling to the green fringes of their continent rather than venture into the interior.

"In America, our desert, our West has always inspired us with a sense of freedom," he said. "Maybe because it was the path to California and a new life. But the Aussies have never seen their outback in that same light. This was a convict nation, and the Never Never was like the bars of a prison. They've always been scared of it."

Beneath them the forbidding landscape became wrinkled by deep-scored gorges, cliffs, ravines and mountains.

"I wouldn't want to crash here," she said.

"As a matter of fact this is where my neighbor Holt Martin's plane went down a few years back. He died instantly, and that was probably a lucky thing. The wreckage of his plane was in a ravine and couldn't be seen from the air. He would have needed to climb out of the ravine to signal, and it's almost always suicide for a man to abandon his plane or vehicle in the bush. We're a hundred miles from the nearest cow camp or homestead. Noelle didn't find him for nearly a month."

"Noelle?"

Tad's face darkened. "His American cousin. She's probably behind everything that's been happening."

"You would blame a woman!"

He muttered a low, mercifully inaudible curse. "You would turn this into another one of your sexist battles."

"Why are you so sure it's her?"

"Well, she's a newcomer."

"Circumstantial."

"Do you always make up your mind in an instant?"

"When the facts are as nonexistent as these, yes."

He made a sound like he was grinding his teeth. "All I know is we didn't have any trouble till she got here. Her family threw her out of Louisiana, and it wasn't because she was behaving herself. She's the type who causes problems wherever she goes. Ever since Holt died, she's been poking her nose around where it doesn't belong."

"She sounds like me."

He made a grimace. "That's hardly a recommendation. Before Holt died, she even stirred him up against his brother, Granger. And Granger against me."

"I thought he was buying your land."

"He is."

"Why couldn't it be him?"

"His property's been hit nearly as badly as mine."

"I thought you said he was sick of Australia. Why would he be buying more land?"

"Damn it, if I knew the answers, I wouldn't have a problem."

Turbulence shook the plane, and Tad lapsed into his stubborn silence once more. Hours passed, and he didn't speak again. Not until the sun was so low and so bright he could no longer shield his eyes from it. And then he wasn't addressing her.

"Damn!" he muttered as he squinted into the sun.

At first she thought he meant the sun as he leaned forward. Then she saw a thin, black coil of ominous smoke against the fiery sky.

"What's that?" she whispered.

His mouth thinned, but he said nothing.

Beneath them was an immense two-story house and its outbuildings—the store, office, quarters for the staff men, laundries. They seemed to cower under an eerie, deepening twilight. Beyond she saw the stables and stockyards.

One of the buildings was burning. Men were running about wildly.

"It's the homestead. Jackson Downs is on fire," he said grimly.

Then he set up their approach.

The Cessna bumped its way to an abrupt stop on the dirt runway. Tad threw open the door, jumped down into the whorls of choking dust. Then he turned to help Jess and the others down.

The landscape was bleak, desolate and vast—cut off from civilization by hundreds of miles of dry, baking land. The air was oven hot. The red dust seemed to have settled on everything—the buildings, the scraggly trees, her clothes. Two Land Rovers and a forlorn Jeep looked like they had just come out of a red brick kiln.

The gritty hand Tad gave Jess jerked her roughly to the ground. For an instant her weight dangled against him in an undignified manner.

For a fleeting moment she was aware of how beautiful the house was, even covered as it was with its mantle of dust. It was an oasis in the middle of a desert. The two-story house had adobe walls two feet thick with wide, shaded verandas

along every side. The house was set high on a rise of red
earth and nestled amidst the shade of tamarind trees. Despite the steaming heat and her own wretched exhaustion,
Jess felt drawn to it because it was Tad's home. She was determined to make it hers, as well.

She caught the faint scent of spinifex resin, the stronger
smells of smoke and fire. The desert was like an inferno
suffocating her, making her tongue go dry and tacky in her
mouth.

Nearby horses screamed in terror.

"The stables!" Tad yelled before he cast her aside and
broke into a run.

Jess chased after him.

A huge wooden building with a rusted corrugated-iron
roof was the source of a fountain of orange flame and black
smoke spurting fifty feet into the air and billowing higher.
As they reached the building, Tad shouted at a bulky man
who was fumbling with the locked doors of the stable.

"What the hell do you think you're doing, McBain?"

Ian whirled, his hard face panicked. Tad reached him,
and the two of them managed to shove the doors aside.

A dozen horses stampeded out the open doors. Tad
grabbed Jess and shielded her with his own body. Chasing
after this terror-crazed herd was a tall, dark man whose shirt
was ablaze. He cracked a whip in the air.

As soon as the man got outside, he crumpled to the
ground in agony and used the last reserves of his strength to
roll himself in the dirt.

Tad and Jess reached him at once. His ruined shirt hung
in ribbons upon his broad, muscled back. His handsome
face was contorted with pain and exhaustion and covered
with black grit and red dirt. Rivulets of sweat had etched
crazy grooves into this fierce mask of accumulated grime.
There was the scent of singed cloth and flesh.

Other men came running up, jackaroos, the native children who'd been silently watching the fire. Jess was scarcely aware of them as she knelt with Tad beside the injured man.

"Kirk! You fool!" Tad began to swear softly to himself as he and Ian helped his brother-in-law stagger to his feet. "The bloody bastards!"

"I told you things were heating up," Kirk said, sagging against him. "You damn sure took your time getting back here. What kept you?"

Then Kirk cast his beautiful black-lashed, green eyes upon Jess. "Deirdre . . . You found her . . ."

"No."

"You crazy bastard," Kirk said to Tad.

Black lashes sealed over the dazzling green. Kirk's voice became a whisper as he fainted.

Jess leaned closer and caught the faint name that was the last sound from his lips.

"Julia . . ."

Jess stared questioningly at Tad.

"She's my little sister. His wife. And she's back in Texas, pregnant. If anything happens to him . . ."

"But I thought she died when she was a child."

"That's what we all thought, but she survived the kidnapping. Kirk went through hell to get her back for us. It's a long story." Tad winced as he inspected his brother-in-law's wounds. Then Tad's hand closed over Jess's. His gaze was intense, pain-filled.

"Please," Tad begged, "don't let him die."

Twelve

There is nothing like a medical emergency to give a doctor total power. With horror Tad saw that despite everyone else's terror, including his own, the opportunity to boss him and his employees had put Bancroft in an excellent humor. Her smug little smiles told him that she was enjoying herself hugely, while she mined this rich vein of drama for all it was worth. He could do nothing but grit his teeth and pray she was as good as she conceitedly thought she was.

Tad's scowl was bitter as he watched Jess bark orders and two of his jackaroos scurry away from the sickroom at a dead run across vast expanses of cool, terra-cotta-tiled halls. His two toughest, hardest jackaroos, men who never let a woman boss them, scampered like children every time Jess's voice rose above a whisper.

In less than an hour, Bancroft had taken over his house, his station, his men. What made him maddest was that he was used to being the one in command. She made him feel useless and...yes, jealous. Oh, sure he'd begged her to save Kirk. Sure, he'd done what he could himself. He'd sent his stockmen after the runaway horses and had guards posted at every outbuilding as insurance against another attack. But in everyone's eyes, it was Bancroft who was the heroine of the hour.

While Tad had been occupied outside with his stockmen, Jess had entrenched herself firmly inside his homestead. Every one of his thirty employees, including the lazy, fat Mrs. B., was in complete awe of her. Jess had won the older woman over with a single sympathetic remark about her plight as the victim of oppressive male tyranny. Mr. B. was as gentle as a lamb! Mrs. B. was the wolf!

"More cold towels, please," Jess ordered crisply.

Mrs. B. didn't even frown as she usually did when commanded to do something. Indeed, she nearly knocked Tad down as she rushed past him to obey this order. Hell, never once had she jumped like that to obey one of his orders.

Ian, too, was impressed as he watched Jess gently work over Kirk who lay sprawled on his stomach across Tad's bed. When McBain's hard gaze shifted to Tad's glum face, the lawyer all but laughed out loud at him. No doubt McBain thought this woman was probably running him, too.

Well, wasn't she? But what could he do? As long as Kirk was down, Tad's hands were tied.

Kirk's gray face was beaded with perspiration. Tad had promised Julia that he would get Kirk back to Texas safe and sound before their baby's birth.

"How is he?" Tad muttered ungraciously, conscious of an acute annoyance toward Bancroft because she had proved herself so thoroughly indispensable so quickly.

"He's going to be okay. He's in pain, but his burns are pretty superficial. What he needs now is rest."

Tad cleared his throat, started to say something, thought better of it and slouched deeper into his chair by the bed.

"We need to leave him alone, now," she commanded softly, ushering everyone into the hall. "You, too, Jackson."

"All right. Damn it." He got up quickly. "It's not as if I don't have a million things to do—things that are more important than supervising you." He slapped his thighs and a cloud of red dust issued forth from his jeans.

She watched the dust settle on the furniture, the floor.

"So do I," she murmured with that irritating tone of self-importance. Then she smiled quirkily, cockily, making him even more furious.

Did all doctors think they hung the moon the way she did? Such conceit was insufferable.

"Leave Jackson Downs to me," he growled. "I won't have you taking over."

"I'm here to help you," she whispered defiantly.

Tad was aware of Ian watching them from across the hall.

"Just remember one thing," Tad said. "I didn't invite you here. As soon as this is over, I want you gone." Her face went very white. "I was through with you when you got on that plane. You proved then that this thing between us won't ever work. I don't give a damn how good you are in bed or what you do here to help me."

Her eyes flared brightly with hurt, and although that silent look of pain got to him, he forced himself to go on. "Nothing you do is going to make a bit of difference. You're just too damned bossy—I mean, for a man like me."

"Admit it, Jackson," she said softly. "What makes you maddest is that you know you need me. You know you want me, and not just in bed. Do you really want a woman who'll let you bully her? You walked all over Deirdre, and you weren't happy with her."

"That wasn't the reason!"

"This is a big place. Do you really want to run it all by yourself? Kirk—"

"To hell with Kirk. You're just using him to get power over me."

"Jackson, that's unfair—even from you."

He knew she was right, but he was tired of her always being right, of her always being wiser. Tad stormed out of the room, determined to get as far from her as he could.

But he was aware of her, of her brilliant, pain-glazed eyes, of her competent efficiency, of everything she'd said and done the minute he'd turned his back on her.

Ian stopped him on his way out of the house. "Hey, Jackson, what about the papers?"

Tad was tempted to agree to everything just to be stubborn and show her, but he turned back and saw Jess in the shadows at the far end of the hall. "I'll sign them tomorrow," he muttered roughly.

Jess's low gasp knifed through Tad.

"What?" Ian was about to go on. Then his thoughtful gaze shifted uneasily to Jess and then back to Tad.

"I need a night to sleep on it," Tad insisted.

"But you already agreed."

All Tad could see were Jess's haunted eyes.

"Damn it, Ian. I said I need a night."

Tad slept in the bunkhouse that night, if one could call twisting and turning on that wretchedly narrow, rock-hard bunk sleeping, and it wasn't selling Jackson Downs that was worrying him. The air conditioner that was fueled by his own natural gas wells was broken, and the holes in the screens let in some persistent blowies. They kept up a perpetual buzzing at his mouth and eyes, and he kept up a nearly constant swatting at them. If it hadn't been for the bottle of whiskey he kept taking frequent swigs of, he'd never have made it through the long, dark misery of those hours.

The yellow porch light was on. Every time he opened his eyes, his gaze fell on a poster-sized picture of a sexy nude blonde opposite his bed. The lady was a bit of provocative decoration that the jackaroos had nailed to the wall. The trouble was that this particular big-breasted starlet bore a too-striking resemblance to Jess, and it was torture to look at her and to remember Jess asleep in a soft, clean bed somewhere in his cool house. Only last night he had had her—again and again. She'd been a wanton, wild for him. Sexually they were a perfect match.

Just the memory of her and his throat felt hot and dry, his body tense and aching. He loathed himself for the power she had over him. He liked good, hot sex; it was something he'd done without too long.

It was infuriating that just a female image on a scrap of paper, just an image that only faintly resembled the warm, luscious woman asleep in his house could arouse him so that every time he looked at it his insides quivered hotly.

Damn her. There would be no peace in his life until she was gone.

He kept opening his eyes, staring at the feminine image on the wall that so taunted him, saluting it with his bottle. It was hell remembering, hell fantasizing, hell doing without the one thing he really wanted.

In the end he resorted to drink to dull his senses, but the drunker he got, the hotter he became every time he looked at the picture, until every muscle was so tense he felt like he was going to explode. It was almost dawn when he finally fell fitfully asleep, but in his dreams he couldn't fight her off.

Jess came to him, and her eyes were as darkly passion-filled as his own. When she began to strip, he welcomed her into the narrow bunk. She crawled on top of him and drove him wild, so wild that he awoke thrashing. Ned, who was in the bunk under him, had slugged him in the arm to make him stop kicking their bunk.

"Some dream," Ned joked, his dark, chubby face too close.

"Shut the hell up."

The next day there was no new violence on Jackson Downs or Martin Reach, and yet the unspoken threat of it hung menacingly in the air.

Maybe that was what set everybody on edge. The jackaroos seemed to find special delight in tormenting Tad by speaking with amazement of Jess's accomplishments. Their praise made Tad want to howl with rage over Jess's clever treachery. She was killing him, killing them all with her kindness, with her usefulness.

"MacKay's doing real good today. He was on the radio talking to his wife in Texas for an hour, though. And the doctor's on a rampage, cleaning your house," Ned told him that morning while he was still in the bunkhouse nursing his hangover.

"I liked it the way it was," Tad muttered in a low voice. He plunged his painfully throbbing head into a lavatory and ran tepid water through his hair.

"She's even set Mrs. B. to work."

Tad jerked his head out of the water and banged it into the faucet—hard. "Ouch! Damn it! What?"

Mrs. B., Felicity Binkum, by name, Tad's housekeeper, was well over sixty and had gray hair that looked like she trimmed it with tin snips. Mrs. B. had a forceful, dominating, poor-me personality and was always at outs with her long-suffering husband, Mr. B., the best damned foreman Tad had ever had.

Mr. B. was the only reason everyone on the station was forced to endure the lazy, whiny domination of the incessantly complaining Mrs. B. He was the only reason Tad had endured the sloppy condition of his house for years, as well as the thinly veiled insults Mrs. B. assaulted everyone with—including him.

Every time any new violence occurred she always eyed Tad and muttered to herself just loud enough so he'd be sure to hear, "Some men would do something."

"Boss, you wouldn't know Mrs. B.," Ned taunted. "She's as sweet as sugar. None of her two-edged barbs to-day."

"I don't believe it." Tad was gingerly rubbing the lump on his wet head.

"Believe it, mate. Doctor knows how to handle her."

Damn right, Bancroft could handle her. They were two of a kind—both man-haters from way back.

Tad snorted belligerently, but Ned wasn't one for taking hints. "Mrs. B.'s mopped every floor. Stripped and waxed them. Scrubbed the walls. Washed everything in the house—sheets, drapes, rugs. Got the jackaroos helping her. You wouldn't know the place. She's cooking up some meat pies. Best-smelling pies! Doctor's a damned good vet, too."

"You haven't turned her loose on the livestock?" This was a yell. He tossed his towel on his bed and yanked on his shirt.

"No, but she sure cured Dane's dog. Wheeler fell into the cattle dip and got himself snakebit last week, and if she hadn't treated him, he would have died for sure. The boys and Lizzie sure would've been brokenhearted."

Wheeler, a Queensland Heeler, was a great favorite on the station.

"You ought to see how she is with Lizzie."

"Damn. I don't want to see it."

"Doctor's the busiest sheila I ever saw."

She damn sure was.

"Hey..." Ned's speculative gaze swept from his boss to the girlie picture of the half-naked blonde that had taunted Tad all night. "That looks likes her, don't it, boss?" Ned's white grin became a leer in his plump, dark face.

Jealous rage washed through Tad as his own gaze followed Ned's. How dare Ned think dirty of Jess. It was all Tad could do to keep from going after Ned's thick, sunburned throat with his bare hands. Instead, Jackson's violence found another outlet.

"Damn it," his deep voice boomed. "What the hell do you blokes hang filthy trash like that on the wall for?" With a single, fluid leap of fury, Tad lunged across the narrow room, ripped the paper from the wall, tore it to bits and threw it into the garbage can. He grew aware of his men's lean, dark faces—hard, set, yet intently curious as they watched him, read him—before they averted their gazes to the rude plank flooring.

Afraid of what he might do or say next, he flung the screen door open and strode outside into the thick dust, flies and suffocating heat.

The door banged; he heard their snickers behind him.

"Now what the hell got into him?"

"It don't take no genius to figure that one out, Ned."

There were guffaws and laughter.

"She's one hell of a woman. Nothing like the other one."

"The boss has met his match for once, and it don't seem as if he likes it none too much."

The boss damn sure didn't. Beneath the darkness of his tan, Tad whitened. The smell of livestock was suddenly overpowering. The liquor churned in his belly like acid. The wooden planks of the unswept porch flooring seemed to swim. He felt a hot, nauseous sensation crawl up his esophagus and he had to grab the railing for support.

"Damn them. Damn them all."

Slowly his weakness ebbed, and after it had, Tad felt like going back inside and using his fists to teach them all a thing or to about what he didn't like too much.

Instead he slammed down the wooden stairs and stepped onto the rocky earth. Brawling with his own men was not the thing to do. Especially since the only crime they'd committed was speaking the truth.

At the bottom of the stairs Tad reached in his pocket and brought out a cigarette. Very slowly he lit it and inhaled deeply. The cigarette made him sick all over again, and he threw it to the ground and squashed it violently with his boot heel.

He had known it would be a mistake to bring Jess here. He just hadn't known how quickly she would take over, how quickly she would challenge his dominion over his own world. Over his own men. Worst of all—his dominion over himself.

She got to him worse out here.

Maybe it was because everyone but him seemed to think she belonged.

Tad refused to let himself be driven out of his house forever. So that night he came in for supper. His intention was to get down to business with Ian, sell the place and ignore her.

But her presence was everywhere.

He was a stranger in his own home.

The house was sparkling. So was Mrs. B. The tin-snip hairdo was wavy and almost becoming. For the first time in years she seemed almost happy with Mr. B. Tad found the contented older couple in one of the screened courtyard gardens, sitting beneath the tamarind trees drinking grog together. He left them before they saw him and went in search of Ian.

Jess was in the kitchen.

Tad meant to stride past the open door and avoid her, but the aroma of roast beef, Yorkshire pudding and lemon meringue pie was too much for him. Damn her. Why was she so good at everything that mattered to him?

His boots made hollow sounds on the cool terra-cotta tiles as he stepped inside and then leaned back against the doorjamb. He was hot and dirty, a grim, angry male presence in the neat domesticity of her kitchen. He knew he smelled of dust and the animals he'd been vaccinating. He could still taste the whiskey on his breath from last night.

She looked up from her cookbook, smiled quirkily at him, and said, "Hi, there."

Just "Hi, there," bold as brass, after what she'd put him through. But his heart filled with a wild, thrilling joy.

"Where's Lizzie?" Tad demanded gruffly.

"In her room reading. I got down a book about dinosaurs."

"Oh."

His intense blue gaze couldn't get enough of Jess. She looked fresh and quite glamorous in Deirdre's riding clothes. She'd probably slept like a baby last night—without him. Beneath a lacy white apron, she was dressed in exquisitely cut cream-cord jodhpurs, elastic-sided riding boots and a clingy, red silk shirt.

A searing pleasure coursed through him.

"I missed you," she said as she put down her spatula, undid her apron and came across the kitchen into his arms.

He felt her trembling, and he was tongue-tied at the beauty of her.

For years he had lived in this house, but never until this moment had it felt like home.

He buried his face against the sweet-smelling satin of her throat. His arms closed around her. "Oh, dear God," he said hungrily, defeatedly. "I'm lost. Truly lost."

For years he had blamed Jess for all that had gone wrong between them. But the blame was as much his as hers—for not seeing the truth, for not wanting to see.

"That's exactly the way I felt—all night," she whispered.

"I missed you."

"I missed you, too. Why didn't you come to me?"

"Because..." His large brown hands ruffled her hair. "Because I was too cussed stubborn."

He knew he would never rule her, just as he knew he could never stop trying. They would always have their battles. But in that moment he didn't care. She was precious to him. He had to have her at his side. He wanted to please her—in everything.

"Hell. I shouldn't be touching you. Not till I've taken a shower. I'm the only dirty thing in this whole blasted house."

He started to pull away, but she wouldn't let him.

"Just hold me," she begged softly.

His finger traced the sensitive skin from her jaw to her chin and then back, a caress that tantalized them both. He could feel her pulse throbbing.

She licked her lips.

And then he kissed her.

In that moment he knew that as long as she was with him, he could never sell Jackson Downs. It was no longer a million acres of drought-stricken desert plagued by perpetual violence. It was his home. Hers, too. And he was going to do what she wanted. He would fight for it because she wanted him to.

Even if it cost him everything.

But he was going to fight for it his way.

Not hers.

Thirteen

The three of them were alone in Jackson's tiny office. A thick, noxious spiral of smoke rose from Ian's cigar that he had set down in the ashtray.

"What do you mean—you're not going to sell?" Ian's voice was as violent as a rapier slicing through the hostile silence.

Jess coughed lightly and fanned the smoke away.

The best supper Tad had eaten in years was over and Mrs. B. could be heard in the distant kitchen doing the dishes, for once without complaining.

Ian, Tad and Jess were glaring at one another across Tad's desk, which was stacked high with legal documents.

Tad leaned slowly back in his cracked leather chair. "Hey, hey. Easy, Ian." Tad took a long sip on his beer. "You're just my lawyer, remember? I make the decisions governing Jackson Downs."

Ian shot a telling glance toward Jess. His low voice got nasty. "Not all—apparently."

The jeering masculine insult went through Tad's vitals like a bullet. Ian had known it would.

Bull's-eye, you bastard. There had always been some barely understood, male rivalry lurking just beneath the surface in his relationship with Ian.

Not by the flicker of an eyelash did Tad let the gray-haired man know his slight had hit the mark. Slowly Tad tipped his chair forward and set his beer bottle square in the center of the most important document so that it ringed it. He said only, but with more stubborn determination than before, "I never wanted to sell. That was your idea."

"Nothing's changed since you decided."

Tad reached across the desk, lifted a legal paper, looked at it, considered the months of tedious negotiation that had gone into drafting all the documents, and then flipped it airily toward the wastebasket. He picked up Ian's cigar and stubbed it out in the ashtray.

Ian lifted his bushy black brows.

"Nasty habit—smoking," Tad murmured.

Ian laughed. "You smoke."

"I've quit." He hadn't made up his mind on that issue until that instant.

"That your idea or . . . your doctor's?"

"What does it matter, as long as it's a good one!"

Tad took Jess's hand in his and turned it over and thoughtfully studied the smooth, pale, delicate fingers intertwined with his larger, darker, callused ones.

His icy blue gaze met Ian's. "You're wrong, McBain, about nothing having changed. Everything's changed. I'm not fighting this thing alone any more."

Jess's fingers wound more tightly into his.

Ian sprang to his feet. "I wasted a trip. It'll cost you."

"It always does."

"I only hope you won't be sorry."

Tad attempted a thin smile. "Thanks for the concern."

Tad pulled the half-empty pack of cigarettes out of his pocket, looked at it and then wrinkled cellophane, paper, and tobacco into a ball and pitched it toward the wastebasket. A moment later he brought Jess's hand slowly to his lips and kissed it.

It was nearly four in the morning when Noelle's panicked call came over the radio.

Jackson woke up slowly, not aware at first that it was the radio that had broken through the layers of his unconsciousness. Jess lay beside him. He caught the faint scent of her skin—that lingering fragrance of orange blossoms. He felt her breasts pressed into his side.

They had made love for hours and fallen asleep together in a blissful stupor of exhaustion—a dangerous thing to do under the circumstances. He felt drugged. He wanted to stay beside her forever.

And yet he felt the danger. Nearer than ever before.

He got out of bed, careful not to disturb her, and went to the radio.

Noelle's voice was so soft, and the transmission so filled with static, that he could barely make her out.

"Granger's gone crazy. Jackson Downs, do you read me?"

She sounded terrified. Either Noelle was the best damned actress he'd ever heard, or someone was really after her.

Tad flipped the switch and mumbled something to reassure her.

"Granger's got a gun. Please..."

The sound of a beautiful woman crying out in the night for his help was impossible to ignore.

But it was a trap! Jackson felt it in his gut. Before he could think through what he wanted to do, he heard Jess behind him, flipping the switch again, speaking into the mike.

"Jackson Downs to Martin Reach. Stay calm. We're coming to save you. Over."

Tad whirled, his anger instant and fierce. As always, Jess was taking over. This was no medical emergency. This was his kind of emergency.

Through the red mist of his rage he could barely see Jess's pale face, stricken with fear and alarm. "Why did you tell her that?"

"You can't just leave her out there all alone!"

"What if she's lying?"

Jess flinched. "What if she isn't?"

His vision cleared and although Jess's beautiful face was half in shadow, he saw her for what she was, a frightened woman, pleading for him to help another. And yet he saw her courage, too.

His expression softened. He reached for her and pulled her closer. Mere inches separated their bodies. She wore only that diaphanous, floating nightgown. Her extravagant, voluptuous breasts were clearly revealed. He could feel the heat emanating from her skin. He remembered the way she made his body pulse with passion. She wanted him to help Noelle—Noelle, whom he'd never trusted.

A heavy sigh broke from him, and he paused before answering. "I'm going, then," he said grudgingly. "If that's what you want."

Dark, gold-flecked eyes were shining now as they met his. "Thank you."

"But you're staying."

Her fingers tightened reflexively on his arm. "Jackson...please...I want to help you."

"We're doing this my way—for once." He stared at her long and hard. "This could be dangerous. Very dangerous."

"Okay."

Nothing was ever that simple with her. "Do you really mean that?"

Her eyes shone trustingly, obediently. She nodded.

He was filled with immense male satisfaction. This was the way he wanted her, docile, sweetly doing things his way. "I love you," he said gently. "You're much too precious for me to risk."

"I love you, too." Tenderly she touched his unshaven cheek. "Even now when you're impossibly macho."

He touched her lightly, lifted her chin. Then he kissed her until they both began to tremble. "Oh, Jess..." He murmured her name with a sigh of regret. He didn't want to leave her, but he unwrapped his arms from her warm, lush body and set her away from him. "You're going to stay here and keep Lizzie safe for me. And that's an order."

"Aye. Aye." She gave him a mock salute.

"We're doing this my way."

A funny kind of smile came over her face. Tad was so staggered that for once she'd agreed to obey him that he didn't think to distrust it....

Not till hours after he and his men and his two planes were already at Martin Reach did he distrust it. Not till he'd been shot at. Not till he'd freed a terrorized Noelle from the attic where she'd been handcuffed to a pipe and a time bomb. Not till he'd defused the bomb and was chasing Granger down with one of Granger's own Jeeps did Tad remember Jess's funny, crooked smile. Only then did he know to distrust it.

And then it was too late.

After setting Noelle free and leaving her at Martin Reach, Tad and his men and their Abo trackers chased Granger, their Jeeps making sweeping, zigzag patterns across an endless bleak landscape of night desert. The moon was a sliver, but the Southern Cross was blazing. The two wildly jouncing vehicles raced bumper-to-bumper. Twice Granger had tried to trick Tad into running over the side of a cliff. Panicking, Granger tried to blast Tad's tire with his gun. Tad rammed him in the rear. Granger's Jeep swerved too sharply, and his tires went over an embankment. The vehicle flipped end-over-end, and Granger wound up pinned beneath the roo bar.

The acrid scent of burning upholstery and oil filled Tad's nostrils as he got out of his own Jeep and strode warily, shotgun in hand, toward the upside-down Jeep.

"Pull me out," Granger screamed hoarsely from beneath the torn canvas tatters of the roof.

Tad was breathing hard from the chase. His shirt was wet with sweat; his face black with grime. He wiped his sleeve across his brow. The first shell of lethal buckshot made a hollow sound as he racked it into the chamber. "I'll show you the same mercy you would have shown Noelle if we hadn't gotten here in time. The same mercy you showed when you set my stables on fire and damn near killed MacKay."

"For God's sake, mate," Granger yelled, "it wasn't me. I didn't want any part of that. I never wanted to hurt Noelle. But she kept snooping around."

Tad kicked a rock with the toe of his boot and sent it skittering past Granger's face. "Then who?"

"Help me, please."

"Tell me, and I'll tell Ned and the boys to pull you free."

Granger was a weakling—city-bred. He had always been a coward. His face contorted in fear.

"Tell me or you'll fry to death the way Holt did. Did you kill him, too?"

"My own brother, dear God!" Bitter, hopeless tears were in his choked voice.

Tad swaggered up to the Jeep, leaned down and grabbed Granger by the throat and squeezed his larynx hard until

Granger began to choke. "No use blubbering like a baby. Talk if you're going to. The fire's almost to the fuel tank. I'm not sticking around to get myself blown apart."

Tad let go of him so abruptly that Granger's face fell into the dirt. Granger whimpered with pain. Tad turned on his heel in disgust and strode away until the darkness swallowed him. "Come on boys."

Granger's gaze went to the thread of blue-and-gold flame creeping ever closer. Then he became crazy with terror all over again. "Okay," he blurted. "You win. Jackson... Jackson! Don't leave me."

There was an eerie silence. Twin threads of flame licked the black night.

"Jackson!"

Out of the darkness came two words. "Tell me."

And Granger whispered a single name.

And to Tad that name was a knife blade of betrayal. Because it belonged to the one man in Australia Tad had trusted. Maybe he hadn't always liked that man, but he had trusted him. Jackson's pulse throbbed unevenly, sickeningly. He stood frozen in the darkness.

"For God's sake, get me loose!"

"Let him go, Ned!" Tad hissed. "Quickly!"

Ian McBain. Friend. Confidant. Fighter for justice.

Ian McBain. Murderer. Betrayer. Ambusher. Vandal. Deirdre's lover.

The damned bastard had been bolting MacKay inside the stables, not letting him out of it!

It didn't fit.

And yet it did.

Ian!

Why?

The Jeep exploded, and while he watched it burn, Tad staggered backward. He was remembering Jess's funny, sweet smile.

She had known all along.

She was back at Jackson Downs—with him.

Rage filled Tad, but it was instantly obliterated by a far more powerful emotion that held his heart in a tight-fisted grip—terror.

Ian McBain.

Tad felt like he'd just been punched hard in the gut.

Deirdre must have told Jess something in India.

Something that had made her go to that island.

Something that had made her call Ian in the first place— instead of him—when she'd first come to Australia.

Tad stared a moment longer at the burning Jeep. Why hadn't he seen it?

Tonight Jess had deliberately put herself in danger. She'd put his child in danger, as well as everyone else he'd left behind at Jackson Downs. For that Tad would never forgive her.

She'd done this to him for the last time! She had proved that she could never be trusted. If he got her out of this alive, he was through with her forever.

Jess had betrayed him, betrayed his trust, betrayed him in the single way that could most hurt him. And yet all that he could feel was the same nauseating fear Granger had known as he lay pinned beneath that burning Jeep.

Ian had Jess. Tad remembered what he'd done to Deirdre. Deirdre must have loved McBain. She'd gone to the island, trusting him, and he'd murdered her. What would he do to a woman as mule-headed and feisty as Jess?

Fear was bile boiling in Tad's stomach.

Jackson doubled over, sick with fear, and threw up on that dry, barren ground. Then he started running.

Jess was quite calm as she stole silently through the house with Lizzie sleeping in her arms. Meeta raced behind them, carrying blankets. The feeling of calmness had crept over

Jess gradually as she'd listened to the vanishing drone of Jackson's planes when he'd flown away.

She had deliberately let herself be trapped at Jackson Downs with a man who might be a murderer, with the man who might have cold-bloodedly taken Deirdre's life. It wasn't something Jess had deliberately planned, although Tad would undoubtedly believe she had. That cry for help from Noelle had been real. Jess had had to send Tad to help her.

But now there was no one to save this sleeping child in the trailing purple nightgown, no one to save the others. No one except herself.

She had five minutes. Max. Before Ian made his move. If it was Ian.

Her day of housecleaning had not been in vain. She had discovered beneath the oldest part of the house a cool cavernous basement that was naturally ventilated. With its great doors locked from the inside, it was a natural fortress. In it she had stored food and water, guns and ammunition for just such an emergency.

After she'd placed Lizzie with Meeta on a pallet, Jess went and brought Mr. and Mrs. B. downstairs to guard them.

"You must do as I say," Jess ordered crisply.

The two days Jess had spent bossing everybody about until they were thoroughly under her control had not been wasted. The B.'s would not have argued with her if she had told them to burn the house to the ground and bury themselves alive beneath it.

"Do not open these doors unless you hear three gunshots followed by a fourth. If someone forces this door, shoot to kill."

Mrs. B. picked up the gun and stared at Jess with wonder and admiration. "You would think the men would do something," she muttered.

"It's up to us—to the women," Jess said in a conspiratorial tone that won Mrs. B. completely.

Jess closed the door, and she heard Mrs. B. order Mr. B. to bolt the doors from the inside.

Jess had given Kirk a powerful narcotic. Her belief had been that if he posed no threat to the murderer, he would be in no danger, either.

Jess went back to Jackson's bedroom and locked the door. She pulled on a black shirt and a pair of black jeans. She got the loaded .38 that she had hidden out of the drawer, tucked it inside the waistband of her jeans, and softly raised the window. If she could just get to the desert, maybe she could hide until daylight. Until Jackson got back from Martin Reach.

Outside the sky was as black as old, congealed blood, and a sliver of moon hung in that menacing curtain of death like a wicked dagger's blade.

She threw a leg over the windowsill.

She was halfway out of the window when he seized her.

Ian grabbed her gun and shoved Jess mercilessly forward toward one of the great outbuildings.

He was hunched forward as he walked, his lips drawn back over his teeth in a savagely crazy grin. "You're too smart for your own good. You were on to me from the first."

"Not from the first. Not till now. But I was almost sure, when you were bolting Kirk inside the stables. You killed my sister."

"You won't get a confession out of me."

"I won't need one. Wally's going to find her body with his bulldozers before too long. The black boy saw you kill **her, didn't he**? You've been back to the island, and he saw you then. I don't imagine it will be too hard to get him to talk. He gave me her wedding ring. You were her lover. Why did you kill her?''

"Everybody was her lover."

"But it was you she went to meet on the island."

"Maybe."

"She came to you in the first place because she was afraid of the violence on the station. You seduced her."

"Don't kid yourself there. She was willing."

"Then she came back to Australia because she loved you, and you had promised to follow her if she left Australia. You sent her to Jackson Downs to steal Jackson's operating cash—to cripple him."

"Deirdre couldn't have told you that," Ian said with a smile.

"She told me enough so that I could figure out the rest for myself."

"You should have stayed in India where you belonged."

"I belong here."

He grabbed her arm and held it bruisingly. "No, I belong here. This land was my family's long before the Jacksons."

"It's over, Ian. Too many people are involved now. Maybe this started out as simple greed or revenge. Maybe you just wanted the land the Jacksons took from your family, but you went too far."

He flung open the door to the outbuilding. It smelled of hay and heat and animals.

"A little gasoline and this place will go up like a torch, the same way the horse stables did."

"Why, Ian?" Her voice was pitched higher than she intended. It sounded shrill and hysterical. "You don't strike me as a sentimental man. I can't really believe you want this place because you lived here once. Why did this land suddenly become so valuable to you after Holt Granger died on that mountain? He was a geologist, wasn't he?"

Ian smiled pleasantly and kept pushing her. "You figure it out, Miss Know-it-all." He shoved her inside. "Now it's your turn to answer my questions. I want the kid and the old couple. Where are they?"

She cringed away from him, but he shoved the muzzle of his gun into her belly.

"I can't have any witnesses." His trigger finger jumped, and the gun made a menacing click. "Tell me, damn it."

He grabbed her blouse to pull her closer, and the flimsy material tore. She shuddered from his closeness, from his hot, vile touch, but he yanked her toward him. The back of his hand gripped the creamy top of her lacy brassiere. She stiffened with alarm when she felt his hand, hard as a hot steel claw, there.

"You're a damned beautiful woman," he muttered, drawing her even nearer to his own bulky, powerful body. She shuddered again. "Damn beautiful."

She felt his fingers tighten on her blouse. "Tell me where his kid is. You can die quickly, or you can die so slowly you'll pray for death to come."

She paused and took her time considering both charming possibilities.

Then in answer she leaned forward and sunk her teeth into his fleshy wrist so hard that he flung her back against the wall. A burning pain shot through her head when it bounced off wood. She could feel a hot stickiness trickling through her hair. Everything started to swirl and darken.

"So you want it slow," he murmured viciously.

She had to stay awake. She had to keep him distracted from Lizzie. Until Jackson could get back from Martin Reach.

That could be hours. Hours... It was hopeless. She would be dead by then. More than anything, before she died, she wanted Jackson to hold her. Just one more time.

Her thoughts began to fade.

Dimly she was aware of Ian looming over her, his hands fumbling at his belt buckle.

What was he doing? Something too horrible to contemplate.

She lay in the hay, helpless, broken. No... If he touched her, she would kill him.

Then she heard a sound at the door. Ian must have sensed it, heard the rush of hot wind or seen a blur of ghostly movement behind him, because he turned.

Buckshot was racked into a shotgun chamber. There was an explosion like an incendiary bomb. Then a shotgun blasted wildly a second time into the ceiling.

The silence afterward was numbing, deafening.

A pile of hay began to burn. The flames cast eerie shadows. In the leaping light Jess could make out Jackson's tall, broad-shouldered form just inside the doors. One of his sleeves was torn halfway off his bronzed arm. His handsome features were wild with hate.

"Let her go, McBain." Jackson's hard voice vibrated like angry thunder in the empty building.

Flames raced up the wall behind Jess.

Ian leaned down and jerked her savagely to her feet. She could hear him laughing softly, nastily against her ear.

"I said let her go!" Jackson raged, aiming his shotgun at them. "My men are outside."

"I've got a gun to her head! I don't have to take your orders, you bastard!" Ian shrilled.

"Let her go or I'll kill you, McBain!"

The heat was like a furnace, and Jess began to cough from the billowing black smoke.

"It's the other way around! Throw your gun down! Or I'll kill her!"

The two men were staring at each other across the darkness, the smoke, the flying sparks and the flames, each man screaming crazily.

The atmosphere was insane, highly charged, electric.

Something had to happen, and soon, or they would all die.

But the tense, silent moment dragged itself out in slow-motion while the flames flew higher.

Then a stray spark landed on Jess's blouse and she jumped. Ian ground his blunt nails into Jess's neck and she screamed in terror.

With a cry Jackson threw his shotgun to the ground.

"No," Jess moaned in defeat as she watched Jackson's gun fall. They were lost. Dear God! They were lost.

Ian yanked her closer to his own body in savage triumph.

"You said you'd let her go, McBain."

"I lied." Ian held Jess so tightly she screamed again. Then he pointed his gun at Tad.

"Why, Ian?" Jackson demanded.

They were surrounded by racing, shimmering walls of fire. Sweat ran down Jackson's handsome face in glimmering rivulets.

"I grew up on this land. You Yanks took it. I always wanted it back. That's why I was so anxious to make your acquaintance when you came over here to run things. Holt Granger worked for me. So did Martin. Holt was looking for uranium before he died. After his plane went down, I sent another geologist into Woolibarra with a Geiger counter. There's uranium down there, all right. Mine. I tried everything I could think of to keep you distracted so you couldn't discover it for yourself. I got Martin to make you the offer to buy you out. I already owned his land, you see. He was just a front for me. Martin set up the attacks. But you kept fighting. Noelle kept snooping around, pestering Granger. She got on to him there at the last, and I ordered him to take care of her. Deirdre came to Brisbane seeking my help. She played right into my plans. Not that she knew what I was really up to. I had to kill her when she finally figured everything out. She was more loyal to you than either of us ever realized."

Ian was backing out of the burning building with Jess. Leaving Jackson to die.

"Well, this is goodbye, Jackson. You're too damned stubborn for your own good. You should have cooperated a long time ago. Get over in that corner."

Tad backed slowly into the corner. "Just let her go."

Ian gripped Jess's arm. "No way. I need her to get out of here. Then I'll have to kill everybody."

"You're crazy."

"Don't say that!" Ian smiled. "I need her to get your little girl. If I can break you, I can break the old couple guarding her."

Something inside Jess snapped. She had been listening to everything he'd been saying limply, lifelessly, enduring the unendurable heat. But his last, gloating threat brought the will to fight charging back to life inside her.

Ian was going to kill them all! If she didn't do something, he was going to kill Lizzie!

Long ago, when Jess had been living in Indonesia, her father had taught her how to fight. What had she been waiting for?

For the right moment. For the exact second when the murderer was so sure of his success that he relaxed his grip on her just a fraction.

She screamed, a high-pitched Oriental yell that was louder even than the roaring fire. Then she kicked Ian hard in the groin. She whirled like a dervish, jumped and jabbed her heel into his throat. He dropped his gun. She grabbed it.

Jackson lunged at Ian and sent him toppling. The two men rolled over and over, fighting, grunting, grappling.

Above them the roof was on fire.

Jackson was younger, stronger, and he wasn't writhing in pain from Jess's blows. Jackson straddled Ian and began pounding him with his fists. Then Jackson's fingers circled Ian's thick throat and squeezed until Ian's face turned purple. Jackson's expression was hard and savage with fury.

Jess rushed to them and tried to pull them apart. "No! Jackson! You're killing him!"

Outside the night filled with bobbing flashlights. Jackson's men came running into the barn.

Jess turned to them pleadingly. "Stop him! Please!" Ned lifted her into his dark arms, held her close against his clumsy body, then carried her outside. The other men grabbed Jackson and Ian, pulled them apart and hauled them bodily outside.

They had hardly stumbled to safety when behind them there was a terrible, rending sound, a rupture that sounded like the end of the world. Flames shot even higher into the black ebony of that long night.

Then the roof caved in. The ground shook with an awful thud as the building collapsed.

Jess scarcely felt it or saw it. She had eyes only for Jackson. Jackson would not even look at her.

"Jackson."

His grimly handsome face was streaked with grime. He gave her a long, hard stare.

Then she remembered that she had defied him.

He was done with her. She could see it in his eyes, and his harshness was killing her. He had come back to save her, risked his life to do so. He would have gladly died for her in that burning barn. All that she saw. But he didn't want her any more because she hadn't told him of her suspicions about Ian.

Jackson was too proud, too stupidly masculine.

He turned and began to walk slowly toward the house.

She had never been more aware of how heart-stoppingly virile he was until that moment when he was leaving her.

Through the mist of her tears and pain she devoured that male swagger in those skintight jeans.

Damn him. A sob caught in her throat. She wasn't going to let him just walk out on her. This wasn't just his show. He still hadn't learned, had he? He wasn't the only one who was going to make the decisions in their lives.

She raced across the hard-packed dirt and flung herself into his arms.

For a moment he was stiff, unrelenting.

"I love you," she cried, touching him pleadingly. She felt him flinch when her fingers grazed his shoulder where the shotgun had kicked him. "Whatever I did, I did to save you. I love you. Doesn't that mean anything?"

For a long moment he studied her tear-streaked face. She could feel her hair, soft and streaming in the warm breeze. She was aware of his height, of the way he towered over her, making her feel smaller than usual. She was aware of the tension in him. It seemed that his emotions were strung as tightly as wire.

"I love you," she said. "I would do anything... anything for you. Why won't you see I'm the right woman for you? The only woman..."

The silence between them stretched until it was almost unbearable. After that agonizing length of time, she finally felt the terrible tension drain from him. A gentle, almost loving look came into his eyes.

"Dear God," he muttered.

Her heart skipped a beat.

"Dear God..." His eyes and face took on an expression that made her feel very odd, as though she'd never be able to take another breath. Slowly, carefully he folded her into his arms.

She laid her head against his chest. He held her close, so tightly she could feel the hard rhythm of his heart pounding fiercely in unison with her own. She felt his hands move gently beneath her hair.

"Oh, Jackson," she wept into his chest. "Don't leave me."

"As if I could." There was a new, softer tone to his voice that Jess had never heard there before. He was surrendering to a force that was stronger than he. "I love you, too," he said simply. "You may as well hear the truth although I know it will make you even more unbearably conceited than you already are—and conceit is an abominable trait in a woman. I can't fight this...this...damn...whatever it is...any longer—although I tried mightily. It's in me, through and through, this love thing. I can't fight you. I can't fight myself. I have to have you—even if you are stubborn and impossible and bossy."

She was weeping, just like any ordinary, sentimental woman, and it was almost pleasant because he was cradling her in his arms so gently, so protectively.

"When Ian had that gun on you, I knew if he killed you I'd die, too," he whispered. "You're a part of me."

"I felt the same way," she said.

"My sweet, impossible, meddlesome darling," he murmured, and no love words had ever sounded dearer. His mouth covered hers. He kissed her, holding her tightly.

At last he released her. There was an interval of tender, joyous silence.

Someday he would tell her that it was not her fault that loving came so hard to him. Not her fault that as a boy he'd idolized his own father till his father had walked out on his mother for another woman. He'd felt that his father had abandoned him, as well. Even after his father had come back, the hurt had stayed there, buried. Subconsciously he'd probably felt safer believing the worst of Jess, blaming her. Safer marrying Deirdre, a woman he couldn't love.

"Lizzie?" Tad whispered.

"She and the B.'s and Meeta are locked safely inside the basement. I gave Kirk morphine so he wouldn't get into any trouble."

"If only there was a pill we could give you." But Jackson was grinning down at her lovingly.

"Are you mad because I let you go even though I suspected Ian?"

"At first I was. But I'm still too damned scared to be mad. That was a hellishly stupid thing to do. Maybe later when I calm down, I'll get mad. Then there'll be hell to pay."

"I promise, from now on, I'll do exactly as you say."

"I don't believe you, Bancroft."

She clung to him tightly.

"But you know something?" He tilted her chin back.

"What?"

He was staring deeply into her eyes. "I don't care any more. What really matters is what you did a while ago. No woman's ever stood up for me the way you did. You said you'd fix things in a week, and you damn sure did. I guess I never knew till now the kind of woman a man needs out here. I love you. I want to marry you."

Her heart gave a leap of joy. "Do you really mean it?"

"Honey, I feel sorry for you." His voice was warm, husky, tenderly amused. "Who'll marry you if I don't? Who else in all the world is cussed enough, and stubborn enough, and ornery enough to put up with a woman as impossible as you?"

A tremulous smile curved her lips, a wild song of joy singing through her veins. "There isn't anybody who can hold a candle to you in that contest."

He smiled sexily, charmingly. His hand reached out to tentatively smooth back the tangles of gold at her temple. Her dark eyes glowed in response to the caress.

In the next instant his arms were tightly around her, and his mouth came down hungrily on her lips.

A long time later she said, "Let's go tell Lizzie."

"And after that . . ." he said, his voice thickening.

"Yes, after that . . . we have till dawn."

Her eyes warmed. Her quick smile held the most tantalizing promise.

Epilogue

It was the first of June, and it was Tad and Jess's wedding day, as well. They were in Texas at the Big House on Jackson Ranch, having been married in the family chapel.

The house, the glittering chandelier, the wedding party—everyone and everything was decorated lavishly in purple satin. The groom's cummerbund and bow tie were of that color. Even the bride's gown was the palest shade of lavender. The bouquet was of white flowers and purple ribbons.

Tad had grumbled at first when Jess had begged him to give in to Lizzie's outlandish wish for the color scheme.

"It's my wedding," he'd howled, "you spoiled imp."

"Our wedding," Lizzie had asserted just as firmly. "You didn't even want her to come to Jackson Downs."

"Because I was afraid you two females would put a ring in my nose and I'd find myself led around by you both for the rest of my life."

Jess and Lizzie had merely glanced knowingly at one another and smiled.

Jess was having the most abominable effect on his child. Every day she got bossier and more muleheaded.

The wedding was purple, a child's fantasy of delight, and Tad was no longer against it. The great mansion was filled with an almost childish, fantastic happiness. And filled with familial love, as well.

For the first time in years Tad felt at home. Almost satisfied to be in Texas. It seemed a long time ago that he'd grown up here, a lonely child, a younger brother, who'd idolized his father and felt abandoned when his parents had separated. With his father's absence, Jeb, his masterful older brother, had begun to dominate everything until Tad had felt he no longer belonged. Later Deirdre hadn't fit in, either.

But now with Jess everything seemed different. He was at peace with himself and with his family, as well. His parents were happier than ever before, and marriage to Megan MacKay had mellowed Jeb.

Upstairs the nursery was filled with babies. Mercedes had shown off her brood of grandchildren to all the guests. Amy and Nick's tiny daughter, Merry, lay napping in a crib beside Jeb's feisty son, Jarred. Kirk was upstairs with Julia, guarding their own newborn son, Jack. Tad swore that it wouldn't be long before he had a son of his own.

Tad asked Jess to dance and soon they were dancing down the length of the ballroom toward the solarium. He could smell her bouquet of orange blossoms. Purple streamers fluttered against his neck and shoulders as Jess waltzed. Suddenly, he was aware of Noelle Martin's shining, dark gaze. She was watching them intently, sadly, from where she stood arm-in-arm with her famous father who had long been a senator from Louisiana. Her still-beautiful mother was sipping champagne as she chatted with Mercedes and Wayne Jackson.

Noelle had been Jess's maid of honor. It was just like Jess to have defied him and befriended the wild, titian-haired Noelle in Australia.

"Noelle is not what you think," Jess had said enigmatically, "not what you think, at all."

Tad clutched Jess closer and forgot Noelle. For a bossy woman, Jess followed his lead divinely. "I hope Lizzie outgrows this purple thing before she's old enough to get married herself," he whispered into Jess's ear.

"I'll save my dress just in case."

"Jeb won't let up teasing me about you. He says you made us more money in the month you were at Jackson Downs than in the entire eight years I was there running things without you. He said you're a wonderful addition to the family."

"Discovering a uranium mine did help. Still, I'm glad he approves."

"He just approves of you to goad me."

"I'm sure you're wrong."

"I've known him longer than you."

For a long time they danced, until Jeb himself strode across the ballroom and cut in. Tad asked Jeb's wife, Megan, to dance, and he saw his brother Nick dancing with the beautiful Noelle.

All too soon the reception was ending, although not soon enough for the impatient bridegroom.

Tad lounged negligently on the balcony and sipped champagne as he watched Jess teasingly assemble the unmarried girls below in the foyer. Gaily she held her bouquet to her lips and kissed it. Then she turned her back on the cluster of girls and flung the white blossoms and purple satin ribbons high into the air.

Every girl ran and jumped toward the flowers.

Every girl but one.

Noelle stood apart, looking grave and lovely in her purple gown. Tad had seen that expression on her face before, many times. Any time a jackaroo had flirted with her. Any time her thoughts had turned to the past.

Not for the first time his curiosity was aroused. As well as an unwanted pang of sympathy.

The flowers flew through the air, glanced off Noelle's listless hands and fell to the floor at her feet.

Lizzie rushed toward the bouquet. "It's yours, Noelle!"

Noelle shrank from the flowers. "No . . . Give it to someone else."

Jess was there in an instant, seizing command—as always—but more gently this time, though. She quieted the disappointed flock of girls and placed the bouquet in Noelle's hands. Jess's words floated up the staircase. "Seek your destiny." Then she kissed Noelle's cheek.

Jess was rushing up the stairs to Tad.

"You threw those flowers to Noelle on purpose. Why? To defy me?"

"You have a complex about female defiance, my love."

"If I do, you are the female who has given it to me."

She kissed him.

"Why Noelle? Why were you determined to throw the bouquet to her? 'Seek your destiny!' What did that bit of theatrics mean? Tell me, Jess."

"It's a long story. A love story. Very romantic. Very tragic," Jess said mysteriously. "Someday I'll tell it to you. But now . . ."

Her fingers grazing against his tensed in the way he'd come to think of as her nighttime touch.

"Yes, now . . ."

"Have you forgotten that tonight is our wedding night?" Her voice was soft, husky.

His arms went around her, and he lifted her easily and began to carry her up, up those endless darkened stairs to the upper story and the bedroom they would share until they left for their honeymoon the next day.

When he reached the door, he kicked it open. Once inside he swiftly locked it behind them before he set her down.

After weeks of wedding madness—relatives, children, Lizzie—they were alone.

Her dazzling golden hair fell in tumbled disarray upon lavender lace.

She was his wife. Really his. Forever.

At last.

Suddenly he felt a wild thrill such as he had never known—joy, excitement, fear—a powerful happiness surging through him.

He was shaking so badly he couldn't move.

Gently she put her arms around his neck. Her mouth was reaching up to meet his. He felt her lips trembling hotly beneath his. Her fingertips caressed his jaw.

He clung to her. To life. To love.

She was everything.

He knew that as long as he had her, he would never be afraid of love again.

*   *   *   *   *

Noelle's story is coming to
Silhouette Desire in April.
Don't miss SCANDAL'S CHILD—
April's Man of the Month!—
only from Silhouette Desire!

Silhouette Romances

Diana Palmer brings you an Award of Excellence title ... and the first Silhouette Romance DIAMOND JUBILEE book.

ETHAN
by Diana Palmer

This month, Diana Palmer continues her bestselling LONG, TALL TEXANS series with *Ethan*—the story of a rugged rancher who refuses to get roped and tied by Arabella Craig, the one woman he can't resist.

The Award of Excellence is given to one specially selected title per month. Spend January with *Ethan* #694 ... a special DIAMOND JUBILEE title ... only in Silhouette Romance.

Ethan-1

SILHOUETTE DESIRE™

presents

AUNT EUGENIA'S TREASURES
by CELESTE HAMILTON

Liz, Cassandra and Maggie are the honored recipients of Aunt Eugenia's heirloom jewels...but Eugenia knows the real prizes are the young women themselves. Read about Aunt Eugenia's quest to find them everlasting love. Each book shines on its own, but together, they're priceless!

Available in December:
THE DIAMOND'S SPARKLE (SD #537)

Altruistic Liz Patterson wants nothing to do with Nathan Hollister, but as the fast-lane PR man tells Liz, love is something he's willing to take *very* slowly.

Available in February:
RUBY FIRE (SD #549)

Impulsive Cassandra Martin returns from her travels... ready to rekindle the flame with the man she never forgot, Daniel O'Grady.

Available in April:
THE HIDDEN PEARL (SD #561)

Cautious Maggie O'Grady comes out of her shell...and glows in the precious warmth of love when brazen Jonah Pendleton moves in next door.

SD-AET-1R

Indulge a Little
Give a Lot

An irresistible opportunity to pamper yourself with free gifts (plus proofs-of-purchase and postage and handling) and help raise up to $100,000.00 for **Big Brothers/Big Sisters Programs and Services** in Canada and the United States.

Each specially marked "Indulge A Little" Harlequin or Silhouette book purchased during October, November and December contains a proof-of-purchase that will enable you to qualify for luxurious gifts. And, for every specially marked book purchased during this limited time, Harlequin/Silhouette will donate 5¢ toward **Big Brothers/ Big Sisters Programs and Services**, for a maximum contribution of $100,000.00.

For details on how you can indulge yourself, look for information at your favorite retail store or send a self-addressed stamped envelope to:

INDULGE A LITTLE
P.O. Box 618
Fort Erie, Ontario
L2A 5I3